THE
GLORY
OF THE
SOLOMONS

Also by Edwin P. Hoyt:

THE
GLORY
OF THE
SOLOMONS

EDWIN P. HOYT

STEIN AND DAY/*Publishers*/New York

All photographs not otherwise attributed are from the National Archives. The map of the western Pacific Ocean and eastern Asia is from Mark Arnold-Forster's *The World at War*, and is reprinted courtesy of Stein and Day Publishers. The maps bearing the U.S. Marine Corps globe and anchor device and the map captioned "Mop Up Operations" are U.S. Marine Corps maps. All other maps are U.S. Navy maps.

FIRST STEIN AND DAY PAPERBACK EDITION 1984
The Glory of the Solomons was first published in hardcover by Stein and Day/*Publishers* in 1983.

Copyright © 1983 by Edwin P. Hoyt
All rights reserved, Stein and Day, Incorporated
Designed by Judy Dalzell
Printed in the United States of America
STEIN AND DAY/*Publishers*
Scarborough House
Briarcliff Manor, N.Y. 10510
ISBN 0-8128-8109-5

CONTENTS

ILLUSTRATIONS

MAPS

ACKNOWLEDGMENTS

I am much indebted to Dr. Dean Allard, head of the Operational Archives of the U.S. Navy at the Washington Navy Yard, and to Mike Walker of his staff for help in the use of the documents mentioned in the bibliography. James Trimble of the National Archives still picture division helped enormously in the discovery of photographs for the book, as he has with so many of my books before.

I am indebted to Captain David McCampbell (U.S.N. Ret.) for several stories and an assessment of the Japanese fighter pilots he met at the Marianas and over the Philippines.

Admiral Arleigh Burke was very helpful in giving me general information about the Solomons campaign and telling stories about Admiral Halsey.

Mrs. Kakuko Shoji of Honolulu, my Japanese teacher, continued to advance my study of the language and steered me out of error in pronunciation (and phonetic spelling) of several difficult Japanese personal names.

I am indebted to Diana Palmer Hoyt, press secretary to Rep. Daniel Akaka of Hawaii, for securing valuable research materials in Washington.

Tadeo Ohta and other members of the staff of the Japanese section of the Library of Congress were most helpful and cordial to my sometimes foolish questions. They found me a number of valuable works.

My wife, Olga G. Hoyt, also helped me with Japanese translation and, as always, read the typescript for grammatical and syntactical errors.

I am not, however, very grateful to the U.S. Postal Service, which managed to misplace some important Japanese materials so thoroughly that although they were mailed from Honolulu in June 1982, they did not arrive in Maryland until January 1983.

Edwin P. Hoyt
Chestertown, Md.
1983

THE
GLORY
OF THE
SOLOMONS

1

THE SOUTH PACIFIC TIDE

ON the night of February 6, 1943, a long column of Japanese destroyers left their South Pacific base at Bougainville Island and headed "down the Slot" toward the island of Guadalcanal in the Solomons group. They carried few supplies and little ammunition for they expected to be back at base in a matter of hours. Their mission was not to carry out an offensive but to rescue the last of some 17,000 Imperial Japanese troops who were being evacuated from Guadalcanal under the noses of the Americans. After the long battle for control of that island the Imperial General Staff had just brought the bloody contest to an end with their decision to withdraw.

Twenty destroyers took part in this rescue mission, eighteen of them moving to Guadalcanal and the other two to the Russell Islands off Cape Esperance at the upper tip of the big island. They moved skillfully and they were lucky; the American fleet units weren't in the area at that moment, although a large fighting force was at sea. But Admiral William "Bull" Halsey was guarding against a Japanese attack on Guadalcanal or on New Caledonia, and the fleet was patrolling south of the Solomons. This American force was powerful: four battleships, three auxiliary carriers, five cruisers, and a dozen destroyers, but it was in a defensive, not an offensive, posture. Admiral Robert Giffen, commander of the

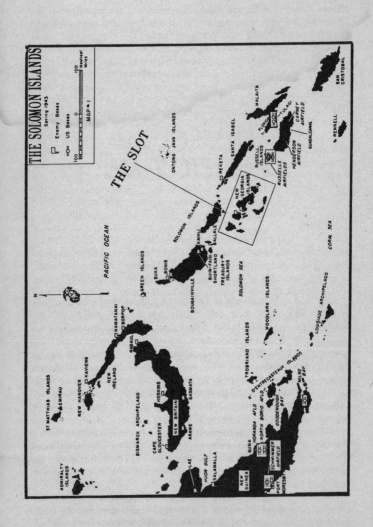

cruiser Task Force 18, was more concerned with the intentions of the Japanese than with launching an all-out search for any enemy vessels. On February 6, Allied coast watchers sighted the Japanese ships and reported to Henderson Field on Guadalcanal, and several air attacks were launched. The bombers claimed to have damaged at least two of the Japanese destroyers, but the planes did not stop them from carrying out their mission. Like gray ghosts, the destroyers slid in toward shore. The pitiful, starving remnants of the Japanese military units swam or floated out and climbed up the cargo nets thrown over the sides of the destroyers. Many men were so weak they had to be helped aboard. And then, long before dawn, the destroyers turned their bows toward Bougainville and were gone. On the morning of February 7, not a single organized Japanese unit remained on Guadalcanal. In three nights the Japanese Navy had removed an entire army force from Guadalcanal without the Americans even having a hint of the master plan. The destroyer *Makigumo* was lost and three others were damaged by Allied aircraft. But that was a small price to pay for saving almost two divisions.

It was several days before the Americans learned the truth, so swiftly and silently had the Japanese moved. On February 9 in Tokyo, Imperial General Headquarters issued a communique about the Solomons battle. Until that time few in Japan knew how badly the struggle had gone, although there had been rumors that the ever-victorious Imperial forces were having some difficulties. But no one expected this communique. Although couched in the most euphorious of terms, it told the story of a dreadful defeat, and the shock of it began to reverberate throughout the empire.

To those who understood the complex Japanese military system, the fact that this communique did not deal with naval matters at all was understandable. Navy and army kept their own secrets, and the navy section of the Imperial General Staff gave out very little information and most of that misleading. (For example, after the serious defeat of the Japanese Navy at the Battle of Midway, the navy concealed even from Prime Minister Tojo the extent of the defeat for an entire month.) The excuse was that it was more important to deny the enemy access to accurate casualty figures about the navy than about the army. But no matter how one read the Imperial communique of February 9, it was bad news for Japan.

For the first time, the government admitted that Japanese forces had been hard hit in the Solomons. The struggle had begun, said the communique, in the summer of 1942, and it had affected the lower section of the Solomons and the New Guinea area. The enemy had arrived in great force and after fierce fighting had forced the Japanese defense units to

The Pacific

Furthest extent of Japanese occupation July 1942

Areas occupied by Japanese on surrender 25 August 1945

0   500   1000 miles

establish new bases for the conduct of operations. In New Guinea, the new base was in the neighborhood of Lae, and from here the Imperial Japanese forces intended to move forward and take all of Papua. This new base had been established in the first ten days of February, and so had several others in the central Solomons. The communique went into some detail about the struggle for Guadalcanal, indicating that a huge American force had simply overpowered the brave defenders of Japan. The communique also gave some comparative war loss figures for both sides, to show that although Japan had been pushed out of Guadalcanal, the cost to the Americans had been enormous. The enemy, said the communique, had lost more than 25,000 men, 230 aircraft, 30 field guns, and 25 tanks. The Japanese had lost only 16,734 men, including those who died from disease, and one hundred and thirty-nine planes. Nothing was said about the navy's situation, except that the navy had fought "a magnificent battle." But about the loss of hundreds of navy planes and of many ships, from battleships to destroyers, Imperial Headquarters said nothing. Even those who could read between the lines could only sense the magnitude of the defeat, and they had no way of knowing that the comparative figures were false.

Moreover, the communique gave no background and failed to mention the enormous argument that was in progress just then in Tokyo about the direction of the war.

The controversy centered around Guadalcanal and the difficulties the Japanese military establishment had encountered for the first time. To meet the American threat, the Japanese had pulled the 41st Division of the Imperial Army out of China and the 20th Division out of Korea. Two other divisions, the 6th and the 51st, were also moved from other southern areas to Rabaul to be committed to the Solomons and New Guinea operations.

Toward the end of December 1942, a growing quarrel between the War Ministry on the one hand and the Imperial Army High Command on the other broke into the open for the first time. In the past, the War Ministry had been responsible for the political aspects of defense, as well as the maintenance of production and liaison between the government and the army. The high command had been given untrammeled authority over operations. If the high command wanted more ships from the civilian economy, it went to the War Ministry and got them—until Guadalcanal. There, when the Americans began sinking ships by the dozen, the problem came into sharp focus. There were not enough ships to go around. The army needed another 300,000 tons of shipping for 1943 to send troops and supplies to Guadalcanal. The war minister looked at the total defense problem of Japan and said no. The army's General Shinichi Tanaka, chief of the Operations Bureau, rose up in fury. Never before had the army been denied a major request. General Tanaka lost his temper with the war minister, forgetting perhaps that the war minister was also General Hideki Tojo, prime minister, and virtual dictator of wartime Japan. Tojo had had enough. Tanaka was transferred out to a front-line command in the south (the equivalent of "banishment to Siberia" for a high-ranking officer of the Imperial General Headquarters). Tojo, having reestablished his control of the army, would never let it go again as long as he held power. He made sure that the officers appointed to control the army were from that time on personally loyal to himself. From that moment, too, he also would be chief of the Imperial General Staff.

The decision to move out of Guadalcanal had been made at the highest level, an Imperial General Headquarters conference in the Imperial Palace, with the Emperor in attendance.

With the capture of Guadalcanal in February, the Americans proclaimed a tremendous victory in the South Pacific. Guadalcanal, they would claim, marked the turning of the tide of the Pacific War.

The American invasion and final seizure of Guadalcanal *was* a victory of great importance. First of all, the six-month struggle for Guadalcanal represented the initial Allied success on land against the Japanese Imperial Army. Until the summer of 1942, the Japanese forces in the Pacific were riding a tide of victory. Hong Kong, Singapore, the oil rich islands of the Dutch East Indies, and the Philippines had all fallen before the "ever victorious" Imperial armies. Admiral Isoroku Yamamoto's Imperial Combined Fleet had destroyed the U.S. Battle Fleet at Pearl Harbor on December 7, 1941, and a few hours later it had knocked out British seapower in the Pacific off Singapore with the sinking of the new battleship *Prince of Wales* and the old battle cruiser *Repulse*. A few weeks later the Japanese carrier force engaged the British Asia Fleet off Trincomalee, Ceylon, sank the carrier *Hermes*, and thus wiped out the most important remaining Allied force west of Hawaii. The last vestiges of organized Allied naval power were destroyed in the Battle of the Java Sea early in 1942.

Burma fell, and the Imperial General Staff was deluged with plans for further expansion, including an attack on India that was supposed to carry the Japanese forces across Afghanistan and the Caucasus to link up with Hitler's armies. Another plan called for an attack on the Russians in Siberia by the crack Kwantung Army, considered to be the best of all Japan's armies. But the Japanese victories had come so much more quickly than expected that the civil affairs people could not keep up. The army and navy were hard pressed to consolidate their victories and build new bases. The most important naval base in the south was Truk, the key to the Bismarck Archipelago, which had been held by the Japanese since World War I and been fortified for a long time. A new base was established at Rabaul on New Britain Island, which had been seized from the Australians. Plans were made to move on to the French territory of New Caledonia and into New Guinea. A few more ships, a few more armies at the outbreak of war, and the Japanese could have seized Australia. That was the navy's dream. But in the spring of 1942 the vast length of the supply line and the spreading of forces began to take its toll.

The first setback of any sort was naval. It came when in the spring of 1942 the Japanese moved to capture Port Moresby in New Guinea. A combined American-Australian force contested the Japanese at what came to be called the Battle of the Coral Sea. The Americans lost one carrier (the *Lexington*) and the Japanese lost one small carrier. In terms of ships sunk, the Coral Sea battle was a Japanese victory, as it was called in Tokyo. But the victory was pyrrhic, for the battle engaged the two big carriers *Shokaku* and *Zuikaku* (the former was damaged) and made it impossible for Admiral Isoroku Yamamoto to utilize them in the next big attack, scheduled for June.

The Coral Sea battle was an American strategic victory only in retrospect, however, because it prevented the Japanese Army, for the first time, from accomplishing an objective: the seizure of Port Moresby, which would have given them control of all New Guinea and a perfect base from which to launch an attack on Australia. It was followed in June by the Japanese attempt to invade Midway Island and the Aleutians simultaneously. Because of the absence of those two big carriers, what should have been an easy Japanese victory at Midway became a stunning Japanese defeat, with four carriers lost and the Midway seizure abandoned, which in turn made the Japanese investiture of the Aleutian Islands untenable and threw the entire Japanese Central Pacific plan askew. The Midway battle was also indeterminate in terms of testing the relative strengths of Japanese and American forces. It was a victory for intelligence, the key being the American breach of the Japanese naval code that enabled the code-breakers to learn when and where the enemy would attack, and enabled Admiral Chester W. Nimitz to organize and launch the most powerful units of his diminished U.S. Pacific Fleet. Midway proved American skill and bravery at sea. Yes, these qualities had actually been questioned by the world after the swift succession of Japanese victories and the apparent inability of the Westerners to fight the Japanese successfully. But Midway did not prove the ability of the Americans to launch an attack and defeat the Imperial Japanese Army on land. Until Guadalcanal, the Japanese had conducted an enormously successful propaganda campaign, based on the assertion that the Japanese military forces were superior to all others in the world. There was some doubt in military circles (though never among the U.S. Marines) whether American troops could match the Japanese in jungle warfare. So the American victory at Guadalcanal was enormously important in America and among America's allies and potential allies as a morale booster.

Midway had another result unknown to the Americans at the Guadalcanal stage of the war: the Japanese loss had disrupted the Imperial Navy's plans to seize the islands of Samoa and Fiji, which were next on the list in the South Pacific. The Samoa-Fiji plan was just being talked up again in August, when the Americans invaded Guadalcanal, and it had to be put on the shelf once more.

The Japanese, however, did not consider the evacuation of Guadalcanal to be more than a temporary setback in their plans for the South Pacific, and the plans never wavered. At the Imperial General Headquarters conference at the Imperial Palace, it was made clear that the Japanese forces were simply changing emphasis. For several months they had been on the offensive in the Solomons area and on the defensive in Papua, New Guinea. This would be reversed.

When it became apparent to Admiral Yamamoto that evacuation of the army troops on Guadalcanal was inevitable, he reorganized his command to begin a new offensive. Vice Admiral Jinichi Kusaka, the commander of the Eleventh Air Fleet at Rabaul, was put in charge of all naval units in the Bismarcks, Solomons, and New Guinea. He began strengthening the bases at Munda on New Georgia and Vila on Kolombangara Island.

One could not say that Admiral Yamamoto did not learn from his mistakes. With the evacuation of Guadalcanal, Yamamoto drew a new "front line," which ran through the middle of the Solomons. This was the line, said the Japanese optimistically, at which the enemy would be stopped. Immediately, the major problem was delivery of supplies. During the last weeks of the Guadalcanal campaign, supply to other bases was sadly neglected and a great accumulation of war materiel had piled up on the docks at Rabaul. The old system, under which the army supplied its own troops in army transports and called for navy help only in emergency, would no longer do. That was the way of a victorious army, unused to serious opposition. In that sense, even the army understood that the war had changed, although the army stubbornly refused to change its basic plans, even after the major setbacks of the previous year at Guadalcanal and Buna on New Guinea, where General MacArthur had stopped the Japanese drive across the Owen Stanley mountains.

The Japanese buildup for the attack on Australia and New Guinea continued. Admiral Yamamoto had moved his advance bases back to Kolombangara and New Georgia islands, which were then to be prepared, under the Japanese plans, to provide the same sort of bases that had been envisaged for Guadalcanal, staging points for air attacks on Northern Australia and the trade routes that brought supplies from America to General Douglas MacArthur's forces in Australia. MacArthur, former chief of staff of the U.S. Army and a distinguished military son of a distinguished father, was well known to the Japanese, and they took seriously his promise that he would return to the Philippines. The movement against Australia was to make sure that MacArthur would be unable to carry out that promise. And although they had lost Guadalcanal, the Japanese retained one distinct advantage in the area. Their aircraft had longer range than those of the Americans, so they could send planes from Rabaul to New Georgia, where they would refuel and then go on to attack the U.S. bases at Tulagi and Guadalcanal, and then return to Rabaul the same way. The American planes—the fighters in particular—did not have the range to reach Rabaul and return to American bases.

With the evacuation of Guadalcanal, Imperial Headquarters in Tokyo made plans to reinforce the area and retrieve the defeat. When the Emperor had agreed at the December 31 conference that Guadalcanal would be abandoned, he issued an Imperial Rescript, to prepare the Japanese public for the change in plans:

> The Emperor is troubled by the great difficulties of the present war situation. The darkness is very deep, but dawn is about to break in the eastern sky. Today the finest of the Japanese Empire's army, navy and air units are gathering. Sooner or later they will head toward the Solomon Islands where a decisive battle is being fought between Japan and America.

Specifically, Imperial Headquarters then took steps to bring new forces south for that decisive battle. The staging area in French Indo-China was enlarged. The China command had promised a new offensive against Chiang Kai-shek for 1943, but that was scaled down to scarcely more than a raiding action. Planes, which were being destroyed at an alarming rate, were shifted from Manchuria and the Burma area to the South Pacific. The Japanese positions at Timor and in Western New Guinea were reinforced. The point, as Admiral Yamamoto knew very well, was to regain the strategic initiative. Yamamoto had no hope for a long campaign, but he wanted to win one major victory, which would stop the Americans and (he hoped) cause them to seek a negotiated peace that would leave Japan in control of her new Pacific empire.

In the past, Yamamoto had thought specifically in terms of a naval victory. Midway was the great opportunity for which he had planned, but after that failure, Yamamoto found himself bogged down in a war of attrition in the South Pacific that demanded the employment of large numbers of troops. That change had to mean a new cooperation between army and navy, because the Japanese Navy had only a few of the special shock troop units that were roughly equivalent to the U.S. Marines. In the assignment of areas of responsibility in the early days of the war, the Imperial General Staff had given the army Formosa, the Philippines, Malaya, the big East Indian islands, and New Guinea. All of these were large land masses, suitable for the employment of armored forces. The navy was given the task of defending the island groups such as the Marshalls, the Gilberts, and the Solomons. But when for the first time a large enemy land force went ashore on Guadalcanal the defensive system was found to be inadequate.

Yamamoto's first major error had been to send in a battalion to drive the Americans out of Guadalcanal. In that sense the American raid on Makin Island in the Gilberts—carried out by Lieutenant Colonel Evans Carlson's Second Marine Raider Battalion at the same time as the beginning of the Guadalcanal operation—was a psychological success. After all, the Americans had never before in this war launched an offensive operation. The Japanese failed to understand that Guadalcanal was just such an operation and not another raid like that on the Gilberts. Also, the Japanese were so used to victory that their intelligence was sloppy, and as a consequence Yamamoto sent in a battalion to do a job that demanded at least a division. When—after several weeks— the Japanese realized that they had a real problem on their hands and decided to rectify it, a whole set of negotiations between army and navy had to be undergone to dispatch the army troops necessary. As noted, the navy's land forces consisted of a few battalions of shock troops that functioned like American marines. To retake Guadalcanal it would be necessary to employ many more men. They had to come from the 17th Army. An entirely new system of cooperation had to be established.

This change was not easily accomplished, because the Japanese military traditionally had not worked that way. An endless series of meetings at Rabaul between Yamamoto's officers and those of the 17th Army brought forth a reluctant collaboration that was never as successful as it should have been. The concept the Americans employed—an area commander had authority over all sorts of troops, ships, and planes— was entirely foreign to the Japanese. The wasteful Japanese system of divided authority would continue. The cooperation in the South Pacific was forced, uneasy, and not completely effective. In the battle for Guadalcanal, the Japanese had learned that transports simply did not have a chance in these waters. In the middle of November the army made its last large-scale logistical attempt in this area when it sent half a dozen transports toward Guadalcanal loaded with troops and supplies of the 38th Division. Only half the transports ever made Guadalcanal, and the remainder were all bombed so severely that they had to be beached there. Many of the troops of the 38th Division arrived all right, but their guns and equipment did not, and neither did most of their food. Instead of an asset, the division had become nearly a liability. Thereafter for the rest of the Guadalcanal campaign, the Japanese supplied their forces only by destroyer and submarine.

As of February 1943, there was no answer but that the Combined Fleet undertake management of the resupply of the forward bases as a regular responsibility. This meant the delivery of supplies to the army forces in the area as well as the navy's own.

The first supply mission to the front lines was dispatched on February 13, 1943, just a week after the evacuation of Guadalcanal. Captain Kintaro Matsumoto was sent down to Kolombangara with three destroyers loaded with food, ammunition, and medical supplies.

The Americans seemed unaware. The ships made Kolombangara without incident, unloaded their supplies, and turned back toward Rabaul. On the return trip they were attacked by eight fighters and fifteen B-17 bombers, but all the bombs went awry and the three destroyers returned without loss. The mission was so successful that it gave the naval command a new sense of security.

As far as the Japanese Army was concerned, the important matter was the capture of all New Guinea. The Solomons were a navy problem, of interest to the army (now that Guadalcanal was evacuated) only because of a relatively small number of army troops stationed at various bases among the islands and because of the enemy air and naval bases at Guadalcanal that could threaten the whole New Guinea operation. The 38th Division, which had been sent near the end of the campaign to Guadalcanal and then evacuated, was moved back to Rabaul to defend that complex of bases and all of New Ireland Island.

The army lost no time in getting back into action, this time in New Guinea. Scarcely had the troops been removed from Guadalcanal when plans for a new operation in Papua were prepared. It would begin in March 1943 with a renewed drive out of Lae.

2

CONFUSION IN COMMAND

IN the area north of Australia, while the Americans did not have the same degree of separation between navy and army as the Japanese, they, too, had their difficulties. The division of the southern Pacific battle region into two area commands was wasteful in itself—the result of the jealous struggle of the army and navy for command of the Pacific War. General MacArthur had been brought out of the Philippines to lead the army forces back. Admiral Nimitz was the Pacific fleet commander, and when Admiral King insisted on the invasion of Guadalcanal to forestall the Japanese buildup, Nimitz employed marines and insisted that the command be in the hands of a naval officer. So the Southwest Pacific Command of General MacArthur and the South Pacific Command of Admiral William F. Halsey, Jr. had come into being as separate entities.

This anomalous situation continued throughout 1942 and into 1943. After Guadalcanal fell, the Joint Chiefs of Staff considered future operations in the area. General George C. Marshall, Chief of Staff of the Army, argued that command of forthcoming operations should be placed in General MacArthur's hands. Admiral King stubbornly refused. But that did not settle the issue. General Henry H. Arnold, commander of Army Air Forces, made an inspection trip to the South and Southwest Pacific and returned to say bluntly that the whole must be put under one commander, and he must be an army officer. Arnold proposed that the Joint Chiefs go to President Roosevelt and secure a presidential decree to that effect. Everyone recognized that General MacArthur's domineering personality was a problem, and several staff officers suggested that he be relieved and pushed into some such job as ambassador to Russia. With MacArthur out of the way, they felt, it would be easier to persuade the navy to accept an army area commander. The argument continued; the army officers complained that the existence of divided commands was counterproductive and confusing. General Marshall told President Roosevelt that further unification of the South Pacific Command and Southwest Pacific Command was badly needed. Admiral King would not give an inch. Roosevelt let the matter lie. So the operations in the Southern Pacific area continued to be divided under the commands of Admiral Halsey and General MacArthur.

On the lower levels, there were other complaints. General Arnold said the navy men did not know how to handle land-based air operations. King ordered Nimitz to strengthen the land-based air command in the South Pacific.

Guadalcanal was invaded by the First Marine Division, with elements of the Second Marine Division in reserve. Two of those regiments, the Second Marine Regiment and the Eighth Marine Regiment, fought in the Guadalcanal campaign. Worn down by heat and disease as much as by the Japanese, most of these troops were supplanted by army units that became available in the area at the end of 1942, and Army Major General Alexander Patch became the field commander of U.S. land forces on Guadalcanal. Here, then, for the first time in the Pacific War, was an army general serving in command of land forces in battle under a navy admiral. Because of Admiral Halsey's enormous ability as a commander the friction was not serious at that level. But lower down it was a constant problem. Major General John Marston, commander of the Second Marine Division, outranked Army General Patch by seniority. Part of his division remained in the fighting on Guadalcanal until the last, but Marston was kept sequestered in Wellington, New Zealand. If he had gone to Guadalcanal, as senior officer he would have taken charge of operations, and the confusion would have been enormous. The American system was superior to the Japanese, but it was far from perfect. The problems of command between marine and army officers would persist through most of the Pacific War.

Late in November, when the tide at Guadalcanal seemed to have turned in favor of the Americans, the Joint Chiefs of Staff gave more attention to the next stage of operations. This would be complicated, the nature dictated by the structure of the commands. There was another problem, which would be resolved in January at the Casablanca conference. There the Allied leaders would decide that the grand strategy of the global war called for continued British and American emphasis on the European theater, and that, during the coming year, again only limited resources could be spared for the Pacific. Given very little with which to work, the Americans were supposed to carry the war against the Japanese—not just stop them but begin throwing them back.

Given such limited resources, the most daring plan of all—to bypass the whole southern area and attack inside the inner empire—was vetoed by Admiral Nimitz as much too risky. The next move was to be up the Solomons, then to the northeast coast of New Guinea, New Britain, and New Ireland. Each operation would involve a task force, and whether this was South Pacific (Halsey) or Southwest Pacific (MacArthur) would be decided in each case by the Joint Chiefs of Staff. As for the overall strategic direction of the campaign—General Marshall proposed that it be MacArthur's. This had been the original plan of the Joint Chiefs of Staff. The South Pacific Command had been ordered only to take Guadalcanal and Tulagi. Marshall recalled this directive. King disagreed again. The next move should be in the northwest, perhaps outflanking some of the Japanese-held islands, and it should be under the South Pacific Command, which in turn would be directly responsible to Nimitz's Pacific Fleet and Pacific Ocean Areas Command.

But Nimitz, in turn, disagreed with Admiral King's haste. He also shared Admiral Yamamoto's premise that the battle for Guadalcanal had not ended and that the island was still in danger of recapture as long as the Japanese held the adjacent Northern Solomons. They had to be cleaned out, and Tulagi had to be turned into a major base for operations. The Japanese string of air and naval bases ran down the Solomons, and they were mutually supporting. It would be too dangerous to bypass Kavieng, Rabaul, Buka, Buin, and the rest. Nimitz urged the Joint Chiefs of Staff to go slow and build up the forces before making a major move.

Admiral Nimitz's assessment of the situation in the Solomons as of February 1943 was very close to that of Admiral Yamamoto, who had retreated no further than Munda, on New Georgia, as his forward point of defense. In meetings in Rabaul, Yamamoto and General Hitoshi Imamura, the Southeast Area commander, worked out their plans: Imamura would be responsible for operations in New Guinea; Yamamoto would be responsible for operations in the Solomons and the defense of Rabaul. As it turned out, this command structure was almost precisely the counterpart of the American, with Halsey in charge of South Pacific operations up the Solomons chain, and MacArthur moving against the Japanese in New Guinea. Like MacArthur, the Japanese Army was more concerned with New Guinea than with the Solomons. The entire purpose of the operation of May that had resulted in the Coral Sea battle had been the investment of Port Moresby in Papua, the southern portion of New Guinea. Only incidentally had troops been landed in the Solomons to build a seaplane base at Tulagi and an airfield on Guadalcanal. The first purpose of the bases would have been to protect the movement into Southern New Guinea and launch raids on Australia to weaken the Allies' capacity to move troops.

The Japanese Army also had its eyes on New Caledonia and Samoa, as points in the ring around Australia and New Zealand. But first of all, in the army view, Papua—Southern New Guinea—must be reinforced and cleared of the Allied troops that General MacArthur had moved in there. The campaign for Papua had begun before that for Guadalcanal. The Japanese had sent an amphibious force from Rabaul in July 1942, and on July 20 the troops had landed under Allied air attack just west of Buna on the north shore of the Papuan peninsula. By the time the American marines attacked Guadalcanal, the Japanese Army was already reinforcing Papua and had about 11,000 men ashore.

General Imamura's attention, then, was focused on this area, which was the next destination in his war plan. That preoccupation was one of the major reasons for the Japanese Army's failure to understand the Guadalcanal threat and to respond to it. Imamura was preoccupied with a striking force he sent over the Owen Stanley mountains from Northern New Guinea to attack Port Moresby, which was defended by only a handful of Australian troops. But MacArthur managed to bring in 10,000 reinforcements, most of them Australians, by the middle of August 1942. The Japanese reinforced their troops again. So did the Allies. The battle raged for months. It was on a smaller scale than that of Guadalcanal but still was regarded by General Imamura as of far more importance. This army myopia continued until December, when a shocked military command learned that for the first time in history the Imperial Japanese Navy could not guarantee resupply of a Japanese army invasion force.

The navy men on both sides, it seemed, thought much along the same lines as did the army men. Admirals King and Nimitz insisted that as long as the Solomons were occupied by the enemy, they were a threat to any operation, and thus they must be cleared. Yamamoto shared their view, although his goal was to regain the lost ground. The first Japanese task had to be to reestablish air superiority, lost in the battle of Guadalcanal.

In February 1943, holding that air superiority in the Southern Solomons, Admiral Halsey was already preparing to attack his next objective: the Russell Islands, just north of Guadalcanal. He wanted these islands as a base for motor torpedo boats. No one regarded this operation as major, but it was still useful to move a little up the chain of the Solomons in a hurry, and nothing could be done about the major moves until higher authority agreed on the command problem. At the moment, there was no way the Joint Chiefs of Staff could come to grips with the problem of area command; the rivalry between army and navy always got in the way. The Joint Chiefs of Staff consisted of two generals and two admirals: General Marshall, the Chief of Staff of the Army; General Arnold, chief of staff of the air command, which was still part of the army and was called the Army Air Forces; Admiral King, who styled himself Commander in Chief of the Navy,° and Admiral William D. Leahy, President Roosevelt's aide and principal military advisor. Equally split, the Joint Chiefs could never agree on the subject of overall command. If there was to be a unified command, the directive would have to come from President Roosevelt, the commander in chief of all the armed forces. At that moment, Roosevelt was primarily concerned with the prosecution of the war against the Germans and all that effort involved. The war in the Pacific was proceeding in a relatively satisfactory fashion, and in his usual way, Roosevelt saw nothing wrong in internal conflict among his departments, up to a point. As an old navy buff (former Assistant Secretary of the Navy) Roosevelt was aware of the intense rivalry between army and navy for the leadership of the campaign against the Japanese. The army plan called for the return through the Philippines. The navy plan called for the move against Japan through the Central Pacific. The matter was further complicated by the emergence of the aerial force in this war as equivalent in importance to an army or a fleet; the air generals and the air admirals vied for control of the land-based air forces that provided most of the striking force. Still, until the resources became available to press in at least one direction, there was no need to decide between admirals and generals.

Given the limited objectives for the first part of the year 1943, Roosevelt saw no need to make any decision about commands, and that is the way he left it. Admiral Nimitz was still commander of the Pacific Fleet, which meant all the ships everywhere. General MacArthur was still

---

°The White House informed King that that title was unacceptable, so the admiral settled for the title Commander in Chief of the United States Fleet.

commander of the Southwest Pacific, which meant the whole area south and west of the Philippines, the original scene of Allied attempts to fight back in 1942. The matter was further complicated by Nimitz's other hat, that of Commander of the Pacific Ocean Areas. Originally this title had been conceived to give Nimitz command of the stray islands in the north and central Pacific Ocean. Admiral King saw far more in the concept. At the same time that King insisted on the absolute need for a fast response to the Japanese at Guadalcanal, he had declared that the Guadalcanal invasion belonged to Nimitz by right of the Pacific Ocean Areas title. That was logical because, since August 1942, King was providing the transports, the bombardment force, the covering fleet and aircraft, *and* the invasion army—the marines; there wasn't much the generals could do about it. Although King's move strained every resource of the navy in the Pacific, it was a brilliant ploy in the political battle for control of the Pacific war effort. It had created the situation that existed in the early months of 1943, when MacArthur could not simply assert the authority given him in the original Joint Chiefs of Staff directive and take command of the new operations. It was all a part of Admiral King's determination that the navy would lead the way to Tokyo through the Central Pacific, with such side voyages as were necessary. Understanding that, his subordinate commanders, admirals Nimitz and Halsey, were willing to make whatever adjustments were indicated.

Staff officers from Admiral Halsey's South Pacific Command flew to Pearl Harbor early in March to discuss the matter of command of forthcoming moves in the South Pacific and Southwest Pacific. Staff officers from General MacArthur's command came up as well. Both sets saw the need for compromise: officially, MacArthur was the overall commander, but he was strapped for ships. The Australians could not begin to meet his needs for cruisers, destroyers, and transports. Earlier MacArthur had inherited the vestiges of the Asiatic Fleet that had been stationed at Manila, but the fleet consisted of a handful of cruisers, a handful of destroyers and support ships, and a double handful of submarines. If MacArthur was to send amphibious invasion forces against the Japanese in New Guinea, he needed ships, and these could come from only one source—Admiral Nimitz's Pacific Fleet.

As for Nimitz, he needed land-based air support for his naval operations in the South Pacific. He had created a land-based air command during the Guadalcanal campaign, but the Army Air Force generals were reluctant to supply units to expand this force, regarding such action as contributing to the navy power base. So Nimitz needed Army Air Force and Australian Air Force commitment to his operations.

At Pearl Harbor the staff men sorted it all out. Nimitz agreed to accept General MacArthur's overall strategic command of the entire

South Pacific. MacArthur agreed that Admiral Halsey would have direct command of the South Pacific (Solomons) operations, though for general direction he would come to MacArthur instead of to Nimitz. Nimitz would retain control of *all* ships, planes, and ground forces of the Pacific Ocean Areas except when they were actually involved in a military operation. That provision made it impossible for MacArthur to commandeer ships for an invasion and then keep them, which he would very much have liked to do.

So the agreement was made, and the division of labor was established for the coming months. MacArthur's forces would continue to peck at New Guinea, and Nimitz would supply the ships and naval personnel. MacArthur would proceed in 1943 to establish airfields at Kiriwina and the Woodlark Islands, northeast of Papua. He would seize the Papuan centers of Lae, Salamaua, Finschhafen, and the Madang area. Later on his forces would attack Western New Britain. This story—the New Guinea campaign—is a subject in itself.

Admiral Halsey would seize and occupy all the Solomon Islands and the southern portion of Bougainville. That campaign is the subject of this book.

Having agreed to the division of authority, Admiral Nimitz took one more step to assure his control of naval operations. It was a part of a general reorganization of naval command. With the growth of the Pacific Fleet Command in the previous year Nimitz was able to designate three separate operating fleets. They were the Third Fleet, Admiral Halsey's command; the Fifth Fleet, which was given to Vice Admiral Raymond Spruance and would become the nucleus of the Central Pacific invasion force; and the Seventh Fleet, which was placed at about this time under Vice Admiral Thomas C. Kinkaid. At long last, MacArthur had the sort of naval force he had been hoping for, but Nimitz had sewed up its ultimate control and retained it in his own hands. Above all he kept control of the growing force of fast carriers, which would be assigned to various fleets for specific operations and then brought back to Pearl Harbor.

The March meeting was greeted with satisfaction by all concerned, and within a month Admiral Halsey made a trip to Brisbane to call on MacArthur and thus attest to MacArthur's overall command and assuage the general's ego. Nimitz had worked it all out so that Halsey could do everything he wanted to do with virtually no interference from Brisbane. Halsey was ready to begin operations "up the Slot."

3

STEP ONE:
THE RUSSELLS

BY 1943 the words *South Pacific* had a magic ring in America. As the campaign progressed—this first offensive action against the apparently invincible Japanese—Americans at home seemed to sense that the war was changing drastically. As the foot soldiers and the airmen turned the tide they found themselves lionized at home. The navy's seesaw battle for control of "the Slot" kept Americans rooting as at an athletic contest. Indeed, one of the most popular American tunes of the day was "Knuckle Down, Winsocki," in which the lyrics urged a mythical school football team on to greater efforts in the face of apparent defeat and heavy odds. The odds began to even as ever more American ships and men were found for the South Pacific battle, and the men came eagerly to the "island paradise," dreaming of dusky dark-haired beauties basking beneath palm trees under a clear evening sky.

The ships came first to Noumea, New Caledonia. This was the headquarters of the South Pacific Command. It was also French territory, and the French here were cranky and unpleasant. To give them their due, the government of the islands was in a most difficult position. Secretly, most of the French sympathized with the home government at Vichy, which was in league with the Germans. For reasons of international politics the Americans and Australians had not simply declared an Allied occupation of New Caledonia, but had chosen the harder road of dealing with the French, who did not like the "occupation." But if the French became too difficult the Americans could simply throw them out (and probably into jail). So the French pretended to "cooperate" with the Americans, but in fact did all they could to make life miserable. They did a thorough job. At first Admiral Halsey had operated from his flagship, the *Argonne*, in Noumea Harbor. Headquarters was then set up in an old warehouse on the waterfront, where the expanding staff was crammed into the tin building like a mess of anchovies. Halsey set up shop in the abandoned Japanese consulate on top of the hill.

As a ship came in from the east to the lighthouse that marked the barrier reef and the channel, the sailors looked dreamily on this land of promise, some of them with the tales of Robert Louis Stevenson echoing in their minds. The ship stopped, and the French pilot came aboard and took them inside to Noumea Harbor to anchor. The harbor was filled with a motley collection of craft—old Dutch transports, Australian and American troopships, battlewagons, a handful of auxiliary carriers, cruisers, destroyers, ammunition ships, and oilers. In all its years Noumea had never been so busy.

From the harbor the white and red and yellow of the city's buildings stood against the green growth of the tropics. It looked lush and inviting.

"This port is attractive when viewed from a distance," wrote one hope-filled sailor as his ship anchored on the edge of the line. "And the climate is ideal. Something like Florida."

That night he and his shipmates basked happily on deck enjoying the new climate. The next day they went ashore for a few hours.

"What a dump!" the sailor wrote that second day. "In comparison, Reykjavik, Iceland, is Nirvana!"

He had seen his dusky beauties in their home environment.

"Splay-footed Melanesians chattering in a patois, some flyblown stores with their shelves empty and a general air of dejected lassitude. . . ." That was his "tropical paradise."

The impression would grow worse. After a few days, his ship headed north toward the war zone. As they moved to Efate, in the New Hebrides, the wind came blasting at them, a searing wind that carried thousands of flies. It was so hot that most of the men abandoned their bunks and tried to sleep on deck. They reached Efate. Another disappointment. Even the officer's club of Havannah Harbor was dubbed "Malaria Manor."

They were now in the real South Pacific, the South Pacific of mud and Melanesians, cannibals and crocodiles, where the green of the jungle dripped water and crotch rot, where "recreation" consisted of swimming offshore from the ship or going inshore to drink warm beer and walk around in the mud.

Guadalcanal, they would find, was the worst of all. The scores of Japanese and Allied warships sunk in Ironbottom Sound sent a constant trickle of oil to the surface of the water and it drifted into shore. And, on those few days when the wind was right and the beach was clear, there was always the danger of sharks and seagoing crocodiles that had developed a nice taste for human flesh in clearing up the results of the carnage of the six months of sea battles.

In the middle of January, Admiral Nimitz arrived in the South Pacific. It was his second visit to the war zone, and this time he brought Secretary of the Navy Frank Knox on an inspection trip. They traveled in Nimitz's big Catalina flying boat. They stayed aboard various warships in conditions that were luxurious compared to those ashore. On the beach, even Admiral Kelly Turner, the senior officer on Guadalcanal, was lucky to have a hut with a plywood floor and half walls.

Mud, flies, mosquitoes, humidity, heat, and fear of Japanese air raids dominated life. Up country, in New Georgia and beyond, it was the same, in reverse, for the Japanese. They had a word for the climate unmatched in English: *mushiatsui*—buggy-hot.

While Secretary Knox looked around, Admiral Nimitz had a chance to talk over plans for the forthcoming operations with Admiral Halsey. They were agreed that it would be three months before a major operation could be launched, but Halsey wanted to keep moving for several reasons, not the least of which was to retain the initiative and maintain the morale he had brought from a dead low to a victorious pitch. When Guadalcanal was secured, he wanted to take the Russell Islands, which lay just thirty miles northwest of Cape Esperance.

In late January, still unmindful of the Japanese plan of evacuation of all troops south of New Georgia, Admiral Halsey expected that the five or six thousand troops reported to be in the Russells would remain and fight. For the safety of the Guadalcanal garrison and Henderson field, they must be dislodged. Then the Russells could be used by American PT boats. That was the official explanation for the coming operation. More important to Halsey was the practice it would offer for his adolescent amphibious force. Admiral Turner, the amphibious commander, had more experience in amphibious operations than any other man in the Pacific. That wasn't saying much. His major effort had been the Guadalcanal landings and resupply, and the conditions of those efforts were not likely to be repeated. The Japanese had been taken by surprise in August when the initial landing was staged. Thereafter they had reacted furiously, and the Guadalcanal campaign had become a slugging match. What Turner must practice were new techniques, using new sorts of craft to land troops in a hurry and get the supplies onto the beaches.

Admiral Nimitz understood what was in Halsey's mind, and he offered no complaint, although it seemed obvious that for its own sake the territory was hardly worth much effort. In Washington, the navy's commander, Admiral King, questioned the whole affair, but Halsey stood his ground, and Nimitz backed him up without telling King precisely why. So on February 7 (the day the Japanese left Guadalcanal), without knowing of the evacuation, Halsey ordered the invasion of the Russell Islands, which consisted of vast tracts of coconut trees belonging to the Lever Brothers soap people and even vaster areas of mud. The Russells were to have a first-class invasion, which was called "Cleanslate."

When Admiral Turner set up camp near Koli Point, on Guadalcanal, even headquarters was built of plywood-floored huts. It was called Camp Crocodile, and it would be the home of the Third Fleet's Amphibious Command for the next year.

Turner's job was to stage an invasion using small vessels. He would test out new landing craft, particularly the small amphibious "amphtracks" that could leave the side of a ship and carry men into the beaches, theoretically without even getting their feet wet.

The composition of the attacking troop force indicated the greatest problem in the South Pacific just then: the shortage of trained units of fighting men. This assault force was as mixed a bag as had ever been sent out: most of the Army 43rd Infantry Division, a third of the 11th Marine Defense Battalion, the 10th Marine Defense Battalion, the Third Marine Raider Battalion, and part of the 35th Naval Construction Battalion (Seabees), a naval boat pool organization, eight PT boats, and a number of small artillery units which had been begged from other commands. The troops and equipment came from New Caledonia, Florida Island, Espiritu Santo, Tulagi, and from the States. The reserve was an Army regimental combat team (undesignated) from the XXIV Corps on Guadalcanal.

On February 9, as Admiral Turner was assembling his far-flung force at Guadalcanal, the word came that the Japanese had evacuated the Russells. But the plan was in motion, and it would continue.

A few days later, a convoy left Noumea carrying a number of the troops bound for the Russells. First they would move to Guadalcanal and then the convoy would become part of the invasion force. The convoy consisted of the transports *President Jackson*, *President Adams*, *President Hayes*, *Crescent City*, and *Tallulah*, accompanied by half-a-dozen destroyers.

On the morning of February 17, as the convoy approached the Solomons from the south, the escorting destroyers picked up several unidentified aircraft on their radar sets. The contacts persisted all day, although the shadowing planes kept carefully out of range. By afternoon the convoy commander, Captain Ingolf N. Kiland, was certain that these were not random contacts but enemy planes shadowing the convoy and that the convoy could expect an air attack. If the Japanese followed the pattern they had already established, the attack would come at dark. Captain Kiland made preparations to fend off an air attack. He ordered additional .50 caliber and .30 caliber machine guns set up on deck and in the landing boats, to be manned by the troops the ships were carrying to Guadalcanal. At six o'clock that evening, in the gloaming, he ordered the gun crews alerted. Using the Talk Between Ships communication system (TBS), Captain Kiland ordered the gunners to open fire without notice on any aircraft they saw.

Just before darkness fell, one destroyer reported clear contact with two planes. At eleven minutes past seven, the black of night was suddenly broken by a bright white flare that exposed the entire convoy.

At that time the convoy was traveling in a closed formation of three columns, the columns a thousand yards apart, and the ships maintaining a distance apart in each column of six hundred yards. The convoy had then reached a position about 20 miles south of the little Solomon island of Santa Anna. The convoy was following the usual zigzagging pattern.

Immediately the convoy commander ordered a radical change in tactics. The zigzag ceased. The ships increased the intervals from six hundred to eight hundred yards, and they began maneuvering violently in 45-degree turns.

That first flare was followed by others and by white float lights dropped on the water on all sides of the convoy. The enemy shadowers were doing a good job of outlining the area. But for whom? As the minutes passed and there was no sign of the enemy but those flares and float lights, the tension grew almost unbearable.

Captain Kiland sent messages to Admiral Halsey's headquarters and to Guadalcanal to ask for air protection.

The destroyers had been operating as an antisubmarine screen, rotating around the convoy at a distance of 2,500 yards. These enemy preparations indicated a bombing attack, so the destroyers were moved in close to the convoy to add their gun power to that of the transports.

The moon appeared bright and clear behind a layer of high cirrostratus clouds that covered the sky, diffusing the moonlight and giving the moon an eerie halo. The minutes crept by, and nothing happened—until 7:43. Then a green flare appeared directly over the convoy and burst into a cluster of eight green flares. One of the destroyers began firing with its main battery. Other ships also began firing, until the gunners realized they were firing at the antiaircraft bursts of the destroyer. The guns all stopped. The tension began again.

At eight o'clock, the radar operators saw seven blips coming in from the south, twelve miles away. The spotter planes were still up there, overhead, dropping more flares. The destroyers began firing again, directed by radar. Captain Kiland moved the convoy away from the angle of attack to make it more difficult for the bombers.

As the Japanese planes began to appear, the Americans saw that they were twin-engined Betty (Mitsubishi) bombers of the all-purpose type. These had been modified for torpedo work.

This torpedo attack was badly coordinated. Good technique called for the formation to stick together until the moment of attack and then for the planes to peel off and come in from several directions, in the hope of confusing the gunners and at least diluting the fire against any one plane. But these torpedo planes split up too soon and thus made individual targets for the gunners. The first plane appeared near the convoy five minutes after the seven bombers had been sighted. At 8:06 the destroyer *Drayton*'s lookouts spotted a plane coming in on her starboard beam, until it was on a line with the transports. The *Drayton*'s gunners opened fire but did not see any hits. When the plane neared the transports, however, they opened fire, and the Japanese bomber turned on a wing and slid into the sea, erupting in a geyser of flame.

Two minutes later that Japanese bomber was followed by another. This one came in on the port bow of the *Drayton*. Her gunners opened fire, as did those of another destroyer nearby, and the plane crashed into the water. Another plane bored in, and another, and the guns of the ships were turned on them as they came. One by one the Japanese planes fell, each flaming into the sea and burning on the water, until five yellow flares had been added to the white ones. The fires spread across the water and continued to burn, and convoy commander Kiland moved away from them, for they silhouetted his ships.

The attack reached its height twenty minutes after it began, and then suddenly it was over, and no damage had been suffered by the convoy. The officers of the destroyers reported hearing the sounds of torpedo propellers underwater and explosions that must have been torpedoes at the end of the run. But only the *Crescent City*'s skipper noted any close explosions. He reported a heavy explosion at the height of the attack, but it did no damage, and he decided it must have been a spent torpedo going off nearby.

Probably the ship most endangered was the *President Adams*. Her captain reported seeing a torpedo dropped four hundred yards off her bow. It came up "porpoising" and then sank just twenty-five yards ahead of the ship's bow. The plane that had dropped the torpedo banked sharply to the right and passed directly over the *President Adams*. The plane had already been hit, and the gunners of the transport saw smoke trailing from its engines. They scored more hits, and the plane glided into the sea, where it caught fire and burned.

Five minutes after the attack ended, two PBY patrol bombers arrived from Henderson Field on Guadalcanal. They were carrying flares, which they expected to drop some distance from the convoy and thus to confuse the enemy torpedo bombers. But there was no need. The attack had ended for the night, a total failure for the Japanese and a most welcome success for the Americans, because for the first time a relatively lightly armored convoy had come through a major attack without a scratch.

The invasion of the Russell Islands was sheer anticlimax. Admiral Turner's ships and small craft and the escorting task force left Lunga Roads at Guadalcanal on the night of February 20, and steamed without incident. They reached the Russells by dawn. An advance force had already announced that the Japanese were gone, and they had not come back. So it was simply a matter of bringing the men and equipment ashore and setting up camp. In the next week, nine thousand men were brought to the islands to begin construction of an air base and naval facilities for PT boats and other craft.

The Japanese, meanwhile, were building up their forces at New Georgia and on Kolombangara, across Kula Gulf. Admiral Yamamoto didn't intend to let the Americans on Guadalcanal rest and was already asking for more planes to reinvigorate his air attacks on Guadalcanal. From four bases located at Rabaul, the bombers and fighters could stage down to little Buka Island at the northern tip of Bougainville, which housed an air base. Another was located at Kahili, near Buin at the southern end of Bougainville, with a naval base and seaplane base. There was another air base on Ballale and then one at Vila and another at Munda on New Georgia.

The tables had been turned, however, in the naval sense. It was now the Japanese who were finding difficulties in running their supply missions to the southernmost bases, through an American air and sea gauntlet. Vice Admiral Aubrey W. Fitch, who had fought the Battle of the Coral Sea, was commander of Halsey's land-based air forces. His headquarters was located at Espiritu Santo, next to the Palikulo airfield. But the main air base for Halsey's assault on the Japanese in the northern Solomons was Henderson Field on Guadalcanal. One fighter strip had been built during the heat of the campaign for the island and another a little later. Bomber strips were now added around Koli Point. Guadalcanal bristled with antiaircraft guns, and the strips were always full of bombers and fighters. Just before the Russells landing, Rear Admiral Charles P. Mason was moved up to Guadalcanal with a brand new job as Commander, Aircraft, Solomons Islands. Halsey now had more than three hundred aircraft on Guadalcanal, and, for the first time since the campaign began, there seemed to be enough of everything. The Black Cat night fighters had made their appearance and they would add a new dimension to the air war. Not nearly as many of the Japanese night fighters, the Gekkos, ever got into action as did the Black Cats. In the air, the tables were almost completely turned on the Japanese, and, at sea, six American task forces stood ready to accept any Japanese challenge. It was the Americans now who came by night to bombard Japanese airfields as the Japanese had bombarded Henderson Field in the summer and fall of 1942.

In February, planes from Admiral Fitch's force and others from General MacArthur's command bombed the Japanese airfields from Rabaul to Munda. But the Japanese were as determined to keep their fields in operation as the Americans had been in the bad days of the previous summer. The moment the bombers left the pitted airstrips, the troops were at work, filling them up with coral. The Americans destroyed the ground installations, so the Japanese moved underground. The American bombers didn't catch many planes on the ground at the southern bases because the Japanese kept most of them back at Rabaul. But in February and March there was no way of assessing the damage save through aerial reconnaissance, and that didn't show what was going on underground.

The second Japanese resupply mission was sent down from Rabaul on February 19, the day before Admiral Turner's amphibious forces invaded the Russells. This time, lulled by their success on the first mission, the Japanese employed a transport, the *Yokuwaru Maru*. She was escorted down to Kolombangara by No. 22 minesweeper and No. 25 subchaser, without incident.

In the middle of the unloading, however, enemy planes interfered. A number of fighters carried out a strafing attack, and in maneuvering to escape them, the ships had about ten percent of their supplies smashed up. There was no other damage. The *Yokuwaru Maru* completed her unloading, and the minesweeper and subchaser took her back again safely to Rabaul.

Then came the landings in the Russells, which the Japanese scout planes discovered immediately. That move created a whole new problem for the army and the navy "cooperators." There were more meetings at Rabaul, and this time it was decided that the resupply system must again be changed. With the Allies so near, building naval and air bases in the Russells, such direct resupply must be abandoned. In the future, the supply ships would run in during the ten days of the dark of the moon. If there were any questions by the army, the navy scout plane report of February 20 ought to answer them. The scout plane pilot counted 180 aircraft on the fields of Guadalcanal that day. The meaning was clear: the Americans could now attack Kolombangara and New Georgia from sea and air without much difficulty. The 80-mile gap between the tip of Guadalcanal and the south end of the Russells made that much difference. Once bridged, it opened the way for new night-mares for the Japanese defenders. If they were going to hold, the navy told the army, the army would have to reinforce the troop contingents on New Georgia and Kolombangara. Reluctantly, the army doubled the force, to about 10,000 men.

A third, hurried, resupply mission to Kolombangara was necessary to handle the rest of the supplies that had backed up. This mission was dispatched from Rabaul on February 27, just a week after the Americans took over the Russells. Again, a transport carried the supplies. She was the *Kirikawa Maru*. The same team, Minesweeper No. 22 and Subchaser No. 25, escorted her on the run south by night. Again, the nocturnal voyage was made without incident, but at about four o'clock the next afternoon, as she was unloading, a force of eighteen fighters and a dozen dive-bombers raided the anchorage. The Eleventh Air Fleet had assigned a protective air cover to this mission, in view of the changed circumstance of the enemy. A dozen Japanese fighters appeared, challenged the American force, and managed to keep the bombers away from the ships. So again the mission was a success, except that this time, on the return voyage, another set of American bombers found the *Kirikawa Maru* off the Shortlands and sank her. With the increasingly serious shortage of shipping, this loss gave the supply planners something to think about, particularly since in March, the Americans were becoming decidedly more aggressive.

Early in March, the American destroyers *Fletcher, O'Bannon, Nicholas,* and *Radford* were assigned to bombard Munda airfield on New Georgia. On the night of March 5, they came up the Slot, past the Russells, just as the Japanese had come down so many times before; then they turned west to pass Rendova and come in through Blanche Channel to hit the Munda airfield. They fired 1,600 five-inch shells at the airfield that night and retired without seeing an enemy. It seemed to be a most successful mission; the trouble was that it did not put Munda airfield out of commission. The next day the field was operating again as usual.

But that night the Munda mission had a corollary. Rear Admiral A. S.

Merrill was to take his task force of cruisers and destroyers into even more dangerous waters, further up the line, through Kula Gulf, to bombard Vila airfield on Kolombangara. Merrill had the cruisers *Montpelier*, *Cleveland*, and *Denver* and three destroyers. The mission was timed to coincide with that of the four other U.S. destroyers. It also happened to coincide with a Japanese mission given the destroyers *Minegumo* and *Murasame*, by Captain Tadao Tachi of the Second Destroyer Squadron, to supply the Japanese garrison at Vila with food and ammunition. The Japanese ships left the destroyer base at the Shortlands shortly after dark, each carrying a full load of provisions. They were seen by an Australian coast watcher, but in the darkness he could not decide whether the ships were destroyers or cruisers, and he reported both possibilities to the American base at Guadalcanal.

Admiral Merrill was steaming up the Slot on the night of March 5 when a radio message from Guadalcanal warned him that the two enemy warships were at sea, moving into the area for which he was headed. A few minutes later he received word that the pilot of one of the three Black Cats acting as his air cover had spotted the enemy ships. They were heading for Vila.

The *Murasame* and the *Minegumo* were quite unaware of the shadowing night fighters. They steamed down past Vella Lavella Island and up through Blackett Strait. They arrived off Vila at 11:30 that night and transferred their cargoes to barges. Had they turned about and returned to the Shortlands by the same route, they would have missed the American ships, but the senior officer, Lieutenant Commander Tokuno of the *Minegumo*, decided to make the faster run up through Kula Gulf to the Shortlands. That course took the Japanese straight toward the American force.

In the night battles off Guadalcanal, several months before, the Japanese usually had the best of it, because they were carefully trained in night-fighting techniques, and when they came down the Slot in those early days, they were always looking for a fight. But this night it was the Americans who were looking for a fight, and because of the new techniques coming to the South Pacific, they were ready for it. They had been warned about the enemy's presence, and they had radar to plot their course and spot the enemy ships. The American radar picked up the Japanese destroyers very nicely, and the American cruisers suddenly opened fire. The sixth salvo struck one destroyer. The Americans said it was the *Murasame* and that she was hit by the guns just before a torpedo fired by the destroyer *Waller* also hit that ship. Some projectile must have hit the magazines of the destroyer in question (the Japanese said the *Minegumo* went down first) because she exploded and went down immediately.

The second destroyer (the Japanese said it was the *Murasame*, the Americans said it was the *Minegumo*) tried to escape to the northeast. Her captain still did not know what he faced. He had seen the enemy only as a few pinpoints of light and he didn't know what sort of ships he faced or how many. He never had a chance to find out, because the radar shifted to his ship, and the cruisers began firing on him. He had no chance even to fire back. The cruisers' six-inch guns began to find the ship, and in three minutes she was dead in the water. One or more shells blew a hole in the plating at the engine room, and it began to fill. The ship started to sink. The captain ordered the ship abandoned. Just then a pair of the ship's guns, set off by the American shells, began firing independently and gave the Americans the impression that the destroyer was firing back at them. The surviving Japanese swam for it as the American ships moved in and bombarded Vila airfield. From both destroyers, only ten warrant officers and about 160 men survived to swim ashore and gain shelter with the Vila garrison.

The Americans were long gone, having sped triumphantly back down the Slot to Guadalcanal to report the sinking of a pair of Japanese cruisers. It was a signal victory for two reasons: it was accomplished with ease by the quick and accurate fire of the radar-controlled guns, and it was the first time the *Waller* had done something to rescue the dismal reputation of the American destroyer men in night fighting and particularly torpedo action. The *Waller* had fired five torpedoes, and one of them had done the job on one destroyer. The American navy had started the Guadalcanal campaign at a considerable disadvantage but in six months had caught up remarkably in every department, and the improvement in radar mechanics and techniques was from this point on to put the Japanese enemy at an enormous disadvantage for the rest of the war.

4

NAKED POWER
IN THE AIR

FEBRUARY 1943 was marked by very little land fighting in either New Guinea or the Solomons. Japanese troops from Salamaua did try to capture the Australian air base at Wau, but the Japanese force in the area was not powerful enough to overwhelm the defenders. So the army command decided to send reinforcements. A convoy of three ships made it safely from Rabaul to Wewak and landed supplies on February 19. The Allies had air patrols out, and they bombed and strafed Japanese installations and ships they could find at sea, but they didn't show any unusual air power at the time.

Thus the Japanese had no real conception of the American air buildup that was occurring in the South Pacific and Southwest Pacific that month. General George C. Kenney's Fifth Air Force was expanding, and that meant more fast P-38 twin-engined fighter planes, more medium B-25 and A-20 bombers, and more heavy B-17 and B-24 bombers. Until the last days of the Guadalcanal campaign, the Japanese airmen had little respect for the American army air forces. The army pilots were flying the old P-400 fighter and the P-39. The latter was regarded by the Japanese Zero pilots as a "pigeon," and there was nothing they liked better than to get into a fracas with a flock of those pigeons. The results were too often negative for the Americans. As for the heavy bombers, they had a dismal record. The pilots had been trained in techniques designed for Europe's high-level bombing missions. But when they were brought to the Pacific and employed against shipping, the high-level bombing proved so fruitless that several Japanese convoy commanders boasted that they had absolutely no fear of a B-17 attack because the big bombers never hit anything they aimed at.

From Tokyo that month, interspersed among the awkward explanations of the advance to the rear in the Solomons, were promises that the Japanese airmen and navy would soon be mopping up the enemy. But General Kenney was as much aware of the deficiencies of his air units as were the Japanese, and he had already taken steps to correct them. The Allied air forces in Papua had grown to number more than 200 bombers and 130 fighters.

Normally the version of the B-25 Mitchell medium bomber sent to the Pacific carried the bombardier in a plastic bubble in the nose of the plane to operate the Norden bombsight. But Kenney decided the planes would use a low-level approach and thus did not need that sort of precision. The bombardiers were taken out, and in each nose bubble, eight .50 caliber machine guns were substituted. Even the bombing techniques had undergone major alteration. The medium bombers were armed with five-hundred-pound bombs fitted with delayed action fuzes, so that the plane could come in low, bomb, and get away before the bomb exploded. No more high-level drops. From now on the bombing against ships would be by skip-bombing, coming in at low level and dropping the bombs so they struck the water in front of the target; the bombs would either explode close to the ship or skip into the sides—either way the effect was more like that of a torpedo. These techniques had been practiced by enough pilots against Japanese targets for the Americans to know that they worked, but the Japanese higher commands were serenely unaware of them or of the major buildup of American and Australian air forces in the area.

There was a good deal of the self-delusion of arrogance within the Japanese military establishment; and that is the main reason that the extent or the portent of the defeat at Guadalcanal had not yet struck home.

In February 1943 the first result of the new set of war plans evolved by the Imperial General Staff was a renewal of the drive to capture all of Papua. To this end, the Australian possession of the Wau airfield was even more of an obstacle to the orderly occupation of the Huon Gulf area, and army and navy commanders at Rabaul agreed that it must be removed. More troops were needed and so a convoy was arranged to carry reinforcements from the Japanese Army's 51st Division to Lae. Eight transports and cargo ships were loaded with soldiers and provisions, including aviation gasoline in drums. These ships would be escorted by eight destroyers, and the whole effort would be under the command of Rear Admiral Masatomi Kimura. Vice Admiral Gunichi Mikawa, commander of the Japanese land-based air forces, promised all the air support that would be needed.

The convoy sailed at eleven o'clock on the night of February 28. On March 1 the convoy seemed protected by the squalls of a storm front as it moved at seven knots down the Bismarck Sea toward northern New Guinea. Their major concern was submarine watch.

Until the afternoon of March 1, the voyage was as successful as Admiral Kimura could wish. The ships moved under the cover of the storm, and no submarines appeared. But then the weather changed, the storm passed off into the Solomon Sea, and the cloud cover began to loosen. Suddenly out of the clouds appeared a single B-24 bomber. The radio operator soon had sent word to General MacArthur's headquarters that a convoy of enemy merchant ships was at sea, protected by half-a-dozen destroyers. The B-24 shadowed them that afternoon and until dark, when it lost contact.

Rabaul was as good as its word and sent air cover as soon as the news of the American plane was flashed. The next morning, March 2, the air cover was resumed, but so was the shadowing. The convoy was now nearing Vitiaz Strait, which runs between New Britain Island (Rabaul) and the Papuan peninsula of New Guinea.

The next morning a number of Allied bombers took off from fields on Papua. There were twelve B-17s and seventeen B-24s, escorted by sixteen P-38s of the 39th Fighter Squadron at Port Moresby. The weather over northern New Guinea was cloudy and full of thunderheads. The P-38s had a hard time keeping track of their bombers and lost them before they ever reached the vicinity of the convoy. They did spot a flight of three Japanese army planes (Oscars) and shot down one of these, but that action had nothing to do with the convoy. The army command was sending small raiding flights over the Allied positions almost every day for harassment.

As the convoy steamed along, out of the sky came seven B-17s to launch an attack. Three of them bombed from an altitude of 10,000 feet, the old technique. The destroyers and merchant ships immediately began "stitching the sky" with gunfire, as the Japanese historians put it later. At an altitude of about 6,000 feet, the B-17s leveled off and dropped their bombs.

The transport *Kyokusei Maru* took direct hits on the No. 1 and No. 2 holds. Aboard this ship were troops of the 115th Infantry Regiment. The direct hits caused fires to break out in the ship and twenty minutes later the troops abandoned her. Fifty minutes after that she sank.

The transport *Saiyo Maru* was in the right-hand column, and the *Kenbu Maru* was on the left. Both vessels took near misses that caused serious damage to the ships. The destroyer *Asagumo* rescued 819 men from the sunken transport. The destroyer *Yukikaze* took on the staff of the 51st Division, and these two destroyers left the convoy and put on full steam to deliver the passengers at Lae after dark. The destroyers turned about, then, to hurry back and join the convoy. They were lucky not to reach it before the battle was joined.

Thus far the attack had been no more than normal and by Japanese standards a very lucky one for the Allies. But on the afternoon of March 2 a new element had entered the picture. From early afternoon, Admiral Kimura and the convoy commander were aware of constant shadowing of the main force by enemy aircraft, which in itself was unusual. And during the afternoon they were attacked by another six B-17s. These were driven off by friendly planes dispatched as air cover by Admiral Mikawa, but not before they had bombed the convoy, killing a number of men on each transport. After the attack, the shadowing from long distance continued.

As the convoy moved on, the Japanese air cover was intensified and although another four planes attacked that afternoon, they were driven off without doing damage. As evening neared, the convoy was off Uinbari Island. That night enemy planes dropped flares above the convoy, but no attack came. Admiral Kimura spent a watchful night, for the Japanese now expected enemy action at any time. But the really dangerous time, all agreed, would come when the convoy reached the narrow Dampier Strait. Once they negotiated that channel, they were virtually at Lae, and the voyage was completed. Traveling at nine knots, the convoy expected to arrive at the destination shortly after daybreak. The convoy moved on and reached Uinpoi Island, on the eastern side of Dampier Strait. They were more or less in Japanese territory from that point on.

The activity began just before dawn. The gloom of the predawn sky was just lifting when the lookouts reported low-flying enemy scout planes around the convoy. When a look at the clearing sky showed that the weather was certain to be fine, Admiral Kimura prepared for trouble.

With the dawn came the heavy air cover that Admiral Kimura had hoped for: 42 Zeroes, Hamps, and Oscars (the latter two types were also variants of the Zero fighter) from Rabaul circled the convoy at high altitude. On the basis of experience, they were in the right place to counter an American high altitude bomber attack.

But the Americans were becoming innovative. Early on the morning of March 3, the Allied planes began to take to the air. Sixteen P-38s of the

39th Squadron and sixteen more from the 9th Squadron were assigned to escort the bombers in. When they reached a point about 30 miles from the convoy, they saw the high altitude cover and moved to engage. Suddenly, those on the decks of the Japanese ships saw the sky full of planes. The lookouts counted a hundred aircraft in the sky above them. The flight of B-17s that appeared at about ten o'clock that morning came in at medium altitude. Following doctrine, the convoy commander kept his ships moving steadily on, ignoring the heavy bombers.

But then, at mast height, in came dozens of A-20 and B-25 bombers and Beaufighters of the Royal Australian Air Force to bomb and strafe the convoy and the escorting destroyers.

At Guadalcanal the Japanese had adopted a defensive technique to counter torpedo planes. It called for the skipper to turn into or away from the attacking planes, thus presenting the narrowest possible target for torpedoes. This is what Admiral Kimura's skippers did that day, as the Allied air attack began.

The activity began before dawn. (Since in these next pages I am following a Japanese account for the most part, the time is Japanese or Tokyo time, rather than the time frame used by the Americans, which was two hours later.) The darkness was just beginning to lift when the lookouts of the protective destroyers reported seeing low-flying Allied patrol planes not far from the convoy. Admiral Kimura looked at the lightening sky. It was going to be a lovely day, clear as a bell—worse luck. The Japanese waited.

At about eight o'clock (Tokyo time, as compared to ten o'clock in the time the U.S. forces used) the attackers arrived. They had formed up over the Papuan airfields early that morning, two squadrons of P-38s to escort twenty-five B-17s and forty A-20s. These were the first attackers to appear. Then in came another group of B-25s, those specially equipped B-25s with the eight .50 caliber machine guns in the nose.

The Japanese air command at Rabaul had made sure that the convoy was covered from before sunrise. But those fifteen planes up above, flying high altitude circles around the convoy, had been there a long time, and they were running short of gas. It was time for a change, and right on schedule up came their replacements from Rabaul. They arrived almost simultaneously with the first air attack on the convoy.

Following the air doctrine evolved in dealing with B-17s, the Japanese fighters stayed high and prepared to attack. About fifteen of the P-38s peeled off to keep them away from the bombers. Flying at medium altitude, then, the Japanese planes were completely surprised when the A-20s and the B-25s appeared, so close to "the deck" that the slipstreams of the powerful engines churned up wakes in the sea. From Admiral Kimura's vantage point, the attack had the look of a torpedo plane strike, and the transports and warships took action accordingly, turning into the enemy planes, to minimize the size of the target they presented. It was just what the American bombers wanted. Down they roared over the ships, machine guns spitting. The ship's gunners along the sides of the vessels could not bring their weapons to bear; only the bow and stern gunners could get fleeting shots at the attackers.

The tracers and explosive shells of the machine guns started fires and killed many men aboard the ships, but this was only the beginning. After the first pass, the pilots turned and raced back, again at mast level, and this time they dropped their bombs as they came. The bombs struck the water, skipped, and smashed against the sides of the ships, tearing jagged holes, or exploded below the water line with the effect of a torpedo.

In half an hour it was all over. Every ship of the convoy was damaged—seven transports and six destroyers—and the convoy was spread halfway over Huon Gulf. The convoy commander had hoped to land his troops at Lae that day, but the only ones who would get there would be those who could make it by small craft and those troops carried in by the destroyers *Asagumo* and *Yukikaze*.

The landing craft and barges were aboard the transports, but the speeding and dodging of the helmsmen to try to save the ships made it virtually impossible to put any of them over the side as long as the attack lasted. Then it was over. The Allied planes had run out of ammunition and bombs. The air and the sea became suddenly quiet. Up above, even the skies were clear. The B-17s, having lost one of their number to Japanese fighters, had gone home. So had the A-20s and the B-25s, and the Royal Australian Air Force Beaufighters, which had come down lowest of all to strafe. Three P-38s had gone down and at least five Japanese fighters.

One of the first ships of the convoy to sink was the destroyer *Shirayuki*, flagship of Admiral Kimura. The *Tokitsukaze* was also set afire and started sinking; and she carried members of the staff of the 18th Army. The next warship to feel the bite was the destroyer *Arashio*. As she floundered, dead in the water, her sister ship, the *Asashio* came up to lend a hand.

The American and Australian planes went back to their bases for gas and ammunition, and they would soon be on the attack again. The situation of the convoy as a military force was now hopeless. It was scattered and the ships were sunk or sinking. Only one of the transports hit that day had actually gone down, but several were burning, all were badly mauled, and there was no way that the force landing schedule could be met. What could be done was to move the troops into the landing craft and barges and get them ashore as swiftly as possible, and all efforts were turned to this end.

It was apparent to the captain of the *Oigawa Maru* that his ship would never make it to Lae. She was badly holed and barely navigable. But at that moment there was nothing to do but wait.

From the Japanese Navy point of view, too, at 8:30 that morning the situation was nearly hopeless. It was obvious that the enemy had severely hurt the convoy. The destroyers had suffered nearly as badly as the transports. The *Shirayuki*, Admiral Masatomi Kimura's flagship, had been sunk. So had the *Tokitsukaze*, and those staff officers of the 18th Army. The *Arashio* had become unnavigable, and the *Asashio*, standing alongside to conduct rescue operations, was attacked by the second wave of American bombers.

When the second enemy attack came, the *Oigawa Maru* was sinking, and that raid finished her off. She went down fast, and to the surface came all sorts of flotsam: life rafts, cases of provisions and clothing, as well as a large number of floating bodies. Oddly, one group of about twenty bodies came up all together and drifted together in the current.

The *Oigawa Maru* had sunk right in Dampier Strait, where the current was running at about 1.5 knots toward the south. At about nine o'clock the surviving destroyers moved in among the wreckage and began rescue operations.

Back at Rabaul it was recognized that the Lae landings were completely out of the question because of the destruction of the transports and thorough confusion of the escorting vessels. The army operations command in the *Yukikaze* could no longer function. The army commander was landed at Finschhafen.

At Rabaul the 8th Area Army Command and the 18th Army Command called on the Southeast Area Naval Command for help. But at that time it was virtually impossible for anyone so far away to be helpful. Rabaul did radio Truk, and two submarines, the *I-26* and the *I-17*, were ordered to the scene. But the *I-26* was on her way out to patrol along the east coast of Goshu Island. It would take more than a day to get to the scene. The *I-17* was just about to return to Truk from patrol when she got the message. She turned around. Other than the dispatch of those two I-boats, the navy felt it could do nothing. The high hopes of the army were smashed.

In the convoy, or what remained of it, at about 10:30 that morning came a report from Rabaul that a large force of enemy planes were heading toward the battle area. The three destroyers, *Uranami*, *Shikinami*, and *Asagumo*, suspended rescue operations then and moved away from Dampier Strait, heading north around the end of Rongu Island.

At 11:20 the men in the water and on the sinking ships were heartened to see Japanese fighters overhead. These were elements of the 12th and 14th Army fighter squadrons. At 10,000 feet they gave air cover to the men in the water as the destroyers sped off to the north. But it was not long before the American planes arrived, and then a battle began at high altitude. Other American planes swooped down low to attack the remaining ships, boats, and rafts in the water. From above, the fliers could see the enormous spread of flotsam, bodies, survivors clinging together, the sinking ships, and the destroyers struggling to escape. "It overwhelmed the eye," one Japanese observer wrote.

Soon Japanese navy planes appeared on the scene as well and added their strength to the fight. But their problem was the same as that of the previous day: the Japanese were at the disadvantage of being far from home base, which gave them a limited time to carry on the battle; then if they did not wish to land in the sea or on an outer island, they must speed back to Rabaul. This was one of the first of the aerial operations in which army and navy planes were called on under the new directives to "cooperate." The degree of cooperation was not of the sort practiced by the Allies. Army and navy units operated totally independently; cooperation meant that the navy planes showed up to help, over what was essentially an army area of operation. Several flights of Zeros came in, tangled with the Americans, and then went off again.

But the American strength was far greater than the Japanese air commanders had expected it to be. At 1:15 in the afternoon a whole new group of fighters and bombers appeared over Dampier Strait and began mixing it up with the Japanese defenders, attacking what was left of the forces on the sea. The Japanese airmen saw more B-17s, more A-20s, and a large number of P-40s, which did not have the range to join in the original battle at sea but were admirably suited for attack and strafing operations under the circumstances that existed around Dampier Strait. They literally tore apart any remaining cohesion of the surviving Japanese units. Rafts, boats, and the listing, sinking ships were worked over time and again. Japanese navy planes from Rabaul tried to protect the men in the boats and in the water, but they were badly outnumbered. Half a dozen Japanese fighters went down that afternoon over Lae. A number of boats were making for the shore and they were perfect targets for the P-40s. One of the P-40s began an attack on a landing barge loaded with troops from one of the transports. Seven Japanese fighters got on his tail. Other U.S. fighters came in to help and a dogfight began. At least two of those seven Japanese planes were shot down. The slaughter did not end until 4:30 when the Americans again were forced to return to their bases. The *Shikinami* and *Uranami* then turned back toward Rabaul with 2,700 survivors. They left behind the *Yukikaze* and *Asagumo* to deal with the remaining survivors in the water.

As the night of March 3 came to Dampier Strait, so did the American PT boats. The Japanese army and navy planes had to head for home by the time the PT boats came out, seven from the base at Tufi and three from Kona Kope. As darkness fell, they were moving into Kula Gulf. Two of the boats hit debris from the day's battle and had to turn back. The other eight boats went on, arriving off Lae shortly before eleven o'clock that night. Two of them found the burning hulk of *Oigawa Maru*, already abandoned by her crew and passengers, and put two more torpedoes into her. Without ado she sank. The other PT boats scoured the water for ships but found none. The only Japanese ships left in the gulf that night were the sinking destroyers *Arashio* and *Asashio*. The others had picked up the survivors they could find and had headed back for Rabaul.

The American PT boats then began searching for smaller craft, turning their 40 mm, 37 mm, and 20 mm guns on them. Those guns were of little use against a destroyer, except to sweep the decks, but against a life raft or boat they were devastating, and hundreds of Japanese soldiers died that night. Their craft were sunk, and they were gunned to death as they tried to swim for the coast at Lae. It was not one of the more gallant nights for the U.S. Navy, but in this war there was little gallantry. The Japanese had established the nature of the war in the beginning, with their "death marches" in the Philippines, Malaya, and Indonesia, which had been designed to impress the local people with the superiority of the Japanese over the Westerners. Also, at Guadalcanal the Americans had learned a great deal about their enemy; particularly that surrender was disgraceful to him, and that a Japanese soldier would pretend to be wounded or to surrender, and then attack when the American guard was down. It did not take many such incidents to create a state of mind that could accept the shooting of unarmed men in the water, and Admiral Halsey's urgings to "kill Japs" gave more or less official sanction to the slaughter.

On March 4, the Japanese put an air umbrella over Kula Gulf, but the Americans penetrated, and at daybreak the bombers were up again. They bombed the hulks of both the *Arashio* and the *Asashio* and sank the latter. Late that afternoon, the B-25s were back, and they sank the crippled *Arashio*. That afternoon, Japanese patrol planes sent an urgent message to Rabaul. They had spotted a large group of survivors (of one of the destroyers) floating in the water 55 miles southeast of Buin. But who was to save them? To dispatch more destroyers from Rabaul into the teeth of that Allied air attack was obviously foolhardy, and the navy refused. They could try to put an air umbrella over the survivors and they did. Early on the morning of March 5, navy and army planes flew over the area, dropping life preservers and circling to keep Allied aircraft away. That morning the *I-17* and *I-26* arrived on the scene and began their rescue attempts. The *I-17* surfaced and picked up 156 survivors, which was all she could carry. She submerged and returned to Truk, to deliver them safe and sound. The *I-26* also surfaced and started her rescue operations. She picked up fifty-four men, and was getting ready to bring alongside three more landing craft, with a hundred survivors aboard, when out of nowhere appeared two American PT boats. They fired torpedoes at the surfaced submarine. The *I-26* crash-dived, and got away, but the PT boats moved in among the landing craft, strafing and dropping depth charges. The Japanese boats sank. The PT boats circled until no more heads showed in the water.

The *I-26* hung around the area for a while, but when she surfaced again, the water was empty. The PT boats had made further rescue attempts useless. That night she landed the survivors at Lae. She headed off on patrol and remained out until the first of May. She returned to Truk to claim two 7,000-ton Allied freighters sunk.

The actual number of Japanese troops who made the shore was never known. Hundreds of survivors did swim to Lae, but they were unarmed and disorganized, and easy prey for Allied patrols and the unfriendly natives. Other survivors made land as far away as Guadalcanal, 700 miles away, only to run across American soldiers—who were not taking prisoners. A handful survived to tell the tale.

Back at Rabaul, it was the tenth of March before the shaken army and navy commands could properly assess the magnitude of the tragedy that had befallen the Lae convoy. Nearly seven thousand men had been aboard the eight transports, including the crews. Of these, 1,200 had been landed at Lae by the destroyers. Another 2,700 survivors had been returned to Rabaul, but 3,000 men were missing, and four destroyers were lost. It was a thorough shock to the Southeast Area Command, and it changed the nature of the war in the South Pacific. From this point on, Rabaul decided, all reinforcement would be done by barge. Never again would a big convoy of ships try to negotiate Kula Gulf.

5

YAMAMOTO'S OFFENSIVE

IT had never been in Admiral Yamamoto's mind to yield the Solomons to the Americans. In the spring of 1943 he could not devote all his efforts to the recapture of the Southern Solomons because he was committed to supporting the Japanese army operations in New Guinea. He did, however, devote a good deal of effort to maintaining his position in the Central Solomons, extending as far south as New Georgia Island. The American move into the Russells made it more difficult, but, even so, during the month of March the Japanese carried out seven resupply and reinforcement missions in the Central Solomons.

The sinking of the destroyers *Murasame* and *Minegumo* on March 5 was a great setback to the Japanese naval command, for the belief persisted in Truk and Rabaul that one Japanese could lick seven Americans. From the command's point of view, the mission was still something of a success since the ships had unloaded their supplies. Yamamoto was certainly not going to let the loss of two destroyers shake him. He would try again.

The next Japanese supply mission to the south was dispatched just three days later, on March 8. The destroyers *Asagumo*, *Yukikaze*, and *Nagatsuke* carried 130 tons of ammunition and provisions to Kolombangara. Part of that would be ferried across to New Georgia for the defense buildup there.

They also brought seven new antiaircraft guns and their crews. Again three days later, March 11, two other destroyers, the *Minezuki* and the *Ayazuki*, were dispatched to resupply the seaplane base at Rekata Bay in the Shortlands with forty-six tons of food and ammunition. Considering the fact that at that moment the Japanese at Rabaul were preoccupied with their attempt to reinforce Lae in New Guinea by convoy, the resupply of the Solomons was going quite satisfactorily. The conventional American belief is that the use of destroyers indicated Japanese fear of using (and losing) merchant ships, but at this time that was not quite an accurate assessment. The real reason the Japanese used destroyers (as the Americans had at Guadalcanal) was the shortage of merchant shipping in the area. Some of the resupply missions were carried out by army transport. But after the Lae convoy disaster the army was extremely short of transports in this area, and Imperial General Headquarters had turned a deaf ear to the request for more transports for Rabaul.

Sometimes there was trouble. On March 29 a six-ship supply group was attacked by American planes, and one subchaser was sunk. Its captain and twenty-nine men were killed. But during March and April "The Tokyo Express" continued to run regularly, although not without difficulties. On April 2, at Buin Anchorage, the destroyer *Kazegumo* was badly damaged by a mine the skipper swore had been laid by American planes a few hours earlier. The port had to be closed until the area was swept.

The tempo of the Japanese resupply voyages stepped up during the last ten days of April, because General Imamura of the 8th Area Army ordered immediate reinforcement to prepare for the attack everyone knew was coming sometime. Field hospitals, field artillery, and several battalions of infantry were all brought down to the Shortlands, to Munda, and to Kolombangara. The striking force of the 51st Division was brought back to Rekata Bay from Rabaul, where it had been sent with the fall of Guadalcanal.

After the mining of the *Kazegumo*, all went well until the end of the first week in May. The war was in a lull, and in April Admiral Yamamoto took every advantage of the lull.

In February and March, as he rebuilt the Eleventh Air Fleet at Rabaul, Yamamoto made sure that Guadalcanal was bombed as often as could be managed. The bombings did not prevent the steady American build-up of the Guadalcanal base, as he had hoped to do, but they did keep the soldiers, sailors, and marines on their toes. For example, the First Special Construction Battalion arrived at Koli Point on March 21 to begin construction of new beach facilities. Two days after the Seabees came, before they had gotten around to building "permanent" foxholes, they were bombed by the Japanese.

The really serious bombing of Guadalcanal began again on April 1. It was the result of a revised war plan established in Tokyo by the Imperial General Staff.

The Imperial Japanese High Command had never wavered from its original concept of the war in the southern regions of the new empire. The key to forward movement was the capture of the whole of New Guinea, and since this was a major island, suitable for Japanese army tactics, the army was in charge. Since the army had its own troop transports, (those eight transports lost in the Lae reinforcement operation were army transports), Admiral Yamamoto's official responsibility to the army had been only to provide protection to get the army troops ashore and to protect the ships sent to supply them. His efforts to resupply the army troops on Guadalcanal had been prompted by the emergency there.

The occupation and protection of smaller land masses was regarded as a navy matter. Thus, theoretically, the navy would defend the Central Solomons, and the army would worry about New Guinea.

After the debacle at Lae, 17th Army's chief of staff flew back to Tokyo to report to Imperial General Headquarters.

One of the new difficulties perceived was the retraction of aircraft carriers and destroyers from the operational zone to Truk. Admiral Yamamoto was conserving his strength, still hoping for the one big battle that would cripple the U.S. Navy and bring the Allies to the conference table on Japan's terms. After the Lae affair, the army argued that the Papua campaign had first priority and that Admiral Yamamoto was to support that effort above all. Yamamoto argued that it was essential to knock out the American base at Guadalcanal before undertaking major naval operations. Since the Imperial General Staff was dominated by the army, the outcome was predictable. But the Imperial General Staff did agree to allow Yamamoto to make an air effort to destroy the American buildup in the Solomons, with the understanding that the effort would also be directed against the New Guinea area and that there would be no major military move to recapture the Southern Solomons until New Guinea was secured.

The first step in the new effort in the Solomons was to be Operation I, a massive air campaign to knock out Allied air superiority in the Solomons and New Guinea. That decision was reached on March 25. Day after day aircraft came down "the pipeline" of interconnecting air bases that ran along the various islands from Tokyo to Rabaul. Yamamoto also brought to Rabaul the carriers *Zuikaku, Shokaku, Zuiho, Junyo,* and *Hiyo* to send some of their planes in with the land-based aircraft of the

Eleventh Air Fleet. The planes were concentrated on the airfields around Rabaul. From that point they would take off, stop at the subsidiary fields for fuel, and then go on to attack the Allied bases. This divorce of the carrier planes from their carriers was necessary because of the enormous losses in pilots suffered by the Eleventh Air Fleet. It was a gamble—carrier operations could go badly from that time on, if many of these highly trained pilots were lost in the next few months' air battles.

The first of the new series of air battles occurred on April 1, when the Japanese sent a fighter sweep to Guadalcanal to knock out American fighter power. But the Allied coast watchers were on duty as usual, and as the waves of Japanese Zeros passed over Bougainville, Choiseul, Vella Lavella, and New Georgia, they reported the southern movement. As the planes neared Guadalcanal they were picked up by American radar in plenty of time for the fighter units to "scramble" their planes and intercept. The Japanese sent down about sixty fighters, and the Americans put up about forty. Over the Russells, the Zeros met a mixture of navy and marine F4Fs, F4Us, and Army P-38s. In the melee that followed, eighteen Zeros were destroyed, and six American fighters were lost.

From that day, Japanese air and sea activity around Guadalcanal increased markedly. The Japanese resupplied Vila on April 1, using a convoy of supply-laden destroyers. The American heavy bombers from Southwest Pacific bases attacked that night but didn't do much damage to the ships unloading off Blackett Strait. The next day a group of P-38s set fire to one small transport north of Vella Lavella Island, but the resupply mission was a success. So were several other destroyer convoy runs to Vila that same week.

On April 3, at Rabaul all was ready for Operation I. The Japanese carriers had contributed 160 planes to the operation. The navy and the army at Rabaul mustered an additional 190 planes. Since Imperial General Headquarters had decreed joint operations from this point forward, Yamamoto would also have army and navy planes from a number of other bases: specifically, Buka, Buin, and Ballale. Thus, to begin the attack, Admiral Yamamoto could put forward 350 fighters and bombers at Rabaul and hundreds more at the other bases, probably something over 600 aircraft.

Although Yamamoto had been commanding the Combined Fleet from his flagship, the enormous battleship *Yamato* in the harbor at Truk, he traveled often, usually by flying boat, to the fleet offices at Rabaul to make his own evaluations of military affairs. He was famous in the fleet for his "front-line inspections."

At dawn on the morning of April 3, Admiral Yamamoto and Vice

Admiral Matome Ugaki, his chief of staff, flew down to Rabaul. As was Yamamoto's custom, they took two flying boats; in case of disaster one of them should survive to maintain continuity.

Admiral Yamamoto's purpose in this visit was to inspire the pilots and aircrews to special efforts before they began this important operation.

The first and most important of these bases was Rabaul itself. Yamamoto went to the Rabaul field where the 204th Air Group operated. This was a fighter group, flying Zeros, and had been in the thick of the battle for Guadalcanal. Captain Yochiro Miyano had assembled his men outside the operations hut, and Yamamoto and his staff mounted the platform that had been constructed for them. Yamamoto gave obeisances to the Emperor and was greeted with cheers.

He announced Operation I.

The men were excited by the news of the coming offensive, and there were more cheers.

He spoke of the great hardships the fliers had undergone and would undergo. As he spoke, he glanced around at the men and surveyed them slowly.

"Now," he said, "we are approaching an understandably difficult battle, a sequel to the last. However difficult a time we are having, the enemy also has to be suffering. Now we must attack his precious carriers with Rabaul's great air strength, and cut them down so they cannot escape. Our hopes go with you. Do your best."

There were more cheers and promises of undying effort. The visit had obviously produced precisely the effect Yamamoto wanted. Seeing the effect, he planned to repeat this performance all the way down the line a few days later.

Operation I was divided into two parts. The first effort was to knock out the assembled American air power at Guadalcanal. The second effort would be made against New Guinea.

On the morning of April 7, the Japanese mounted a major air attack on Guadalcanal. First they sent hundreds of fighters and bombers down to the staging fields in the Central Solomons. High-flying American reconnaissance planes that morning took pictures of 114 planes at Kahili airfield on Bougainville; another 100 were located at Ballale. More planes were staging into the airfields at Buka, Vila on Kolombangara, and Munda on New Georgia.

A total of 170 planes were assembled on the field at Rabaul and ready to go.

Among these were planes of the 204th Naval Air Group at Rabaul. It was a measure of the importance headquarters put on this operation that this first mission of Operation I was led by Captain Miyano himself.

Everyone at the airfield knew what was happening and excitement

filled the air that morning. Some of the ground crews had worked all
night to get the planes ready. The aircrews had arisen at three o'clock in
the morning and put on the new underwear issued the pilots when they
went into battle. They had eaten hastily and assembled at the operations
hut for briefing on the weather and enemy dispositions, and for final
instructions. But no instructions were needed, really. The officers and
men were primed to the point of fearlessness for this major effort. They
knew it would be costly in terms of pilots and planes. Many of the pilots
had written "last" letters home, and included hair and fingernail clip-
pings, which would forever symbolize their presence within the family.
Among these was Captain Miyano who did not expect to come back.

As the fliers of the 204th got ready to man their planes, a message from
headquarters reached the field. Reconnaissance planes flying over
Guadalcanal just after dawn reported that the Americans had amassed a
force of five heavy cruisers, ten destroyers, and ten transports at Guadalcanal. When the pilots heard this, they cheered. They picked up the
new white scarves they had all been issued that morning and headed for
their planes.

Everyone knew it was more than a normal mission. The sides of the
field were lined with base personnel again, and again Admiral Yamamoto was there, in spotless starched white uniform, standing quietly on
the sideline, watching. His presence aroused in the young men a determination born of the military system, which imbued all soldiers and
sailors with one thought above others: every man's life belonged to
emperor and country, and it was an honor above all others to die in
battle.

"Their hearts were filled with resolution to see their great chief
standing there," said one squadron member.

The takeoff that morning was just like all the others of the past, except
in number of planes. The weather was closing in, gray sky above, and a
rain squall hit the field as the first planes began taxiing along the apron.
Everyone was anxious to get off. Now the pilots hurried even more.

Captain Miyano had not said much before he climbed into his Zero.
His plane handlers noticed that when he got into the cockpit and
adjusted his instruments, he did not, as he usually did, pull on the
parachute harness. He ignored it. No one said anything.

One by one the planes took off, the Zeros first, and they formed up
over the field and circled as the slower bombers got going. It was six
o'clock when all the planes were in the air and ready to head for the
battle zone.

The roar of engines was deafening, as one plane followed another off
the ground. Then, suddenly the field was quiet, except for the drone of
engines up above. The men lining the runway began to drift away in

little groups. One lonely figure stood to the last, waving as the planes went out of sight—Admiral Yamamoto.

Over Rabaul, the Zeros circled and eighteen of them peeled off to head for Buin to pick up a force of dive-bombers. The remainder moved down toward Buka, where they would refuel before going on to Guadalcanal.

They landed at Buka at about nine o'clock and waited while the ground crews refueled the planes. The 253rd Air Group was doing the same. At a little before ten o'clock the 204th was ready to go again, and 52 Zeros took off and headed toward Guadalcanal. It was a long way, 500 miles. The 204th and the 253rd kept together, at high altitude. Indeed, they were flying at very high altitude, 15,000 feet, to avoid detection before they reached their objective.

An hour and a half out of Buka they passed high over the oblong shape of Choiseul Island, a green and brown mass outlined against the blue of the ocean.

From Choiseul on, the Japanese were in territory where they could expect Allied air opposition. The flight leaders began to keep an even warier eye turned around the horizon, lest they be jumped by American fighters. Just before 12:30, the 204th Group's planes reached the Russell Islands, and flak began to fly up at them. One or two planes were hit. They saw a small formation of enemy aircraft off to one side, going the other way. There was no way of getting to them.

Admiral Yamamoto had arranged for the airmen to have some help from the submarine force. One I-Boat was assigned to lie off Cape Esperance at the northwest corner of Guadalcanal Island and send radio signals that would guide the planes in on target. With the shortage of fuel that all the airmen felt, this was to be a big help. But the night before the attack the submarine got involved in a fight with a destroyer and finally went up on a reef off Cape Esperance; the crew abandoned ship. All this was unknown to the high command and to the airmen. As they came in toward Guadalcanal, expecting guidance, they heard nothing at all.

Down south, at Henderson Field on Guadalcanal, the Americans were already getting information about the incoming attack.

At noon, Allied coast watchers on New Georgia reported that the sky was gray with Japanese aircraft. Guadalcanal radio broadcast the warning of an impending air raid, largely for the benefit of the dozens of ships that stood in Lunga Roads. Rear Admiral W. C. Ainsworth's cruiser task force was just weighing anchor, preparing to move north along the Slot to bombard Munda again that night. With several hundred torpedo- and dive-bombers coming down the Slot, Ainsworth decided that was no place to be, so he took his ships out toward

Indispensable Strait and the safer waters to the south. But dozens of other ships still lay in the waters of Guadalcanal and Tulagi across Ironbottom Sound. The Japanese observation planes that morning had counted fourteen transports as well as the task force, most of them on the Guadalcanal side. Across at Tulagi lay fifteen PT boats and their tender, the *Niagara*, seven small transports, eight new Landing Craft Tanks (LCTs), the 14,500-ton tanker *Kanawha*, the tanker *Erskine Phelps*, three tugs, and several visiting New Zealand ships.

Most of the ship captains got the message. But there was nothing they could do except wait for what might come.

They waited.

From the fields of Guadalcanal, Admiral Mason was able to mount 76 fighter planes, and they orbited in small attack units in the Savo Island area to the north. At two o'clock in the afternoon, Radio Guadalcanal announced "Condition Red"—an air raid was coming. A few moments later the announcer added his unofficial emphasis: "Condition Very Red." It was not long before all concerned could see for themselves what he meant: the sky was filled with black dots. Scores of planes were boring in to attack.

At Henderson Field, the operations office marshaled its forces. The American fighters were to concentrate on the Zeros, and they began peeling out of their orbits and heading in to attack the Japanese fighters. While they did so, the Japanese bombers headed straight for the ships in Ironbottom Sound.

The tanker *Kanawha* was most conspicuous down there on the water, because she was throwing a white wake. She had just gotten under way, heading out toward Indispensable Strait, escorted by a patrol boat and the destroyer *Taylor*.

Fifteen Aichi dive-bombers came after her. They screamed down and dropped their five-hundred-pound bombs. The bombs tore through the tanker's skin and started fires. One bomb smashed into the engine room and put it completely out of commission. There was no chance of her moving further. In moments the tanker was ablaze from one end to the other. After five planes had bombed the tanker, the Japanese flight leader was so pleased with the results that he diverted the other ten planes to hit other targets.

The tanker seemed to be lost. The *Taylor* abandoned her, and the patrol boat stayed far off. Even the skipper of the *Kanawha*, Lieutenant Commander Brainerd N. Bock, agreed with the Japanese flight leader, who had decided the *Kanawha* was finished. He ordered the ship abandoned.

The engines were dead but the ship was still sliding through the water, away from the trail of burning oil. Some men found rafts to push off the deck into the water, but the burning oil kept most of the men from getting near those makeshift lifeboats. Men went over the side and began to swim.

As the men of the *Kanawha* tried to save themselves, dozens of other bombers screamed in across Tulagi harbor. The New Zealand corvette *Moa* was fueling from the *Erskine Phelps* that afternoon. As a result of a breakdown in Allied communications procedures, her radio was not tuned in to the Guadalcanal radio channel. She did not get the advance word of the impending air raid. The first her crew knew of it was at that moment when the scream of the dive-bombers assailed their ears. The Japanese were aiming for the tanker, but they hit the corvette and she went down in a few minutes. Fortunately, all but five men of the crew were saved.

Other dive-bombers attacked the tanker *Tappahannock*, which had been unloading aviation gasoline in Lunga Roads. But her skipper had heard and heeded the warning. He had cleared the area and was moving out of Lengo Channel when the dive-bombers came in. She was escorted by the destroyer *Woodworth*. The Japanese attack on these ships was not very skillful, and the antiaircraft gunners on the destroyer and ashore were effective. Seven dive-bombers concentrated on the tanker, but she managed to avoid all the bombs.

The destroyer *Aaron Ward* also came in for attack. One of the dive-bombers put a bomb into her aft engine room and two other near misses did more damage. She sank later in the day.

The fighting was furious. The Zeros did their job almost perfectly, keeping the American fighters engaged so that most of them never had a chance to go after a dive-bomber. When it ended, the fliers of both sides returned to their bases to make exaggerated claims about their victories. The Americans claimed a total of more than 100 planes shot down. Officially, pilots and antiaircraft gunners together were credited by their own authorities with shooting down twenty-seven Zeros and a dozen dive-bombers. The Japanese denied that so many of their fighters had fallen. They admitted to the loss of only nine, although Japanese figures agreed with those of the Americans on the twelve bombers.

The Japanese fliers were just as prone as were the Americans to exaggeration. Their pilots came home to claim the sinking of a U.S. cruiser, three destroyers, eleven transports, and thirty-one American fighter planes. The American figures showed one destroyer, one corvette, and one tanker sunk, and seven marine fighter planes lost.

As for the tanker *Kanawha*, as the battle faded, the tugs *Menominee* and *Rail*, two LCTs, and a minesweeper came out to rescue the survivors. They picked up all but nineteen men, and as the flames died down a little the navigator, Lieutenant C. W. Brockway, gathered a group of volunteers from the *Rail*. They boarded the burning tanker and got the fires out. The *Rail* towed the tanker to the west side of Tulagi and beached her. It seemed that she might be salvaged.

But the Japanese bombers had done their work well. Even though the fires were out, the tanker was taking water and dropping down by the stern. During the night her aft end filled to the point that the bow popped up, and she slid off the bank and sank in Ironbottom Sound.

Having had his swipe at Guadalcanal, Admiral Yamamoto was now obligated to serve the army's ends by taking his next attack to New Guinea, where the U.S. Fifth Air Force was operating. The first strike was made against Oro Bay because observation planes had reported the presence of a dozen ships. The Japanese came in silently, and the Allies had only five minutes warning. The bombers sank one freighter, put another up on the beach as a wreck, and damaged an Australian minesweeper. They lost six planes in the fight.

On April 12, the Japanese from Rabaul again hit New Guinea—Port Moresby this time. A force of 175 planes made the attack. Once again the Zeros did their job admirably, engaging the Allied fighters so their bombers could get through. But the pilots looked down on the shipping and found an unimpressive collection. Only a few small craft were in the harbor that day, so the big effort was largely wasted.

The Japanese were back on April 14, this time to hit Milne Bay, where the observation planes had reported the presence of fourteen transports. But by the time the Japanese attack arrived, all except four of the transports had cleared. This time nearly 190 planes came in from Rabaul.

The bombers again did their work. They sank one Dutch ship that was carrying ammunition and gasoline and damaged another. They damaged a British motor ship and shot up the airstrip near the town, setting off a fire in a fuel dump. Only seven planes were lost in the raid, and the Japanese came back, as usual, full of stories. Rabaul headquarters sent the word to Admiral Yamamoto that his Operation I had cost the enemy one cruiser, three destroyers, and more than two dozen transports, plus a hundred and seventy-five Allied planes. Believing all that was true (which it was not), the Japanese considered the operation a success. Admiral Yamamoto called a halt to the bombing, and the carrier planes were ordered back to their carriers.

So, Operation I came to an end and was officially declared by the Japanese to have accomplished all it set out to do. In the light of the events of the next few months, it seems to have been a waste of Japanese talent, although the losses were not particularly high on either side. If

Yamamoto wanted to go to all the trouble of staging a special operation, then why did he break it off so suddenly, before it had accomplished what he wanted? One reason was not known to the Americans at that moment: the naval aircraft shortage in the South Pacific would not permit much more. The 204th Air Group, for example, suffered a steady attrition of planes, and its commander kept hounding Eleventh Air Fleet for more. But there were no more, and as it soon became painfully apparent to all, there were not enough planes on hand to accomplish the missions planned. A commander would ask for twenty planes, and get six. He would complain about the six and say that was not enough to fly a mission protecting bombers, and the answer was that it would have to be enough. That was the way the war was going in the south, and the airmen were the first to know that it was not good enough. But, as they discovered if they hounded higher authority long enough, there was absolutely nothing to be done about it.

6

THE ASSASSINATION
OF AN ADMIRAL

IT was nine months since the battle of Midway had been won by the Americans because they were able to break the Japanese naval codes. The Japanese still did not know that the enemy could read their most secret communications.

The Japanese returning from Midway had suggested that the enemy must have had some advance knowledge, and suspicion was directed at the code. But Imperial General Headquarters would not believe it. That code, like the German secret codes, depended on a complicated code machine. The developers swore that it was impossible to break the code, and Imperial Headquarters was satisfied.

So the American radio intelligence teams continued to draw enormous advantage from the fact that they could tell what the Japanese were going to do and when. Intelligence alone did not win battles, but it certainly helped.

The radio intelligence section of Naval Intelligence at Pearl Harbor worked diligently, particularly with the submarine service, to give out operational information and yet try to preserve the closely guarded secret of the source of information.

So far, their efforts had been successful, but the maintenance of the secret was one of the big problems for the command, since use could not be made of the material without sometimes threatening to compromise the source.

The intelligence men were careful and lucky. As of the spring of 1943, neither Admiral Yamamoto nor the high command in Tokyo had the slightest inkling that the naval code was not secure.

Thus, on April 14, when Yamamoto planned another front-line tour to bolster morale of the airmen in the South Pacific, Combined Fleet Headquarters had no hesitation in sending the information and Yamamoto's itinerary to all the bases and commands involved in messages using the secret naval code. The message was received at Shortlands, Buin, and Ballale, giving the time of the admiral's departure from the main naval air base at Rabaul and the time and manner of his return.

The message was also received by a United States Navy radioman at Dutch Harbor, Alaska, whose monotonous job it was to monitor Japanese radio traffic. The radioman did not know what he was taking down, but he did know that all Japanese naval traffic was to be relayed to Naval Intelligence offices in Washington and in Pearl Harbor.

When the message about the Yamamoto trip was decoded it created unusual activity in both commands. At Pearl Harbor, Commander Edward T. Layton, the Pacific Fleet intelligence officer, discussed the possibility of assassinating the Japanese commander and concluded that the idea was sound. The radio intelligence team was worried, because it seemed likely that if an attempt was made on Yamamoto at this time, the Japanese would draw the conclusion that their communications had been breached. But theirs was not the decision. The yes-or-no rested in Washington.

In Washington, the information came first to Naval Intelligence Deputy Chief Captain Ellis Zacharias. Soon many top officials were in on the secret, and most of them seemed to agree that the assassination was very much in the U.S. national interest. As the Japanese pointed out in their histories after the war, Yamamoto, although unknown to most Americans, was ranked by those in the know high on the list of Axis "ringleaders." With the U.S. Navy he was inscribed just after Emperor Hirohito and Prime Minister Tojo on the hate list. The reason for singling out Yamamoto for the honor was that he was regarded (quite rightly) as the architect of the sneak attack on Pearl Harbor.

When the unusual message was received, several officials saw the opportunity for revenge. Indeed, the Japanese term for the whole affair was *fukushu saku* (revenge military operation). That motivation certainly possessed America in general, and the politicians in particular. Secretary of the Navy Frank Knox pushed the matter. President Franklin D. Roosevelt liked the idea.

At Pearl Harbor, Admiral Nimitz, with his cool engineer's mind, considered the matter in a different manner. Yamamoto was a professional naval officer, just as Nimitz was. Under other circumstances, the shoe might be on the other foot. What could such a move accomplish? Was it worth the obvious danger of compromising the "Ultra" secret, the knowledge of the Japanese code? In the end he decided it was. Nimitz sent a message to Admiral Halsey at Noumea, saying that if Halsey thought he could manage the assassination he was authorized to begin "preliminary planning." That last phrase indicated that the final decision would be made at a higher level, and Halsey had to be prepared to abandon the plan if the decision was negative.

The war was an extremely personal matter to Admiral Halsey; since the Pearl Harbor attack he had hated all Japanese with a hearty passion, and Admiral Yamamoto was third on his personal "shit list." When the message arrived at Noumea, Halsey was in Australia on a flying trip, conferring with General MacArthur about future operations in the South and Southwest Pacific. The admiral's staff, however, knew the admiral's mind, and in short order the message was sent on to Rear Admiral Marc Mitscher, the new commander of land-based aircraft in the Solomons.

Admiral Mitscher, like Admiral Halsey, was an aggressive fighter. He did not hesitate to accept the challenge, nor did he concern himself with the possible repercussions on the "Ultra" secret of such an assassination. These matters were for higher authority. Within a matter of hours he had conferred with his staff, plotted the possibilities, and returned a message saying that it could be done.

When Admiral Halsey returned to Noumea, he was delighted to learn of the plans. He referred to Yamamoto as "The Peacock" because of the Japanese admiral's enormous dignity and his habit of appearing in public only in full dress uniform, complete with gloves and a ceremonial sword. Halsey's feelings about Yamamoto were perhaps more personal than those against the others. He knew the Japanese admiral from the old days when he had visited Japan as a junior officer with The Great White Fleet that President Theodore Roosevelt had sent around the world. Halsey took the unannounced Pearl Harbor attack as a personal affront.

Not long after the attack on Pearl Harbor, Yamamoto had been quoted in neutral countries as saying he was looking forward to dictating peace in the White House. Rather, Yamamoto was misquoted. What he had said was that the sort of peace he was being asked about by the reporter could only be dictated at the White House, and what he had meant was that only the president of the United States could stop the war. In fact, Yamamoto, alone among the Japanese leaders, had opposed war with the United States until Japanese and American policies had made it inevitable.

Still, although the wheels were in motion, the matter was not decided.

In Washington, Captain Zacharias vigorously advocated the assassination. The Japanese Navy, he said, could claim no other figure so beloved by the men of the fleet and the general public. And speaking technically, there was no other in the Japanese Navy with the flair and dash of Yamamoto. On a military level, said Zacharias, the assassination attempt was as much worthwhile as it was on a political level.

But the decision was still not yet made, and there was only one man who could make it, President Roosevelt. It was one thing to advocate the assassination in principle, and quite another to learn that it was feasible and then put the official stamp on it.

Viewed from hindsight, the decision was anything but chivalrous. But chivalry had no place in World War II. With the outbreak of war, the United States had for the first time joined the advocates of "unrestricted submarine warfare." Atrocities had been committed from the beginning by the Japanese in the "death marches" in the newly captured countries, the beheading of airmen shot down over Japan in the Doolittle raid, and most recently the torture and murder of European civilians in the Solomons.

The Americans had responded in like manner. The "no quarter" character of the war was well established.

President Roosevelt approved the assassination, and when the message went from Washington to Pearl Harbor to Noumea, it bore the signature of Secretary Frank Knox. So, in a matter of hours, the assassination was "on." Admiral Halsey was informed that the matter was cleared. He sent a message to Admiral Mitscher.

Nimitz had asked Halsey if he could make such an interception so far away, because even three months earlier Halsey would not have had the resources to do the job. But those resources had recently become available in the increased number of P-38 long-range fighter-interceptor planes in the South Pacific. A number of them had come up to Guadalcanal for the 339th Army Air Force Fighter Squadron. These planes were most effective against the Zeros, making up in speed, altitude tolerance, and diving potential for the superior turning capacity of the Zero. By spring, the Zero pilots had learned to respect the P-38 above all American fighters, and for good reason. An only moderately skillful P-38 pilot in his superior plane could face up to Japan's best in their unarmored Zeros and have at least an even chance. For a mission such as the one outlined by Admiral Mitscher for the Army Air Force pilots, the P-38 was the ideal plane. The attempt on Yamamoto would be a matter of split-second timing; he would probably be traveling with members of his staff in a Mitsubishi Zero (Betty) twin-engined bomber; the bomber was to be ambushed and shot down at one of the bases as it was preparing to land. The point of the mission was to get in, shoot fast, and get out. It would be the epitome of what the Japanese called a *damashi uchi*—sneak attack.

Thus, within a matter of two days from the interception of the message bearing the Yamamoto itinerary, the military authorities of the United States had discussed the matter thoroughly at every level. Given the resources, there was nothing to stop the operation. The question of the security of the code-breakers was generally disregarded at the political level where the decision was finally made. The green light was on, and when the code-breakers intercepted still another message reaffirming the Japanese plans and timing, Admiral Halsey sent a radio message in his own vigorous style to Admiral Mitscher:

IT APPEARS THE PEACOCK WILL BE ON TIME. FAN HIS TAIL.

At dawn on April 18, at the Japanese air base at Rabaul, all was ready for Admiral Yamamoto's one-day inspection flight. For several days various members of his staff and subordinate commands had tried to persuade the admiral that it was not necessary for him to make this trip just now, and that it was dangerous. One of his officers had even suggested that the Americans might very well find out somehow about the trip and make a special effort to knock him out. As they all knew, the Japanese no longer controlled the air space above the South Pacific islands; even their own bases were subject to bombing attack. Yamamoto, however, would not be dissuaded. The Japanese in forward bases of the islands had suffered too many reverses recently, and they were receiving too little support from home. Whatever he could do to bolster morale was worth the effort.

The commander of the air base at Rabaul had laid on twenty Zero fighters to escort the admiral's plane on the trip, but Yamamoto had refused to accept so much protection. It was not necessary, he said. Those planes were better used escorting bombers or waiting to destroy American attack planes. He insisted that no more than six Zeros accompany the mission.

Just before six o'clock on the morning of April 18 (Tokyo time) the traveling party assembled at the Rabaul's eastern airfield for the takeoff. Yamamoto would ride in one of the attack bombers of the 705th Bombardment Squadron. His plane and Admiral Ugaki's were piloted by experienced fliers. Six Zeros of the 309th Fighter Squadron comprised the escort.

A few minutes after the admiral's party arrived on the field they were aboard and the engines were turning. Admiral Yamamoto's plane took off first, heading out over the east end of the bay above the volcanoes. Ugaki's plane was next, and then the pilots moved into formation. The Zeros took off and joined them. They climbed to 4,500 feet, and two of the fighters moved up ahead and above the formation. Two more fighters covered Admiral Ugaki's plane, and two protected the rear. The formation turned and took a course southeast, toward Bougainville. Admiral Yamamoto moved up to the front of his plane and took over the pilot's seat.

Admiral Yamamoto's subordinates were efficient; his party was precisely following the itinerary established for him.

Six o'clock takeoff had been made, as announced. The first stop would be Ballale, where they were to arrive at 8:00 A.M. (Tokyo time) and spend just enough time for the admiral to address his fighting men.

The pilots tightened up the formation as they moved out to sea and up to five thousand feet altitude. A little scattered cloud appeared, but visibility was excellent. As Admiral Ugaki noted in his diary, flying conditions could not have been better. The pilots were a little nervous with so much responsibility, and they tightened the formation until the planes were flying wing to wing with the tips nearly touching.

They passed over the northern tip of Bougainville and then below they could see the base at Buka. They went on without incident. When they neared Ballale they were particularly careful because that airfield was perched on the edge of the jungle and one false move would send a plane spiraling into the thick mass of trees and creepers. But all of these pilots were experienced fliers, and they had made the trip so many times it almost seemed like a milk run.

Since the admiral was expected, by 9:30 (U.S. time, 8:00 Japanese time), all the base personnel were lined up along the runway, from the commander on down. They waited, watching for the planes.

Aboard the lead bomber, the pilot sent back a message for the admiral. They were ahead of schedule. They would arrive at Ballale at 7:45. Immediately after the admiral had said a few words to the assembled troops, they would head for the harbor, and the subchaser that had been laid on for the admiral's trip to the Shortlands. There was no question about going down there by plane. Shortlands was the site of a destroyer and seaplane base.

It was virtually on the edge of the combat zone and any movement by air might be expected to bring about an American air attack. It wasn't certain, but it was too great a possibility to ignore.

By 9:45, the admiral would have spoken to the men of the Shortlands bases, and he would be ready to board his ship again and speed for Ballale. At 11:00 A.M. he would board his bomber again and, escorted by the six Zeros, would make the ten-minute flight to Buin where he would lunch with the assembled officers of the naval command and naval air command.

At 1:00 P.M. he would be in the air again, on his way back to Rabaul, and would arrive at 3:40 P.M. U.S. time. The result of this busy day, Admiral Yamamoto knew from experience, would be to put new life into his front-line defenders. Despite the doleful warnings of his colleagues, Yamamoto knew that at this time morale was the most important asset his command could have, and so he had never wavered in his insistence on making the dangerous trip.

The air flight down had been so uneventful that even the worried Admiral Ugaki had relaxed. He had written in his diary and napped until warned by the crew of his bomber that they were approaching landing.

At Henderson Field on Guadalcanal at 7:00 A.M. (5:00 Japanese time) Admiral Mitscher was sitting in his jeep on the apron of the runway as eighteen P-38 pilots came trooping down to the flight line and climbed aboard their planes. The American takeoff to intercept Admiral Yamamoto's flight just before it landed at Ballale had to be earlier than the Japanese takeoff from Rabaul because the distance was greater. For the American effort, Mitscher had chosen the 339th Army Air Force Fighter Squadron because he had come to respect that unit's abilities in the two weeks since he had come to take over command of the land-based air forces in the Solomons. These fighter pilots knew their business and their record against the recent Japanese air raids showed it. Also, the P-38 almost seemed to have been built for just such a job as the interception of Admiral Yamamoto's flight.

The problem, from the moment that Mitscher had Halsey's message about the Yamamoto trip, was to figure out how many planes to send, what opposition they might expect, and how they were going to get to Bougainville and back, a straight-line round trip of about 650 miles. It meant that someone was going to have to do extremely accurate dead reckoning navigation and that auxiliary gasoline tanks would have to be brought in for the P-38s. (They were not normally used by fighter planes at Guadalcanal at this time because of the short range of most missions and the added danger of fire.) It also meant flying "down on the deck" most of the way, to avoid detection by Japanese radar. That requirement made the mission even more difficult; the P-38 was designed for high altitude, and down on the deck the engines consumed three times as much fuel. Some of the pilots might have to ditch on the way home.

When the preliminary plans had been made, Major John W. Mitchell, the commanding officer of the 339th had been called in and given the assignment. Admiral Mitscher had particularly asked that four specified pilots be sent on the mission. They were captains Thomas Lanphier and Rex Barber, and lieutenants Joseph Moore and James McLanahan. They had performed very well in the big Japanese raid of Operation I on April 7, claiming a total of seven Japanese planes shot down. On that same day the marines, flying Wildcat and Corsair fighters, had lost seven planes to the Zeros. The outcome of that air battle, then, had showed the superiority of the P-38 and the excellence of this particular group of pilots.

The planners at Henderson Field had worked meticulously, even to the point of anticipating that Yamamoto's plane would arrive at Ballale fifteen minutes early because on the morning of April 18 the usual southeast wind would not be blowing, so they would have no head winds to buck.

The Americans decided to use eighteen planes, even though they had no knowledge of the size of the Japanese force of Zeros that would be covering Yamamoto and had to assume that they would run the danger of being jumped by all of the 100 army Zeros based on Bougainville. But only eighteen P-38s were available. Other fighters could come along and cover the rear, but their value would be to stop a chase by Zeros after the fact. They couldn't keep up with the P-38s.

Nor could the P-38s slow down for their companions. Major Mitchell, figuring his logistics, estimated that if they flew at optimum speed, they would have about five minutes in the target zone before fuel became critical. The route he planned made the trip a third longer. To avoid detection he would bypass the New Georgia group and fly out of sight of land. The distance then would be four hundred more miles to the target, but the extra tanks should take care of that. The success of this mission depended on getting in and getting out in a hurry. Just a few hours before the mission was to begin, Major Mitchell learned (from a new intercepted message) that the Japanese escort would be only six Zeros, but that did not mean the 100 Bougainville Zeros would not be primed to look for enemy incursion.

At 7:10 U.S. time Mitchell's P-38 took off, followed by the three others of his flight. Admiral Mitscher waved from his jeep as the planes passed the apron on their way to the runway. The next four planes were the "shooters," led by Captain Lanphier. On takeoff, McLanahan's plane blew a tire, and his flight was scrubbed. There was not a minute to wait for him. Now there were seventeen P-38s.

In the air, the planes circled until all had taken off, and the squadron joined up at 7:25 and headed west. Half an hour out, Moore's plane refused to respond to a switch to the drop tanks, and he had to turn back. Mitchell motioned two other pilots, Besby Holmes and Ray Hine, to move up to join Lanphier's flight. They would be the new "shooters."

Now the strike force was down to sixteen. The planes droned on. Mitchell took them down "on the deck." This was dangerous flying, and they learned how dangerous when one P-38 very nearly crashed into the sea. There was no way of controlling absolute height at high speed and in the winds. Some planes flew at ten feet above the surface and some at fifty. One fell so low that prop wash from the plane ahead drenched the windshield and blinded the pilot. He was lucky to be able to climb above the danger zone. They were so low—all sixteen planes—that their propellers left wakes like those of power boats, so low that the pilots could see big fish, including many sharks, swimming in the clear Pacific water.

The whole flight was over water, far to the west of Kolombangara and New Georgia. Mitchell had chosen this course to avoid detection by Japanese coast watchers who were just as effective as the Australians.

At 8:20 Major Mitchell changed course, and half an hour later he changed course again. The planes passed around Vella Lavella Island and turned to the northeast, still right down on top of the water. By this time, with half an hour still to go, the pilots were growing restless. They had flown a long way without seeing anything but their own planes. The strain of keeping the planes so close to the water made them nervous. None of them had ever spent so much time out of sight of land before.

Suddenly, the mist that had lain over the water cleared and ahead of them they saw Bougainville. Mitchell made out the landmark; they had come in just southeast of Empress Augusta Bay, which had been his point of aim. They were one minute ahead of schedule.

But where was Yamamoto?

Lieutenant Douglas Canning was the first to see other aircraft, just off to the left and higher than they were. The Americans counted. There were the six fighters, as unwittingly advertised by the Japanese. But there also were two—not one but two—Betty bombers. Mitchell had not been prepared for this development. It seemed questionable that the four P-38s assigned the "shooter's" role could take on both bombers. But there was nothing else to be done. Mitchell turned to parallel the course of the Japanese and began to climb.

It was time to drop the auxiliary tanks, which could now only impede maneuverability and increase the danger of fire and explosion. Mitchell dropped his. Several pilots had trouble with theirs, including Holmes, who moved out of formation and maneuvered his plane to try to shake the tanks loose. Hine joined him in the approved fashion, to protect the other P-38, and so two of the "shooters" were out of position. Lanphier and Barber went on, heading out to intercept the Japanese formation.

The Japanese flew on, not seeing anything out of the ordinary, until one pilot finally caught the silvery flash of jettisoned auxiliary tanks in the sky and shouted out the warning.

The Zeros turned toward the enemy planes; Lanphier engaged one of them and shot it down. Meanwhile, Admiral Yamamoto's plane had turned sharply toward Buin and went down on the deck, just above the jungle tops. Admiral Ugaki's pilot turned the other way, out to sea.

Barber was the first to attack. He saw one of the bombers ahead of him and opened fire. Pieces began flying off the unarmored plane, and the Betty made a sharp turn to the left and then plunged toward the beach. Barber never saw it fall; he was too busy with three Zeros on his tail, until planes from the cover above got after them and scattered them.

Lanphier, having tangled with one Zero, then went after the other bomber and nearly collided with a pair of Zeros that were trying to intercept him. He got behind the bomber and began to fire his guns. The right engine shot out a jet of flame and the wing tank caught fire. The bomber began to burn, the right wing came off, and the plane plunged into the jungle and exploded. The two Zero pilots then began to chase Lanphier, but he managed to get into a climb and to outdistance them with the twin engines. When he reached 20,000 feet and looked around, they were gone.

Holmes finally cleared his auxiliary tanks, and he and Hine came in looking for the bombers. They saw one fall into the jungle and another, chased by a lone P-38, which had three Zeros on its tail. They sped to the rescue and began firing at the Zeros. Holmes claimed to have shot down two of them and then he too went after the second bomber, using his twenty-millimeter cannon and the fifty-caliber machine guns.

Admiral Ugaki's bomber jinked and weaved and tried to get away. Down below, at Kahili airfield, every operational Zero was trying to get into the air to join the battle. From his vantage point inside, Admiral Ugaki watched the battle and saw the men in the plane dying as one of the P-38s laced the bomber with heavy fire. He did not realize that the P-38s were shooting cannon, but he did see that the 7.7 mm guns of the Betty could not reach the P-38 while the fighter was working over the bomber. The men inside began to fall—the tail gunner, the crew chief, the waist gunners, and some of Yamamoto's staff.

From above, the Americans saw the bomber disintegrate as it struck the water. But this was not quite the case. The pilot, seeing that he could not escape the P-38 that was after him, pushed the wheel down, and opted to make a crash landing in the sea. The bomber began to fall. As he neared the water, the pilot tried to pull out of the dive to pancake in, but the plane did not respond to the controls, and she struck at full speed. The left wing broke away, which lessened the impact in the fuselage and probably saved Ugaki's life. The plane rolled over to the left and began to sink.

Admiral Ugaki was thrown out of his seat and scrambled up the aisle and out of the broken fuselage. Around him the sea blazed with burning gasoline, but he managed to avoid it. He looked around him. A boat was coming at high speed from the shore. The pilot and one other Yamamoto staff officer, Rear Admiral Kitamura, had also survived. They were all rescued within a few minutes.

Above, the Zeros from Kahili airfield had begun taking off and gaining altitude to attack the American planes. Zeros got above Barber, Holmes, and Hine, and started an attack. Barber and Holmes managed to get away, but Hine was shot down. Up above, Major Mitchell called his pilots to start home. The whole action had taken less than five minutes, but time was short, as he knew it would be. He headed toward Guadalcanal, and the other P-38s turned. Several of them lost touch with the formation and straggled home by themselves.

Major Mitchell brought his pilots home. Lanphier came in alone after several other planes had landed. He was scarcely out of his P-38 than he was shouting, "I got Yamamoto. I got Yamamoto." Soon Barber was on the ground, making the same claim, and then along came Holmes, who landed first at the emergency field in the Russells. He told the whole story on the airstrip to a gang of marines. His version was that perhaps he had shot down the bomber carrying the Japanese admiral.

The whole affair became enormously confused and the number of Zeros claimed by the pilots was far in excess of the three that had gone down. The combat intelligence officers finally straightened out the figures a little. The number of Zeros was reduced to three, but they gave credit to Lanphier, Holmes, and Barber for one bomber each. Since there were only two bombers involved, it was indeed confused. With the exception of the fliers involved, no one cared. The fact was that there was a good chance that Yamamoto was dead.

Mitscher so informed Halsey in a guarded message that referred obliquely to the Yamamoto plane: ". . . Two bombers escorted by Zeros flying close formation. One shot down believed to be test flight. . . ."

When that message was received at Halsey's headquarters the joy was almost as unrestrained as it had been on Guadalcanal when Admiral Mitscher had presented the army pilots with a case of bourbon whiskey. Admiral Kelly Turner let out a war whoop. Halsey pretended it was nothing:

"Hold on Kelly. What's so good about it? I'd hoped to lead that scoundrel up Pennsylvania Avenue in chains with the rest of you kicking him where it would do the most good."

Then Halsey sent a message to Mitscher:

> CONGRATULATIONS TO YOU AND MAJOR
> MITCHELL AND HIS HUNTERS—SOUNDS AS
> THOUGH ONE OF THE DUCKS IN THEIR BAG WAS A
> PEACOCK.

There was nothing Halsey would have liked better than to announce the victory to the world. But what would happen if he did?

During the day, a number of high-ranking officers in Washington, Pearl Harbor, and Noumea began to have second thoughts. Simultaneously several officers realized that there was no way the Americans could have known that Admiral Yamamoto was aboard one of those planes except by intercepting a secret coded message.

Halsey sent a "rocket" to Admiral Mitscher, warning him that the mission must be kept absolutely secret, for fear of compromising the code-breakers. It was a little late. Newsreel cameramen on Guadalcanal had already taken hundreds of feet of film, and reporters had the story in their notebooks.

All the film was confiscated. The reporters were put on notice that their story was censored. Mitscher ordered the P-38s out again the next day to fly a routine mission over Buin just to show themselves, so the impression on the Japanese would be that the Americans had begun regular fighter sweeps in the area.

It was the next day before the Japanese could launch a proper search into the jungle near Buin, and several hours later before the searchers came upon the wreckage of the bomber that had crashed there. The search was interrupted by those P-38s which swept overhead, coming in to strafe Kahili airfield. But in ten minutes the planes were gone, and the search proceeded. The searchers found the plane and the bodies. All aboard had been killed in the crash.

Admiral Yamamoto had obviously been at the controls, and he had been thrown clear along with Admiral Takata of his staff; the bodies of the others in the plane had been badly burned by the fire, but Yamamoto's body was intact, and the white gloves and ceremonial sword he had brought with him on his last flight were there.

The bodies were taken back by litter to the shore and then by submarine chaser to Buin. There, on April 20, the body of Admiral Yamamoto was cremated with the others. The ashes were placed in little boxes and then taken to Rabaul. The flagship *Musashi* came down from Truk with a whole fleet behind it. The urn containing the admiral's ashes was placed aboard in his "Commander-in-Chief's quarters," along with those of the six staff officers killed with him. The fleet left for Truk and after a short stop there went on to Tokyo.

The shock reverberated through the South Pacific.

Something had to be done about command, so Admiral Mineichi Koga was appointed to be commander of the Combined Fleet. But it would not be the same; Japan had lost the great hero of the war.

The military and the public were not told about the death of Yamamoto until the funeral fleet arrived in Tokyo Bay in May. Then Japan gave itself over to a period of mourning.

Only a day or two after the event, army and navy headquarters at Rabaul sent messages to the Imperial General Staff in Tokyo suggesting that the ambush could not have been accidental. The Americans must have broken the secret naval code, they said.

But in Tokyo it was easy for the code experts to assert once again that it was totally impossible for the Americans to break the machine code. They would have to have a code machine of the same sort, on the same settings. There was no way this could have happened, said the Japanese experts. Everyone knew that there had never been a breach of security in this regard. So, although faced with the evidence and warned by the strongly expressed suspicions of the men in the field, Imperial General Headquarters refused to believe, and the Japanese codes remained as they were—the major weakness of the Imperial Navy—throughout the Pacific War.

When the deed was in the making, the Americans involved in the Yamamoto affair were warned to say nothing. The seventeen living pilots who had been assigned to the mission were immediately grounded, sent back to Noumea, lectured by General Millard Harmon, commander of the Fifth Air Force, and then sent back to the United States. At every step they were warned that if they said a word about the mission they would be court-martialled. They got medals and promotions and were assigned to duty in the United States for the rest of the war.

Everyone on Guadalcanal and in the Russells who knew anything about the mission was also threatened with the direst of fates if he breathed a word. Yet the story got out. An Australian newspaper got hold of it and printed it. It was also printed and broadcast widely in South America.

So the Japanese knew that there had been a breach of security. But that arrogance in Tokyo continued. The Imperial General Staff heard the story and dismissed it as they had the complaints of the admirals and generals at Rabaul.

The American secret was saved.

Had the assassination been worth the risk? To be sure, Yamamoto was an important figure, and even the president of the United States had concurred in the affair; one might say that he had passed the death sentence.

The irony is that of all the Japanese leaders, Yamamoto at that period in the war had the most realistic view of the future, and had the war continued to go as badly as it did go, it is conceivable that he could have had a hand in bringing it to an end earlier than August 1945.

But also, as the death of Field Marshal Erwin Rommel also proved, the fact was that no individual in the war was indispensable, or worth the price of that broken code, and had the Japanese leaders in Tokyo recognized what had happened, the course of the war might have been changed. Certainly many ship movements would never have been reported to the submarines, and it is possible that some battles might have had a different result.

In the end, the outcome would have been the same; there was no denying the effect of American production over the long haul. But had the fact of the broken code been accepted in Tokyo, many more Japanese lives might have been saved and many more American lives lost.

In authorizing the Yamamoto mission the Americans had taken a chance that seems much more risky now than it seemed then in the euphoria of the moment.

As it happened it turned out all right for them. They were very, very lucky.

7

ATTRITION

SINCE the previous January, Admiral Halsey and General MacArthur had been building up their forces in preparation for the 1943 Allied offensives in the South and Southwest Pacific theaters.

The military situation was almost the reverse of what it had been six months earlier, when the Japanese in the Solomons had controlled the air and the sea. Halsey's preparations included frequent strikes against the Japanese air bases on New Georgia and Kolombangara islands from the air and by sea, using cruisers and destroyers. But the Japanese doggedly continued to supply their forward garrisons in spite of frequent American air attacks.

Except for the loss of the *Minegumo* and *Murasame*, the spring supply runs had been routine, until March 29. That afternoon Allied planes caught a six-ship convoy at Rekata Bay and sank Subchaser No. 28. The captain and twenty-nine men were killed in the attack. Two days later, three Japanese destroyers visited the same spot without incident. They brought supplies and evacuated twenty-five men suffering from fever. That evening, the destroyers *Samidare, Akigumo, Kazegumo, Yugumo,* and *Asagumo* cleared Rabaul Harbor and headed for the forward bases. At about 6:50 they were attacked by a large formation of enemy planes. As darkness lowered, the planes dropped flares and began to attack all five ships. The destroyers scattered and took evasive action. The only ship hurt in all this action was the *Samidare*. A near miss damaged the riveting in the crew's compartment aft, and the area began to flood. Under the circumstances, the captain of the *Samidare* decided it was too risky to try to unload and perhaps have his ship sink under him, so he turned back toward the Shortlands, but returned to Kolombangara and unloaded his supplies and troops without further incident.

Since in March General Imamura, the commander of the 8th Area Army, had ordered the reinforcement of the Central Solomons bases, several battalions of infantry, field artillery, and specialist troops were sent down, along with field hospitals and more radio installations. The last ten days of April were the period of the dark of the moon, and the Japanese used these days to good advantage in their resupply program. The moonless nights meant less danger from American attack.

Since the Battle of Guadalcanal the situation of Japanese and American forces was reversed; the Americans had the initiative, so they sent the Raiders, and the Japanese tried to respond. The character of that air battle is illustrated by a Japanese naval pilot's story of the Solomons air campaign. The chapter on the air battle for the Northern Solomons is entitled *soromon no sora o ketsu ni somete* or *Blood Bath Over the Solomons*.

After Admiral Koga had taken command of the Combined Fleet, he acted quickly to reinforce Rabaul's battered air force. On May 10, several units were transferred down from Truk to Rabaul, bringing the total number of Zero fighters up to the highest point it had reached since Operation I in March. The 251st Air Group joined the 204th and 582nd Air groups at Rabaul. The reason for the reinforcement was to begin a war of attrition against the Americans at Guadalcanal, and even further afield. Bombers and fighters began almost daily runs down the Slot, that now legendary water passage that runs through the Solomons.

On May 13, the Eleventh Air Fleet sent a large strike south, following a technique just evolved, of moving planes down to the Russells to entice the Americans into battle there. From the Japanese point of view it was preferable to fighting at Guadalcanal; it gave the Japanese pilots a bit more fuel—always a major problem because of the long flight from Rabaul that they had to make before going into battle.

On that day they passed by the western tip of the Russells and headed for Guadalcanal, hoping to catch the Americans by surprise. They were flying at 24,000 feet and had already been in the air for three hours. There was no surprise. The Allied coast watchers had been tracking them all the way down.

Spotting Allied fighters a few miles away, the leader turned, just as the enemy turned to intercept. The Japanese mission leader began signaling his planes.

The leader of this strike was Lieutenant Zenjiro Miyano, commander of the First Squadron of the 204th Air Group. He was a highly experienced fighter pilot (he had fought in the Aleutians before coming to Rabaul). He led twenty-five Zeros from the 204th Air Group, plus seventy more from the 582nd Group and 251st Group.

The Allied unit consisted of about sixty planes from Guadalcanal, Marine F4Us, Army Air Corps P-38s and P-39s, Navy F4Fs, and New Zealand P-40s. The Japanese immediately split up into battle formations, and in a few minutes the opposing forces met. The large formations quickly broke down into flights of four planes and attack units of two planes, and, as was becoming ever more evident, at this technique the Allied fliers excelled. Of necessity they had learned that the way to fight Zeros was to keep formation.

The time was five minutes after eleven (Tokyo time).

The fight could not last more than an hour—the Japanese didn't have enough fuel to prolong the combat. Actually it lasted considerably less. Lieutenant Miyano and a force of three Zeros sat above the conflict, directing, and, when necessary, swooping down to help some Zero in trouble. Miyano kept an eye on his fuel indicator and when the critical moment came he broke off the engagement, formed up his aircraft, and headed back to Rabaul. When the pilots arrived at the debriefing, the attack force claimed to have won. They had, said Lieutenant Miyano, accomplished precisely what they set out to do.

And what was that mission, seemingly so aimless? It was the mission that had been entrusted to the Rabaul air force by Admiral Yamamoto, to destroy Allied air might in the Southern Solomons so that the Japanese effort in New Guinea could proceed without hindrance from that quarter. Lieutenant Miyano's report said that both sides combined put about 130 planes into the air that day over Guadalcanal, and the Japanese returned home in "complete victory," having shot down forty-one American aircraft.

That was not the American recollection. American and New Zealand pilots that day claimed sixteen Japanese planes with a loss of half-a-dozen of their own.

What the battle showed was the continued reliance of the Japanese air forces on outmoded tactics. The arrival of the P-38 in the Solomons changed the whole air war. Yamamoto had been aware of the improving quality of the American fighting equipment, and he had commented that he was very much more concerned about that than about the quality of the American fighting men. But the fact was that both the equipment and the men were becoming more effective at the arts of war.

There was very little the Japanese could do about it, given their limited production capacity. They could and did produce growing numbers of aircraft at home, but that production was based on the use of existing dies. The aircraft manufacturers were continually improving the existing aircraft; for example, Admiral Yamamoto's last bomber had been given a much longer range; it could travel 2,300 miles. But introduction of entirely new types was another matter, and for all practical purposes the Japanese would fight the entire war with the same weapons with which they had started. The Americans, on the other hand, were constantly improving their aircraft. When the war began the P-38 did not exist. Nor did the P-51 which also would make its appearance in Pacific waters; nor the F6F, which went into five versions, each improved over the last; nor the TBF torpedo bomber; nor the Black Cat radar-controlled night fighter. These new aircraft were beginning to come into the American air forces, along with the B-25 medium bomber and the A-20 attack bomber. In 1943 the changes came very fast.

The Japanese pilots became indisputably aware of that fact early in June when observers over the Russell Islands noted that the Americans had completed two airfields there and that both housed marine fighters. The shocking part was that the Japanese bombers had been claiming they were interdicting the American supply lines, and obviously this was untrue. Lieutenant Miyano came back to his unit's base at Rabaul's eastern airfield with a suggestion for new tactics. Since the bombers had failed to stop the building of the airfields, let the fighters undertake the destruction of the fields and the aircraft on the ground. He wanted the Zeros equipped with wing racks to carry 130-pound bombs. The suggestion met with the usual opposition from ordnance officers and purists, but the fact was that some new tactic had to be tried. So the group commander agreed to let Lieutenant Miyano have his way, and on June 7, when the next big mission took place, two Zeros were so equipped. They would fly in with the other fighters, and then while the others lured the Americans aloft, the bombing Zeros would try their luck.

On this day, eighty-one Zeros from the 582nd and 251st Air groups were employed. They flew down across the Russells as was their usual tactic, this time heading from north to south across the islands. There were the airfields below, and indeed they were operational.

It seemed unbelievable to the Japanese that the change could have occurred so quickly, and the implications were not lost; from this time on, the relatively short-range SB2c dive-bombers and F4F and F4U fighters could reach Buin when equipped with auxiliary gas tanks. For the first time the Americans had the ability to strike hard at the interior Japanese bases.

Perhaps, the optimistic fighter pilots thought, they could succeed where the bombers had failed.

The experimental fighter bombers had excellent protection. As they came in over the southern Russell Island airfield, three other Zeros were on their left and four on their right. The other fighters moved on, high, and continued to look for the enemy. The bombing planes moved slowly down to carry out their mission. Suddenly a pair of P-38s flashed in between them and their escorts—the escorting fighters had let just a little too much distance develop between them and their charges—and the bombing planes were shot down. The new tactic turned out to be a complete failure.

That day the melee became general, and once again a swarm of Allied aircraft of half-a-dozen varieties rose up to meet the enemy. Generally speaking the P-40 was not much of a match for the Zero. It did not have the climbing speed, the range, or the altitude capability of the Japanese plane. But in a scrap at low altitude, the P-40 was a plane to reckon with, and that day a dozen of them from the 44th Fighter Squadron were involved.

The Allied planes did well; they shot down twenty-three Zeros or about thirty percent of the force that had come down the Slot. The Allies lost nine planes, and all the pilots were recovered. That was one advantage of fighting above your own territory.

In this springtime of 1943, the attrition among Japanese naval pilots was becoming one of the most difficult problems the Rabaul Air Fleet command had to face. A few, such as Lieutenant Miyano and Warrant Officer Ryoji Ohara, seemed to have charmed lives. Miyano had participated in the original air strikes against Clark Field in the Philippines. He had served aboard the carrier *Junyo* with skill enough to merit one of the Japanese fleet air arm's rare promotions.

Ohara had flown from Buin. He had fought in many of the Guadalcanal and New Guinea battles. On May 13 he had been involved with a pair of F4U fighters and had shot them down, then made a forced landing at Kolombangara. He had been in the middle of the fracas with the P-38s that day and escaped unscathed.

Another very skillful pilot was Ensign Yoshio Oki of the 251st Fighter Group. He had already shot down a dozen enemy planes and had served a tour of duty in New Guinea, had then been returned to Japan for treatment of wounds, and was now on his second South Pacific tour.

The dreadful disaster of the convoy to Lae, the death of Yamamoto, and the sure knowledge that more and better Allied aircraft were arriving constantly in the South Pacific brought a subtle change to the morale of the Japanese fliers. They now spoke of the air lane between Rabaul and Guadalcanal as "cemetery alley" and sometimes of their aircraft as flying coffins. There was no more talk about "ever-victorious forces" around the airfields. There was no shirking. The fliers went out day after day as bravely as ever and fought as hard as ever. But many of them now considered themselves to be doomed. They had no hope of seeing their homeland again.

Morale was lifted with the arrival of an improved version of the Aichi dive-bomber. (The Americans called the new arrivals Vals.) The pilots felt they had a little better chance of survival in the new planes. And some new Zeros were also coming down the pipeline from Japan. They were faster and had a longer range than the Model 11 that many of the pilots had been flying. Still, the designers and factories were producing basically the same sort of aircraft as before—fast and maneuverable, but extremely vulnerable. Probably there was no way to make a basic change to protect the pilots without sacrificing the Zero's best qualities. The new Zeros, like the old, burned with the ferocity of welding torches once they were hit in the vitals.

Early in June, the 204th Air Group got a dozen of the new Zeros. The shipment was part of the buildup for the new air war Admiral Koga had decreed to advance the Japanese cause in the Solomons and New Guinea. The 204th also got a new commanding officer, Lieutenant Commander Tomo Oyama. This officer's arrival was indicative of the Japanese Naval Air Force's biggest problem: adequately trained personnel. Lieutenant Commander Oyama had been fighting for a long time. His experience went back to the early days of the war in China. He had flown a fighter in the initial attack on Clark Field in the Philippines and had served in that entire campaign. He had also fought in the Celebes, Borneo, Java, and Timor. He had then been sent back to Japan to become a test pilot. Now he was coming back to the front to fight again because the Navy needed experienced men.

The new Zeros had an immediate impact on morale. On June 3, several of the most experienced pilots escorted a flight of bombers out of Buin in an attack on Guadalcanal. There were twenty-four Zeros in the force that day; they ran into several packs of F4Us and F4Fs and came home to claim six American planes shot down with no losses to themselves. The American record does not bear out any such one-sided victory, but as usual pilots in combat are not very good judges of such matters.

Elated by the "victory" of June 3rd, the pilots of the 204th Fighter Group returned to Guadalcanal the next day; in fact, they would be fighting almost steadily for the next twelve days, along with the 251st

Fighter Group and the 582nd Fighter Group, either around Guadalcanal or over New Guinea.

Then came June 16, which was to go down in the Rabaul records as one of the bloodiest and most disastrous days of the whole war for the Zero squadrons.

The Japanese were waiting to deal a decisive blow to the American buildup they had been watching in the Russells and at Guadalcanal, where Admiral Kelly Turner's amphibious landing organization was operating out of a camp near Lunga Point. As the Japanese observation planes reported, something was about to break. There were too many American cargo ships in the harbor and just too much activity for the lull in the land war to continue.

Admiral Koga hoped to head off an American invasion of the Central Solomons by prompt and decisive action. After wearing out the Americans by attrition, he would then launch an attack of his own, combined with an army move, win a fleet engagement, retake Guadalcanal, and force the Americans to the peace table. If that plan sounds peculiarly like one of Admiral Yamamoto's, why it was; Admiral Koga was a disciple of Yamamoto.

The next Japanese effort, he said, was to be a major attack on the four major airfields on Guadalcanal and in the Russells and destruction of the vessels lined up in Lunga Roads.

On June 10 a troop convoy was spotted by Japanese search planes. This convoy aroused the pilots' interest because the scouts also saw a carrier. She was the escort carrier *Suwannee* and, like all carriers, a prize coveted by the Japanese navy pilots. A strike from Rabaul sent half-a-dozen twin-engined bombers to attack the carrier, but all of them were shot down that day by American fighters from Guadalcanal.

Later in the day, Admiral Kusaka's Eleventh Air Fleet sent a much larger force to sink the carrier and the six transports she protected. More than sixty Zeros escorted twenty-four dive-bombers to make the attack. But the coast watchers, the radar, and the American fighter pilots were waiting for them. The Japanese fighters did their job magnificently, sacrificing themselves to let the bombers get through. But when the bombers did get through the American fighter screen, they found the antiaircraft guns on Guadalcanal and aboard the ships took a heavy toll, and only half-a-dozen bombers got anywhere near the targets with their ordnance.

The cargo ship *Celeno* was hit twice and was so badly damaged that she had to be beached. But at least she did not sink. LST 340 was badly hit and the soldiers she carried were ordered to swim for shore. But as the attack wound down, two other LSTs came up with fire-fighting equipment, and they managed to save the vessel.

Few of the Japanese fighters and fewer of the bombers got home that day. One pilot reported exuberantly that they had sunk all six of the transports, but the next morning the scout planes reported the true situation off Lunga Point. The big ships were all still there, unhurt.

Two days later, the Japanese tried again. Another dozen bombers came down the Slot, escorted by about thirty fighters. Again the effort was repulsed by the fliers from Guadalcanal, with heavy losses for the Japanese.

But Admiral Kusaka did not quit.

Before dawn on June 16, the Japanese scout planes were over Guadalcanal, and they reported seeing five large transports and twenty-eight smaller vessels in the open sea between Cape Esperance and the southern tip of the Russells. At Rabaul, Japanese intelligence recognized the signs of a forthcoming invasion effort, and at Eleventh Air Fleet Headquarters, the orders went out: this would be the day for the big air battle.

The weather could not have been better for flying that morning. The sun came up in a cloudless sky, and there was virtually no wind. It was hot already—the middle of the hot season—but no one noticed it. The whole Rabaul base was alive with excitement, for this "great battle" had been a topic of conversation for weeks. After all the casualties the Eleventh Air Fleet had taken in the past two weeks, all the Japanese pilots knew that many would not come back that day, but they were all resigned, even lifted to a sort of exaltation by realization of the nearness of death. They lined up on the runways beside their planes. The ground crews came out and delivered box lunches and soda pop—three bottles per man—and they made ready to take off.

At ten o'clock, twenty-four dive-bombers from the 582nd Bombardment Group took off, followed by forty-eight Zero fighters from the 204th and 582 Fighter groups. They would be climbing to gain altitude all the way to Buka, where they would link up with twenty-five fighters from the 251st Group, making one attack formation of nearly a hundred planes. They would fly high above the Solomon Sea, to Guadalcanal to destroy the Allied flotilla.

Lieutenant Miyano was leading the 204th Fighters in their watch over the bombers. Over the sea as they approached Guadalcanal, he noticed that two of his fighters were having trouble because they had throttled back so tightly to maintain speed with the slower bombers. There was nothing below them but water, and it was many miles to the nearest friendly territory. If they went into the sea, then it meant two more airmen lost. Miyano ordered the bombers to speed up; when one plane began to lose power and sink toward the sea, Miyano dropped down to head the pilot toward Kolombangara Island, the last possible field for an emergency landing.

The mission went on.

Miyano led his fighters all the way. When the ships came in sight he would give the order to attack.

At 12:30 the Japanese force was over the Russells. The warnings went out at Henderson Field and American fighter pilots began to scramble for their planes. Soon they were in the air, P-38s, P-40s, F4Fs, F4Us, and even some vintage P-39s, which could be effective only at a low level.

The 339th Fighter Squadron made the first contact with Miyano's force. Lieutenant Murray J. Shubin was leading a flight of four P-38s northward, when he spotted the big Japanese formation fifteen miles from the western end of Guadalcanal. Here the altitude capability of the P-38 proved an advantage. The Japanese were coming in at 24,000 feet, but the P-38s were at 27,000 feet, prime position for an attack. Lieutenant Shubin did not wait for reinforcements. He led his flight down in a charge on the last dozen Zeros. The Americans came from above and behind the Japanese and when they reached firing range, they began shooting. That first surge knocked out five Zeros before they could react. Then, one by one, the P-38s were also hit, or ran out of ammunition and zoomed away from the battle. This action was of the sort that led the Japanese to believe that they were shooting down Allied planes when they were not. Actually at the end of fifteen minutes, all the P-38s had left the battle except Shubin's. He continued to fight for another forty minutes and in a series of furious battles shot down three more planes and damaged another. That one P-38 accounted for at least five Japanese Zeros that day. It was no wonder that the men of the Eleventh Air Fleet had such high regard for the P-38—with its 20 mm cannon.

By the time Shubin left the scene, scores of other Allied planes had joined the battle, coming up from the three Guadalcanal and two Russells airstrips.

Twenty-one P-40s from Henderson Field got off the ground shortly after the P-38s met the enemy up north. By the time these U.S. planes were airborne, the Japanese dive-bombers had arrived over Guadalcanal and were preparing to attack the ships in Lunga Roads. The P-40s and two flights of P-39s began to work over the dive-bombers. The Zeros peeled off to meet the threat and took most of the punishment, so that the bombers would have a chance at their targets. By this time the fight had moved out over the channel between Lunga Roads and Tulagi, as the bombers went after the shipping. Lieutenant Miyano was leading, watching and directing. Warrant Officer Sugida's Zero was just behind him. Suddenly out of nowhere appeared an F4F. The pilot put one short burst into Miyano's Zero, and it nosed over, burst into flame and crashed into the sea.

Warrant Officer Sugida took over leadership of the mission and somehow got the survivors back to Rabaul. A number of planes dropped off at Kolombangara Island to make emergency landings. The Allied planes did not pursue, having used much of their fuel in the aerobatics of fighting. The Japanese came home from the raid sad because of Miyano's death but not dispirited. They claimed to have sunk six transports. Actually they had hit three and done considerahble damage to them and to shore installations. The Japanese also admitted to heavy casualties. The Americans claimed to have shot down sixty-six of the one hundred Japanese planes with a loss of six Allied aircraft.

But the fact is that the raid was not a failure, by the Japanese standards of the day.

By American standards it was damaging, but not as damaging as the Japanese believed it to be. Another factor had entered the Pacific war equation: the American industrial machine was in full gear, and more war materiel was being sent to the Pacific than before. Therefore in terms of replacement possibility, the Japanese damage on this and other raids was much less meaningful than it would have been had the positions been reversed.

The Japanese belief in the success was not pretense. Lieutenant Miyano was mourned throughout the Eleventh Air Fleet. Further, he received one of the most meaningful of Japanese Navy accolades— posthumously he was promoted two grades, to become Commander Miyano. It was a very real honor in a service where promotions were sparse. He had flown 228 missions and shot down sixteen Allied planes. He had been shot down by a tyro in one of those flukes of war.

The death of this highly competent and experienced fighter pilot was indicative of the Japanese naval aviation problem that would grow worse each month. The best men were dying as the Allied plane strength increased by great leaps. The Japanese plane production machinery was just about keeping up, but the air training program was not producing pilots fast enough to replace the dead.

The big raid of June 16 marked the end of the Japanese Eleventh Air Fleet effort to halt the American move north. The truth was that temporarily the attack potential of the Rabaul air force was nearly exhausted. As of June 20, the fleet had been reduced from the high point reached in the spring to fifty-three twin-engined Betty bombers, thirteen Val dive-bombers, and eighty-three Zeros. Admiral Koga's air offensive, really a continuation of Admiral Yamamoto's Operation I, had come to an end. It had failed to slow Admiral Halsey's progress.

8

RENDOVA

FOR the first time since the beginning of the Pacific War, the Allies were on the offensive. After the fall of Guadalcanal, Admiral Halsey proceeded in an unhurried fashion to prepare for the attack up the Solomon chain, while General MacArthur did the same in New Guinea.

The Japanese regarded what was happening as a breathing spell. That was a major miscalculation. All the while the Allies seemed to be resting, they were bringing tens of thousands of tons of supplies and tens of thousands of new and rested troops into the South and Southwest Pacific to carry on the 1943 operations.

To be sure, the Russells were taken with a very mixed invasion force, but that was the last of such operations. The planning for the invasion of New Georgia was thorough and leisurely as such things went.

The first objectives were to be four spots in the New Georgia area, to be taken for their tactical value in the main invasion.

One was Wickham Anchorage on the southeast coast of little Vangunu Island. This would become a fuel station for PT boats and other small craft from the Guadalcanal area.

The second objective was Segi Point on the south coast of New Georgia, which the Seabees were to turn into a fighter strip in short

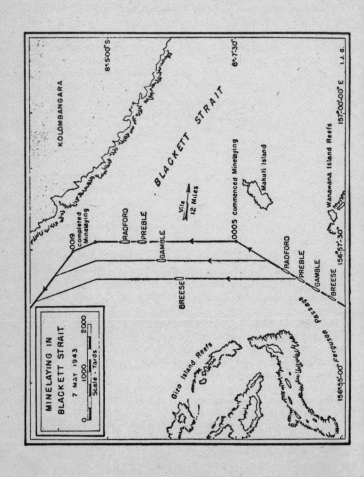

MINELAYING IN
BLACKETT STRAIT

7 MAY 1943

0   1000   2000

Scale - Yards

Gizo Island Reefs

DASH

156°55'-00' Ferguson Passage

BREESE

BREESE

RADFORD
PREBLE
GAMBLE

156°57'-30"

Wanawana Island Reefs

157°00'-00" E

Makuti Island

0005 commenced Minelaying

Via
12 Miles

BLACKETT STRAIT

GAMBLE

RADFORD
PREBLE

0019
completed
Minelaying

KOLOMBANGARA

8°-5'00"S

6°-7'-30"

order. That would eliminate the need for long flights from Henderson Field or from the fighter strips on Guadalcanal and the Russells.

Third, Viru Harbor, up the coast from Segi Point, would become a safe harbor for the small vessels.

Fourth, Rendova Island, across the Blanche Channel from New Georgia, was large enough to become a PT boat and artillery base.

The plans were made in February. The Joint Chiefs of Staff approved the operation at the end of March, and in April and May a steady stream of materials began moving up from Noumea, and later directly from Pearl Harbor and the United States. The ships came first to Lunga Roads; then many of them were sent on to the Russells, which was eighty miles closer to the objective.

The Japanese, as noted, had watched the steady buildup of the Russells bases when they flew over during their many air raids on Guadalcanal.

On the islands of Pavuvu and Banika, the Americans built their PT boat advanced base. At the end of May a number of boats moved up there. Nightly, they ran patrols up to New Georgia.

That spring, the harassment of the Japanese in the Central Solomons became a way of life, one that Admiral Halsey found most satisfying because of the results. One night early in May, four destroyers moved into Blackett Strait, which runs between Kolombangara Island (where the Japanese had many troops) and Arundel Island. The strait was part of the primary route for Japanese supply ships bringing troops and supplies to Kolombangara.

The destroyers were the *Radford, Breese, Gamble,* and *Preble.* The last three were old four-stack, coal-burners, nearly obsolete for such tasks as convoy or submarine hunting, but valuable nonetheless, as they showed on this mission. The task was to lay mines in Blackett Strait. On May 7 they laid 250 mines between the Gizo reefs and Kolombangara. Two days later the Japanese destroyers *Oyashio, Kurashio, Kagero,* and *Michishio* set out on a resupply mission to the south. As they had done many times before, they came down through Blackett Strait. But when they reached the middle of the strait, the first three destroyers struck mines. The *Kurashio* hit so many that she sank; the *Kagero* and *Oyashio* caught fire and lost power. The *Michishio* began rescue operations. An Allied coast watcher spotted the ships from shore and sent a message that brought a 60-plane air strike from Guadalcanal the next morning. Most of the planes failed to find the target because of bad weather, but about twenty got through. The *Kagero* sank after colliding with mines, but the enemy planes sank the crippled *Oyashio.* The loss of life was 85 men for the *Oyashio,* 81 for the *Kurashio,* and 18 for the *Kagero.* The *Michishio* escaped with some damage and returned to Rabaul.

These were just the latest Japanese ships to suffer from American offensive mining operations. Mines laid in Kavieng, Buin, and Munda all brought more Japanese casualties. The destroyer *Kazegumo* was damaged by American mines while moving through what had previously been safe waters. A number of merchant ships were sunk or damaged. Several I-boats that disappeared during this period may have fallen victim to the mines.

The fact was that by May 1943 there were no more "safe waters" for the Japanese fleet south of Truk.

Still, the Japanese continued to move men and supplies—by destroyer, by submarine, and by barge to New Georgia and Kolombangara, and by road and trail on the islands. Belatedly, in May, the Japanese Southeast Command at Rabaul began to recognize the immediacy of the need for heavier reinforcement. Even then, they had not gotten used to the idea that this war in the South Pacific was going to be fought in terms of divisions and not battalions.

Early in May, General Imamura sent Major General Minoru Sasaki down to New Georgia with the title of Commanding General, Southeast Area Detachment. Sasaki was a highly trained and highly regarded member of the officer corps. He was then fifty years old.

His career had begun in the cavalry. He had studied in the U.S.S.R. and in Poland. He had gone to Army General Staff School, served in the very important Military Affairs Bureau of the War Department, which actually made army policy, and in 1936 had joined the Army General Staff. Since his promotion to major general in 1939 he had served in the field continuously until 1942, when he again went to Tokyo as head of the mechanized department of the army.

From this post he came south to take over the defense of New Georgia. On his insistence, the flow of supplies and men increased sharply.

When the Allies became aware of this new Japanese policy, Admiral Halsey ordered bombardment of the Japanese bases at Vila and Munda. The first attack was carried out on May 12.

The bombardments were successful only in the sense that none of the Allied ships was sunk. They stood offshore first at Vila and then at Munda and fired away for several hours, using up 10,000 rounds of ammunition. The damage to Japanese installations was minimal.

Minelayers came along and laid more mines in Kula Gulf. Like the bombardment, the minelaying was uneventful.

But there were some accidents, as aboard the cruiser *Nashville* when a shell exploded inside a gun turret, killing several men and wounding several more. And the mines the force laid were effective no more than one day before the Japanese swept them up. The minelaying had hurt the Japanese when it came as a total surprise. But after the initial surprises, the Japanese brought more minesweepers down from Truk, and the mine damage ceased.

The results of such operations were not productive, as Admiral Nimitz saw immediately when he reviewed the action reports of the units involved. He ordered Halsey to stop the marginal operations and get on with the invasion of the Central Solomons.

Halsey already had the idea. His operation plan was drawn, and he was nearly ready to go. The plan had the great virtue of simplicity. Rear Admiral Richmond Kelly Turner was told to start working up the Solomons chain. He was not told how to do it. In essence, Halsey gave the ball to Admiral Turner and told him to run with it.

One of Admiral Halsey's peculiarities of operation was that he insisted on maintaining tactical control of his forces although he remained at Noumea. That was not as difficult as it may seem because radio communications kept the admiral in constant touch with events. That was the way he wanted it.

Turner was named commander of Task Force 31, which consisted of big transports of the President class (*President Hayes, President Jackson, President Adams*) plus a number of LSTs, destroyers, minesweepers, and smaller invasion craft such as LCTs, LCIs, patrol boats, PT boats. Three infantry units were part of the force, too: a western landing force, built around the Army 43rd Infantry Regiment, and an eastern landing force, built around the Army 103rd Infantry Regiment, and a reserve of Marine Raiders. The Second Marine Air Wing would be responsible for getting planes into New Georgia as soon as possible and operating out of there. The whole invasion area would be generally protected and policed by Task Force 36—the battleships, carriers, cruisers, and destroyers of the Third Fleet, which Halsey kept under his own direct command.

Kelly Turner's mission was stated very simply:

This force will:

(a) On D-Day, capture RENDOVA ISLAND, the VIRU HARBOR, SEGI POINT, and WICKHAM ANCHORAGE areas, capture or destroy enemy garrisons, and develop these positions for offensive operations.

(b) At the first favorable opportunity thereafter, when directed by the Commander Third Fleet, capture in succession MUNDA, KOLOMBANGARA, and other enemy positions in the NEW GEORGIA group; and capture or destroy enemy garrisons.

(c) The purpose of these operations is to prepare for further operations up the SOLOMONS.

Had the Japanese been given an advance look at Admiral Halsey's orders, they would have thought the Americans were crazy. No one (except the Russians in Manchuria) had ever stood up to the Imperial Army for long. The events of the last months of 1942 had occasioned some changes in the thinking of Japanese officers in the South Pacific, but had made little impression on the staff officers who manned the Imperial General Headquarters (most of whom had never commanded an army or navy unit in battle). Even after the defeats at Buin and Guadalcanal, General Tojo's government still believed that the war could and would be won.

Admiral Kusaka, the overall commander of the South Pacific for the Japanese, and General Imamura, commander of the Eighth Area Army at Rabaul, saw what was coming. On May 22 the navy's aerial scouts had counted 278 planes on Guadalcanal. Over several weeks they had noted and reported on the constant buildup of the bases.

General Imamura sent word to Admiral Koga at Truk that reinforcements and supplies were needed vitally, and he got them. During the month of June, three transports began to ply busily between Truk and the Central Solomons bases, bringing in about a thousand tons of ammunition and supplies.

On June 27 Imamura dispatched reinforcements to Kolombangara. The bulk of one battalion of the Army 13th Infantry Regiment was delivered to the island by the destroyers *Mochizuki, Yunage,* and *Satsuki* that night without incident. That meant another 800 defenders.

But the Americans were aware of the reinforcement and the next day, at two o'clock in the afternoon, the new unit had its baptism of fire when forty-eight American bombers attacked Munda airfield. They destroyed a number of installations and two antiaircraft guns. The antiaircraft gunners claimed to have shot down five Allied planes.

Then, at seven o'clock on the night of June 29, Munda airfield was shelled by two U.S. destroyers. Even so, that same night the destroyers *Nagatsuki* and *Minazuki* delivered more troops and ammunition to Kolombangara. They also delivered the regimental commander, Colonel Tomanori, who arrived with regimental flags flying. It was apparent at Munda, and the word was passed to Rabaul, that an invasion was imminent.

But the old ways died hard. The Japanese referred to what was coming as a *hanko*—counterattack. Technically speaking, that was correct: the Japanese had occupied these islands at the end of 1941, so any attack now was a counterattack. But the army and navy thinking was still overshadowed by vestiges of the past; it was hard to forget the days when the Imperial forces rolled up one victory after another. The self-deception inherent in the use of the word counterattack was one

thing, but military hyperbole was invoked with predictions of "crushin
blows" and "annihilation" of the enemy.

Whatever they called the movement that was coming from Guadalcanal, the troubles of the Japanese in the Solomons were just beginning.

The first move in the invasion of the Central Solomons occurred on
June 20, and in a sense it was inadvertent. Segi Point at the southeastern
end of New Georgia, was regarded as enormously important to the
Allied plans for the next few weeks. Here the Seabees would rush in to
build an airfield to take the pressure off Guadalcanal and the Russells.

For several weeks before the invasion small parties had slipped in and
out of the area, often by submarine, to make contact with the local coast
watchers and familiarize themselves with the terrain.

The Japanese were well aware of the activity but were unable to stop
it. Around the middle of June the activity became so noticeable that the
Japanese garrison commander at Viru sent a large detachment southeast
over the mountains to capture and hold Segi Point, then to build an
airstrip there.

But the resident Allied coast watcher, D. G. Kennedy, had already
proved to be as much a guerrilla fighter as a watcher. He kept a
schooner in a little bay and had been known to fight pitched battles with
Japanese patrol craft. He maintained a force of local warriors who had
remained loyal to Britain throughout the year and a half of Japanese
occupation. They had ambushed small parties of Japanese from time to
time, and when Kennedy learned from the island telegraph that the
Japanese were coming, he prepared to ambush this party as well. He did
so, killed a number of the Japanese, and scattered the rest, and
captured the notebook of Major Hara, the commander of the detachment. The notebook gave all the details of the Japanese plan to hold
Segi. That night Kennedy sent a radio message to Guadalcanal with the
news.

"Strong enemy patrol has approached very close, and by their
numbers and movement, it is believed they will attack. Urgently sug-
gest force be sent to defend Segi."

Admiral Turner responded by sending Lieutenant Colonel Michael S.
Currin with companies O and P of the 4th Marine Raider Battalion on
the night of June 20 in the destroyers *Dent* and *Waters*. The Raiders
were to hold Segi Point.

The destroyers had some difficulty getting into these restricted
waters, and both scraped bottom. Luckily the bottom was mostly mud,
and the most serious damage done was to the *Dent*'s port propeller,
which took a mauling.

The Raiders were landed just after six o'clock on the morning of June

...urs later their defenses were declared secure. On June 22, the ...yers *Schley* and *Crosby* brought two companies of the Army ...3rd Infantry Regiment and a naval survey party that was to do the preliminary work for the building of the airstrip. The Japanese sent patrols around the island, but they were kept under watch by the Solomon Island soldiers, who reported every move to coast watcher Kennedy. The area was regarded as so secure that four days later war correspondent Clay Gowran of the *Chicago Tribune* was brought into Segi aboard a PBY seaplane.

On the evening of June 27, the marines turned Segi Point over to the army troops and moved off to begin the second part of their advance operation. They were to cross the five-mile strait in rubber boats and land on New Georgia at Segi, then move overland to Viru Harbor, where they were to assault the small Japanese garrison. (Allied intelligence indicated that the garrison consisted of about 100 men; there were actually 229). The marines were to take possession to prepare for the official invading force which was to land on June 30 from the sea.

The advance unit landed in the early minutes of June 28 and bivouacked for the night. At 6:30 the marines were going again, in single file, along the narrow jungle trail heading north across the mountains. Three hours later the rear guard encountered a Japanese patrol, and in the firefight that ensued four Japanese were killed, and one or two escaped into the jungle. The marines suffered no casualties, but it was apparent that they would not make Viru Harbor by the morning of June 30 as they had hoped. They sent a message to coast watcher Kennedy back at Segi Point to relay to Admiral Turner.

Forty-five minutes later, the rear guard of the column was hit by a larger enemy patrol, this one armed with machine guns. The jungle became bedlam. When the noise of the firing subsided, Sergeant Sudro and four men from Company P were missing.

That night the Raiders bivouacked on the Mohi River. At 6:30 the next morning they moved out again. The sergeant and the four men had not shown up.

Again, at 11:15, the Japanese hit the rear guard. Lieutenant Brown's platoon took the worst of it. When the fight was over five marines were dead and one man was wounded. They counted eighteen Japanese bodies. Lieutenant Colonel Currin decided to deal with the problem at the source. He detached Company P, except for the weapons platoon, to attack the village of Tombe, where the Japanese were concentrated. Captain Walker was in command. With him were Lieutenant Popelka, Lieutenant Brown, and a hundred men.

At nine o'clock on the morning of June 30, the main body crossed the

Viru River, and the next morning it approached the village of Tetamara, the location of the Japanese garrison for Viru Harbor.

Admiral Mitscher's Guadalcanal air force cooperated and sent dive-bombers to plaster the village that morning, but even so, when the marines came up the Japanese were ready to fight, disposed before the village and out on both flanks. The marines approached and the struggle began.

This time Colonel Currin heard heavy machine gun fire. The marines began to take casualties. After an hour they had advanced about 100 yards, and there they were stopped until the colonel moved machine guns forward. At one o'clock in the afternoon, the force managed to get around to the south and take possession of the ridge there, with a ravine on the right front. The Japanese sent out flanking forces. Colonel Currin sent demolition squads with satchel charges to both flanks to deal with the heavy machine guns that were beginning to harass the men again.

At 3:30 P.M. the Japanese decided to charge the marine position and began working themselves up to it with screams and yelling:

"Marine, you die. . . ."
"Tenno Heika, Banzai. . . ."

But the assault failed, and half an hour later the marines overran the enemy positions. At 4:30 that afternoon they had sole possession of Tetamara village. At 5:00 P.M. the LCTs of the invasion force landed. Colonel Currin brought in his six dead and seventeen wounded marines. They did not then count the dead Japanese. They assembled the captured equipment: six light (.25 caliber) Nambu machine guns, four .31 caliber machine guns, six field guns. Captain Walker and his men arrived from Tombe to report no casualties. They had killed a dozen Japanese. During the night two of the wounded marines died. The next day a thirty-man patrol, sent out to "mop up," killed two more Japanese soldiers.

On the Fourth of July the Americans had good news. Sergeant Sudro and the four marines missing after the first Japanese ambush had made it back to Segi Point.

From then until July 9, the marines patrolled the area and killed several more Japanese soldiers. At 5:30 A.M. on July 9 they embarked in landing craft for Guadalcanal, turning Viru over to the army troops. The marines had taken twenty-eight casualties, thirteen of them killed. In turn they had killed sixty Japanese and wounded another 100.

Most of the Japanese garrison escaped into the jungle and began working through the bush toward Munda.

At Munda the rains had begun in earnest on June 23. There it was fog and drizzle, but at Rendova, where the northern part of the island is largely flat red clay plainland, the constant rains of the next few days created a quagmire. Everything was flooded.

For three days at the end of June, the American bombers and fighters seemed to hover almost constantly over New Georgia and Kolombangara islands. The airstrips at Vila and Munda were pitted from constant bombing. No Japanese planes could get in during the daylight hours. Any trying to get out would have met a wall of gunfire.

There was also a good deal of activity on the ground behind the Japanese lines, as advance U.S. parties moved in and out of the areas that would soon be attacked, in order to make plans for rapid buildup of the bases once the Japanese were driven out. This sort of movement was not as dangerous as it seemed because the Japanese never controlled the entire islands, but only pockets where they built their bases. Guided and guarded by the coast watchers and their native troops, the Allied surveyors were relatively safe.

On the night of June 29, Admiral Merrill brought his destroyers and cruisers to the shores of New Georgia to shell the Rekata Bay base and lay mines.

Japanese headquarters at Truk and Rabaul knew what was coming before the troops did. On the night of June 29, the submarine *RO-103* was patrolling west of the Russell Islands, when her captain sighted a large force of warships and transports moving northwest. They had to be heading for the Central Solomons.

Still, the Japanese naval headquarters at Rabaul was caught off guard. On this same day, General MacArthur's troops were landing at Nassau Bay, seventeen miles from Salamaua on New Guinea. At the same time they were landing in the Trobriand Islands, off the New Guinea shore.

The Allies were conducting an enormous troop buildup that did not go unnoticed at Rabaul. The problem was that there were too many rat holes to watch. From the middle of June onward, the Japanese were aware of the danger from Guadalcanal. They knew that the Americans were poised for action. But the Japanese had planned their defenses and their strategy—which called for concentration on New Guinea, rather than the Solomons—and they made no attempts to change them.

The Japanese were totally unaware of the first set of landings, at Wickham Anchorage. Admiral Halsey wanted this location for a PT boat staging point, because the three hundred Japanese on Vangunu Island, south of New Georgia, were located on high ground to the east of Wickham.

Two destroyers and seven landing craft took part in this landing before dawn. The operation was badly managed, the craft got in the way of their own boats, and six of the boats were lost. If there had been any Japanese at Wickham Landing, the results might have been disastrous.

Meanwhile the main landing force was moving further northwest.

Then, on June 30, came the dawn at 4:45. At that moment the sun poked through the rain clouds, the visibility for a moment was perfect, and the Japanese defenders looking out on the leaden sea saw six transports and a whole fleet of boats facing Rendova's North Point, about three thousand yards out. The Allied invasion of the Middle Solomons had begun. It was just before seven o'clock in the morning, U.S. military time.

Actually the first landings were made on two small islands that overlooked Blanche Channel, the waterway the transports would use to approach Rendova. The destroyer *Talbot* and the minesweeper *Zane* landed two companies of the 169th Infantry Regiment on these islands. There were no Japanese present, so the going was easy enough, except that the *Zane* ran up on the reef and stayed stuck until pulled off later that day by the tug *Rail*.

Then the "shock troops," special jungle-trained men of the 172nd Regimental Combat Team, "the Barracudas," were landed in the wrong place. Their mission was to land in Rendova Harbor and wipe out the Japanese garrison before the main landing. But their "ferryboats"—the destroyers *Dent* and *Waters*—took them to the wrong place, and when they landed and found no Japanese, they were temporarily out of the fight.

The other men of the 172nd RCT were put in the right place, without a doubt. They landed by the early light, and it was not long before the lost men of the first landing showed up. Since several thousand Americans had landed, to oppose fewer than 400 Japanese in total, the issue was never in doubt. In half an hour the Americans were storming one point after another. It got down to hand-to-hand fighting.

Almost immediately Japanese communication between Munda and Rendova was cut off. Munda, of course, was next on the list that day. The Japanese had no way of combating the enemy concentration of ships and troops except in the air. But no Japanese aircraft appeared.

From the lookout station atop the point, the defenders of Munda watched what was happening across the strait. Munda Cape housed half-a-dozen navy 12-centimeter and 14-centimeter guns and these began firing on the enemy ships.

The command ship and transport *McCawley* and the destroyers *Dent* and *Waters* landed the first waves of troops to hit Rendova's beach. They were the targets of the Munda guns.

The destroyer *Gwin* was hit in the aft engine room by a shell from a shore gun. Three men were killed and seven were wounded. Immediately the *Gwin* began making smoke to screen the transports from the shore guns. The warships found the sources of shore fire, and one by one the batteries were silenced. By eight o'clock U.S. time, all of the Japanese shore batteries on Munda Cape were knocked out.

Ashore on Rendova, the fighting was furious but brief. The Japanese garrison seemed at first to be confused, but a young naval officer, Lieutenant Senda, seized command and led the men in fighting to the last. It was an uneven contest. How uneven is shown by one small event: a boat returned to the *McCawley*, carrying one wounded soldier—the sum total of U.S. casualties that could be rounded up.

At eight o'clock that morning the fighting was over on Rendova. A handful of Japanese escaped into the jungle. From the naval and army commands at Rabaul came an order to withdraw from Rendova. It was picked up at Munda and a bugler blew three blasts to tell the survivors on Rendova that their mission was finished. Still, no help had come for the Japanese.

At that moment at Rabaul there were seventy-one Zeros, twenty dive-bombers, forty-one torpedo bombers, and five scout planes available. And because there were two landings in two widely separated parts of an extremely broad front facing the Rabaul command (New Guinea and the Central Solomons), Admiral Kusaka's Eleventh Air Fleet could respond to the American landing only with a fighter sweep. At nine o'clock (Tokyo time) that morning, twenty-seven Zeros got off the ground and headed for Rendova.

The first indication of their arrival came at eleven o'clock when the task force off Rendova went to battle stations in response to a report of "bogies" coming in. A few minutes later the Japanese fighters were engaged in an air battle with a larger group of American fighters from Guadalcanal, somewhere between thirty and forty fighters. The fighting was carried out at high altitude, 21,000 feet above the invasion fleet, and not much was seen from the water or the ground. But the Allies (Americans and New Zealanders) had the best of it, claiming sixteen Zeros. Several Allied planes were shot down, and one pilot was rescued by a boat from the *McCawley*. The destroyer *Buchanan* picked up two more pilots.

By noon, Admiral Kusaka had his bombers armed and ready to make a major attack on the American invasion force, with twenty-four fighters and twenty-six twin-engined Mitsubishi (Betty) bombers fitted for torpedo work. The Japanese came down the Slot, to Rendova Harbor, but found that the invasion fleet had landed its troops and supplies, and moved off, heading back toward the relative safety of

Guadalcanal. The American fighter cover over Rendova began trailing the force and sniping at the "tail-end Charlies" and managed to pick off a few. But just after 3:30 in the afternoon, U.S. time, general quarters was sounded aboard the *McCawley*. The Japanese were closing fast. Up above, forty-one American fighters moved to intercept.

The Japanese followed their usual tactics: the fighters lured and engaged the American fighters, while the torpedo bombers tried to get down under the screen to attack the ships. Some of the American F4Fs and F4Us managed to come down with the bombers and shot down at least five of them by Admiral Turner's count.

The torpedo bombers bored in on the invasion fleet, splitting into small attack units so they could approach from different directions. At 3:50 Admiral Turner ordered the ships to begin firing. Three minutes later he ordered an emergency ninety-degree right turn.

Several torpedo planes headed for the flagship, the *McCawley*, and dropped their torpedoes as they came in. The captain of the *McCawley*, Commander Robert H. Rodgers, was already in the ninety-degree turn ordered by Admiral Turner, but he made another ninety-degree turn inside that, to try to comb the wakes of the torpedoes. He almost made it, but not quite. One torpedo struck the *McCawley* amidships, just as the gunners were shooting down two of the torpedo bombers. The ship began to list to port and went dead in the water. The reports from the damage control center indicated that the engine room was flooded.

With their ship lying helpless, the men of the *McCawley* watched in horror as another torpedo headed directly for the disabled flagship. But the torpedo ran just alongside the ship, from stern to stem, and sank, just beyond the bow. From their grandstand seat, the men of the *McCawley* watched the rest of the attack. From the American point of view, it was very satisfying: seventeen of the attacking bombers were shot down, and no ships other than the *McCawley* were hit.

Admiral Turner was taken off the stricken ship by the destroyer *Fahrenholt*. Rear Admiral T. S. Wilkinson, his second-in-command, remained aboard the command ship to try to salvage her. Fifteen men had been killed and eight wounded by the torpedo explosion, and the wounded were transferred. The *McCawley* was taken in tow by the transport *Libra*. Later that day the tow was transferred to the tug *Pawnee*, which had a difficult time of it, and lost the tow that night. While Admiral Turner was considering the problem, something came out of the night and put two torpedoes into the *McCawley*. There was no further need to worry about a tow. She went down to join the scores of other ships sunk in these embattled waters. (Later, to the chagrin of all concerned, the commander of the local PT boats came into port boasting of the sinking of an "enemy" transport in Blanche Channel that night. Admiral Turner was not known for his patience in such situations. He took immediate personal command of the PT boat operations.)

The other landings succeeded, although not particularly brilliantly. The marine Raiders under Lt. Col. Michael S. Currin who had landed at Segi Point ten days earlier were supposed to move up to Viru Harbor and eliminate the Japanese garrison there, but the planners had not taken proper cognizance of either the weather or the terrain. The mud and the rain and the swollen rivers slowed the troops down in their overland march, and they had to stop and fight off Japanese harassing attacks as well. So, when the Viru occupation force arrived at the mouth of that little harbor on June 30, it was greeted by fire from a naval shore gun and backed off. Its troops were taken back south and put ashore at Segi Point.

From the Japanese seaplane base in the Shortlands, that evening a group of seaplane bombers took off to attack the Rendova Anchorage. When they arrived they found no ships and so retired.

That same night of June 30, Allied bombers attacked the Japanese air bases on New Britain and New Ireland, causing enough damage to put a serious crimp in the next day's operations. In recent days the bombing of Japanese bases by Admiral Mitscher's land-based aircraft and General MacArthur's Fifth Air Force had been severe, as had been the losses over the Solomons and New Guinea.

As of the night of June 30, the Rabaul air force was reduced to a total of thirty-five Zero fighters, six torpedo bombers, ten twin-engined bombers, and two scout planes. That night the Eleventh Air Fleet called on Truk for more help, and Truk ordered the 21st Air Group down to Rabaul. That would add sixty fighters, forty-eight torpedo bombers, and sixteen scout bombers to the force.

On July 1, after the two companies of the Fourth Raiders arrived at Viru they soon had silenced the shore gun and scattered its operators. Dive-bombers from Guadalcanal gave them a hand, and by afternoon the Japanese at Viru were eliminated.

On July 1, the Japanese again launched several air attacks from Rabaul, to strike at the second section of the American landing force. Thirty-five Zeros and six Aichi torpedo bombers carried out the assault. They went home claiming to have sunk a destroyer and a cruiser, but the fact was that they did not sink any American ships. They also claimed to have shot down twenty-seven American fighters with a loss of five Japanese fighters and three bombers on the mission. The Americans claimed to have destroyed half the Japanese planes.

The U.S. Navy had a more accurate claim for that day's work: that night the American destroyer *Radford* discovered the submarine *RO-101* on the surface and attacked and sank her.

On July 2, Admiral Kusaka took advantage of the new dictum from Imperial General Headquarters and called on the army to provide the planes for his mission against the American landings. He sent two dozen army bombers and thirty fighters, most of them army planes. They kept low on the water all the way down and came in low across the mountains of New Georgia to swoop down on the beachhead.

American radar failed to detect them, and the first thing the men on the beachhead knew of the attack, high explosive bombs were falling on them. Right around the beach the Americans suffered 150 casualties and serious damage to landing craft and equipment. The Japanese claimed a major victory in the air and on the land and sea: nine American fighters shot down and three probables, and no damage to the Japanese air force.

That night the cruiser *Yubari* and six destroyers moved south through the Slot, with an air cover, and attacked the Rendova beachhead. Their intelligence was faulty, however, and near the shore most of the shells fell in the jungle beyond.

Three American PT boats were out that night, but they were quarry, not hunters. The destroyer commander herded them into a circle and prepared to gun them down. They saved themselves by making smoke and sneaking out of the circle to safety, firing six torpedoes without effect.

Early on the morning of July 2, at Rabaul, General Imamura sent a helpful suggestion to Admiral Kusaka. Why did the naval air force not launch a massive attack against the shipping in Rendova Bay to destroy it *in situ* and thus isolate the west side waterway and make it impossible for the transports to move? An ambush was what was wanted.

There was just one problem with that suggestion. How was it going to be accomplished? The Japanese naval air force was having a hard enough time just making normal attacks. The Americans obviously had air superiority and naval superiority over the island and about 3,500 troops ashore at that time. There still were not enough planes available for the sort of operation the general wanted. Despite the "cooperation" between army and navy, the army was extremely sparing in its allocation of aircraft to meet Admiral Kusaka's requests.

That morning at Rabaul General Imamura paid a call on Admiral Kusaka. They agreed together that the suggestion was eminently sound, given thorough cooperation, and in their enthusiasm suggested that the chances were "ten thousand to one" that it would succeed.

**RENDOVA HARBOR
AA DEFENSES**
4 July 1943

90mm AA
40mm AA
20mm AA
50 Cal AA
155 mm guns

If it did not succeed, then they would have to give serious consideration to new strategy, but the blame (this was inherent) would be shared equally.

At about this same time, Admiral Halsey at Noumea was making some command decisions as well. The success of the Rendova landing was complete. While Halsey knew that they had to expect a Japanese reaction in the air and at sea, it had not come yet, and the scout planes flying over Rabaul reported only a handful of Japanese naval vessels in that harbor. So perhaps the Japanese were not going to react for a while.

Once the troops were on the ground in the Central Solomons, command passed from Admiral Turner to Army Major General John H. Hester. Admiral Halsey ordered him now to move against Munda, on July 5. Meanwhile, Marine Colonel Harry Liversedge had been ordered to move up with 2,600 troops to occupy Rice Anchorage on the northwest shore of New Georgia, opposite Kolombangara Island.

The purpose of this move was to forestall any attempt by the Japanese to reinforce the Munda area from the Kolombangara base at Vila. These troops were to move on the night of July 4. So were the Japanese troops who were coming down to reinforce Munda. Hence, three days after the Allied invasion of the Central Solomons, the stage was set for a major confrontation.

9

THE BATTLE
OF KULA GULF

AT Segi Point, before nightfall on June 30 the U.S. Navy Seabees began working in the rain to build that airstrip. Admiral Halsey wanted the airstrip—and he wanted it in a hurry. They had a two-week deadline, so neither bombing nor bad weather stopped their work for long.

On June 30 Rendova Harbor, beneath the 3,400-foot mountain, became a busy advanced base for the PT boats. Lieutenant Commander Robert B. Kelly set up the base. The troops lived and worked in the rain. On July 1 it rained all day. The men rose after a night of rain that poured into their pup tents and foxholes to build new foxholes and reestablish their tents.

The roads left by the Japanese and the planters of the past had turned into sticky masses of mud and even these were completely blocked most of that first day. The artillerymen were moving 155 mm guns into position, and they bogged down time after time. By afternoon the entire area above the beach was one great mire, and the only way to carry supplies was on human backs, through the mud that was at this point thigh deep. The men had to labor uphill and down, and cross two swollen streams to reach higher ground. The men redug foxholes and replaced their pup tents. That night it rained and Japanese snipers on the perimeter banged away at them until dawn.

Back at Noumea, the quick success of the American landings at Rendova persuaded Admiral Halsey that the Japanese were off guard, and he decided to take advantage of this situation by pressing ahead. What he wanted was the quick capture of Munda, which meant he would have the first major Japanese air base in the Central Solomons and one that would put Rabaul very definitely within regular attack range. So Halsey ordered General Hester to move up the timetable and start the assault on Munda. The general was to do this by ferrying troops over in landing craft from Rendova to New Georgia.

At Rabaul, Admiral Kusaka and General Imamura were talking about retaking Rendova, and that day the army and navy staffs were conferring on various plans. Immediately, Japanese army and navy units would undertake a cooperative reinforcement, to bring more troops down to strengthen the defenses of Kolombangara and New Georgia islands. These troops would be brought by destroyers from Buin and Buka and landed at Vila. Then those bound for New Georgia would be ferried by barge across to Bairoko, the port for the Munda airfield.

On July 2, General Hester undertook the task of moving troops to New Georgia. For several days army patrols had looked for a suitable landing place near Munda, but they had not found one closer than five miles away. That place was Zanana Beach. The real problem was that, by landing there, the army troops would have to make their way through five miles of jungle before they could attack. Five miles of jungle threatened to be hard on field guns and heavy equipment—just how hard Admiral Halsey did not quite realize.

The landings at Zanana began on July 2 and continued, as the U.S. Army infiltrated men through in small boats and in small numbers. It was no way to move any but highly trained Raider battalions in the South Pacific jungles.

Meanwhile, Admiral Halsey had learned that the army troops threatened to bog down. He had assembled a force of 2,600 men under Marine Colonel Harry Liversedge, and they were assigned to move to Rice Anchorage, across the strait from Vila, and there to block off any Japanese attempts to reinforce the Munda area from Vila, the Kolombangara base. At the same time, Rear Admiral W. L. Ainsworth was assigned the task of "quieting" Vila, by a bombardment with the cruisers *Helena*, *Honolulu*, and *St. Louis*, and four destroyers.

At approximately the same time, the Japanese at Rabaul had the same idea about Rendova. The plans to retake that important base were in the works. First of all, the American positions had to be worked over. Earlier attempts by the Tokyo Express to attack ships in the harbor had been unlucky: every time the Japanese showed up, the American supply missions had either just left Rendova or were at the other end of the line just starting out.

So on July 2, the army and the navy decided to try their first really combined bombing mission. The bombers were army bombers and the fighters were navy fighters from Rabaul. There weren't too many of the latter, about two dozen, because the Eleventh Air Fleet had been ground down to the nub in the recent weeks of fighting. The army supplied twenty-four heavy bombers.

For once the weather was just about right, cloud cover to protect the fliers' entry into the target zone but clear weather over Rendova. The fighters stayed up high, and the bombers came in and dropped their bombs on the beach since they could find no shipping in the harbor. They caught the U.S. troops completely by surprise. The Rendova garrison, so newly arrived, had only one radar set, and it was down for repair that day. The troops were lined up for the noon meal in the mess area near the beach. The bombers caught them there and caused a hundred and twenty-five casualties. They also wrecked the field hospital and knocked out two 155 mm guns, one 40 mm antiaircraft gun, and two tractors. One or two bombs hit the gasoline dump and started a fire that destroyed a hundred drums of gasoline.

The Japanese Eleventh Air Fleet got some help at last. In response to Admiral Kusaka's insistent pleas for reinforcements, Admiral Koga sent down about fifty planes from Truk. On July 3, the Rabaul air force sent an all-navy fighter sweep over Rendova. They encountered about forty Allied planes, many of them P-38s, and claimed to have shot down nine without any damage to the Zeros. The army was supposed to contribute another group of fighters to this sweep, but they never arrived at the rendezvous. The army excuse was that the weather was so bad many of the planes were forced to make emergency landings at various fields and the others did not find the rendezvous point.

The story is probably true; one of the factors in the air war was the enormous difference in caliber of training between army and navy. The army pilots were perhaps expert at low-level troop support, but they had little experience and not much apparent taste for the traditional fighter sweep, and because island defense had originally been assigned to the navy, the army bombers had little practice in conducting long-distance flights.

On July 4 came the second combined army-navy air operation. Seventeen army Aichi 97 dive-bombers and forty-nine navy Zeros set out to attack the American transport fleet at Rendova, flying by way of Anbanba and Lubiana islands. Most of the army bombers got lost in the thick cloud cover and did not perform at all. The few that made it all the way soon discovered that the American antiaircraft fire from land guns and the ships in Rendova Harbor was fierce and accurate. The returning planes reported they had sunk five transports and set several supply dumps on fire. Actually they had put bombs between LCI 23 and LCT 24 and caused so much damage that the two ships were beached. But they were not destroyed. The returned Japanese fliers also claimed that their unit had shot down fourteen American and New Zealand fighters but had lost only six bombers. The army's official account of the action credited the six as *jibaku*—suicide explosions, which could mean that those pilots chose to dive on an objective when their planes were damaged, or could have simply been an honorific way of accounting for the loss of the bombers. The concept of the suicide dive of a distressed plane was always with the Japanese fliers, but at this point in the war the suicide dive was a matter of personal desperation, not official policy.

Once again, concerning the raid of July 4, there is enormous disparity between the accounts of the Japanese and those of the Americans. Brigadier General Francis P. Mulcahy, commander of the New Georgia air force, which was just setting up shop at Rendova, claimed that the U.S. antiaircraft guns knocked down 12 twin-engined bombers with the expenditure of only 88 rounds of ammunition. If so, it must have been the most accurate antiaircraft action of the war. General Mulcahy's statement also seems a bit euphoric in the claim that American fighters shot down five Zeros too, "and only one escaped."

As of July 4, then, the Japanese and the Americans were of the same mind: reinforce their positions in the Central Solomons in preparation for new attacks.

On the afternoon of July 4, Colonel Liversedge's troops were embarked in seven destroyer-transports. They were a combination of men of the 1st Marine Raider Regiment and the army's 145th and 148th Infantry regiments. The destroyers moved north toward Kula Gulf, and shortly after midnight on July 5 they rounded Visu Point on New Georgia and headed into the gulf. Just then they caught sight of gun flashes: Admiral Ainsworth's bombardment force was in action.

After working over Vila for a few minutes, the ships turned across the channel to Bairoko Harbor on the New Georgia side. The Japanese usually brought their supplies down to Vila and then small craft and barges ferried them over to Bairoko for New Georgia's defense.

This reinforcement was the task of Rear Admiral Teruo Akiyama, and for the task a special reinforcement group had been brought together. On July 4, shortly before sundown, four of the destroyers sallied forth from Buin, loaded with troops and ammunition and supplies for Vila. At 11:30 (Tokyo time) they were in the process of unloading when the flashes of the American bombardment group's guns alerted them, and they hastily put to sea, abandoning the landing. From long distance the destroyers fired spreads of torpedoes at the American shapes and then turned and scurried away for the safety of the open sea. No destroyer squadron skipper was fool enough to take on a force of cruisers and destroyers, particularly when his decks were loaded with men and supplies.

All this while, the seven American destroyer transports were moving up the New Georgia shore toward Rice Anchorage to deposit their troops. Suddenly—the time was half an hour after midnight—the destroyer transport *Ralph Talbot* picked up two blips on the radar screen where no blips ought to be, about five miles away to the northwest, moving north at a speed of 25 knots. Two minutes after the blips appeared, they disappeared from the screen—out of range.

The ships indicated by the blips were part of Admiral Kusaka's reinforcement team, a fact the Americans discovered ten minutes later when the destroyer *Strong* of the bombardment force was hit by a torpedo that seemed to come out of nowhere. The blast opened up the destroyer like a sardine can, flooded the engine rooms, and wrecked the forward fireroom. The *Strong* listed to port and skidded to a halt, her back broken.

The destroyers *Chevalier* and *O'Bannon* rushed to the rescue of their fellow destroyer. Then the Japanese shore batteries from Bairoko and Enogai opened up on the destroyers. One shell hit the crippled *Strong*, and the *O'Bannon* suspended rescue operations to take on the shore batteries. Other shells from the Japanese guns fell around the transport-destroyers, arousing concern lest they be hit. Meanwhile, the men of the *Chevalier* were working to take off the crew of the *Strong*, which was sinking. In less than ten minutes they brought 241 men across from the stricken ship, under fire all the while by the enemy batteries, which were putting shells all around them. The *Strong* began to settle, and the captain of the *Chevalier* moved his ship away just in time to avoid entanglement with the sinking ship. The *Strong* went down like a stone, her depth charges began to explode, and some of the men still aboard struggled in the water after she was gone. Other destroyers picked up more survivors and some swam to the beach, but forty-six men were lost.

At one o'clock in the morning the American bombardment group had finished its job, and all the surviving ships hauled out for Guadalcanal. The transport group stayed on to unload.

The destroyers moved to a point about 1,500 yards off the Rice Anchorage and began to disembark men and equipment into Higgins boats and rubber boats. Each Higgins boat towed one ten-man rubber boat in to shore. The Japanese batteries at Enogai Point then shifted their fire to the transport destroyers, and 150 mm projectiles began falling around the landing area. The destroyers *Gwin* and *Radford* took the Japanese batteries on Kolombangara under fire and silenced two of them. The other two guns continued to fire during the landings but did not score any hits.

The landing was completed by six o'clock, and the transport group retired. On the way out of the strait, the *Ralph Talbot*'s lookouts spotted an American whaleboat and pulled up alongside, to rescue eighteen more survivors from the *Strong*. Then the *Ralph Talbot* caught up with the other ships and they all retired to Guadalcanal without further excitement.

On the morning of July 5, the Japanese high command at Rabaul recognized the significance of the previous night's maneuvering. The appearance of that Allied landing unit in Kula Gulf had to mean that the enemy was preparing to assault Munda airfield. At seven o'clock on the morning of July 5, Rabaul headquarters had word from the navy special landing force troops (marines) that the Allied forces were moving overland.

Colonel Liversedge had with him the 1st Marine Raider Regimental Headquarters, the 1st Marine Raider Battalion, and the 3rd Battalion of the Army 145th Infantry and the 3rd Battalion of the Army 148th Infantry. Leaving two companies of the 145th and some quartermaster personnel at Rice Anchorage to handle beach defense and resupply, Liversedge took the remainder of the force marching toward what they called Dragon's Peninsula. Company D of the 1st Raider Battalion was sent ahead to secure a bridgehead across the Giza Giza River.

On July 5, Admiral Akiyama was back at his task, moving south to reinforce Kolombangara and New Georgia with the army troops assigned by General Imamura. Shortly after sundown, three different groups of destroyers left the advance base at Buin to head for Vila.

American intelligence was working well this day, and, in the middle of the afternoon, Admiral Halsey had the word that a large number of Japanese destroyers at Rabaul were loading and getting up steam to go someplace. It did not take Halsey long to figure out where. He informed Admiral Ainsworth's cruiser force, which was in Indispensable Strait, off the southern tip of Guadalcanal. Ainsworth turned around and started back up the Slot. There was no time to fuel, but luckily he did not need fuel at the moment.

Ainsworth had with him three cruisers, the *Honolulu*, *Helena*, and *St. Louis*. His destroyer force had also been brought back to strength (after the loss of the *Strong*) by the assignment of the *Radford* and *Jenkins*, which were just then loading fuel at Tulagi after their strenuous night off Rice Landing. They hurried and caught up with the cruiser task group shortly after dark.

The Japanese captains had been complaining that the suddenness with which these resupply operations were launched and the orders changed, created a lot of confusion. The Americans could have said the same: the two new destroyer captains were not familiar with the task group commander's orders; it was another rump group that was expected to perform like a trained squadron. But there was no help for it. Events were moving too fast in the Central Solomons to go by the book.

Admiral Ainsworth was confident. So was Admiral Akiyama. The Americans had two distinct advantages.

First, they were sending cruisers with their six-inch guns, which could stand off at long range and blast the enemy destroyers without taking gunfire in return.

Second, all the American ships in this group were equipped with radar.

Admiral Akiyama was confident because just the night before he had sunk an American ship in that brief engagement off Kolombangara. Also, he had no great respect for the American ability to fight at night.

The weather had continued to be foul, and this hampered the American search planes during the day and that night. The Americans sent out radar-equipped night fighters on search missions, but they did not find Admiral Akiyama's force. Furthermore, even though the Japanese had made exceedingly good use of their "long-lance" torpedoes in virtually every destroyer encounter since the beginning of the Guadalcanal campaign, the American naval authorities still had not come to understand the nature of the Japanese weapon. The torpedo was oxygen-driven. It had a range of 22,000 yards (12+ miles) at 49 knots, or 44,000 yards (25 miles) at 36 knots. It was about twice as powerful as the American torpedo. The sinking of the *Strong* the night before ought to have been an object lesson—it would have been virtually impossible for an American destroyer to have duplicated this feat. But the scurrying and confusion of the times let such lessons go unstudied. Admiral Ainsworth was secure in the knowledge that his six-inch guns outgunned the 4.6-inch guns of the enemy. Admiral Akiyama was secure in the knowledge that his torpedoes outgunned the six-inch guns.

Just after midnight (which made the date July 6), Admiral Akiyama detached the destroyers *Mochizuki*, *Mikazuki*, and *Hamakaze* to hug the coast of Kolombangara and head for Vila. He took his other seven destroyers down the middle of Kula Gulf. Thus, if there were any enemy ships about he would be likely to meet them, while Captain

Tsuneo Orita, with the smaller force, got about the business of landing his troops and supplies at Vila.

As the Japanese group began to split, the blips showed up on the radar screen of Admiral Ainsworth's flagship, the *Honolulu*. The Japanese were about sixteen miles away from the American task group. Admiral Ainsworth ordered the ships into battle formation: the destroyers *Nicholas* and *O'Bannon* leading, the three cruisers in line, followed by the other two destroyers, the *Jenkins* and *Radford*.

Akiyama's change in disposition puzzled the Americans. What were those three Japanese destroyers doing, turning off to the right? Besides, at this range, the high mountains of Kolombangara tended to foul the radar screens, and Admiral Ainsworth was not quite sure how many or what sort of ships he faced. He came to the conclusion that there were at least seven enemy vessels, perhaps nine. He still did not know what class ships they were.

When the range had closed to six miles, Admiral Ainsworth decided to open fire, using his radar for fire control. He chose the second group of ships in the Akiyama force. These were the *Amigiri*, *Hatsuyuki*, *Nagatsuki*, and *Satsuki*. The cruisers would attack these ships and so would two of the American destroyers. The other two American destroyers would fire on the leading Japanese ships, which were directly under Admiral Akiyama's control. They were his flagship, the *Niizuki*, the *Suzukaze*, and the *Tanikaze*.

But five minutes after the American ships had changed to battle formation, Admiral Akiyama's new radar set aboard the flagship picked up the enemy vessels. He ordered the Japanese ships to speed up to 30 knots and prepare to launch torpedoes.

At three minutes before two o'clock, the Americans began firing. The first shells from the cruisers were aimed by radar at the *Niizuki*, and they struck home, knocking out her steering and dealing her a mortal wound. She began taking water immediately. But the *Suzukaze* and *Tanikaze* launched sixteen torpedoes that headed for the American force.

The cruisers continued to fire at a high rate of speed and the enormous racket and lighting up of the sky convinced Admiral Ainsworth that he had the enemy on the run. He was sure he was obliterating the Japanese ships. But the fact was that he was doing nothing of the kind.

The *Suzukaze* was hit by several six-inch shells, and some fires started and three men were killed. But the most serious damage was the loss of her searchlight, for the Japanese dearly loved to confuse the enemy by lighting them up. The *Tanikaze* was hit only by a dud six-inch shell in the forecastle and it spoiled a number of bags of rice. That was all.

Having made their torpedo attack, the two Japanese destroyers turned, made smoke, and ran out of the battle zone to reload torpedo tubes.

The American destroyer skippers charged with attacking the lead ships wanted to fire torpedoes, but Admiral Ainsworth had told them to use guns first, so they withheld the torpedoes. They lost their slim chance to once more show their proficiency with these weapons, but this time it was not their fault; they were at the orders of a big ship admiral.

The difference between the Japanese and the American tactics soon became painfully apparent. Seven minutes after the Japanese ships had fired a spread of sixteen torpedoes, they began to arrive in the American area. Within three minutes the cruiser *Helena* was hit by three torpedoes—her bow was blown off and her back broken. She folded up like a jackknife.

Admiral Ainsworth did not even know what had happened until a few minutes later when the *Helena* failed to answer signals. The signals called her to join an attack on the other four Japanese destroyers, loaded with troops and supplies for Vila, which were eight miles away and going along at 30 knots.

Admiral Ainsworth then made a move that should have won the battle—he crossed the enemy T. Now the Japanese ships were moving in a column against the American column at a ninety-degree angle. That meant all the American ships could fire on all the Japanese destroyers, but only the first destroyer in the Japanese line could fire at the Americans. But for some reason the American shells failed to hurt the *Amagiri*, first in line, and she pulled out of the suicidal formation. The *Hatsuyuki* was second in line. She was hit by three shells. All of them were duds, so the damage they caused was not fatal. Only five men were killed; the worst problem was the destruction of the bridge steering station, which forced the captain to switch to emergency steering. He ordered the *Hatsuyuki* out of line, the line broke, and the Japanese destroyers scattered to head for Vila.

At this point, the American ships lost track of the Japanese and so the engagement ended. Admiral Ainsworth had the impression that he had sunk several ships and damaged others, and that the Japanese were in flight back toward Rabaul. Therefore it did not occur to him to go poking around Vila, where he would have found them. He detailed the destroyers *Nicholas* and *Radford* to rescue survivors of the *Helena* and headed back toward Tulagi. It was just as well that he had not gotten into a new fight with the Japanese. His cruisers were nearly out of ammunition and could not have fired more than ten shots from each gun.

The *Helena*, having taken three torpedoes, began to sink just as a fourth torpedo hit. That one was a dud, but it didn't matter, for the *Helena* was just then going down, her bottom ripped apart and her bow broken off. She went down in 1,800 feet of water.

The Japanese destroyers *Suzukaze* and *Tanikaze*, which had retreated to a safe distance from the American cruisers to reload torpedoes, finished that job and turned to come back into the fight. But by the time they returned to the battle zone, all was quiet on the surface of the sea. The Japanese destroyer captains looked around, saw nothing, and headed back for Buin.

The troop-carrying destroyers stopped at Vila as they were supposed to do, and unloaded 1,600 Japanese troops and ammunition and supplies for the garrisons and for Munda. Only the *Nagatsuki* got into trouble. Cutting across the familiar waters to reach Vila more quickly, she ran into something unfamiliar: a reef. She ran hard aground on the reef. The *Satsuki* tried to tow her off, but it was no go. The *Nagatsuki* sat, stuck fast on her reef.

The *Amagiri* stopped long enough to pick up survivors of the sunk *Niizuki*, and then caught sight of the *Nicholas* and *Radford*, which were rescuing *Helena* survivors. The Americans were already watching Admiral Akiyama's ships on their radar and plotting attack figures.

The Japanese *Amagiri* fired torpedoes. So did the American *Nicholas*. None of them struck home. The American destroyers, aided by their radar, began firing their guns and one shell exploded in the radio room of the *Amagiri* and did other serious damage. The Japanese skipper decided he was at too much of a disadvantage, and sped off toward home, leaving some three hundred survivors of the *Niizuki* to make shore alone or drown. Among those lost was Admiral Akiyama.

The *Amagiri* made smoke as she left the scene and the Americans decided she was mortally wounded. Two of the Japanese troop-carrying destroyers chose to go out Blackett Strait and moved around the far side of Kolombangara to get home safely. But the *Mochizuki*'s captain, assuming that the action was over and the Americans had retired south, decided to hug the coast of Kolombangara on the Kula Gulf side and was picked up by the radar of the *Nicholas* and *Radford* as they were continuing the rescue of the *Helena* crewmen. For the second time they left the scene and sought battle with the Japanese. Both sides fired, but no damage was done. The Japanese ship retired in a cloud of smoke, which convinced the Americans that she was hard hit. As the morning grew bright, the captains of the *Nicholas* and *Radford* began to worry about a Japanese air attack and left the scene of the *Helena* sinking for Guadalcanal and safety. Four boats stayed behind to continue rescue.

The Japanese planes came, and so did the American planes. When they got to the scene of the battle, all they saw were the whaleboats moving around in the oily waters above the *Helena*, and the *Nagatsuki* hard aground on her reef off the Kolombangara coast. The Japanese were heavily outnumbered—39 American planes to their seven Zeros—but they tried to protect the *Nagatsuki*. They fought hard. The odds were great but in a way they succeeded, because while the Americans claimed to have shot down four of the Zeros, they did not manage to destroy the *Nagatsuki*.

That accomplishment was left to a flight of B-25 medium bombers which arrived in the afternoon when no Japanese air cover was present. The B-25s bombed very effectively, setting the ship afire in several places. That evening her magazines went up and the *Nagatsuki* was a wreck. The remains of the crew, who had stood off the morning attack with their antiaircraft weapons, left the ship and went ashore to join their fellows on the overland trip through the jungle of Kolombangara to Vila.

So the battle the Americans called the Battle of Kula Gulf came to an end. The Americans claimed a victory, misreading great plumes of smoke for ships that were burning. The Japanese said only that the results of the battle were indeterminate.

The battle was reminiscent of another, the Battle of Tassafaronga. In the last days of the Japanese tenure on Guadalcanal, Rear Admiral Raizo Tanaka was roasted by Admiral Yamamoto after scoring a brilliant victory at the Battle of Tassafaronga, sinking an American cruiser and damaging three others without losing a destroyer. Yamamoto was furious then because Tanaka failed to carry out his assigned mission, which was to resupply the troops ashore.

In Admiral Akiyama's case, while his forces had lost an admiral and two destroyers, and suffered damage to others, they had sunk an American cruiser, carried out the mission faultlessly, and landed 1,600 reinforcements. So by the hard standards of the Japanese high command, the late Admiral Akiyama had to be given credit for victory at Kula Gulf.

10

JUNGLE WAR

THE Japanese naval and army commands at Rabaul had been taken completely by surprise by the Rendova landings. The main reason for the surprise was the speed with which the Americans were able to act; the Japanese simply had underestimated the enemy and for a time longer continued to do so.

The failure was largely that of the army; the Japanese navy had been taught by Admiral Yamamoto to respect American productivity, and the Battle of Midway had erased any doubts in the minds of his adherents. They were still the men in control of the Combined Fleet. But just now, in the early period of the "cooperative" operations by army and navy in the South Pacific, they were not prepared for the sort of land action that the Americans were ready to undertake. Nor would it have made any difference, because the army did not take advice from the navy.

The size of the Japanese garrison on Rendova—just about three hundred men in total—was an indication of the degree of the surprise. From some of the captured diaries of Japanese soldiers and sailors came glimpses of the views of the men in the field. They wondered privately why they were not reinforced.

The main reason was that army and navy could not decide what was to be done by whom. The army's position had always been that the navy was responsible for defense of these little islands where large-scale military tactics were of no use at all. Despite the new orders from Imperial General Headquarters, the old ways died hard. And so, as of the end of June, the Japanese still had done virtually nothing to reinforce the Central Solomons although they had plenty of warning from the airmen, who came back day after day to report new installations going up in the Russells and on Guadalcanal.

Thus, the landings on New Georgia caught the Japanese with but a single regiment to protect the entire island, and of course General Sasaki chose to concentrate most of this force at the northern end of the island, in the Munda airfield perimeter, because as everyone knew, this was the vital point of the island and the key to defense of the Central Solomons.

With the landings at Rendova, General Sasaki warned Rabaul that the enemy would move swiftly against New Georgia and asked for reinforcements. They had been coming, but more slowly than he would like, and because of the nature of the ports on Kolombangara and New Georgia, most of the troops were brought first to the Vila base on Kolombangara. That island possessed three piers capable of handling seagoing vessels. Vila's was by far the best, and the only one capable of taking a destroyer.

New Georgia had two piers, only one of them truly useful for supply, and that at Bairoko Bay. Thus Colonel Liversedge's mission to capture that area was extremely important to the success of the Allied cause.

Colonel Liversedge's jungle fighters—marine and army—were called the Northern Landing Group to differentiate them from General Hester's troops who had crossed to New Georgia via the narrow strait from Rendova and were making their way laboriously across country. The Northern Landing Group had bivouacked on the bank of the Giza Giza River on the night of July 5, and early the next morning they crossed the river and began moving toward the Tamoko River, their next natural obstacle.

Both crossings were difficult because the constant rain of the past two weeks had made torrents of streams that in other times of the year were down to the creek level. The land was mostly swamp, and where there was hard ground it was no longer hard but sticky mud.

The 3rd Battalion of the 148th Infantry was diverted to move toward the Munda–Bairoko Trail and there to set up a trail block. That barrier should keep the Japanese from bringing any reinforcements or supplies overland to the airfield at Munda from Vila.

The main body then continued along the trail to Enogai Inlet. At this inlet, Colonel Liversedge expected to meet the Japanese. Already a bombing raid on the Japanese garrison at the inlet had been staged from Guadalcanal to support the overland operation.

Just about eight miles away as the crow flies—but eight miles of rugged mountain territory covered with thick jungle—General Hester's troops were not doing very well. They had the advantage of the heavy artillery back on Rendova, but in the jungle this was not as much help as it might have been elsewhere.

The Japanese defenders, well-trained troops of the 229th Regiment, had dug in along the Sho River, not far from Zanana.

The Japanese watched the movement of the Americans for several days, beginning on July 2, and estimated that they had brought 11,000 troops to the island. But the Americans did not launch the attack that was expected. Instead they, too, dug in along the Sho River, closer to the mouth. The Japanese plan called for attack on July 7.

At that point the American 172nd Regiment Combat Team was on the left and the 169th Infantry Regiment was on the right. As the Americans moved toward the Bairoko River, the Japanese gave ground slowly. They made excellent use of the jungle and seemed to have snipers everywhere.

Actually this whole defense against General Hester's large force was carried out by the 11th Battalion of the 229th Infantry Regiment—less than a thousand men. In the evenings, they infiltrated the American lines and carried out what they called *shinto joran kodo*—literally, infiltration commotion action. According to the official Japanese war history, the operations here were extremely successful, far more than they had been against the marines on Guadalcanal. The Japanese troops crawled through the jungle like crabs, making rustling noises in the jungle. They made animal noises, and gave birdcalls, to unnerve the Americans. They attacked foxholes screaming like idiots, and once inside the American perimeter they rushed about stabbing and strangling the soldiers in their foxholes until cut down. They used many flares to signal each other, not only for informational purposes but for the psychological effect they had on the enemy. By July 8, they felt that they had succeeded and that the Americans were extremely edgy and their morale damaged badly enough to affect their fighting capability.

How right they were: the Americans got virtually no sleep for three nights in a row, they fired at everything that moved in the darkness, and they killed and wounded some of their own men.

The Japanese record, from the after-action reports of the 229th Infantry Regiment, was extremely laconic, but also revealing—as shown by the following sample.

July 6. Enemy contact maintained.

July 7. At about 8:30 A.M. the enemy commenced an advance, having been reinforced. The [Japanese] Battalion held the trail on the right bank against the enemy. We held our own.

July 8. The enemy brought in still more troops. Mountain artillery fire fell close by our No. 1 trail. A fierce fight developed.

General Hester's advance was badly bogged down. In four days his 169th Regiment had moved only a mile and a half inland along the trail to Munda. He did not seem to be able to make up his mind about what to do with the 172nd RCT, so it was stalled at Zanana. Finally the general tried to move the men of the 172nd along the coast to Laiana. The Japanese soon had them pinned down, too.

Japanese jungle tactics had little effect on Colonel Liversedge's northern assault force, largely because the Raiders had been trained to fight under just such circumstances. On July 7, the main force moved toward Maranusa I and got there without meeting any resistance. Twenty minutes later, however, the advance unit, moving out toward Triri, ran into a Japanese patrol, and killed two of the enemy. These were identified as naval troops (Japanese marines), members of the Kure Fifth Special Landing Force. These were the troops who served the Bairoko port and they were fighting along with the Japanese army but under entirely separate command and orders. Although Tokyo, Truk, and Rabaul had all ordered "cooperation," it just did not get down to the regimental level.

All was quiet for a time, but at one o'clock in the afternoon firing began again, and it was apparent that the Japanese were launching an attack. When it ended, ten Japanese were dead, including one officer, and the marines had one prisoner, badly wounded. In that action the Americans lost three men killed, and four men were wounded.

The most valuable adjunct to the action was the discovery that the officer had a map of the Japanese defense positions at Enogai and Bairoko.

During the daylight hours, the Guadalcanal air force was giving the troops all the support it could, but most of the bombers and fighters went to General Hester's area, where the Americans were in trouble.

General Sasaki had every right to be pleased with the way his small force in the Zanana area was holding the Americans. He was, in fact, impatient to be in action on a much larger scale. To his knowledge, day after day the enemy was bringing troops and armaments to Rendova, which meant the enemy strength was being multiplied several times.

Sasaki was expecting new orders from Rabaul, but he did not get them. From Rabaul he did not even get any information as to a plan to drive the Americans out of the Central Solomons, although that was the reason for which General Sasaki was brought down to New Georgia in the first place.

At the moment, the Americans were not giving him a great deal of trouble. General Hester's force had proved so inept as not to require anything like his maximum effort, but he could not expect that situation to continue indefinitely. He had to expect another landing closer to Munda, and an all-out attack on Munda if he did nothing to stop it. At the moment he did not have the resources to launch a counterattack. That night of July 7 he considered the problem and asked Rabaul for orders.

While General Sasaki waited for an answer, the minor actions continued. They were little more than skirmishes by his standards.

On July 8, the Japanese sent a company against the Americans at Triri, and that morning the marines and army troops fought two sharp actions. At eleven o'clock the Japanese withdrew toward Bairoko and the 1st Raider Battalion continued to move toward Enogai along the west shore of the Enogai Inlet. Triri became the base of operations. The 145th Infantry's detachment established headquarters here and Major Girardeau of the Medical Corps set up his aid station here, too.

By midafternoon on July 8 it became apparent that Colonel Liversedge had made a bad guess about the terrain along the Enogai Inlet.

The Japanese had no intention of letting the Americans set up shop at Triri. At four o'clock in the afternoon they attacked again, and this time the fighting was harder than ever. Only when a company of the 1st Raiders came up and hit the Japanese on the left flank was the issue resolved. They were the advance unit of the force that had gone toward Enogai. The 1st Raiders came back, announcing that they had reached absolutely impassable territory. It was all deep swamp. They started out again, but this time moving uphill along drier ground to the west. The Japanese then moved back toward Bairoko, leaving many dead in the field.

If General Sasaki needed a nudge, the results of the day's fighting gave it.

The American pressure was increasing and the hour of decision was coming near. Something had to be done. That afternoon Sasaki composed a message for Eighth Area Army Headquarters at Rabaul giving a digest of the current military situation and an explanation of his views. At 2:57 it was sent off, with an informational copy to the Japanese Eighth Fleet.

General Sasaki warned Rabaul that every day the enemy's superiority in troops and equipment became greater than his own. In fact, the longer Rabaul delayed, the more his own battle force would be dissipated (even if he won every engagement).

Further, the enemy pressure was compressing the perimeter toward Munda, Bairoko, and threatened to force him to evacuate to Kolombangara. To continue to delay, he warned Rabaul, could be nothing but suicidal.

What he requested was an early decision authorizing him to undertake a counterattack, first to destroy the Northern Landing Group, and thus to frustrate the enemy's planned attack on Munda. He needed reinforcement by way of Kolombangara and Bairoko. He would then attack the Americans on their flank and force a major battle.

If the reinforcements were forthcoming, he would undertake this action on the morning of July 9, and he expected a decision (in his favor) before nightfall.

This setback ought to slow the Allies up considerably and give a chance for a more ambitious attack to be put in motion. It would be very helpful, said General Sasaki, if, in addition to reinforcements, he could have a massive air strike to cover his operations.

Having sent that message, General Sasaki waited for results.

A few hours later came the answers:

From Eighth Fleet Headquarters: "Most reasonable sentiment. Agreed."

From Eighth Area Army Headquarters: "The very best possible plan. Highest confidence and expectations in the attack."

Inherent in these replies were agreements to supply the support General Sasaki had requested.

At that moment General Sasaki was looking to troops of the 13th Regiment, stationed on Kolombangara. There were two plans to get them across to New Georgia; one, to bring them over via Bairoko and then overland to Munda, and two, to move them directly by barge and small boat to Munda.

Moving them down south and bringing them overland from the Sho River area had one advantage: it was safer. Munda was constantly watched by the enemy, and moving them over the short route from Kolombangara to Bairoko meant the danger of running afoul of the troops landed by the Americans at Rice Anchorage.

But the plan for moving the troops south—despite the fact that General Sasaki had no great fear of what General Hester might offer— presented a huge problem: the Japanese had never used the coastal road, and they simply did not know the terrain.

Thus, although turning over plans in his mind, General Sasaki finally opted to move the troops via Bairoko, following familiar routine. But those troops must move quickly if they were to catch the enemy off guard.

On the evening of July 8, then, Colonel Tomonari, the commander of the 13th Regiment on Kolombangara was informed that he was to begin sending troops across to Bairoko by barge. That night the troops moved, and by dawn one battalion had gone across and two battalions were ready to move to Bairoko. But they would not be moved until nightfall protected the small boats from the prying eyes of the Americans.

That night of July 8 Colonel Liversedge had good news: Lieutenant Colonel Delbert Schultz of the Army 148th Infantry had put his troops in position in the roadblock to keep troops from coming in from Kolombangara.

That was about the only good news of the day. Liversedge's force had made no progress toward Enogai because of the misreading of the terrain (no decent maps) and the Japanese harassing attacks. In the first three days Liversedge had advanced seven miles. In the past twenty-four hours he had not gotten anywhere. He had run out of supplies. The only food the men found in the Japanese camp at Triri was some maggoty rice. Doctor Girardeau was trying to treat the wounds of more than twenty men without adequate medicine.

The need for food helped push the Raiders out the next morning toward Enogai. They marched on empty stomachs. The Japanese officer's map that had fallen into their hands proved its value; they were able to bypass several Japanese defense points on the way to Enogai until they came to Leland Lagoon. At eleven o'clock they made their first contact with the Japanese.

From that point on the contact was constant. They fought all day long sporadically, trying to reach the Japanese supply dump at Enogai. They did not make it that day. They dug their foxholes and went to sleep hungry for the second night.

The 3rd Battalion of the Japanese Army 13th Infantry Regiment reached Bairoko during the early hours of July 9. The troops moved out the next morning, heading down toward Munda, and Colonel Liversedge's trail block.

Major Seishu Kikuda, the battalion commander, had a rude map, a woodblock print on rice paper, which gave him the information he needed.

As far as the major knew, the plan was for the 13th Infantry to assemble in the plantation area about five miles from Munda, and from this point, on July 11, to stage a major attack on General Hester's troops.

Those American troops in Southern New Georgia were confused and so badly beleaguered by July 8 that Admiral Turner ordered up a dawn bombardment from the guns that lined the shores of Onaivisi Island, just three miles away. At the same time he sent a sixty-plane bombing raid against Munda, as well as four destroyers to bombard the airfield area.

In an hour the 155 mm howitzers on Onaivisi poured 5,800 rounds into the jungle where the Japanese were supposed to be. The destroyers used 2,300 five-inch shells against the airfields, and the bombers dropped seventy tons of bombs. The result, reported to Rabaul by General Sasaki, was nine men killed and ten men wounded.

Back at Triri, Colonel Liversedge was not happy. The campaign was not going well, and he needed some help that he could not ask for. His only operative radio had been crushed by a falling tree.

At Guadalcanal on the night of July 9, Admiral Turner's staff figured out that there was something wrong when the hours went by and they had no word from Liversedge. They knew Liversedge must be short of supplies. They moved to help, and on the morning of July 10 came a welcome air drop. It consisted of K rations, chocolate, and ammunition.

As soon as the bundles were picked up and opened, Liversedge rushed a detachment up toward Enogai to supply his forward troops.

That morning those hungry marines had tightened their belts and started the attack again at seven o'clock. They fought like hungry tigers, and by three o'clock in the afternoon the Japanese were driven from Enogai and the rice warehouse belonged to the marines. At last they could eat.

But not rice. Just then, Captain Morrow of the 145th Infantry came hurrying up with a detachment loaded down with rations and ammunition.

The Raiders passed out the latter and dug into the former. They had been without food or water for thirty hours.

Raider Captain Clay Boyd then led his D Company in a push through to Enogai Point, and as darkness came, the Raiders set up a defense perimeter. Two small pockets of Japanese were contained within the general perimeter. They would be dealt with the next morning. But already they had possession of the position and the Japanese heavy artillery batteries.

Major Kikuda's battalion of the 13th Regiment marched all morning on July 10, heading from Bairoko down toward Munda along the narrow twisting trail. The major was a careful officer, the main body was preceded by a point group, and on each side flankers made sure that they would not be ambushed by the enemy. At three o'clock in the afternoon, however, they hit the roadblock.

In China, these Japanese troops had learned the psychological value of noise. They began whooping and shouting—banzais, threats, and obscenities—at the Americans. The Japanese harried the tired and bewildered army troops all afternoon. But they could not remain forever in a static position. Colonel Tomonari was behind them, with the other battalions of the 13th Regiment, and they had to clear the way. That meant driving through the American line. All went well until they encountered a small stream that was not on the map, and there they had trouble. But they had to break through, and after heavy fighting they did, with a hundred casualties. They were then led down toward Munda by a patrol under Lieutenant Furakawa who had been sent out by General Sasaki's command and had fought his way through the enemy lines.

The 3rd Battalion continued south, in contact with the enemy much of the time, punishing the enemy and moving them out of the way so that Colonel Tomonari's troops would not be hit by them.

They arrived in the plantation area at about 5:30 on the afternoon of July 12 and set up camp. They were met there by a staff officer from General Sasaki's command, and he gave them their orders. The Japanese bedded down in the recently fortified area of the Lambeti Plantation. Others had arrived earlier, and others would be coming in constantly for the next week or two.

It appeared that they were going into battle almost immediately. But the men were tired from their long trip and half day's battle. They needed a break before going up into the line to join the troops of the 229th Regiment outside Zanana.

On the afternoon of July 12, a young lieutenant from the Imperial Army 229th Regiment showed up at the camp with tears in his eyes, bearing a plea from Colonel Genjiro Hirada for reinforcement of several positions, particularly those where the Liversedge column was operating. He had a sad story to tell of Japanese troops being overwhelmed by the enemy. He asked for help to go with him right away.

Several young officers encouraged the lieutenant. They grew very excited and talked of "annihilating" the Americans. They came up to the command post and said they were ready to move out to start the attack immediately.

But the camp commander intervened.

The troops were exhausted, he announced. Much as he would like to help, he could not send these men into battle this day. They had been marching for two and three days, they had suffered through nerve-wracking crossings from Kolombangara, and they had fought their way down to the plantation from Bairoko. They would soon enough be "annihilating" the enemy in the major attack in the south. They must have at least a little rest.

The young lieutenant from the 229th Regiment was so distraught that he undertook to argue with his superiors. Usually such action would mean immediate discipline, even to the point of death. But in this case the senior officers were sympathetic. The young lieutenant had obviously been through much. His uniform was stained and torn, and he had none of his equipment except his pistol and his samurai sword.

But on the matter of rushing off to save a detachment of the 229th, the senior officers were adamant.

The men could not go. Not yet.

The lieutenant took one last despairing look around, and then he slipped away through the coco palms of the plantation into the gloom of the jungle.

When General Sasaki learned of the plight of the 229th command post, he ordered the 1st Battalion of the 13th Regiment to relieve Colonel Hirada and then return to the plantation to participate in the general attack.

The 1st Battalion of the 13th stepped out, but what happened next is not known. The records of the 229th Regiment were destroyed with the Munda base there on New Georgia. It is not even known where the fighting was occurring at that moment—but it must have been in Colonel Liversedge's area, for on that day he claimed to have killed many Japanese, and General Hester's forces were making no such progress.

Early on the morning of July 11, Colonel Liversedge's troops at Enogai began to advance again. By eight o'clock that morning they had wiped out the small Japanese pockets. Then they set about tidying up the Enogai camp as an American installation.

At that point, Colonel Liversedge added up the results of his campaign so far. His marines and soldiers had killed 350 Japanese. They had lost forty-seven men killed, eighty wounded, and four missing. They had captured four big 140 mm field guns, three antiaircraft guns and eighteen machine guns, rifles, grenade launchers, two diesel tractors, and a searchlight.

At Rabaul, Admiral Kusaka had the word of the loss of his Enogai base within a matter of minutes after the last troops moved out. The Eleventh Air Fleet sent an air mission against Enogai almost immediately on its capture. At ten o'clock that morning Enogai was bombed, and again at 11:30 the Japanese came over. They did a little damage, knocked out some equipment, and killed three marines and wounded fifteen.

Liversedge had been worrying about his wounded, whose condition was not improving any in the field, and so it was a great relief when three PBY seaplanes landed at three o'clock in the afternoon to take the wounded back to Guadalcanal. But the PBYs had scarcely landed than they were bombed and strafed by two Japanese float planes from the

Shortlands base. Fortunately the small arms fire from the shore drove the Japanese planes off without any damage, and the PBYs took off late that afternoon with all the wounded.

That night, at nine o'clock, seven Higgins boats filled with supplies came up from Rice Anchorage. Enogai, then, was secure and supplied. Now Colonel Liversedge could turn all his thoughts to moving on against Munda.

Back in the Zanana area, General Hester was still bogged down. Japanese snipers were holding up his advance with remarkable skill. In order to shorten the supply route, General Hester decided to send the 172nd RCT to take Laiana, on the southeastern tip of the Munda peninsula, very close to the defense perimeter of the Munda airfield garrison.

General Sasaki moved his units around, and soon had the Zanana–Laiana Trail cut off as completely as was the Munda Trail. In desperation, General Hester asked for naval artillery support, and Admiral Turner sent him a task force to bombard the enemy. But General Hester was not used to working with naval gunfire support, and he was afraid that the bombardment would hit among his own troops. Thus his designated targets were so far from his own lines that the naval bombardment force sent up under Admiral Merrill could do him little good. The Japanese simply moved forward close to the American lines, and the shells passed over their heads.

Merrill brought four cruisers and ten destroyers, and they made a magnificent racket for forty minutes. They fired 8,600 five- and six-inch shells, which was enough to stun a regiment. They then turned and went away. The result was a lot of chopped up jungle but no Japanese casualties.

The most serious effect of the bombardment on the Japanese was to keep them up late. But the same had to be said for the Americans of the 172nd RCT.

On the morning of July 12, General Hester's men got moving again on the trail to Laiana, but the Japanese harried them all day long. Then before dark the enemy also cut the trail behind the Americans, taking them out of contact with the 169th Infantry altogether. The move left the 172nd deep in the jungle without food or water and with a quarter of a mile of muddy swamp between them and their objective, Laiana Beach.

On July 12, Colonel Liversedge moved his forward headquarters to block the trail that led from Bairoko, the landing point of Japanese troops ferried over to New Georgia from Kolombangara. He had now accomplished his primary missions. Unfortunately he was unaware of the two lesser trails that led from Bairoko Harbor to join up with the

Munda–Bairoko Trail below his block. But there was nothing more he could do at the moment. Enemy patrols were active around Enogai that day, probing for weakness. One patrol was driven off and two Japanese were killed.

The next assault had to be on Munda, and Colonel Liversedge did not have the force to undertake such a mission. He had to wait for reinforcements. General Hester's force was to be just that, but those troops had not arrived and it did not look as though they would in the near future.

Meanwhile the Japanese were doing very well with their limited resources. They had managed to continue to resupply their troops, using the trails unknown to the Americans. They began building up defenses on the eastern shore of Bairoko Harbor, in preparation for the big assault.

On July 13, Colonel Tomonari joined up at the plantation camp. More of his troops had been brought across Kolombangara Island after they had been landed on the wrong side during the big naval battle of Kula Gulf. The troops had ferried across the strait to Bairoko and followed the path carved out by the advance troops.

General Sasaki was getting ready to move.

11

THE BATTLE OF KOLOMBANGARA

FINALLY, the Japanese command back at Rabaul was taking the problem of New Georgia seriously. Early on the morning of July 12, a large force set sail from Rabaul for Kolombangara. It was led by Rear Admiral Shunji Izaki in the cruiser *Jintsu* with some destroyers of Destroyer Squadron Two (*Yukikaze, Hamakaze, Yugure,* and *Kiyonami.*) They were escorting the destroyer transports *Matsukaze, Satsuki, Minazuki,* and *Yunagi,* which were carrying the 1,300 troops of the 13th Regiment destined for the New Georgia battle.

The Allies' coast watchers saw the Japanese ships moving and sent the word posthaste to Admiral Halsey, who ordered Admiral Ainsworth to go up the Slot that night and intercept the enemy force. For this mission Halsey gave Ainsworth additional destroyers, so that he left Guadalcanal with ten, plus the cruisers *Honolulu, Leander* (of the Royal New Zealand Navy), and *St. Louis.*

The Americans moved toward Kolombangara with the confidence of radar-equipped fighters. The Japanese moved south with the confidence of experienced night fighters. The Americans had the advantage of night fighters of another sort—in the air. Just after midnight one of the Black Cats announced the approach from the north of a cruiser and five destroyers about twenty-five miles away. This was Admiral Izaki's escort force. The Americans intended to attack by radar, fully expecting to be able to do so before the Japanese discovered them.

However, the Japanese had already discovered the Americans as Admiral Ainsworth's ships swung into a single battle column, with five destroyers ahead and five destroyers behind the three cruisers. No, the Japanese did not have high-quality radar, but they did have electronic equipment to detect radar and to plot its emanations. Thus Admiral Izaki knew the position and movements of the Americans for two hours before they arrived.

At one o'clock on the morning of July 13, the American radar picked up the Japanese flotilla—one big blip and five little ones. Admiral Ainsworth ordered the ships to speed up while turning to the right, to put the Japanese ships on the starboard beam: thus all the American warships would have a crack at the enemy.

One of the problems of the Kula Gulf engagement had been the failure of the destroyers to use their torpedoes. That would not be the case this time; just before 1:10, Admiral Ainsworth ordered the destroyers to start firing torpedoes at the blips on the radar.

At the moment that the American ships became visible in the moonlight, at about eight minutes past one in the morning, Admiral Izaki ordered the destroyers to begin firing torpedoes. They did, and the "long lances" were on their way toward the American column. Secure in his radar, Admiral Ainsworth came on for another few moments, then unleashed the six-inch guns of the cruisers. As usual, all three American cruisers began firing on the biggest blip on the radar screens, the light cruiser *Jintsu*. In less than ten minutes they fired 2,600 shells at her. Perhaps twenty of them struck home, and they did the job. The *Jintsu* lost her steering, and then her firerooms were hit and flooded and she went dead in the water. At about this point she was struck by two of the American torpedoes, and she broke in half. The two halves of the ship drifted apart, both burning. She had been able only to fire a few salvoes at the Allied ships before she sank, taking down the Admiral and nearly all the crew of 480 men.

One of those salvoes had been aimed at the New Zealand cruiser *Leander*, and one shell at least hit her, knocking out her radio aerial. That was not very serious damage to accept for the sinking of an enemy cruiser. But Admiral Ainsworth had underestimated his enemy. Those early torpedoes came on. The admiral belatedly ordered a turn to the south. In making the turn the *Leander* caught a torpedo, which put her out of the battle. Admiral Ainsworth detached the destroyers *Radford* and *Jenkins* to stand by the *Leander* and protect her from further attack.

At this point the Japanese cruiser *Jintsu* was sinking. Four of the support force destroyers turned immediately after firing their torpedoes and retreated for a reload. The *Mikazuki* stood by the stricken flagship for a few minutes, then saw her danger and the impossibility of being much help to those two flaming pyres that had so recently been joined in one ship. She, too, turned and scudded north to reload.

Above the battle, the pilot of a Black Cat night fighter watched and reported to Admiral Ainsworth that the Japanese were retreating north at high speed. If that was not quite the case, still Admiral Ainsworth had to believe what the pilot saw. He also believed the reports from his ships, which claimed to have hit six separate vessels and left them all burning. As the night wore on he began to revise these figures downward, but he was still of the opinion that the battle was over and all that remained to be done was to mop up.

The destroyers *Nicholas*, *O'Bannon*, and *Taylor* were sent off northward, told to chase the enemy as far as the Shortlands if necessary and sink them if they could. But they did not get the whole message, and although they moved out, they soon turned and headed back down the Slot, in the belief that Admiral Ainsworth had retired for the night. They were out of the battle.

The enemy, in fact, was not retreating toward the Shortlands; rather Captain Yoshima Shimai had led the ships into a squall not far to the north, where they slowed and completed their torpedo reload in just a little over fifteen minutes. Then they turned and came down at high speed to seek out the Americans again. Meanwhile, the four troop-carrying destroyers had moved in close to the Kolombangara coast, turned around the island, and were now discharging the 1,300 troops of the 13th Regiment at Sandfly Harbor on the far coast. Although Admiral Izaki had gone down with his ship, his mission was already a success. Now Captain Shimai set out to make it more so.

There were no blips on the American radar, but Admiral Ainsworth had those reports of burning enemy ships, and he turned north again to find them. Just before two o'clock in the morning the radar of the flagship *Honolulu* picked up blips a little over twelve miles away.

What ships were these? Were they the destroyers he had sent north? Were they the enemy?

There seemed to be only one way to find out. Ainsworth began calling up all his destroyers to discover their whereabouts.

Meanwhile, Captain Shimai was moving his destroyers south at high speed, prepared to attack as soon as he could make out the enemy. Five minutes later, Captain Shimai saw the American force and ordered the torpedo attack. Earlier that night, the American fleet had turned sharply to the right to begin firing. The captain guessed that they would do so again, and ordered the torpedoes sent a little off to the right of the oncoming line of vessels. The Japanese destroyers fired their torpedoes, swung around, and raced away.

Just at this point, Admiral Ainsworth had completed his roll call and decided that the ships on the radar screen had to be the enemy. He ordered the cruisers to open fire and once again to make a sharp right turn to be sure they all had good firing position.

The sharp right turn took the American force squarely across the tracks of the Japanese torpedoes. A lookout aboard the *Honolulu* saw the first one pass by and shouted out the word. But by that time another torpedo had smashed into the *St. Louis,* and the *Honolulu* took the third in the bow, then a dud in the stern. The stern torpedo made a hole, but the bow torpedo spread the *Honolulu*'s forepart out like a shark's mouth. As the damage control parties ran to their work, the bridge of the *Honolulu* was exposed to a dreadful sight; another torpedo smashed into the destroyer *Gwin,* just ahead of the *Honolulu.* With a roar and a blinding flash, the *Gwin* blew up in the middle. The crew tried to save her, but there was no saving this night. As dawn began to appear, the destroyer *Ralph Talbot* stood by to take off survivors (all but two officers and fifty-nine men), and in the bright morning light she was scuttled.

Admiral Ainsworth retired to the base at Tulagi. He had sent ahead the word that he had scored an enormous victory, which had been true before he went back into the fight to go after the Japanese destroyers. By the time he got to Tulagi he was thoroughly depressed by the extent of his losses and damages, but at the base the cruiser men were greeted as conquerors by a brass band and all sorts of congratulations. Ainsworth's self-esteem was also raised when the Americans rescued one of the handful of survivors of the *Jintsu,* and he swore up and down that the Americans had sunk most of the Izaki force.

It was not true, of course, but in a way the Americans had scored a victory even in defeat. They could afford to have three cruisers damaged, one so badly that it was out of the rest of the war. They could even afford to lose a destroyer. The American production machine at home could absorb this easily enough. For every ship sunk, three came along.

There was no brass band to greet Captain Shimai when he returned to Rabaul. There was not even much talk of victory. That was not the Japanese way. But the feeling that a victory had been won ran high, and the Japanese, too, exaggerated the extent of the American losses, claiming all three cruisers sunk plus several—not one—destroyers.

The press at home in Japan trumpeted as usual. Within the Japanese naval establishment, the memory of Admiral Izaki was criticized because he repeated a mistake that (the Japanese believed) had already cost the Japanese the battleship *Hiei*. At the start of the battle, to confuse the enemy he had turned on his searchlight. But instead of confusing the Americans, the searchlight (said his detractors) had given them an aiming point.

That claim was not really true. The Americans were firing by radar and not by visual observation. The Japanese criticism of their commander showed a basic misunderstanding and underestimation of the enemy's capability, just as the continued American carelessness about Japanese torpedoes showed an American failure.

Writing shortly after the war, Samuel Eliot Morison expressed wonder that the American navy had not, by the summer of 1943, come to grips with the nature of the Japanese torpedoes. No one in authority in the South Pacific seemed to understand what the Japanese had, although since the beginning of the Tokyo Express runs down the Slot the Japanese had scored victory after victory by using these torpedoes. Admiral Ainsworth went into the Battle of Kolombangara believing that the destroyer *Strong*, sunk only a few days earlier, had been the victim of a submerged submarine, not of a destroyer torpedo fired from a distance impossible for an American destroyer to duplicate. Some officers had heard rumors about the effectiveness of the Japanese torpedoes, but they were just that, rumors. Commanders did not make policy based on rumors, and there were no official directives nor any high-level understanding of the problem. This was true even though (Morison reported) a "long lance" torpedo came ashore at Cape Esperance on Guadalcanal, was taken apart and examined, and the facts were sent on to Pacific Fleet Intelligence at Pearl Harbor. There the report was apparently bottled up—one of the vital bits of information of the day—and the war went on.

The fact was that the Japanese at Kolombangara had again outfought the Americans and defeated them in terms of damage done.

But it was also a pyrrhic victory. The loss of the cruiser *Jintsu* was a high price to pay for a Japanese Navy that was already feeling the results of the long battle of attrition in the Solomons.

12

MUNDA

FROM the Japanese army point of view, the Battle of Kolombangara had been a complete success. The navy's protective force had done just what it set out to do, drawn the American attack away from the troop landing, and 1,300 badly needed reinforcements were on their way to New Georgia. But once again the Japanese Army made a vital mistake: it brought too little power forward to do the job.

For example, just then Admiral Turner was pressing Admiral Halsey for about 25,000 more troops to throw into the battle. The Japanese were thinking in terms of battalions, the Americans in terms of divisions.

Later in the war the troop shortage would plague the Japanese; just at this time, that difficulty was not paramount. The Japanese could have sent the whole Sixth Division to reinforce General Sasaki, and the idea was suggested at Rabaul by junior staff officers. However, the commanders looked to New Guinea and worried about their two-front war. They made the mistake of ignoring the suggestion that strong manpower at this juncture would do wonders in the defense of New Georgia.

In the air, Japanese and American planes fought nearly every day as the American Solomons air force met the Japanese Eleventh Air Fleet. The Japanese sent flights of bombers and occasional single planes. In the evenings the seaplanes from the Shortlands were out. Kula Gulf was the scene of activity on both sides night after night.

The difference between the war at this stage and that of a few months earlier at Guadalcanal was that Kula Gulf, unlike Ironbottom Sound, was a real no-man's land. Japanese and Americans moved in those waters constantly by night, and there were many "minor encounters" in which men died. Scores of planes were lost on both sides, as the pilots bombed and strafed the waters of the gulf. For example, on July 14, a whole flight of four P-39 Airacobras simply disappeared over southern New Georgia. Whether they fell afoul of a flight of Zeros or ran into bad weather was a matter for intelligence to try to figure out. Those four pilots were just statistics in a war so hot that only the major actions have been chronicled.

At Enogai, Colonel Liversedge was bogged down. He had taken this point, as directed, but he could not move until someone else did. The "victory" of the naval forces at Kolombangara did not seem like much of a victory, since all this while the enemy was continuing to infiltrate more troops while his help still did not come up from the south. For the next three days, from July 13 to July 16, his men went out on patrol. Usually they encountered some of the enemy, and a few shots were exchanged. During the whole period Liversedge lost one man killed and one man wounded. On both sides the sparring was cautious. General Sasaki's troops were busy digging in for the assault against Bairoko that they expected.

They were also preparing a counterattack against General Hester's force between Laiana and Zanana. The Japanese referred to this area as the Sho River, and this is where General Sasaki planned to attack. On July 13, the staff officer from Sasaki's Headquarters handed Colonel Tomonari his orders:

> The 13th Infantry Regiment with all speed will move to the Sho River upper stream area [where the 169th Regiment was bogged down]. You will disembark on the shore in the Suzumoko vicinity [west of Zanana] and make a flank attack on the enemy's main force to destroy the pressure on the shore. After this, immediately, you will move to the upper water of the Sho River in the Fujita Bridge area and relieve the troops of the 229th Regiment there. You will secure the river crossing and then destroy the enemy main force in the upper river region. You will be accompanied by a platoon of engineers to the Sho River crossing and they will be responsible for your crossing. Then you will leave the Sugi artillery reserve corps in com-

mand of the Fujita Bridge, and through the wireless squad as well as the telegraph squad, you will report on these actions to this headquarters.

Following these orders, the 13th Infantry began to move out from the plantation area near Munda. On July 14 one company left at 10:00 A.M. This advance guard would move first to the Sho River upper stream crossing mentioned in the orders. They were to scout the enemy and report on the topography. After that the attack plans would be made final.

Except for wireless communication, from this point on the unit was to be out of touch with General Sasaki's headquarters. There was no way that Sasaki could be in touch with them because the distance was too great, but he was not dismayed. He had every confidence in Colonel Tomonari and the picked troops that made up the 13th Regiment. On July 14 and 15, headquarters had two sets of situation reports. The regiment reached the operational area and made contact with the enemy. Colonel Tomonari reported then that something strange was going on in the Rendova Bay area. A large force was being brought over to the Sho River (Zanana). What this meant Colonel Tomonari was not quite sure, but it seemed to him that the time had come to strike.

That message was sent at 7:29 on the morning of July 14.

General Sasaki agreed. He sent off a message to Rabaul, with a duplicate addressed to Buin just in case the Rabaul message was not picked up. He gave details of his new plan for an offensive.

He announced that the time had come for the offensive to stop the enemy's buildup and destroy the beachhead at Zanana and Laiana. This was the psychological moment to attack, he said. It must be done within the next ten days or the defense of New Georgia was in jeopardy, and for the second time the Japanese would suffer tragedy. (He was obviously referring here to Guadalcanal and the error of sending too little too late that had cost the Japanese that island.)

What General Sasaki wanted was not just permission to attack—he already had that. What he wanted was massive air and naval support plus more troops.

The messages went off but they were never acknowledged. Apparently neither one was picked up. So General Sasaki's new plan of attack was never revealed to Rabaul, and no support was to be forthcoming at the outset.

Meanwhile, General Sasaki was having just about as much trouble with his local communications. After a few days' rest, the men of the 13th Regiment were pronounced ready to face fire again, and they moved out. Major Kikuda's 3rd Battalion set off on July 14 for the

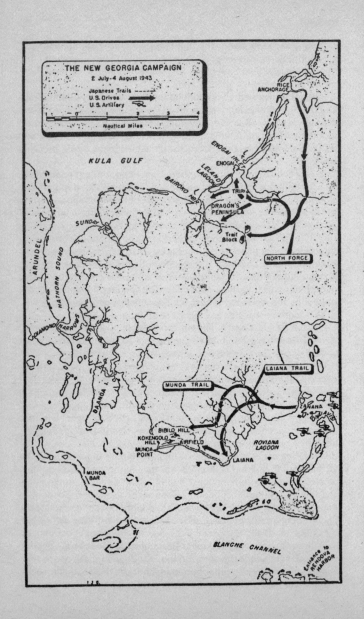

THE NEW GEORGIA CAMPAIGN
2 July-4 August 1943

Japanese Trails ------
U.S. Drives
U.S. Artillery

Nautical Miles

KULA GULF

RICE ANCHORAGE

ENOGAI INLET

ENOGAI

LELAND LAGOON

BAIROKO HBR.

TRIRI

DRAGON'S PENINSULA

SUNDAY

Trail Block

NORTH FORCE

ARUNDEL I.

HATHORN SOUND

DIAMOND NARROWS

BAANGA I.

LAIANA TRAIL

MUNDA TRAIL

ZANANA

BIBILO HILL

KOKENGOLO HILL

AIRFIELD

MUNDA POINT

ROVIANA LAGOON

LAIANA

MUNDA BAR

BLANCHE CHANNEL

Entrance to
HENDOVA
HARBOR

Zanana area. They began crossing the mountains—up one hill, and down the dale—the never-ending slogging along in dense jungle all the way. The major soon found that the map he had was of no use. They navigated by compass, heading east.

Colonel Liversedge's men continued to "organize" the ground in the American northern force's area. Every night they were bombed by Washing Machine Charlie, which meant one or more of the Japanese float planes from the Shortlands. Sometimes there were a few casualties. For the most part the bombs knocked down palm trees.

Colonel Liversedge waited, but the Japanese failed to make a pass at his roadblock along the Bairoko–Munda Trail. He did not realize that the enemy had begun using shortcuts. It was certainly true that the roadblock had been useful in preventing the Japanese from reinforcing the Enogai garrison when Liversedge was attacking it, but it had not cut off supplies to Munda, as he hoped. At the end of this time, the roadblock forces were withdrawn to Triri. For a week planes had been supplying them by air, but most of the supplies went into the jungle and a lot of them were recovered by the Japanese. Since nothing much was happening, it seemed best to bring the men up to safety. On July 15 the wounded were moved to Enogai, whence they could more easily be evacuated to Guadalcanal. The roadblock was abandoned, and Colonel Liversedge waited for his reinforcement.

It never came. Finally Major General Oscar Griswold, the commander of the XIV Corps, announced to General Millard Harmon, Halsey's ground forces commander, that Hester would have to have another division of troops to move forward on New Georgia. The fact was that the assault had been bollixed up more thoroughly than any maneuver in the South Pacific to that date.

General Hester had split his regiments, one taking the upper trail and one staying along the coast. Finally, on July 13, the badly mauled 172nd Infantry did reach Laiana. But then General Sasaki, who knew the terrain, moved a battalion of the Imperial Army's 13th Infantry in between the two American regiments. The 169th was cut off, deep in the jungle, and its supplies were exhausted. The troops were subsisting on air drops, with many of the bundles falling into the hands of the enemy.

When Admiral Halsey had the word that more troops were essential, he sent General Harmon up to New Georgia to find out exactly what was going on. When Harmon arrived, he was dismayed at the state of morale of the two regiments and the confusion of General Hester's command. Virtually on the spot, he relieved General Hester, and he told Griswold that in the absence of any other the corps commander would also have to take over the assault force.

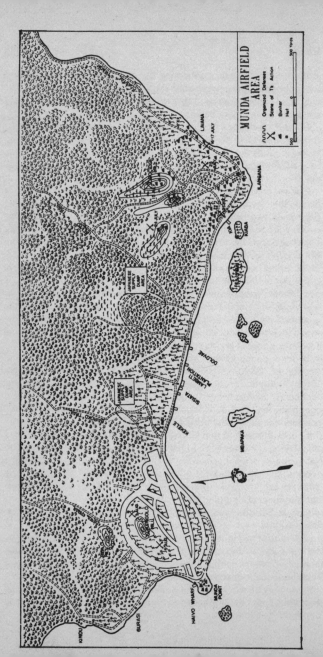

MUNDA AIRFIELD AREA

﹏﹏﹏ Organized Defenses
✕ Scene of ¾ Action
▲ Bunker
● Hut

The problem, as it would be again, was the inadequate training of the army troops assigned to the New Georgia operation.

In the beginning of the South Pacific battle, Admiral Turner had employed the marines. They had been trained for this sort of warfare, particularly the Raider battalions. Indeed, at San Diego the navy maintained an amphibious school, and out of this would come Major General Holland Smith to take over the Central Pacific invasions. The army troops (General MacArthur's command excepted) had been trained for European-type operations. As the navy claimed, its men had been given training on Guadalcanal, but that was minimal, and obviously it was not as well done as it should have been. The officers of the New Georgia assault force were not as expert and confident as they should have been. In their war history of the South Pacific, the Japanese make much of the powerful effect their noise-and-confusion tactics wreaked on the enemy at New Georgia.

When General Griswold took tactical command at New Georgia, he saw that he needed fresh troops from Guadalcanal, and he estimated that it would take ten days to get the offensive going again. He began moving troops into the Zanana area as rapidly as possible, and this activity was the subject of Colonel Tomonari's report of July 14.

That day the 3rd Battalion had its difficulties. Major Kikuda set out from the plantation area with his map, assuming that it would be an easy march. But he found no trail, and although he heard shooting he saw nothing. Soon the battalion was lost. Kikuda tried to get oriented by using a compass, but even that was not very satisfactory; he and his men kept coming back to points they had already passed.

They really did not know where they were until suddenly, quite by accident, through a clearing in the jungle the major caught the sound of surf. And then they saw below them a dense mangrove swamp. The seacoast must be nearby. The battalion made a ninety-degree turn off its old course, and after an hour's walk the troops found themselves on a hill overlooking the seashore. Below them, not a hundred feet away, they could see half-a-dozen American troops. They must be near the American landing area.

They found Colonel Tomonari and reported. As night approached, they assumed their defensive positions so that they would not be surprised on the evening before their attack by a night counterattack from the Americans. At five o'clock that evening, the battalion leaders went to the regimental command post to get their orders from Colonel Tomonari for the next day's action.

It was July 16, two more days after Colonel Tomonari's request to stage the attack, before the permission came and the wheels were put in motion. During that time, although the colonel was moving his force into position, the Americans did not even know he was there.

The 1st Battalion would kick off from its bivouac area. The 3rd Battalion would deploy to the right to cover the flank of the main attack until it was launched, and then join. The time was set for six o'clock, just as the sun was setting.

The fortified positions of the 229th Regiment were all around them. The enemy knew there were Japanese troops up the hill, and as the evening came the artillery began to fire on the hills. At a signal, the men of the 13th Regiment began to move forward, crawling and creeping, with their heads down. It was rough country, covered with century plants whose spikes stung their cheeks as they moved along.

When the 1st Battalion had reached a point about a hundred feet from the American lines, they were discovered, and rifles and automatic weapons began to open up. Still, Colonel Tomonari did not get up.

Now the heavy cloud cover that had moved around the island all day long began to spill rain, heavy showers that drenched friend and foe alike. During one of these downpours, Colonel Tomonari decided the psychological moment had come and gave the order.

Attack!

The first up was a platoon leader of the 2nd Battalion, Cadet Ensei Azachi, and he charged forward until he was shot down. The Japanese lost men, but this attack was a success. The 13th Regiment had driven the Americans back, causing them to leave tanks, machine guns, and scores of 155 mm artillery pieces in their wake. Among other things, the Japanese captured a supply dump, which was more than welcome because they were cut off from their own supplies by the speed with which they had marched and the constant interdicting action of the American air forces. But now they were resupplied with food at least. That night the troops spent clearing out the old enemy battle camp and making it habitable for themselves.

Act one in the drama of the 13th Infantry's mission had been successfully completed.

The weather continued to be stormy, and the 13th Regiment was out of touch with General Sasaki's headquarters for several days. During this period the American artillery and air forces did what General Hester's infantry had been unable to do—they kept the Japanese at bay. The constant bombardment and bombing by American planes was hard on morale. That first major attack had left the elements of the division badly scattered, and it was all Colonel Tomonari could do to bring them together again under the heavy impact of the American fire. But the Japanese held the positions.

On the night of July 17, Colonel Tomonari staged another attack against the American troops on the shore. By this time the 43rd U.S. Army Division had arrived, and its command post was located not far from Zanana. Colonel Tomonari ordered the new attack; it was carried out in the same manner as the first, and before the Americans knew it, the Japanese were inside the perimeter and inside the command post. Colonel Tomonari had advanced to within 400 yards of the sea, the regiment reported back to General Sasaki. It had scored a complete victory.

The historians of the U.S. 43rd Division have challenged this contention, and they say little about the attacks of this period. But the fact is that from the first of July until nearly the end, the American land forces in southern New Georgia were badly in disarray and were neither advancing nor winning any battles. The 13th Regiment attacked again and again—and won ground every time.

Fresh troops from the Army 148th Regiment were brought to face them and open the Munda Trail. Only then could the weary troops of the 169th Regiment be rescued from the upper trail to Munda. They had been cut off for two weeks. The only way they were surviving against the Japanese who attacked from all sides was by clustering together and with the help of air drops and air support.

The most important factor in holding the Japanese down during this period was the heavy American artillery operating from Oniavisi Island across the Roviana Lagoon, just three miles away. Had it not been for these big guns, the entire bridgehead would probably have been destroyed.

The first evidence of General Griswold's contribution to the battle was the appearance of marine light tanks. Six of them came in to push upstream and relieve the 169th Infantry. But it did not take the tankers long to learn that this was not good tank country.

Soon the six operating tanks were in action. They moved along rapidly from the beach at Laiana to the western outposts and up the hill, knocking out several Japanese coconut log bunkers. But then they began encountering the prepared positions of Colonel Hirada's men, which included sunken concrete pillboxes. In a fashion that would become more famous on the islands of the Central Pacific, the Japanese had built a complex system of connecting trenches, and they could move rapidly from one to another. At one place near Bairoko they were reported to have dug a tunnel through the hill, six feet high, three feet wide, and three hundred feet long.

From such formidable defenses, the Japanese soon began knocking out the tanks, one by one. They had no antitank weapons, so they adapted land mines to the purpose. They also used a flame thrower.

Soon they had damaged three tanks, which were forced to withdraw. They were not replaced in this struggle.

To keep the Japanese at bay during this uncomfortable new buildup period, General Griswold called on Guadalcanal for artillery, naval, and air support—and he got it. But how much good it did above the harm is perhaps questionable. The harm was that in the dense jungle the Japanese had no hesitation in coming to close quarters, and the bombs and shells were about as likely to fall among the Americans as among the enemy troops.

Very early on July 18, Colonel Liversedge finally got reinforcement, but it did not come from the army troops down south. Despairing of that situation, Admiral Turner sent Liversedge the 4th Raider Battalion, under Lieutenant Colonel Currin, who had taken Segi Point and then Viru.

The men of the 4th Raider Battalion came up in six destroyer-transports, and these were escorted by five other destroyers. While on the way, just after midnight, the U.S. destroyer force received a report of three unknown destroyers dead in the water, not far off the Kolombangara coast.

Obviously these were Japanese destroyers, unloading more troops. The American destroyers moved in to attack, but the Japanese avoided them and made smoke. The attack fizzled out. The next excitement came just after two o'clock in the morning when a violent explosion buckled plates and shook the destroyer *Lang* from end to end. She had been hit by a bomb that had come out of nowhere; some men even thought at first it was a torpedo.

Washing Machine Charlie was at work again.

The bombing had created enough damage in the engine room to force the *Lang* to slow down. The radar reported many enemy planes and this situation continued for two hours, although the *Lang* was not bombed again. She was able to complete the escort mission and then returned to Tulagi for repairs.

She had been in battle, but the results were muddy. Who and what had been out there, in the air and on the sea, were not known to captain or crew. This is the way it was night after night in Kula Gulf as Americans and Japanese set out simultaneously to reinforce their positions and yet prevent the enemy from doing the same.

At one o'clock on the morning of July 18, after their wild ride, the 4th Raiders arrived at Enogai Inlet.

The reinforcement did not mean as much as it seemed because Currin's unit arrived two hundred men short.

The destroyer-transports that brought the marines in also took all the wounded and sick men out, and when all heads were counted, Colonel Liversedge did not have many more men than he had begun with in the Rice Anchorage landing. Still, Liversedge was itching to get moving, and he called a conference of his battalion commanders (two marine and two army) and that afternoon made plans for an assault on Bairoko, the Japanese port of entry for reinforcements from Kolombangara. Tentatively, he scheduled the attack for July 20.

To soften up Bairoko he asked for, and got, air attack. The Japanese positions were bombed and strafed by aircraft from Guadalcanal on July 19. But for that matter so was Enogai, bombed twice on the evening of the 19th. In the first raid nine men were hit; none was hit in the second raid.

That day, Liversedge embroidered the plan, gave each battalion its instructions, and issued verbal orders that they could mull over while the written orders were prepared. They were to be ready to move out at 7:30 A.M. on July 20.

On July 20, Colonel Liversedge started his offensive against Bairoko. On the right hand, or north, were the troops of the 1st Raider Battalion and the 4th Raider Battalion. On the left was the 3rd Battalion of the Army 148th Infantry. The 3rd Battalion of the Army 145th Infantry was left back at Enogai in reserve.

Liversedge's drive ran up against the Japanese at about 10:15 A.M. He

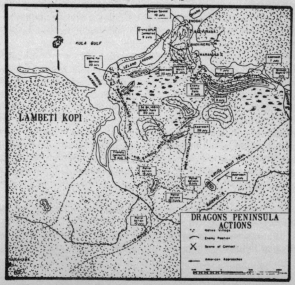

DRAGONS PENINSULA
ACTIONS

found that the enemy had made good use of the time when the Americans had been held up waiting for reinforcement. The Japanese had built emplacements of coral and logs and had dug in behind them. The positions were constructed with an eye to cross fire, and snipers had taken to the coconut palms above, where they sat, quietly, their camouflaged uniforms enhanced with bits of palm frond and dirt that broke the human silhouette. As the Americans came up, the Japanese opened up with machine guns and mortars and the snipers began their work.

Colonel Liversedge quickly discovered that he had moved into a hornet's nest. The Japanese defense was four tiers deep, with interconnecting trenches. The Americans approached with enormous firepower, and the din of automatic weapons was deafening. One observer who had been at Bloody Ridge on Guadalcanal swore that the volume of fire at Bairoko was more intensive.

Liversedge's troops discovered the extent of the Japanese defenses when they breached the first line, only to find that the second line was as strong. They broke through the second line at 2:30 that afternoon, after Liversedge had committed his local reserves, the 4th Raiders, and half the demolition platoon. The position looked good, on high ground, within view of Bairoko Harbor. But there were two more lines of defense to be broken. And here Liversedge began to run into real trouble.

At 3:47 Liversedge asked for the last of the reserves. He was ready to make his final push. The Japanese seemed to be on the run, and many were seen without weapons. He figured he could take the point in short order and then control Bairoko Harbor. The move looked a lot easier than it turned out to be.

One reinforced platoon began to move up to the west along the narrow spit north of Leland Lagoon. They moved forward as far as the west end of the lagoon, but there they were stuck, held down by mortar and rifle grenade (knee mortar) fire.

(Actually the knee mortar was not a rifle grenade but a true small caliber mortar designed to be operated by a single infantryman. The long narrow tube handled an ordinary Japanese grenade.)

At 3:30 the Japanese began their countermove, with something the Americans did not expect. It started with a heavy (90 mm) mortar barrage on all units, and especially the command post. The Americans began to take more casualties than Liversedge had expected. He could not reply in kind; he had no heavy mortars.

By five o'clock the last of his reserves had been committed, and he was no further ahead than he had been an hour before. It was remarkable: the Japanese were pinned into a small defensive perimeter, not more than 300 yards from east to west and 600 yards from north to south.

But those 90 mm mortars were fired with speed and accuracy and without apparent regard for expediture of ammunition.

Shortly after 5:00 P.M. the American left flank reported that a Japanese counterattack seemed to be building up. Liversedge continued the firefight until 5:15 and then decided he was getting nowhere. He moved the casualties out, and gave orders to withdraw to the high ground, 500 yards east of the harbor. Half an hour later the withdrawal was under way, with the Americans losing some ammunition but saving all weapons and all their wounded. The walking wounded, eighty of them, began the long, long trek back to Enogai, a mile away. Two companies of the 4th Raiders covered the withdrawal and stayed up on the high ground until 6:00 P.M. when they were ordered back to Enogai. They returned, reporting that just before they left, two barges loaded with Japanese reinforcements entered Bairoko Harbor. They were just the first of the small boats to come in. The Japanese stream of reinforcements had not even been slowed down.

As night fell, Colonel Liversedge had a report from lieutenant colonels MacCaffery and Schultz, who had been sent off that same day with a column to move around to Triri and then down to Bairoko to flank the Japanese and support Liversedge. They had run into a strong Japanese force three miles outside Triri and had been pinned down. Liversedge ordered them to dig in for the night.

He then counted noses. He had lost forty-nine men killed, 206 wounded, and one man missing. The 4th Raiders had taken the worst beating, with 205 casualties. They had reported thirty-three dead Japanese, but that was all they knew about the defenders' casualties. The attack had been anything but a success. There was no way Liversedge could attain his objective without substantial reinforcement.

On July 21, the wounded were evacuated by three PBYs from Guadalcanal. After Liversedge reported on his troubles, a massive air strike was brought in to hit Bairoko. From ten o'clock in the morning until dusk, American fighters came in every hour to strafe and SBD dive-bombers to bomb the Japanese positions there. The Japanese retaliated in kind. At 4:30 that afternoon a strong force of Zeros hit Enogai Inlet and the marine positions, and damaged one PBY. And that night, Washington Machine Charlie was back again.

The battle for Bairoko seemed to have reached a stalemate.

13

IN THE BALANCE

THE American troops in Southern New Georgia were in disarray, and two men knew it very well. One was General Griswold, who was fighting time to bring in the new force that could move up to help Colonel Liversedge take Munda. The other was General Sasaki, whose pleas to Rabaul for an immediate major effort in the air and on the sea were going unanswered.

The U.S. 169th Regiment was dawdling on the Munda Trail, cut off from the beachhead by the Japanese, and virtually encircled. One battalion actually was encircled, and with that the regiment's snaillike pace up the Munda Trail came to a halt. The Japanese ambushed the trail parties that tried to take casualties back to the Zanana beachhead. They whooped and hollered all night long like savages and cut the throats of the soldiers in their foxholes on the perimeter.

Day after day more Japanese troops infiltrated through the PT boat-infested waters of Kula Gulf to Bairoko and then trudged their weary way overland to the plantation encampment north of Munda, where General Sasaki's officers parceled them out to the areas where they were needed most. A growing problem for the Japanese would be the lack of artillery replacement. Their system of resupply did not allow for much movement of heavy equipment, so they continued to be without antitank guns and howitzers for the troops of the line. But they had plenty of light and heavy machine guns, grenades, and heavy mortars at whose use they were expert. And, at least for the moment, in Southern New Georgia, the Japanese had the initiative.

What kept the southern situation from becoming a rout of the Americans was air support. Both sides were throwing as many planes as possible into the air to hit enemy land positions, but the Americans had more planes. In the air, dogfights were not as common as they had been during the old Guadalcanal days, when the American fighters went up to shoot at anything they saw. Now their major mission was to escort the bombers to the target and protect them from the Zeros. The Japanese were doing the same, except that they sent many more fighters, in attempts to lure the P-38s and F4Us into combat.

Their usual ploy was to lurk over Kula Gulf, simulating dogfights among themselves in the hopes that they would thus seduce U.S. fighter pilots into the web. It did not work very often, as the fighter pilots began to obey Admiral Mitscher's stern orders to stick to the business at hand, which was to blast the daylights out of the Japanese troops on New Georgia.

One of the most exasperating efforts of the Japanese was Washing Machine Charlie. The troops half-joked about the tinny sound of the float planes that harried them night after night, dropping a bomb here and there, but killing and wounding enough men to keep the joke from being funny. These night raids cost the troops sleep by night and cut their efficiency by day. The only weapon effective against them was the night fighter, but there were not enough of these to make the patrols up and down Kula Gulf, and the Slot, and intercept the lone bombers. However, the night fighter situation was growing better for the Americans. The navy had its Black Cats—PBYs equipped with radar for night operations—and the army had P-70s, which were A-20 attack bombers, fitted with a radar set in the nose and four 20 mm cannons. These ranged above New Georgia in the night time and shot down some of the Washing Machine Charlies. They were much more effective against the twin-engined Betty bombers the Japanese sent down on some nights.

The American air strikes against Japanese positions and shipping were sometimes effective, sometimes not. On July 17 Admiral Mitscher had word of a large concentration of shipping at Bougainville's Tonolei Harbor, and he sent up a giant air strike reminiscent of the Japanese strikes against Guadalcanal six months earlier.

Up went 220 planes, including four-engined B-24 Liberator bombers, dive-bombers, and torpedo bombers, covered by 114 fighters. This time the situation was reversed: the American fighters protected the bombers while the Japanese Zeros tried to get at them, and then the bombers ducked under the fighting and tried to do their work. Their success was not enormous: they sank the destroyer *Hatsuyuki*, but not much else.

But two nights later the American air forces did claim prey in a big way. The Japanese had sent another of their resupply missions toward Kolombangara that afternoon, and late at night a Black Cat discovered the convoy, which consisted of three heavy cruisers, one light cruiser, and nine destroyers, under Rear Admiral Shoji Nishimura. The convoy was so large because the Japanese had been frustrated in their last attempt to resupply the troops fighting on New Georgia, and they wanted to make sure that this one did not fail.

The three supply and troop-carrying destroyers headed in for Kolombangara's shore and were chased and bombed by the night fighter, but without effect. But half-a-dozen bombers from Henderson Field attacked the cruiser-destroyer force and dropped 2,000-pound bombs from low level. They sank the destroyer *Yugure* with one direct hit and damaged the cruiser *Kumano*. Sure that his supply mission had been successful, Admiral Nishimura headed back home, leaving the destroyer *Kiyonami* to rescue survivors of the sunk destroyer. But the next morning two flights of B-25 bombers skip bombed the *Kiyonami* and left it sinking.

On July 22, the Japanese sent a routine reinforcement mission to the Shortlands. It included three destroyers laden with troops and supplies, and the seaplane-carrier *Nisshin*, which was carrying an artillery battalion and its equipment. American bombers caught the convoy in broad daylight in Bougainville Strait and sank the *Nisshin* with all that heavy equipment. The three destroyers made it safely to Buin and the troops were moved down to the Shortlands by barge.

There was nothing wrong with the Japanese method of resupply and reinforcement of the troops in the Central Solomons except that it was far too costly in terms of destroyers and other valuable ships.

The ineffectual attack launched by Colonel Liversedge's northern landing force had left him short of supplies, but on the night of July 23 Admiral Turner sent up a large convoy: two cruisers and five destroyers protecting four supply destroyers. They sneaked into Enogai Roads and managed to unload their supplies and take on the wounded without any more of an incident than the harassment of the landing by Japanese shore batteries on Kolombangara.

Colonel Liversedge wanted more troops, but General Griswold was too badly bogged down in the south to give them to him. The fact was that both Americans and Japanese were operating on shoestrings. The American naval situation had improved marvelously since the Guadalcanal days because the European War, which was paramount in the plans of the Joint Chiefs of Staff, did not call for an American naval buildup. But the shortage of Allied troops was serious, because the European Theater of Operations devoured divisions as a dragon devours maidens.

The Allied Combined Chiefs of Staff were looking forward to the Normandy landings of the following year, and this meant bringing a million Americans and all their trucks and tanks and heavy artillery over to England. There was precious little left for the Pacific commands. And the Japanese, too, were facing shortage, at this point mostly of ships and planes, but later of troops as well.

Their population base was less than half that of the United States. True, they had more men under arms at the beginning of the war, but most of them were tied down in China and Manchuria, and they continued to be.

Just now, faced with the problem of reinforcing the South Pacific, they were drawing on China, where over a million troops were operating, and the Kwantung Army of Manchuria, which numbered about 700,000 that year. Some units, particularly aviation, were moved in from China. But the Imperial General Staff was not inclined to strip these areas, which it considered to be far more important, to bring reinforcements to the south.

For these reasons, the South Pacific campaign continued to be a limited war. Just how limited is indicated by two encounters between Admiral Halsey and Captain Arleigh Burke, commander of a U.S. destroyer squadron. When Burke had come to the South Pacific, he had reported in to Admiral Halsey as did all senior officers, in the office at the old Japanese consulate in Noumea.

Halsey had fixed him with those blue gimlet eyes of his and given the captain a brief indoctrination. He did not care much about spit and polish discipline. What he wanted was fighting men and fighting ships, he had told Burke. And he did not want anything else.

Burke had gone into action. (He had led those four supply destroyers into Enogai on the night of July 23.) So far from a real dockyard, his ships had quickly become troublesome, and the engineering gang had their work cut out for them to keep the vessels going at high speed. One of the destroyers in particular needed work—and equally, the destroyer chores of the Solomons campaign needed every ship, and the men of the destroyers needed a break from the constant tension. But Halsey was hell on anyone who came up crying. So the situation continued until one day Burke, in desperation, simply sent his raunchiest destroyer down to Sydney without saying anything to anyone at Noumea.

Halsey's antennae were always out and scarcely had the ship returned to base when Captain Burke was called on the carpet, and he came in great trepidation to Noumea.

Admiral Halsey was sitting behind his desk with a black look on his face as the captain came in the door. He speared Burke with a glance.

"Tell me, captain, in the name of great thundering Hades, what business you had sending one of your ships down to Sydney, without asking ME!"

Burke fidgeted. But there was no way out. He summoned his courage.

"Well, sir," he said, "we ran out of whiskey and beer, and the men . . ."

He got no further. Halsey's face cleared. He grinned. Then he laughed.

"Well, thank God," he said. "I was afraid you were going to say you sent her down there for repairs, and then I was going to have to bust your ass."

So Captain Burke went away and about his business, which was to fight the Japanese.

The battle for New Georgia—and that meant the airfield at Buna—went on, and on.

Inside the Munda defense perimeter, the battle was beginning to wear seriously on the nerves of the Japanese defenders. Nearly every day they were bombed once or twice by dive-bombers from Guadalcanal. American warships bombarded them at night, keeping the Japanese defenders short on sleep. By July 17, ninety men had been killed by these attacks and 636 wounded. Worse, more than a thousand men were ill with fever and other tropical diseases. There were a hundred cases of "war neurosis." So a good part of the garrison of about 3,000 men could not be depended on for defense.

Starting July 19, the character of the American attacks changed noticeably. The attacks grew in intensity and length, and several times each day the Munda area was hit by ten or twelve planes, heavy bombers, dive-bombers, medium bombers, and fighters.

General Sasaki realigned his defenses. He decided to give priority to the attack on the American buildup at Zanana above all else and sent a staff officer to inform Colonel Tomonari that the 13th Infantry was to make a second attack there on July 25.

The 13th Infantry was to assemble on the right flank of the 229th on July 23 and prepare to cross the Sho River and drive the Americans off the beachhead. All well and good, but on the evening of July 23, General Sasaki changed his mind. He called on the 13th Regiment to go into a defensive pattern, tightening its lines up against those of the 229th.

General Sasaki seemed to have sensed that the Americans were preparing for a major onslaught, and this prompted him to change his strategy in midstream, a decision that brought considerable criticism by Japanese historians after the war. Having decided on a solid and aggressive stance, at this point General Sasaki seemed to have thrown judgment to the winds, and without apparent reason to have dumped his plan.

But in one way General Sasaki was quite right. The Americans were gearing up for an all-out effort against Munda. General Griswold was under enormous pressure to get the drive against Munda going again. He had to get that done in a hurry, General Harmon informed him, so that they could go on to the next step. For the South Pacific operations of 1943 had been geared in with the Southwest Pacific operations of General MacArthur. The two commands had to share landing craft and destroyers and air support for their offensive operations; so it was essential that the schedules set down in March be kept as well as possible, and the New Georgia operations was far behind.

Sasaki was again seeking reinforcement. On July 23 he sent a message to the Eighth Fleet in Rabaul, asking for a change in the reinforcement pattern. He wanted the entire 2nd Battalion of the 235th Regiment to come to Munda, instead of Bairoko and then the 13th Division operations area. Furthermore, instead of having them fed in company by company, he wanted the whole battalion at once.

The message was sent and received, but the junior officer on duty in Rabaul that night was not paying attention to business, and the message was never delivered to the command. So, when the destroyers came down that next day to deliver the troops to the south, they dropped off only the 235th's 7th Company instead of a battalion. It was to make a considerable difference in the defense of Munda.

Somehow—possibly because of the bombing and the never-ending tension—the euphoric feeling that had permeated the Japanese camp with the victory (even if not followed up) of the first Tomonari drive against Zanana suddenly switched to a deep gloom. General Sasaki could see nothing but deterioration in his battle situation. His troops could scarcely move within their own perimeter because of the attacks, and it was becoming ever more difficult to use the No. 1 Trail which brought in troops and supplies. As for actual casualties, they were not too high. By July 23 the 229th had 104 dead, 135 wounded, and fourteen missing; the 13th Regiment reported 153 dead, 140 wounded, and three missing, and the 22nd Field Artillery and the Bairoko base unit reported another fifty dead, eighty-three wounded, and four missing. Those figures, of course, did not show the sick or the dispirited.

Meanwhile, in the other camp, that successful attack of Colonel Tomonari's 13th Regiment against the Americans on the beachhead had brought an immediate call for help, and the response had been the dispatch in a hurry of part of the 148th U.S. Infantry to Zanana.

Their orders had been to move up and open the Munda Trail to get the 169th Regiment out of its pickle. On July 18, 19, and 20 the Americans had tried to move up, with ever-increasing forces, but had been ambushed and driven back each time by the troops of the Japanese 229th Regiment, whose long occupation of this territory had produced deep fortifications, pillboxes, interconnecting trenches, and interlocking fields of fire. It had taken three new American battalions to finally force a lane through the Japanese so that the 169th Regimental Combat Team could be withdrawn.

General Sasaki's offensive of July 25 did not get going, but General Griswold's did. Early that morning, Captain Burke's destroyers came whooping up to the shore off Lambeti Plantation, the Japanese staging area, and plastered the landscape with five-inch explosives. They fired four thousand rounds. Then Admiral Mitscher laid on a bombing raid that covered the shoreline between the American positions and Munda. All this while the army artillery fired patterns of 105 and 155 mm high explosives into the area. One would think that all this gunpowder would wipe out anything that lived.

But as the Americans were to learn so much more decisively that fall at Tarawa, the Japanese defense constructors knew what they were about, and many pillboxes that had received direct hits still stood. The Japanese had the neat trick of moving up close to the American lines to escape the bombardment, but in this case moving into the jungle was enough. When the bombardments were over, the Japanese returned to their defense positions, and when the American infantry and the tanks tried to move ahead, they found themselves under intense fire and had to give up for the day.

Nonetheless, the enormous quantity (by Japanese standards) of shells and bombs that the Americans were able to expend did take their toll. The next morning the U.S. troops moved back, and the artillery plastered the no-man's-land thoroughly. This unexpected action caught the Japanese by surprise, and they suffered many casualties in the bombardment. Then tanks and shock troops with bazookas, flamethrowers, 75 mm pack howitzers, 37 mm antitank guns, machine guns, grenades, and rifles went after the pillboxes.

It was rough work, but at the end of this day the Americans had destroyed seventy-five pillboxes. At least, they thought they had. That night the Japanese infiltrated through the Americans lines and reoccupied many of the pillboxes. So the next day much of the demolition work had to be done over again.

The terrain between Zanana Beach and the Munda defense zone is hill and jungle, with the flatter coastal plain covered by palm plantation. Each of the hills had to be scaled. And each, the Americans discovered, was a Japanese defensive position, set up to withstand just such attack. A good example was the hill the Japanese called Three Corner Hill. The single company that had arrived from the 230th Infantry in the comedy of errors about transportation was immediately sent by Colonel Hirada of the 229th on July 25 to take over Three Corner Hill. The company started out in the middle of an American artillery barrage, not having gotten the word that it was about to begin, but managed somehow to make it to the position and there the troops settled in.

They held off the enemy on July 25. On July 26 the marines brought up six light tanks, and they attacked Three Corner Hill. The Japanese drove them off. Soldiers rushed out with grenades and satchel charges, trying to knock the treads off the tanks. If a tanker stuck his head up, it was liable to be blown off by a blast of automatic small arms fire, or he might fall back with a neat round hole from a sniper's bullet in his head. The ground had to be gained, foot by foot, and the casualties on both sides were not negligible. Two tanks were disabled, and the others grunted down the hill to reorganize. They started up the hill again, with a much larger force, moving along the south side of the hill. It soon became evident that that particular position could not hold out much longer, so the Japanese retreated.

Where the 169th and the 172nd had failed, the fresh and better trained 148th Regiment gained ground slowly, supported by the marine armor. The assault along the coastline was the hardest. The troops that had relieved the 169th to open the Munda Trail were in the position of flanking the Japanese defenses, and their way was easier.

The Munda defense was built around the nine hills that protected the airstrip. The closest of these, towering above the field, was Bibilo Hill, which commanded the airfield and the coastline. On July 27, the 148th's advance units were within a half mile of Bibilo Hill (the Japanese called it Diamond Hill). But there the Japanese dug in and began a stubborn battle. By day the Americans passed over hidden pillboxes. By night the Japanese came out of the pillboxes and fought their way to their own lines. They always left one man behind when abandoning a position, and he might cause a dozen casualties and hold up a unit for half a day until he was routed out like a mole.

This was a new sort of fighting for the Americans, and it took some getting used to; it was unlike anything that had occurred on Guadalcanal. The marines would get all the public credit for facing this sort of defense in the drive across the Central Pacific. It was unfortunate that General Howland Smith, who was planning the invasion of the Gilbert

Islands, had not been exposed to this campaign in the Central Solomons. He was aware of the Japanese last ditch stand on Attu Island in the Aleutians in May, but this Solomons campaign was in its way even more desperate, and certainly much more effective from the Japanese point of view.

One reason for the slowness with which information filtered out was a natural reluctance on the part of the American high command to publicize their situation, for as of the end of July the New Georgia campaign was anything but a success. The ease of the occupation of Rendova had fooled them all, and now Munda was still holding out and the whole drive north was imperiled. With control of the air and a superiority on the sea that had not yet been seriously challenged, Admiral Halsey was itching to get on with the invasion of Bougainville, a much more extensive Japanese base complex. But until New Georgia was in hand there was no way Bougainville could be approached.

As of July 27, General Sasaki saw the end of his resistance in sight and warned Rabaul. The enemy was steadily closing in on his positions.

A patrol sent down to the beach area close to the American camp discovered that the Americans had relieved their pressure on the pillbox-defended positions on the hills—for the moment—but a new attack on July 29 seemed to be mounting. His message to Rabaul indicated what to expect in the future:

> The enemy moves more and more troops to the left flank of his main force, in the Horse-hoof Hill vicinity of the ridge line. Every day the bombardment increases as the opposition moves through the jungle. The losses of the 229th Regiment continue to increase. Present headquarters full force about twenty men. Reserves are declining also. But the fighting will continue to the last man.

General Sasaki's situation was already hopeless and he knew it. He sent regular messages to Rabaul, but he did not get replies. He was out of touch with Commander Saburo Okumura's navy unit in the north that was attacking the Americans from the other side, but which had now been badly chewed up.

By July 27 General Sasaki could see that the loss of Munda, and that meant New Georgia, was simply a matter of time. The requested naval and air support from Rabaul had never materialized.

The Americans kept moving slowly but steadily ahead. The penetration grew so dangerous at the mountain pass in the Hanaya vicinity that General Sasaki detached a platoon from the 15th Air Defense Battalion down at headquarters and sent them up to reinforce the troops there.

They did strengthen the defenses, and the Americans tried hard but failed to dislodge them. The two most heavily hit spots were called by the Americans Bibilo and Kokengolo hills. As noted, the Japanese had their own names, Diamond and Bombshell hills.

As of July 29, the attack seemed to be intensifying but on the same lines as before. The Sasaki reports to Rabaul mentioned heavy artillery bombardment, with the heaviest attacks coming on the north, and constantly increasing pressure.

Then suddenly, at dawn on July 29, all the shooting stopped. On the crest of Batore Hill the enemy abruptly vanished, leaving some equipment behind. It was an enormous surprise and an opportunity for the Japanese to reinforce the various positions. But the rub was that there was very little reinforcement possible, because General Sasaki had gotten about one-third of the troops promised him—and a lot less than one-third of what he had requested.

As of that date, Sasaki's strength at Munda was reduced to 1,200 troops.

What was happening, of course, was that General Griswold was girding for a final move. Goaded by General Harmon and Admiral Halsey, he *had to* move, and move fast.

During the next two days the Japanese abandoned some positions and strengthened others. The hills remained, with their pillboxes. But inside the Japanese camp everyone knew that it would take a miracle to save Munda.

14

AWKWARD VICTORY

ON August 1, the war on New Georgia Island started up all over again with renewed fury.

The Japanese had consolidated their defenses and abandoned many points that could no longer be held. General Sasaki was not getting as much help, even from Kolombangara, as he wanted, for even before Sasaki saw the handwriting on the wall, the high command at Rabaul had seen it and had begun diverting its efforts to strengthening other points, such as Buin on the southern tip of Bougainville. But Sasaki was getting some reinforcement, and he was determined to hold out and make the American victory as costly as it could be.

Indeed, the entire South Pacific strategy had been turned toward delaying and, if possible, containing the Allied drive.

The Japanese navy forces in the South Pacific were growing ragged with the enormous responsibility pushed onto them. The Eleventh Air Fleet had lost dozens of Zeros and its best pilots. The drain on destroyers was constant. The older ones were used when possible for ferrying troops and supplies, but some of the new destroyers also had to be pressed into this service. The result was serious disruption of naval combat operations in the area.

The heat was on New Georgia, so resupply of the other Japanese bases was virtually unnoticed by the Americans. On July 26, the destroyers *Arashikaze, Yugure,* and *Hagikaze* set out from Rabaul to carry on the reinforcement program. First they delivered sixty men and seventy-seven tons of meat to the naval air station at Rekata Bay. Then they took 840 men of the 23rd Infantry Regiment to Buin. That major base was being reinforced because the high command expected the Shortlands to be the next invasion point, and they knew very well that their chances of holding that outpost were slim.

The Rekata–Buin mission went like clockwork. The three destroyers pulled into Rekata Bay at ten minutes past midnight on the 27th, and within an hour they had unloaded what they were leaving there and were under way for Buin. Most of the time, they were covered by planes from Rabaul and Buin.

But that sort of air coverage could not always be managed, particularly down in Kula Gulf, where the fighting was growing hotter and hotter. As far as the resupply missions for New Georgia were concerned, the most troublesome nettles were the American PT boats, which came out night after night to harry the Japanese.

By the end of July the Americans had more than fifty PT boats operating from two bases in the area. They were—or could be—quite effective against the barges the Japanese used to bring troops across from Vila to Bairoko. But the PT boat captains liked to live dangerously, and they were forever on the lookout for Japanese destroyers. Sometimes they found them.

On the afternoon of August 1, the Japanese destroyers *Amagiri, Arashi, Hagikaze,* and *Shigure* set out from Rabaul with 900 more troops and 120 tons of supplies to try to tip the scales at Munda. They were instructed to move down through Vella Gulf, because a mission a few days earlier had used that route. Kula Gulf was just getting too hot.

The four destroyers moved in through Blackett Strait without difficulty, unloaded their cargoes, and then headed home at thirty knots. It was a night so black the officers on the bridge could scarcely see the bows of their ships—just what was wanted to keep out of trouble. But trouble was afloat, in the character of half-a-dozen American PT boats hanging around Blackett Strait and Vella Gulf. Among them were *PT 159, PT 157, PT 109,* and *PT 162,* lying in positions that might bring them into contact with this supply mission.

The Japanese destroyers were charging along at what at least one of their captains considered to be totally dangerous speed in these narrow waters, when suddenly the command ship, the *Amagiri,* encountered a black shape dead ahead, and at thirty knots. The destroyer smashed into *PT 109,* cut the boat in half, and sped on.

The following destroyers fired on the wreckage. The crew struggled in the water and tried to swim to land. Eventually eleven members of the thirteen-man crew, including the skipper, Lieutenant John Fitzgerald Kennedy, were rescued through the efforts of a coast watcher, Lieutenant Arthur Evans.

It was just another unimportant bit of the South Pacific day's work, except that in this case it involved a man who would much later become President of the United States.

As for the war at hand, the incident was almost entirely meaningless and, if anything, tended to confirm the belief of destroyer and cruiser sailors that the PT boats were more nuisance than anything else. Admirals Merrill and Ainsworth had standing orders that when their ships were operating in Kula Gulf the PTs were to stay home. That was the result of the unfortunate incident weeks before when a PT boat had mistakenly sunk a crippled American ship. The "small fry" were a long time in living that down.

The PT boats could be effective when taking on opponents of their own size, and they did create difficulties for the Japanese resupply missions. For instance, one night in late July three PT boats engaged half-a-dozen Japanese barges trying to reinforce Munda. They didn't sink any barges, but they did delay the landing and caused some casualties.

On July 29, during the respite in the fighting on New Georgia Island, Major General John R. Hodge replaced General Hester as commander of the 43rd Division (a post Hester had held as well as that of invasion troop commander). Thereafter the Americans began to move much more smartly. But even with better morale, leadership, and increased number of troops, the going was tough. An advance of 1,200 yards in a day was excellent, for the Japanese contested every foot of land.

Around Munda, one by one the strong points fell to the advancing American troops. On August 2 the U.S. 43rd Division pushed across Lambeti Plantation and reached the east end of the airfield. General Griswold advised Colonel Liversedge's force at Enogai that he had broken the Japanese hold on Munda and that many of the troops from the defense perimeter were now fleeing north. He asked that Liversedge cut them off.

Liversedge was not in camp at the moment; he had gone back south for conferences. But he was in touch with the battalion commanders by radio and that night sent the troops of the 148th Regiment back to the roadblock. The increase in Japanese activity was notable as the Munda troops began filtering north. It meant more alerts and more sudden skirmishes, which usually ended up with a handful of U.S. casualties, a number of dead Japanese, and some prisoners. During and after the war, a myth persisted that no Japanese ever gave up—wounded or not.

But the fact was that American intelligence officers counted about 700 Japanese prisoners of war during this campaign (most of them wounded so severely they were captured without knowing it) and so were in more or less constant contact with Japanese prisoners, who were a primary source of information.

On August 4, the troops of the U.S. 37th Infantry Division broke through the pillbox line about 600 yards north of the airfield.

Back at Guadalcanal, the command was concerned about the number of Japanese reinforcements that had been getting through to Kolombangara. On July 15, Rear Admiral T. S. Wilkinson had replaced Admiral Kelly Turner as commander of the South Pacific Amphibious Command. (Turner was returning to Pearl Harbor to prepare for the U.S. invasion of the Gilbert Islands that fall.)

Admiral Wilkinson decided the best antidote to the Japanese movements would be a destroyer sweep of the area around Kolombangara. He called on Commander Frederick Moosbrugger, the commander of Destroyer Division 12, to make just such a sweep that night.

Actually Admiral Halsey was looking forward to the next move after New Georgia. At Pearl Harbor, Admiral Nimitz had suggested that the prospects of working the American way up the chain of the Solomons were most uninviting. If every island cost as much in terms of time and resources as had New Georgia already, then they would be forever getting to Rabaul. So he wanted Halsey to bypass Kolombangara, the main Japanese base, and land next at Vella Lavella, to the north. Vella Lavella offered an airstrip and landing facilities.

Once Kolombangara was bypassed, the Japanese would have no reason to keep moving men and supplies down that far, and Halsey could anticipate that the Kolombangara garrison would be left to wither. So it was partially in preparation for the forthcoming new invasion, and partially to stop the movement of troops and supplies between Kolombangara and New Georgia, that this naval operation was conceived.

On August 5, the fighting on New Georgia was all over, as far as organized opposition was concerned. General Sasaki evacuated as many troops as he could, by way of the trail and Bairoko. The troops in the last two hill positions were surrounded and could not be gotten out, so they were told to fight to the death and left behind. Their rear guard action allowed many more Japanese to get away than otherwise might have made it. Virtually all the survivors as of the first days of August got out.

At 1:40 on the afternoon of August 5, the Liversedge force was told by General Griswold to stick tight where they were and not try to move south along the trails. The general wanted them to be prepared to stop as many of the escaping Japanese as possible. And all the Japanese who could escape were doing so. The days of suicidal stands were still to come in this war, except, of course, when a Japanese unit was cut off, in which case the national military tradition held for death rather than the "dishonor" of surrender.

On August 6, the Americans began counting the Japanese bodies and announced that they had killed 2,000 enemy troops in the siege of Munda. American losses in the ground fighting were put at 1,150.

The Japanese continued to hold Bairoko and through that port to evacuate their troops, about 1,300 in all, including General Sasaki.

Within a matter of hours after the capture of the Munda airfield, Seabees and army engineers were moving into the island to begin the reconstruction of the field, so that it could be used by Admiral Halsey's forces in the drive up the Central Solomons.

The Japanese Navy continued to make efforts to resupply Kolombangara Island, in the belief that it would be the next target of the Americans. On August 4, just such a mission was planned for four destroyers, and before dawn on August 6 the *Hagikaze, Arashi, Kawakaze*, and *Shigure* set out from Rabaul for Vila, carrying more than a thousand troops and fifty tons of supplies for Kolombangara. Their plan called for after-dark arrival in the area controlled by American aircraft. But that same afternoon at 2:30 they were spotted by an American plane off Buka, and the radio operators aboard the ships could hear the plane operator flashing an urgent message to someone.

The task group of American destroyers was lucky. Its sweep had been ordered on August 5 on the intelligence tip from Pearl Harbor that a Tokyo Express trip ought to be shaping up just then. And Commander Moosbrugger on the morning of August 6 had met with Commander Rodger W. Simpson of Destroyer Division 15, who would be along on this mission. They planned a two-pronged attack on whatever Japanese force they encountered. Commander Moosbrugger would lead the mission with his *Dunlap, Craven*, and *Maury*. Commander Simpson would be responsible for the *Lang, Sterett*, and *Stack*. Moosbrugger would attack first if the vessels they met were destroyers, because his destroyers were up to strength on torpedoes. Simpson's ships were short on torpedoes, because they had been fitted out for operations against the Japanese barges and carried a number of 40 mm guns, in addition to their five-inch guns and 20 mm guns. If they encountered a barge flotilla, the Simpson group would attack first.

At 11:30 on the morning of August 6, the American destroyers were on their way from Tulagi up the Slot. In late afternoon they had the search plane's report of a Japanese "fast fleet" heading south, and knowing

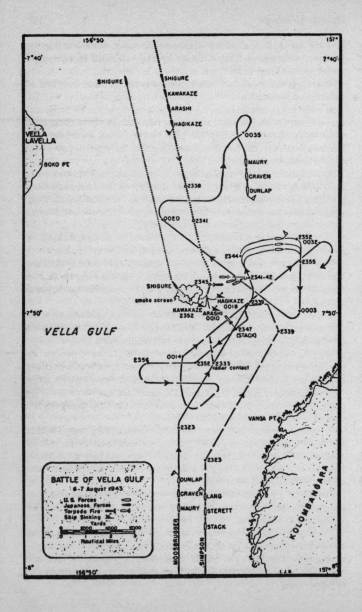

BATTLE OF VELLA GULF
6-7 August 1943

U.S. Forces ······
Japanese Forces ·-·-·
Torpedo Fire ⊏⊐
Ship Sinking ✗

Yards
2000   4000   6000
0   1   2
Nautical Miles

how the Japanese operated, Commander Simpson estimated that the Japanese would be in Vella Gulf by midnight. He and Moosbrugger made plans to meet them there.

Thus forewarned, and with their radar, the Americans already had an enormous advantage.

At 7:00 P.M. (Tokyo time) the Japanese entered Bougainville Strait and speeded up to thirty knots for the fast run through those dangerous waters to reach their objective. Not quite two and a half hours later they were northeast of Vella Lavella Island. Then Kolombangara came up on the starboard bow.

The Americans were coming up fast from the south. They moved in through Gizo Strait, made a sweep around the waters between Gizo Island and Kolombangara, then headed northward up Vella Gulf. They were in battle formation: the *Dunlap* leading, then *Craven* and *Maury*, with *Lang*, *Sterett*, and *Stack* in another column off to the right of the first column. It was about 11:30, U.S. forces time, when the *Dunlap*'s radar operator first reported blips on his screen: four in a column.

This time the Americans had all the advantages: they were ready; they had their torpedo tubes prepared; they had located the enemy and he had not become aware of them, nor would he do so until he made visual contact.

At 11:41 the American destroyers began firing torpedoes, and the enemy still had not seen them. The *Dunlap*, *Craven*, and *Maury* each fired eight "fish" at the Japanese ships from 6,300 yards.

They had disconnected the magnetic exploders of the torpedoes. By this point in the war, the magnetic exploders on American torpedoes had become suspect because of malfunctioning. In the submarine force the discussion led to hot argument, but not in the surface force. The torpedo officers of these destroyers had disconnected the magnetic exploders without making an issue of it.

As the Japanese vessels neared their destination, they were looking for trouble, but in the form of PT boats, not enemy destroyers. In their encounters with the U.S. fleet, they had nearly always bested the American destroyers, and the Japanese did not believe U.S. destroyer men knew much about torpedo fighting.

Finally, the Japanese did see the shapes of ships and moved swiftly to attack with their own torpedoes. But it was much, much too late. The American destroyers had already fired torpedoes and turned.

The captain of the *Hagikaze* saw something and ordered the helm turned hard aport, but before the destroyer could respond, two torpedoes smashed into her. The *Arashi* caught the next pair, and at least one torpedo hit the *Kawakaze* in the vitals causing her forward magazine to explode.

The *Shigure*, alone, was saved—by the irony of the fact that she was the oldest and wheeziest of the destroyers and had been unable to keep up with the modern ships on their dash down the gulf. She had fallen half a mile behind the others, and when the lookouts reported that torpedoes were coming in, Captain Tameichi Hara was able to turn in time and save his ship. The American torpedoes slipped by his sides and went on harmlessly.

All but one. The turn seemed to take forever, and in the middle of it, Hara would have sworn that he had not made it in time, that his ship was hit. There was no explosion, just a dull thud, and then the rudder seemed to begin acting up. Hara was puzzled, and then he forgot the incident but he did not forget that the destroyer was badly in need of dry dock attention.

Weeks later, when the *Shigure* went into dry dock, the workmen discovered a neat round hole through the rudder, which accounted for the destroyer's sluggish action after that night of August 6.

The other Japanese ships that night did not fare nearly so well.

In the darkness no one was quite sure what had happened. The burning *Kawakaze* lit up the sky, and the Americans thought they had hit a Japanese cruiser. The *Arashi* burned too, although not as furiously.

The second group of American destroyers, led by Commander Simpson, saw the ships on the radar screens and began firing with their five-inch guns. They put the finishing touches on the *Kawakaze*, or at least so it seemed, for as the shells began to hit, the Japanese destroyer rolled over and sank.

Meanwhile, Captain Hara's *Shigure* completed the sluggish turn and then moved into position to fire torpedoes. These did no damage because the American ships had turned in time.

Hara moved away, ordered the men to reload the tubes (which they did in a hurry), and came back. However, by this time his three fellow destroyers were all but gone, so he turned and got out of those dangerous waters as quickly as possible.

As he went, he saw the *Arashi* explode and sink. All six American destroyers opened fire with their guns on the *Hagikaze*, and she burned and blew up. At that point, although the gulf was full of wreckage and men swimming, the radar screens of the Americans ships were clear. Moosbrugger brought his destroyer through the wreckage on the water and saw hundreds of heads. For once there was no danger and he attempted rescue, at least for intelligence purposes. But the Japanese swimming in the sea refused to approach the American destroyers as they inched through the water. Of the seven hundred destroyer crewmen aboard the three ships and the eight hundred troops, only three hundred and ten men were listed officially as surviving. These men had somehow found their way to shore and had been rescued by Japanese troops from Kolombangara.

On the way home, the *Shigure's* captain announced the disaster to Rabaul and called for rescue of the men. But it never came. Some made it to the islands around the gulf, but no one would ever know how many beyond those rescued by the Japanese, or how long they were able to survive. During the next few weeks, the coast watchers reported that Solomon Islanders ambushed and killed many unarmed and ragged Japanese and brought in others as prisoners of war.

Captain Hara returned to Rabaul and unloaded the two hundred and fifty troops aboard the *Shigure* and the supplies. He went ashore with details of the dreadful story of the worst single defeat the Japanese had suffered at sea since Midway. It was clear-cut and frightening.

For the first time the Americans had shown themselves masters of the torpedo attack, which seemed almost unbelievable to a Japanese destroyer fleet that had become exceedingly arrogant because of success.

Just now that arrogance was beginning to disappear in what would be a stream of news reports of one Japanese defeat after another.

The American air attack in March on the Lae convoy in the Bismarck Sea had shown what could happen to Japanese vessels deprived of air superiority. But this latest American victory had come *at night* in restricted waters, and air power had played no role except (as it had functioned for the Japanese earlier) as a weapon of intelligence. The Japanese had not fired an effective shot. The physical superiority of the American navy was beginning to show, in this victory of radar. The most serious injury suffered by any American in the action was to a gun loader on the destroyer *Lang*, whose hand had been crushed by accident. Ever since the early string of Japanese victories at sea had ended, the Japanese had been telling themselves that the American mechanical advantages could be overcome by fighting spirit. After the night battle of Vella Gulf—although Captain Hara at first claimed to have sunk an American cruiser with his own torpedoes—there were many in the Imperial Navy whose confidence was never again restored.

The success of this particular mission gave the Americans a new confidence in their destroyers, and they came out again three nights later. Admiral Wilkinson supposed that the Japanese would again be ready to try a reinforcement mission to Kolombangara, based on the pattern of the recent past. But the high command at Rabaul had decided that the cost of these forays had grown too high, and never again would they send destroyers into those waters to reinforce the army. The American destroyers did encounter a number of Japanese barges, still moving troops out of New Georgia to the safety of Kolombangara. The destroyers were too big and too unwieldy to do much damage. In an encounter with three barges, three destroyers managed to sink only one; the others ran circles around them and escaped.

After Munda had been captured and New Georgia was declared to be in American hands, there was plenty for the U.S. foot soldiers to do. Hundreds of Japanese still remained on the island and on the smaller islands that were a part of its orbit. They had to be driven out or killed.

The American air forces hit Bairoko every day. Colonel Liversedge's men poked around the perimeter, killing a few Japanese on each patrol. The Japanese, in turn, continued to bomb Enogai and other American positions in the north.

On August 8, troops of the U.S. 25th Division made their way up the Munda–Bairoko Trail to meet the Liversedge force at the roadblock. Theoretically, the Japanese were sealed off in the jungle, but actually they were using subsidiary trails to get away even yet.

The Japanese maintained control of Bairoko until August 18, when a combined force of army and marine troops made the final assault. The battle for Bairoko lasted until August 24, when the marines and army troops enveloped the port and overwhelmed it. General Sasaki had left for Vila on one of the last barges.

Kolombangara now became the center of resistance in the area. Many Japanese, however, were in the jungle, operating as guerrillas.

Some troops remained on smaller islands of the New Georgia complex, and they had to be routed out by foot soldiers. It was always tough going and the casualties were high on the American side. On the Japanese side the casualties were higher, for the spirit of Bushido did drive most Japanese to prefer death to capture, and they had been so prompted by their superiors.

What is called the New Georgia campaign did not finally end until the middle of September 1943. There were too many holdout spots, too many little enclaves such as those on Arundel Island, where the Japanese could control the entrance to Kula Gulf through heavy artillery. They had to be routed out.

American intelligence in August estimated that there were only 200 Japanese on that island, but, as the New Georgia campaign ended, General Sasaki sent more of them down to Arundel.

The 172nd Infantry was assigned the task of clearing Arundel, but they could not do it. After more than two weeks, which ended in a Japanese counterattack that caused many casualties, General Griswold sent in more troops and tanks. It took them until September 20 to push the Japanese off Arundel Island. As far as the Americans were concerned, the casualties had been heavy, and the 172nd Infantry's combat force of 1,000 men had suffered more than 775 casualties.

The Japanese had lost several thousand men, probably closer to the three thousand figure that the Japanese army history indicates, than to the twelve thousand that one Japanese naval historian claimed. About 8,000 Japanese were involved in New Georgia, as compared to 30,000 Americans.

Actually, although at the time Admiral Halsey was impatient about the length of time the New Georgia operation took, it turned out to be more or less average for assaults on the Japanese islands up the chain toward Tokyo. This was the first offensive operation since Guadalcanal. There was no book to go by.

What New Georgia showed, even more than Guadalcanal, was that to defeat the Japanese the Allies would have to write new pages in the textbooks of island warfare.

In the writing, the campaign for New Georgia and Munda air base can be concluded neatly. It was not that way in the action; neither the Japanese nor the Americans considered the Munda and New Georgia battles to be definitive. They were just part of the long campaign of attrition that at that time threatened to become endless. If the Americans had to take every single little island all the way up the Solomons chain, the effort and the expense in lives and material would be enormous. There had to be a better way, and it was up to Admiral Halsey to find it. In Washington and at Pearl Harbor the argument was for "leap-frogging," and Halsey himself believed this was the way to go. But there was another school, which said that a wise commander never left a powerful enemy force in his rear.

The original planning had suggested that the next attack would be on Kolombangara. That island was indeed a powerful Japanese position, much stronger and housing more troops than New Georgia. Kolombangara and not New Georgia had been the major Japanese southern base. Admiral Halsey's original plans for the capture of New Georgia had indicated that it should be accomplished in a matter of days. He had also indicated that the troops were to move on swiftly to Kolombangara.

The experience at New Georgia was indeed sobering. Given the greater strength of Kolombangara, Halsey could expect a much more protracted battle.

Various officers had suggested the leapfrog technique. General MacArthur's headquarters mentioned it. So did Admiral Nimitz. Halsey took it all under consideration. He was the man in charge and his responsibility was to tighten that ring around Rabaul, the major Japanese base in the South Pacific. How he did it was his business.

15

VELLA LAVELLA

AFTER the fall of New Georgia, it would have been logical to expect that the Japanese Combined Fleet at Truk would emerge to seek battle with the Americans. The Combined Fleet was still the most powerful force in the South Pacific. But Admiral Koga had many problems. He had taken the fleet back to Japan that summer for some major maintenance, and at that time he had had meetings in Tokyo.

What had to be decided was the manner in which the Combined Fleet could be best used against the enemy.

Admiral Koga had given up part of his carrier planes to the Eleventh Air Fleet at Rabaul for use in missions against the Allied forces in the Solomons and in New Guinea. Should this practice be continued at the expense of the carriers?

Such discussions were a part of a more important process of decision: the navy general staff in Tokyo was just then engaged in a great debate with General Tojo about the conduct of the war. Tojo had never paid a great deal of attention to the southward advance of the Japanese forces, because all this was primarily a navy enterprise. From the days when he had served as chief of staff of the Kwantung army in Manchuria, he had been preoccupied with the Asian continent.

With the fall of New Georgia, Prime Minister Tojo began talking about withdrawal to a perimeter running from the Marianas to Truk to Wewak, and forgetting the Solomons altogether.

Admiral Koga had argued that the Pacific must be defended and he explained to Tojo the historic American navy war plan (Plan Orange, which was generally known to the Japanese Navy) and its emphasis on the Central Pacific.

Tojo and the generals were no more than half convinced that the Americans would try to pull it off, but they did agree to continue the war effort in the south, while at the same time building up the bases elsewhere for counterattack in 1944.

Finally, they settled on a defensive perimeter that ran from the Marianas to Truk to the Central Solomons, to New Guinea and Timor. Rabaul would continue to be the center of activity against the enemy, but it was understood that Rabaul was no longer regarded as primary. The revised war plan for the Central Solomons was defensive.

These Tokyo decisions in the summer of 1943 marked the basic change from offensive to defensive strategy on the part of the Imperial General Staff.

The army and navy in the South Pacific were now instructed to wear down the enemy while the Imperial General Staff built up strength for the new effort to come.

The army immediately would build seventeen new airfields in eastern New Guinea. The army and the navy together would hold the Northern Solomons (with as little reinforcement as possible). The Combined Fleet would wait for suitable opportunity, when the Allies made an important landing, and then the Combined Fleet would sally forth and demand that "decisive battle" that Yamamoto had talked about for so long. So the dead hand of Admiral Yamamoto was still guiding Japanese policy.

At the moment, Admiral Koga said and General Tojo agreed, the most important need to be filled was that for aircraft. New efforts were devoted to increasing aircraft production.

The need was emphasized by the demands of the program of attrition in the Central Solomons. During the Munda campaign and after, the Japanese never let up the pressure from the air. The Eleventh Air Fleet's strength ebbed and flowed, but, since it was operating on two fronts the attrition was obviously great. The number of planes would rise to about 250, and then after a big air battle or two it would fall by as many as a hundred planes.

Still, the air battle over the Solomons continued day after day.

On August 7, forty-eight Zeros led a dozen dive-bombers to attack the

Admiral Mineichi Koga was Commander in Chief of the Imperial Japanese Navy's Combined Fleet from April 1943 to April 1944. (*U.S. Navy*)

Vice Admiral Jinichi Kusaka served as Commander in Chief of the Southeast Asian Fleet from December 1942 to August 1945. *(U.S. Navy)*

Vice Admiral Tomoshige Samejima in a staff car. He was commander in Chief of the Eighth Fleet from April 1943 to August 1945. *(U.S. Navy)*

Lieutenant General Takeshi Takashina (right) and Colonel T. Suenaga *(U.S. Navy)*

General Hitoshi Imamura, Commander in Chief, Japanese Eighth Army *(U.S. Navy)*

General Douglas MacArthur

Admiral Chester W. Nimitz

Rear Admiral Marc A. Mitscher, Commander, Air, in the Solomons

Rear Admiral Richmond Kelly Turner commanded amphibious forces.

Troops loading onto landing craft

In the Solomons campaign, the DUKW, the amphibious tractor, came into its own. Had it not been for such vehicles, the American troops on Vella LaVella and Bougainville might have bogged down entirely.

First the LCVI ran up onto the beach and then men poured out. If they were lucky, they got ashore and had some time to string communications wire.

During the campaign for Guadalcanal, it had been the Japanese cruisers that ran up and down the Slot, apparently at will. But during the second stage of the Solomons battle it was the American cruisers that bombarded the Japanese positions.

The Americans land on Rendova.

American troops race across a Rendova beach, supported by a fighter plane.

The incredibly beautiful and rugged Solomons terrain provided ample strongpoints and hiding places for determined Japanese defenders.

A U.S. Marine patrol examines a dead Japanese soldier.

Marine Raiders

An American PT boat on patrol

An American B-25 bombs a Japanese ship in Rabaul Harbor.

A Japanese transport burns off Kavieng at the northern tip of New Ireland.

A B-25 bombs a Japanese ship in the Bismarck Sea battle.

A U.S. Marine radio installation at Torokina

The Japanese were only one enemy for the Marines on Bougainville; the other was mud.

The resting place of a U.S. Marine on Bougainville.

Rendova Anchorage. Since there was nothing in the anchorage at the moment but small craft, the damage was minimal.

The attrition campaign worked both ways. On August 9 the Americans launched a 170-plane attack on Kolombangara, part of Admiral Halsey's ploy to convince the Japanese that the next invasion would, indeed, be at that island. The Japanese put up an air cover and fought back.

On August 12 the Americans raided Buin with 145 planes. The Eleventh Air Fleet responded with every Zero it could put in the air, and the attack turned into a major air battle. The problem with such air battles was still the paucity of accurate reporting of the results, and in this the Japanese were far more prone to exaggeration than the Americans.

On this date they claimed to have shot down thirty-three American planes, while losing only one of their own. The real problem with such reporting was that it gulled higher authority into believing that the air war was going much better for the Japanese than the pilots knew it was. The Japanese were becoming the victims of their military system, which demanded victory at all costs. With that sort of pressure, army, navy, and airmen all stretched the truth remorselessly and the result was a growingly distorted picture of the war at Rabaul, at Truk, and in Tokyo.

Admiral Koga and the Combined Fleet had returned to Truk early in August, so the "decisive battle" could come at any time. Only one element was missing at the moment: enough major American ships to make the risk worthwhile.

In the landing to come in a few days, Koga was going to be disappointed, for the force assembling in the waters of Tulagi and Guadalcanal consisted largely of troop-carrying destroyers. But these days there were almost always a few big transports in Lunga Roads. Japanese scout planes had been watching a buildup, and on August 12 they announced that it was reaching a peak. So the next day the Eleventh Air Fleet set up a raid of half-a-dozen torpedo bombers out of Buin. They took off in the afternoon, without escorts (in order to be less conspicuous) and flew at wave-top level past Choiseul and the east side of Isabel Island.

Shortly after dark they arrived over Lunga Roads, and there below the pilots saw the assembling amphibious force. The torpedo planes sped in low, dropped their torpedoes, and sped away before the air raid alert system had time to react. (If there was one failure of ground-to-air radar in 1943 it was the inability to pick up low-flying planes.) The imaginative Japanese pilots claimed to have torpedoed three American ships, but American records showed only that the supply ship *John Penn* was hit and sunk.

The Japanese were still waiting for the invasion force to set out for Kolombangara, and the reinforcement of that island continued. General Sasaki was there, organizing his defenses.

But after much consideration, Admiral Halsey had definitely decided to try the leapfrog technique. On that night of August 12, while the Japanese float planes were snooping on the American flotilla at anchor off Guadalcanal, Admiral Wilkinson sent four PT boats to Vella Lavella to check on the situation of that island.

After the sinking of the American cruiser *Helena*, a number of American sailors had swum to Vella Lavella and remained there for ten days. The only people they saw were some of the 2,000 Solomon Islanders who lived there. The Japanese had never thought the island worth occupying, so it remained a sort of no-man's-land, where shipwrecked sailors of both sides ended up waiting for rescue.

The PT boat force was attacked by the Japanese float planes that roved at night, but the Japanese did not realize that this group of PTs was anything out of the ordinary. Actually it was a survey party, going ahead to set up beach markers at the most likely landing spots. One boat was hit and four men were wounded, but that was all. The party landed and did its work. From the natives the Americans learned that there were a number of bands of Japanese on the island, survivors of various ships and soldiers who had been passengers. They were poorly armed, but numerous enough to cause some trouble.

The advance party gave this information to headquarters, and the next day, August 14, the advance party was reinforced, while Admiral Wilkinson started his slow-moving LSTs for the island. So geared were the Japanese to watching for activity at Kolombangara that they missed the American invasion fleet although it sailed steadily on during the daylight hours.

The landings were directly under the command of Admiral Wilkinson, who came up riding in the destroyer *Cony*. When the landing force was ashore and the beachhead secured, then Brigadier General Robert McClure would take command of the occupation force. As the troops were prepared to land, they were told that the Japanese had command posts at several spots on the island, but that it was really only used as a staging point for barges coming down the Slot.

General McClure estimated the number of enemy troops ashore at about 100, but indicated there might be as many as 250 Japanese there. Considering the fact that he was landing with 4,600 troops, the number of the enemy did not seem to be much of a problem.

The landings began shortly after six o'clock in the morning. There was

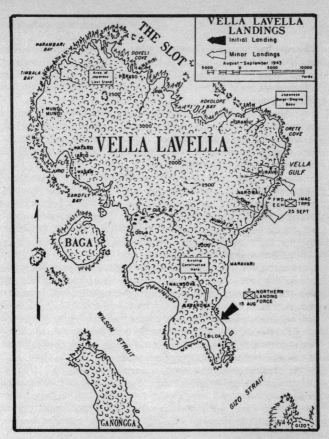

some difficulty involving the shallow lagoon and coral reef, but with the aid of bulldozers to scrape up coral, the landing craft were brought in and their men and equipment gotten ashore in good order. The Americans worried about a counterstrike from the air or the sea, but they need not have. Not until early on the morning of August 15 was the alert given to Rabaul, and by that time the destroyer transports were landing their troops at Vella Lavella's Barakoma Beach, under a heavy fighter cover.

The Japanese were stunned. Their whole new strategy was built on the concept of delaying action. Kolombangara was ready. It had not occurred to General Imamura or Admiral Kusaka that the Americans might go "around end."

The American destroyer wave of landings was completed before seven o'clock in the morning, and the first Japanese planes did not arrive until nearly an hour later. When they came, however, it was apparent that the Japanese had pulled the plug to put out every available aircraft that day. Before the day was out they sent 140 Zeros, thirty-six dive-bombers, twenty-three Betty bombers, and twenty seaplanes to hit the landing forces.

The first wave consisted of six dive-bombers under Zero escort. They came in high, and the Zeros headed for Admiral Mitscher's fighters that were orbiting around the landing area. The Zero pilots did a good job of sucking the fighters away from the destroyers that were to be the target of the bombers, and they soon had most of the fighters engaged.

The bomber pilots approached very professionally from the east, so that the sun was in the eyes of the ships' gunners as the bombers came down. All six made the run, all six dropped their bombs, but here the question of attrition once again came into play. These Japanese bomber pilots, for the most part, were replacements of replacements. They had not gotten the training and they did not have the experience of the first-line fliers of six months earlier.

The bombers made excellent runs, but their aim was poor. The best they could do was score near misses, which sent up huge showers of water, but did not sink or even seriously damage any of the invasion craft.

Not all of those bomber pilots got home that day, by far. Three of them were shot down by fighters over the landing area. But the pilots who did get home boasted of another great victory and claimed to have sunk several cruisers, destroyers, and transports. The fighters also claimed to have shot down twenty-four American planes, while losing a total of seventeen fighters and bombers. So Admiral Kusaka continued to send planes that day.

The second wave came in just after noon. It was ineffectual. These pilots were obviously the third team. The planes were driven off by the fire from the ships and shore, and they suffered several losses.

The third bombing attack was no more effective. The day ended without any serious mishap to the American beach, except about sixty casualties from Japanese strafing and bombing. The ships offshore were unhurt. The Americans claimed to have shot down forty-four Japanese planes.

By nightfall the American beachhead was as well established as anyone could wish. General McClure had ashore his 4,600 troops and 2,300 tons of supplies, which was enough to maintain this force for fifteen days. The guns had plenty of ammunition. The troops had dug in and placed machine guns and large and small antiaircraft guns around the perimeter.

At Rabaul the Japanese had to decide what action they would take in the face of this new development. Admiral Kusaka wanted the army to provide at least a battalion to make a counterlanding. (As usual he spoke of a force far too small to do the job.)

General Imamura said no. Commitment of a single battalion against General McClure's force would be "like pouring water on a hot stone," he said. (It evaporates.) As for making a major landing—using a regiment perhaps—he already had the answer from Tokyo two days earlier.

Imperial General Headquarters had instructed him to start the gradual withdrawal of troops from the Central Solomons. They were to fall back slowly, taking as much toll of the Allies as possible, and finally to defend only Rabaul to the last.

So there was never any question of launching a major offensive to stop the Americans at Vella Lavella. The Japanese actually did not expect to hold Kolombangara, or the Shortlands, or even Bougainville. Even Rabaul was already written off in the strategic books of the Imperial General Staff. The line at which the Americans would be stopped had been established, and the closest point was Truk.

The important tactical matter at this stage of Japanese thinking was the salvation of the troops and equipment on Kolombangara. To guarantee this, they needed a base nearby, and the northern tip of Vella Lavella Island, at the opposite end from the American invasion, was the logical point. Admiral Kusaka and General Imamura agreed that a base should be established there immediately. Two days after the American invasion, two companies of troops and a navy unit were moved south in a number of barges. Rear Admiral Matsuji Ijuin took four destroyers to accompany them and protect them from American attack.

This troop move marked a new Japanese naval policy in the South Pacific, which came as a direct result of the sinking of three Japanese destroyers in the battle at Vella Gulf a few days earlier. Indirectly, the change reflected the loss of some forty destroyers in the past year or so in Solomons waters. Admiral Ijuin had recommended that, in future, destroyers be used only for escort and that they not seek battle in addition. Also, the modern destroyers should not again be used for troop transport.

The command at Rabaul and Truk had listened to him.

Just before sailing, Admiral Ijuin had conferred with his destroyer captains. He told them of the changed policy. Instead of seeking action under any conditions, the destroyer captains were to remember that their mission was to get the troops ashore, and that was the end of their mission. It was a distinct departure from the past.

The four ships left Rabaul during the hours of darkness on August 17, bound for a rendezvous point where they would meet twenty barges carrying 400 troops for Horaniu on Vella Lavella. They had not gone

100 miles from Rabaul, however, when the radio operator of the flag-ship intercepted an American scout plane report, and they knew the enemy would be out looking for them. Ijuin radioed Rabaul for more air support.

Sure enough, that scout plane sent the message to Admiral Wilkinson that four Japanese destroyers were coming south, and Wilkinson ordered Captain Thomas J. Ryan to take four American destroyers up the Slot to meet them. When they got to Gizo Strait they were spotted by a Japanese float plane, which in turn warned Admiral Ijuin that the Americans were coming their way.

Meanwhile Admiral Mitscher at Guadalcanal had sent out eight TBF Avenger bombers that attacked the Japanese ships as they neared Vella Lavella. The planes bombed, the ships fired at them—no one scored. Two more American planes attacked and missed.

Meanwhile a Japanese float plane spotted the American destroyers and gave position, course, and speed to Admiral Ijuin, while the Americans found the Japanese ships on their radar screens. So far it was a toss-up.

The float plane bombed the American ships, ineffectually, and soon the air was disturbed by flying shells as the two flotillas exchanged fire. The Japanese also fired torpedoes at long range.

What came next was an exercise in maneuvering on both sides, which ended with the Japanese destroyer *Hamikaze* hit and the destroyer *Isokaze* damaged by near misses. The *Shigure* fired torpedoes at short range at one American destroyer, but missed. Then, to the disgust of Captain Ryan, Admiral Ijuin disengaged and went speeding off at thirty-five knots to Rabaul. The Americans found it hard to understand why the Japanese had declined the battle, but Ijuin had done his job. In the confusion, nearly all the barges got into the Vella Lavella shore where they holed up in coves and waited for the enemy to go away. The next day they moved to Horaniu and delivered their passengers. Within a week the Japanese had a new barge base there. The American de-stroyers did knock out a few of the small craft escorts of the barges, but by any standard the reinforcement mission had to be regarded as a success. And these days the Japanese were willing to settle for a limited success in such endeavors.

Captain Hara of the *Shigure* went back to Rabaul believing he had sunk an American cruiser but he had not. That night, however, the Japanese did do some serious damage. Faced with the problem of American air superiority over the Central Solomons, the Japanese had begun to evolve some new techniques of attack. Most effective of these was the night attack by small units of bombers flying low to avoid the radar.

On the night of August 17, the second group of Americans coming in to Vella Lavella were hit by the Japanese air force. A group of three bombers came in low and dropped their bombs on the cluster of LSTs off the beach. The ships headed out to sea for the night but Japanese planes trailed them and attacked again. This time they scored a number of near misses, one of which later caused a fire and explosions that blew *LST 396* apart. *LST 339* was bounced up on the beach by a near miss. The destroyers *Waller* and *Philip* maneuvered at high speed to lay a smoke screen and collided. The *Waller* had to go back to Tulagi for repair.

The lumbering (ten-twelve knots) LSTs were the easiest targets the Japanese had yet had, and the bombers made the best of it. In the next few days they scored a number of hits on the LSTs and even more near misses.

But the LSTs were tougher than they looked, and all of them survived after that first mishap. The Japanese air attacks were troublesome, but the acid test came in the Japanese high command assessment at the end of those first few days: "The enemy landing was not dislodged."

With the American invasion of Vella Lavella, the admirals and generals at Rabaul decided to shorten their lines of communication. They began the process of withdrawing troops and equipment from the major front-line bases: Kolombangara, the Shortlands, Santa Isabel Island, and several other spots where they had maintained air and naval bases and stations for communications and island traffic.

Now, in August 1943, began a renewed period of attrition that was grinding on the men of both sides. The situation of the summer of 1942 was almost precisely reversed: the Americans had the preponderance of power in the air and on the sea, but not enough to destroy the enemy. The result was a constant series of air raids and sea raids involving relatively small forces and accomplishing very little. The Japanese, in one sense, accomplished more than the Americans. They began to get their troops out of these zones that were to be abandoned, staging them northward in small craft that moved like Chinese river pirate junks, holing up in jungle country by day and venturing out across small bodies of water by night, whipsawing back and forth on the way north to safety.

As for the larger craft, both sides used them with caution. Admiral Ijuin had a healthy respect for the American radar. It had changed completely the odds in destroyer night fighting, and the improved training of the American destroyer men had brought a new element into such combat.

For the Japanese, the trouble was that the American radar made it hard to close with the enemy. For officers who had served in the halcyon days when every encounter was a victory, it seemed hard to adjust to these new times when the high command urged them to be cautious and stick to the narrow limits of their missions rather than seeking battle.

But after all, as Admiral Ijuin put it, it did not pay to sink an enemy ship if it cost too dearly in men and Japanese ships.

The Japanese evacuation of Santa Isabel began on August 17 and proceeded almost without incident. The evacuation of Rekata Bay came next. There the Japanese had maintained their effective seaplane base, manned by about 3,400 men. That evacuation began a day or two after the move at Santa Isabel. It was hampered by Admiral Wilkinson's cruisers and destroyers, which roamed the seas of the Central Solomons. One night in mid-August, a heavily laden Japanese destroyer force set sail from Rabaul, prepared to deliver supplies to Rekata and take off a thousand men. The ships' commander then learned that American cruisers were lurking off that seaplane base, and they turned back.

But the major difficulty for the Japanese came from the air. Almost every destroyer heading south on a rescue or supply mission was bombed at some point in its journey. Rabaul grew short of destroyers again because so many were in the shipyards or sent up to Truk for repairs of bomb damage. Several of the ships that had been serving for many months in the South Pacific were examined, found to be in terrible condition, and sent back to Japan for major overhaul. That again created complications.

The Americans took their share of bombing punishment too. At Vella Lavella the beachhead was bombed every day. In the first two weeks of September, the Japanese made forty-two separate raids on the beachhead, most of them after dark.

The operation of clearing the Japanese from the island was not moving as rapidly as Halsey had expected. Finally, Admiral Halsey decided to clear out all the Japanese on Vella Lavella and brought in fresh troops to do the job. These were men of the 3rd New Zealand Division under Major General H. J. E. Barrowclough. Their task, which looked easy on paper, was to drive the Japanese into a pocket on the northwest tip of the island and seal them off.

Barrowclough's troops began their push, but the Japanese did what they had done on New Georgia. They dug in and resisted in a manner that must have gladdened the hearts of the Imperial General Staff. Some days the New Zealanders made six hundred yards. Those were good days. Some days they made two hundred yards. And every yard meant blood and battering.

Meanwhile the Seabees came into Barakoma to build an air base, which was one of the main reasons for moving against Vella Lavella in the first place. When it could be put into operation fighters could go all the way to Rabaul with auxiliary tanks, something the Americans had not been able to do before.

To make even better use of Vella Lavella, Admiral Halsey decided to put a marine staging base there for future attacks up the Solomons chain. On the morning of September 17, the I Marine Amphibious Corps sent a detachment under command of Major Donald M. Schmuck to land at Ruravai, up the coast of Vella Lavella, and set up this base. There was some difficulty in landing because of the beach terrain, but the troops got ashore successfully, and so did the guns and trucks and other equipment.

Suddenly out of the sun came fifteen Japanese dive-bombers and twenty Zeros.

The marines manned their guns. They shot down one dive-bomber which burst into flames and crashed into the sea. But the other Japanese bombers came boring in and dropped five-hundred-pound bombs on the beach. The marines shot down two more bombers, which crashed in the jungle, and another went off trailing smoke. But the raid had to be called a success for the Japanese. One 40 mm gun was destroyed. Every man of the crew of another gun was killed by one bomb.

As the bombers flew off, the Zeros came flashing across the beach, strafing. They did a lot of damage before the U.S. combat air patrol appeared to chase after them as they flew northward.

Schmuck's force was hit fairly hard: thirty-two dead and fifty-eight wounded. It would have been worse had he not insisted that every man dig a foxhole as soon as he got ashore, before beginning work on unloading and moving equipment around.

Such Japanese attacks came so frequently and did such damage that in a few days Major Schmuck arranged to have all supplies unloaded at Barakoma, where the marines had brought in 90 mm and 155 mm guns. The Japanese had quickly learned respect for the heavy antiaircraft fire there and let the beachhead alone.

So by mid-September the Allies were ashore in force on Vella Lavella, and the issue was not really in doubt. But the Japanese were not yet finished, and although they could not win, they could exact a heavy price in lives and equipment.

This was the agony of the war of attrition.

16

THE BATTLE FOR VELLA LAVELLA

BY September 1943, the ragged edges of the New Georgia campaign were smoothed out, and the Allies held the whole island. However, there was still hard fighting on Arundel Island, across Hathorn Sound.

As long as the Japanese held any of this territory, they could bring in field artillery and cause all sorts of damage, from shelling Munda airfield to sinking ships. General Sasaki knew this very well, and he had already shown it. His artillery on Kolombangara was harrying Munda Point.

The American campaign on Arundel went like no other. The 172nd Infantry landed and found absolutely no organized Japanese resistance. There were only about 250 Japanese on the island, a single company of the 229th Regiment.

The 172nd, after a bad time at Zanana, was reinforced and somewhat rested, and the troops moved in with the contained vigor of veteran jungle fighters. But here, unlike New Georgia, the Japanese dissolved before them. That reads like easy work, but it was quite the opposite. The Japanese emerged after dark to cut lines of communication—and throats.

When General Sasaki learned that the Americans had landed on

Arundel in force, he countered with force. He began sending in the Japanese 13th Infantry from Kolombangara to Arundel with instructions to harrass the Allied troops as long as possible. After the Vella Lavella landings, when it became apparent to Sasaki that the Americans were bypassing Kolombangara, he sent in more troops of the 13th Infantry, with instructions that they were to hold out until the Kolombangara forces could be evacuated back to Rabaul.

The new commander on Arundel was Major Kikuda, who had performed nobly with the 1st Battalion of the 13th Infantry on New Georgia. He began by organizing an ambush, and thereafter on Arundel dealing with ambushes became a way of life for the invaders.

Admiral Halsey's plans for the future movement up the Solomons chain depended on reduction of any and all points that could cause trouble for the future. At Arundel nothing seemed to go as planned. After two weeks on the island the troops of the 172nd were bogged down and generally on the defensive.

But the Japanese were not in such good shape either, although the Americans did not know it. By September 5, Kikuda's force was short of supply. They had run out of salt, flour, soy sauce, and powdered bean paste—all the things that made a Japanese soldier's diet palatable—and were subsisting on rice. They were ragged, and many of them went barefooted.

Back on August 20, the Japanese Navy had announced by radio that it would resupply Arundel by September 7. But by September 5 there had been no further word, although there should have been.

The reason the supplies had not come was traceable to the change in policy by the naval command, after the serious losses of destroyers in recent weeks. Destroyers were to be withdrawn as much as possible from the supply system and small boats were to be used to do the job. In fact, seventy boats were sent out, carrying fish, ammunition, and other supplies. But some were sunk, some capsized, some ran aground before they reached the area, and some—captained by seamen unfamiliar with the waters—simply got lost and never arrived.

The Japanese on Kolombangara suffered: the figures showed that 220 tons of supplies were shipped out for that island but that only fourteen tons arrived during this period.

As for the detachment on Arundel Island, they got nothing at all and soon were nearing starvation. There was only one solution: steal the food from the enemy. In a series of night raids they did just that, stealing enough to keep themselves going. During this period the nightly whooping and shouting and shining of lights was not primarily to kill the Americans but to distract them so that other Japanese could get into their supply dumps.

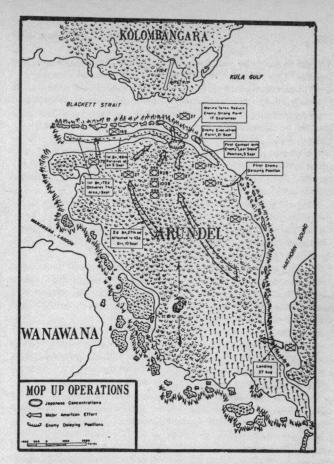

MOP UP OPERATIONS

〰 Japanese Concentrations
⟸ Major American Effort
〰 Enemy Delaying Positions

KOLOMBANGARA

KULA GULF

BLACKETT STRAIT

WANAWANA LAGOON

ARUNDEL

WANAWANA

HATHORN SOUND

Marine Tanks Reduce
Enemy Strong Point
17 September

Enemy Evacuation
Point, 21 Sept

First Contact with
Enemy Last Stand
Position, 5 Sept

First Enemy
Delaying Position

1st Bn, 169th
Relieved on
5 Sept

1st Bn, 172d
Occupies This
Area, 1 Sept

2d Bn 27th Inf
Attached to 43d
Div, 10 Sept

Landing
27 Aug

Arundel Island was in a uniquely difficult position to receive supplies from any point but Kolombangara. Surrounded by American-held territory, except on the north, its waters teemed with enemy craft, and most of the supply boats sent toward Arundel were lost. But by constant effort, General Sasaki managed to get enough food and ammunition across to continue the battle.

Also, all this while, troops of the 13th Regiment were filtering into the island, and by September 10 the Japanese were stepping up the action against the Americans. This was a classic delaying tactic, and it was working.

On September 10, the commander of the 13th Regiment, Colonel Tomonari, visited Arundel and inspired the troops there to further glory. On the morning of September 15, the Japanese staged a counterattack so strenuous that it completely stalled the American advance along the island. The 172nd Infantry had to ask for reinforcement.

When General Griswold heard of the difficulty, he assigned the 27th Infantry and a number of marine tanks to Arundel to clear off that island so the advance up the Solomons chain could begin again. On the night of September 16, the tanks came ashore in a blinding rainstorm and went into position. The next morning they attacked during a rainstorm, supported by the new 27th Infantry troops. They surprised the Japanese completely and managed to gain 500 yards that day. At the rate of 500 yards a day, the Allies would have been able to clear the northwest section of the island in about ten days.

Colonel Douglas Sugg of the 27th Infantry was so pleased with the advance of the 17th that on September 18 he tried the same performance again. But this time he found that the Japanese had brought in two 37 mm antitank guns and placed them in a position that commanded the only tank approaches.

The Japanese opened fire beyond the range the tanks' guns could reach, and before the attack had gotten well under way two of the tanks had been knocked out. The marines escaped from the vehicles only because the U.S. infantrymen were able to lay down a devastating field of fire on the whole Japanese area.

The next day the advance began again. This time the infantry was all around the tanks and shot at anything that moved. The Japanese, who constantly tried to come up close with magnetic mines to stop the tanks, were unable to get close enough. That day the attack made great progress toward the northern tip of Arundel.

When General Sasaki learned of the American reinforcements and the progress of the attack, he decided the 13th Regiment had done all it could, and he withdrew the remaining troops on the night of September 20. His casualties had been high, about 350 dead and about 500 wounded. But they had done precisely what he had asked: they had held up the American advance for more than three weeks, giving General Imamura and Admiral Kusaka time to build up the defenses of Rabaul. He had preserved the bulk of his force in two campaigns, New Georgia and Arundel, and they were ready to be moved north to fight again.

American casualties had not been too high, 44 dead and 256 wounded, because of the enormous fire power of the infantry units. The real casualty had been time.

By the third week of September, the mass evacuation of Japanese from the old forward bases was well under way. They were removed from Buka and all the other bases south of Bougainville. The Japanese were certain this island would be the next point of invasion. They were prepared once again for the same sort of battle of attrition designed to slow the Americans down while Imperial General Headquarters hopefully but not very realistically worked out a new offensive program.

Hopeful Tokyo certainly was, the government guided largely by army officers who had virtually no experience with western powers. Unrealistic it was also, as Admiral Yamamoto and a number of other military figures had pointed out before the war. Japan had extended its resources to the utmost to conquer what it had; there was not enough steel, not enough aluminum, not enough oil to build a new armada and equip whole new armies to fight in the South Pacific.

The Japanese were now moving more rapidly, pushed by the Americans. They harried New Zealand troops advancing through the jungle of Vella Lavella in the same way they had harassed the Americans on Arundel and for the same reason: buying time for General Sasaki. The Allies captured the Japanese barge staging base at Horaniu on September 14. Thereafter Vella Lavella had no further value to the Japanese. All that was left was to evacuate the six or seven hundred Japanese troops left in the northwest corner of the island.

On the day that Arundel Island was evacuated by the Japanese, General Sasaki also moved the troops off Gizo Island to Kolombangara. There were, then, about 10,000 Japanese army and navy personnel on the latter island, and it was the responsibility of General Sasaki and the navy to get them off safely.

Here is the course of events, from the official Japanese history of the war:

September 23. The planning for the Kolombangara Island garrison's withdrawal began. From dawn on, B-24 bombers struck the small boat harbor. The American heavy artillery at Munda bombarded the Vila defense perimeter, destroying one 13 cm gun and killing nine men. From Arundel Island all day long could be heard explosions and engine noises.

September 24. The battle situation was the same. Eight men were killed by sporadic bombardment from Wanawana and Arundel islands. The commander of the 2nd Small Boat Flotilla came to make contact [with General Sasaki] and returned to Choiseul. The time of withdrawal approached, accompanied by heavy American pressure.

September 25. A formation of 59 American bombers attacked. Two 13 cm gun installations were completely entombed by the bombing. In the morning the promontory guns' powder magazine suffered a direct hit and a whole series of explosions began.

Admiral Ijuin was given the responsibility of taking the Japanese troops off Kolombangara. This was to be done in several runs by twenty-five Japanese destroyers during the last, moonless nights of September. They would come to Tuki point, on the north shore of Kolombangara, pick up troops, and then escort the many barges northward.

Given the services of the Pearl Harbor code-breakers, Admiral Wilkinson had advance information that they would do just this, and on September 22 he sent Admiral Merrill's cruiser force up to the waters off Kolombangara to look for the Japanese. The cruisers and destroyers went up the next night and the next, but radio intelligence intercepts could not give them everything, and at first they concentrated on the wrong area and found no Japanese.

Then, on the night of September 25, they were steaming along when a raft of torpedoes began appearing, and one very nearly struck the cruiser *Columbia*. Admiral Wilkinson remembered what had happened to too many American cruisers under similar conditions, and he withdrew the Merrill force. He substituted a destroyer patrol. But when the destroyers came up at night, they were snooped on by the Japanese float planes. The airmen dropped the special flares that warned the Japanese that American destroyers were about—and dropped them right over the destroyers for the most part. This spotlighting impeded the Americans no end.

In fact, the Americans were singularly blind to the Japanese evacuation system, as the events of the next few days showed.

September 27 was the beginning of the heavy traffic out of Kolombangara. That morning the Americans began a whole series of air strikes against the island, indicating the buildup of the sort of pressure that in the past had signaled an American invasion.

The pressure was particularly felt in the stepped-up American air effort against troop concentration points, to try to stop the withdrawal. That day American planes hit Kolombangara all day long. The east wharf was attacked at 7:54 in the morning by seventy-seven bombers, then by a lone P-38, next by a B-25, again at nine o'clock by four F4Us, and by another four navy fighters early in the afternoon. The Jaku base was hit just about as frequently.

All this American effort really did not put much of a damper on the withdrawal. When evening came, two groups of daihatsus (armed barges, something like American LCIs) set out from Choiseul bound for Kolombangara. The plan called for them to go into shore, load up with troops, and then meet their covering destroyers just offshore. Obviously proper timing was an essential to the success of such a program.

The No. 2 Barge Squadron set out from Choiseul Island at 5:30 P.M. for Kolombangara. At about ten o'clock the Tanegashima unit encountered four PT boats and what they thought were four American destroyers. The destroyers were actually five: Captain M. J. Gillan's *Ausburne*, *Claxton*, *Dyson*, *Spence*, and *Foote*. In the resulting action three Japanese army barges were lost and one navy barge was sunk. Personnel loss was limited to fifty-one men, because Ensign Gidan Takenaka had the presence of mind to beach the other boats. He was helped immeasurably by the float planes' bedeviling of the U.S. destroyers.

The timing worked very well. Precisely as written in the orders, the barges arrived in two sections. They picked up 800 men and moved outside Gatsu point, where the destroyers were waiting. The destroyers escorted them to Buna. They did not see an American craft or plane, and there was no hitch of any kind.

The next day, September 28, even bigger plans were afoot. The barges picked up 2,685 troops that night and took them out to the destroyer transports *Satsuki*, *Minazuki*, *Ayazuki*, and *Amagiri*, which were waiting just offshore. The destroyers then sped north toward Rabaul, since they had most of the sick and wounded from the last of the New Georgia campaign on board.

Immediately after the destroyers had left, a number of American PT boats showed up and attacked the daihatsus. Although they were too late to affect the troop withdrawal they did play hob with the Japanese barges. Two of these ran aground in their frantic maneuvering to get away. Within the next two days they were bombed and strafed and wrecked by American planes.

The next big mission, six destroyers again, moved out from Taihei Beach. The destroyers anchored offshore, and the daihatsus brought the troops out. This was an aspect of the evacuation that the Americans missed—they believed that the whole evacuation was being carried out by daihatsus and that the only function of the destroyers was to guard the flotillas of smaller craft. The fact was that the Japanese followed both schemes.

Sometimes there was trouble. On September 29, the daihatsus came into Jaku Bay to pick up a number of troops. The procedure then was to move on up to the north cape of Kolombangara, where the destroyers were waiting for the small craft and their human cargoes. But in this case the plan was disrupted by American PT boats, and the daihatsus had to hole up in bays along the shore. And the next day, they made their way cautiously across to Choiseul.

The moment one trip ended, the destroyers turned about and came back. At Tsukino Point, the navy's Tanegashima Daihatsu Squadron picked up five hundred men, and at Shonami Harbor they picked up four hundred men. They missed the destroyer contact and had to make their way across a mirror sea, brightly lit by the full moon. The trip from Kolombangara to Choiseul took six long, fretful hours. The squadron commander felt very lucky that every boat arrived safely.

The next to last rescue mission of that day, September 29, set out just before 8:00 P.M. from Kolombangara. Suddenly, up came a force the skippers identified as three American destroyers and a cruiser. The Japanese craft scattered like leaves in the wind, each skipper getting every last surge of power out of his engines as he moved to get away. Then up came several American PT boats to add to the confusion.

Meanwhile, with all the activity there, the last mission, consisting of four other daihatsus, moved in to Tsukino Point and took off 329 men without incident.

The U.S. PT boats were always a problem for the Japanese daihatsus, if they were about. On September 30, off Kolombangara's North Point, several PT boats completely disrupted the attempt to move the troops out to Choiseul.

The American craft discovered the Japanese at 7:45 P.M. The No. 1 Daihatsu was hard hit but made it to the west side of Sunbi Island, where she got her sixty-five men off before sinking like a stone. The No. 2 Daihatsu managed to land seventy-three men at Sunbi after she was damaged. The No. 3 boat, which was carrying ninety men, was sunk offshore, but her men were rescued. The No. 4 boat arrived safely having managed to sneak away from the PT boats. In all this action, the Japanese claimed that only six men were lost.

That last mission on September 30 brought an end to the first phase of the Kolombangara evacuation. At that point, the Rabaul high command decided on a change in direction, because the evacuation of the ten thousand men on Kolombangara was taking far too long. At Rabaul it seemed far too dangerous to continue going on the way they had for the past few weeks. The American air and naval pressure grew stronger every day. At Rabaul the staff officers predicted that they would soon run into disaster, which meant loss of ships. And ships were like diamonds these days.

To the men involved in carrying out the withdrawal, the new policy came as a dreadful shock.

Higher authority decreed that the withdrawal should be *suspended*, because the program was straining the fleet's destroyer resources. What somebody up top was talking about, obviously, was abandoning all the men south of Bougainville to the mercies of the enemy. The commander of the 8th Fleet gave the order.

Many officers saw in the delay the death warrant for eight thousand men still on Kolombangara.

For two days the debate continued at Rabaul, until finally the matter was decided. General Imamura and Admiral Kusaka were convinced that it would be worse than useless to leave those men to die. So the command issued reaffirming orders:

Every man on Kolombangara will be rescued.

And so, on October 1, 1943, the rescue missions began again.

At Rabaul the destroyer command made preparations for the first trip, which would bring the destroyers to the north end of Kolombangara. They would continue for the next week, on an emergency basis. Having set the policy, Rabaul command was going flat-out to do the job.

It all worked almost like clockwork, under the noses of the Americans, just as the Guadalcanal evacuation had been carried out.

By the end of the week, the Kolombangara withdrawal was complete; virtually all of the ten thousand men had been taken off safely and moved either to Bougainville or to Rabaul. The command boasted to Tokyo that not one man in a hundred had been left behind.

Given the Japanese decision to make the ultimate effort, what would have happened if Admiral Wilkinson had persisted in maintaining the cruisers up north is a matter for conjecture around the winter fire. Quite possibly he would have lost a cruiser or two without seriously impeding the Japanese action, because the Japanese technique of evacuation eliminated the need for the destroyers to stand in dangerous harbors and wait like sitting ducks. The Japanese destroyers were ready to fight to protect the troops in the small boats. Certainly it would have been useful to the Allies to have stopped the retreat of those ten thousand men, but they were not in a position to do so, particularly since the Japanese were prepared to throw everything they had at Truk into the scale to accomplish this evacuation.

The Americans continued routine patrols, and in these the U.S. destroyers did sink some barges; they also caught the submarine *I-20* on the surface and sank her. Once or twice they chased Japanese destroyer groups, and in one running fight they put a few holes in the topside of the destroyer *Samidare*, but they did not really accomplish much.

Historian Samuel Eliot Morison faults the U.S. Navy for not understanding the Japanese evacuation techniques and for misuse of planes, ships, and PT boats. It all went back to the basic unfamiliarity of the Americans with night-fighting techniques. Planes and PT boats and ships got their signals mixed up, and the cruiser and destroyer officers were perhaps afraid of being torpedoed or bombed as much by their friends as by their enemies. The Americans were still not very comfortable in fighting night naval actions, although by far the majority of the fighting in the South Pacific had been, and would be, at night.

In view of later developments in the southern islands, it comes as something of a surprise to learn the extent of the effort the Japanese devoted to rescuing six or seven hundred men from Vella Lavella in the face of an approaching enemy.

The Americans were literally swarming around Vella Lavella. Yet the Japanese were to employ nine destroyers to defend the barge and subchaser flotilla that would actually take the troops from Vella Lavella to Buin, a distance of about fifty miles.

The whole fleet numbered nine destroyers, four subchasers, and twenty barges. Admiral Ijuin was again in command. There is an interesting comparison between the manner of operation of Admiral Ijuin and one of his predecessors, Admiral Raizo Tanaka, who was, on the record, the best destroyer commander the Japanese ever had.

Tanaka had been given the first of the "special missions" during the Guadalcanal days. At that time the Japanese Navy expected him to fight and deliver troops and supplies, and while placing a high priority on delivery, higher authority did not relieve the commander of the responsibility for winning a naval action at the same time.

After several dangerous missions, Tanaka had the temerity to argue with Admiral Yamamoto that the use of destroyers to land supplies and reinforce troops was a misuse of weapons. Thereby Admiral Tanaka wrecked his career. Yamamoto hustled him out of the South Pacific and he ended up running a sleepy navy yard in Rangoon.

Admiral Ijuin was working under no such handicaps. He had already shown that he felt his primary responsibility was to his ships, and if necessary he would abandon a mission or delay it to keep out of a battle that might diminish the South Pacific's already strained destroyer fleet; and what Ijuin was doing was completely acceptable to his superiors. So much had the Pacific War already changed. The high officers of the Japanese general staff still refused to think of themselves as on the defensive, except temporarily, but the facts spoke for themselves to the officers in the field.

Before dawn on the morning of October 6, Admiral Ijuin set sail from Rabaul with six fighting destroyers, escorting three transport destroyers. Along the way they would pick up a number of subchasers, torpedo boats, and barges. They would then evacuate the troops from the tip of Vella Lavella to Buin.

Admiral Ijuin was commanding the force from the destroyer *Aki-*

gumo. He was operating with a simple plan that he had used before successfully: his first group of four fast new destroyers (*Akigumo*, *Kazegumo*, *Yugumo*, and *Isokaze*) were all rated at thirty-five knots. They would search for the enemy and engage him if he came out to attack the transport train. Meanwhile Captain Tameichi Hara, with the slower *Shigure* and *Samidare*, would be prepared to strike the enemy from another angle. And while the fighting destroyers kept the enemy at bay, the transports would slip off and do their work. This plan had worked to perfection several times in the past few months and so was highly regarded at Rabaul.

The problem, of course, was that the Americans had enough experience with this sort of operation to know what to expect. That was Captain Hara's argument, but it went unheeded.

October 6 was the sort of day the Japanese liked, dark and squally, which gave the Japanese a greater feeling of security against air attack as they moved down along the east coast of Bougainville. But their sense of security was misplaced. Their operational plan had been broadcast to the commander of the Combined Fleet, and the American radio interceptors had picked it up. At Pearl Harbor the message was decoded long before the ships set out, and Admiral Halsey soon had the word. He advised Admiral Wilkinson that the Japanese would be coming down the Slot to Marquana Bay to reach Vella Lavella, and he told when they would come and in what number.

Sure enough, on the afternoon of October 6, an American search plane spotted the Japanese ships as they moved south, and a report was sent to Admiral Wilkinson.

Admiral Wilkinson had a serious problem: the American destroyer force was heavily occupied just then in escorting convoys to Guadalcanal and Munda. The only three destroyers actually uncommitted were the *Selfridge*, *Chevalier*, and *O'Bannon*, under command of Captain Frank Walker, which had been assigned to the patrol of the Slot against Japanese troop movement. But since there were so many more Japanese ships involved, Wilkinson also detailed Captain Harold Larson with the *Ralph Talbot*, *Lavallette*, and *Taylor*, to leave his convoy and hurry to Marquana Bay to intercept the enemy.

In midafternoon, when the Japanese knew they had been spotted by the American plane, they altered their formation, increasing the distance between ships and between the three groups of ships.

They expected air attack within a matter of hours. But the weather was so foul that no air attack arrived, although off Choiseul they did become aware of a number of planes that could not find them in the squalls.

At sunset Admiral Ijuin detached his fast destroyers from the rest of the group and sped along with them toward Vella Lavella. He intended to intercept any Americans who were about. The other ships, as ordered, slowed to nine knots and stood toward the Shortlands. The barges and patrol craft were to come out soon after dark, and these other destroyers would escort them to the rendezvous and stand guard while they and the troop carriers picked up the sailors and soldiers on Vella Lavella.

After dark, also, the ubiquitous Japanese float planes were out, and they came close enough to Captain Walker's force that he figured he had been "spooked" and thus deprived of the element of surprise. That was not quite true. But the Japanese did make visual contact with the Americans before the American radar caught the Japanese. The reason was probably the moving of the squalls that tended to distort the radar reception with static.

Admiral Ijuin then considered how to deal with the American destroyers. (He believed there were four of them.) As he was making a plan, his radio officer announced receipt of a message that four enemy cruisers and three more destroyers were moving west around Vella Lavella.

This report gave Admiral Ijuin a great deal of concern. His destroyer force was not capable of dealing with four cruisers very satisfactorily. So the Admiral issued an order to his captains to be prepared to reverse course (abandon the mission) on a moment's notice.

Actually, that second report referred to Captain Larson's group of three destroyers and represented bad reporting by an inexperienced pilot.

Captain Walker's three destroyers moved steadily toward Marquana Bay, and at 10:30 that night they made contact with the Japanese. The two sides then began maneuvering, while the transports moved in to Marquana Bay to pick up the troops.

Admiral Ijuin led the enemy away from Marquana Bay.

When they were about six miles apart, Admiral Ijuin suddenly ordered his ships to turn left and prepare to attack with torpedoes. At the same time, Captain Walker prepared to open fire with his guns and did. The shells began heading toward the lead Japanese ship, the *Yugumo*. Some began to strike. One or two disabled her rudder.

Then the Americans fired torpedos, and one of these headed toward the *Yugumo*. Her captain could not maneuver to escape, and the torpedo struck her squarely in the side. The ship began to burn brightly and slow down. The Americans shifted their fire to the *Shigure* and the *Samidare*. But they made the mistake of thinking the *Yugomo*, which was obviously dying, was out of the fight. The *Yugumo* fired torpedoes, and one of these hit the American destroyer *Chevalier*.

The torpedo struck her in the port bow, just opposite the forward magazine, and the combined power of torpedo and ammunition blew apart the entire forward part of the ship as far back as the bridge. The engines kept turning, and the forward motion threatened to drive the *Chevalier* under until the captain got a message to the engine room to back engines. At the same time he told a signalman to use his blinker to warn the *O'Bannon*, which was just behind.

But the signalman, who had been knocked about by the blast, fainted before he could send the message. The *O'Bannon* came charging up as the *Chevalier* backed, and the *O'Bannon* rammed into the starboard side of the ship, her bow penetrating the *Chevalier*'s aft engine room.

Probably the failure of the signalman made no difference. In the heat of the battle and given the sudden slowing of the *Chevalier*, the collision would seem to have been inevitable.

The *Selfridge* continued to try to close on the Japanese. But the range was too great for the American torpedoes to reach the Japanese ships beyond the *Yugumo*. It was not, however, too great for the Japanese torpedoes. Earlier, during the wild maneuvering, the Japanese destroyers *Shigure* and *Samidare* had launched sixteen torpedoes. The *Selfridge* ran smack into one of these, and the explosion caused her to slow down and take water. There were many casualties, but fortunately no vital parts were destroyed nor were the magazines hit.

By this time the three original American destroyers were out of the fight, but the three commanded by Captain Larson were just nearing the scene so they could get into it. As they came up, they were spotted by one of the Japanese float planes, which warned Admiral Ijuin. Believing that at least three American cruisers were now descending on him, Admiral Ijuin turned and headed back for Rabaul, and the battle for Vella Lavella came to an end.

The result was a victory for the Japanese in every sense. The troop transport destroyers had broken off at the first sign of action and headed for Vella Lavella's north shore base. Within the hour of arrival they were loading the six or seven hundred troops and an hour later were under way. Vella Lavella was evacuated without the loss of a man.

The loss of life aboard the sunken Japanese destroyer *Yugumo* was believed to be complete, but in fact about a third of the crewmen were rescued by American PT boats. That is remarkable, first that the Japanese would submit to rescue, and second that the Americans would

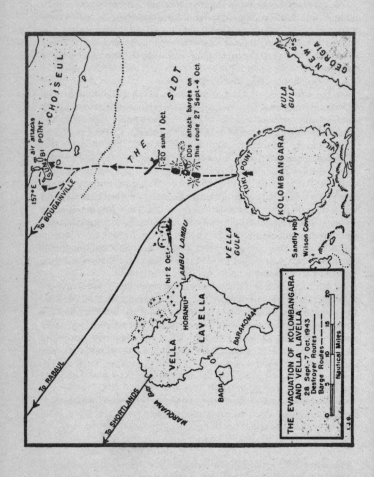

THE EVACUATION OF KOLOMBANGARA
AND VELLA LAVELLA
28 Sept.-7 Oct. 1943
Destroyer Routes ———
Barge Routes +++++
Nautical Miles

continue the task after one Japanese crewman rewarded an American sailor for a cup of coffee by killing him.

When the battle ended, the *Yugumo* was sunk. The American *Chevalier* had to be sunk by a torpedo from the *Lavallette*. The *Selfridge*'s crew managed to make temporary repairs and get their crippled ship back to Tulagi. The *O'Bannon* made her way back, crippled bow and all, and a few days later was sent home to the United States for a breather and major repair.

Japanese and American intelligence were some time in truly assessing the battle. It was a typical encounter in this campaign of attrition. The Americans came back claiming three destroyers sunk with damage to three or four more. Admiral Ijuin went back to Rabaul believing he had faced a reinforced cruiser force and had sunk two of them, as well as three destroyers.

The Japanese had "won" the engagement, but they had lost another destroyer. The high command was not pleased when Admiral Ijuin reported in. In Japanese fashion, he was not chided, but with considerable fanfare Admiral Kusaka held a party at the officers' club. He and Admiral Samejima, commander of the Eighth Fleet, made much of the presentation of a ceremonial sword and daggers to three of Ijuin's subordinates, without a word for Ijuin's performance.

So much had the war changed that Admiral Ijuin, who had fought his battle and won, was nearly as badly disgraced as had been Admiral Tanaka, who had also won.

Tanaka had knocked out a far superior force but had failed to complete his mission of supplying the Japanese troops on Guadalcanal. Admiral Ijuin had won his battle and carried out the task of withdrawing the troops brilliantly, and still he was in trouble. The official displeasure could be attributed to a growing realization that the war was going badly. And, for the Japanese, indeed it was. With the Battle of Vella Lavella, the campaign for the Central Solomons was over. In spite of the attrition, the Allies had won and were now prepared to move ahead against the Northern Solomons.

A few more victories such as Admiral Ijuin's, said the wags at Rabaul, and the Japanese Navy would lose the war.

17

THE INVASION OF BOUGAINVILLE—1

ADMIRAL Halsey had the Central Solomons, although there were times during the struggle for New Georgia when the campaign had threatened to become a fiasco. The worst problem for the Allies had been the misreading of the difficulties.

The amphibious command had asked for about three times as many troops as it got. The request was rejected because the troops were not available. That lack has to be weighed against the apparent incompetence of the ground command and inexperienced troops.

Furthermore, the Americans still had a good deal to learn about fighting the Japanese at sea. In spite of the enormous advantage of radar, the Allied navy was still not winning all the sea victories by far. The Japanese Army had withdrawn its air forces from the region during the New Georgia campaign. The army claimed the planes were needed to protect army installations and support army moves in New Guinea. The real reason was the same sort of antagonism that had caused the navy pilots to blame the army for the death of Admiral Yamamoto. The cooperation ordered by Tokyo between services was never more than skin deep except under the most rigorous circumstances.

Despite the loss of the army planes, the naval air force was still potent. In fact, the Japanese Army Air Force never did amount to much in the

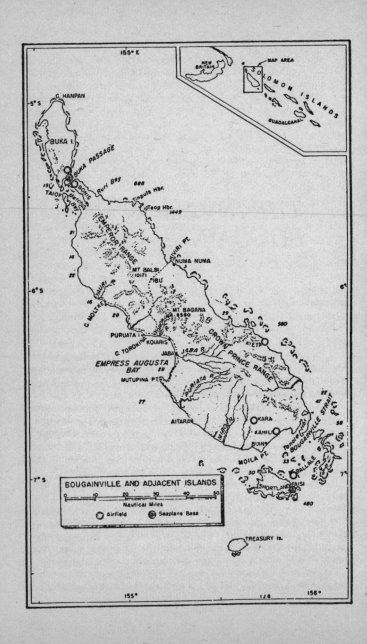

BOUGAINVILLE AND ADJACENT ISLANDS

Solomons campaigns. Its pilots were simply not well enough trained in that sort of combat. Perhaps encounters with the Japanese army pilots accounted for the "easy" victories claimed by many American fliers. In any event, Americans tended to overexaggerate their victories and underplay those of the enemy. (This was a weakness shared by the Japanese, at great cost to themselves.) The most serious American error, perhaps, was to overestimate the numbers of Japanese casualties and underestimate the Japanese ability to withdraw troops. Admiral Halsey, who was fond of hyperbole, asserted that all Americans could fight better than all Japanese. How much better they were supposed to be depended on the mood of the moment; the degree of superiority ranged as high as twenty times better.

In the fall of 1943, there was still reason for this exaggeration, however. Halsey had ended the Guadalcanal campaign with the assertion that the Japanese were not "supermen," an opinion Tokyo's propagandists had fostered successfully throughout the world in the first halcyon days of their war. A subtle fear that such might be the case had penetrated deep into the American psyche, as Halsey knew so well. His constant stream of verbal abuse against the Japanese ("The little yellow bastards . . . kill Japs, kill Japs, kill more Japs . . .") was really carefully measured propaganda for troop and American home consumption, for Halsey understood the American press and its relationship to the public better than any other commander except MacArthur.

In spite of the difficulties, Halsey had pulled off the victory and in October 1943 was ready to take the next step toward Rabaul—the capture of Bougainville.

As the Japanese in the South Pacific knew very well, the battle for Bougainville was going to be far more difficult than the one for New Georgia and even more difficult than the battle for Guadalcanal, because Bougainville is the premier island of the Solomons, a hundred and thirty miles long and thirty miles wide, with about the land area of the big island of Hawaii. It was not the land area but the large number of bays and landing places that would give trouble.

Weeks before the evacuation of Kolombangara, the Japanese had known what to expect. Soldiers moving around on Bougainville had found carelessly discarded American K-ration boxes at several points near the coastline. Japanese intelligence deduced that the Americans were searching for the most favorable point to stage a landing. Fortunately for the Americans, the boxes were found at widely disparate points, so they did not tip off the location of the coming landings.

For Japanese morale, it was just as well that the Japanese soldiers and sailors in the South Pacific were not aware of the futile nature of their defense activities. In the spring, before the New Georgia landings, the Imperial General Staff had, as noted, written off the whole area south of Truk and Rabaul. That was the reason for Admiral Kusaka's hesitation in completing the evacuation of Kolombangara. But on September 30 Imperial Headquarters had instructed Admiral Kusaka and General Imamura to hold as long as possible all along the southeastern front. Despite talk of "victory" the Imperial General Staff was under no illusions. The orders did not call for any last-man stands. The orders were in no way peremptory; they used such terms as "make every effort" and were, in fact, most reasonable.

These new instructions from Tokyo indicated that Rabaul must be the center of this defense line. The Japanese in the field were asked to make that "effort" to "repulse all enemy attacks," by "protracted defense" at Bougainville and in Northern New Guinea. These are not the words of winners. The Imperial High Command had in no sense changed its strategic aim of the spring. The generals and admirals had simply persuaded themselves that the Northern Solomons and New Guinea were to be held as long as possible—without real possibility of success— to give Tokyo time. The time was for the buildup and execution of offensives on two other fronts: China, where the Imperial Army was to drive into Chungking, and India, where the army was to attack along the western border of Burma and drive through Imphal, toward Afghanistan.

After the Imperial General Headquarters had laid out the general defense program for senior commanders, they passed it along. General Imamura, commander of the Eighth Area Army, prepared a special message for all the units under his general command. This went out in a package with his own interpretation of the Imperial Staff's policy declaration. On the right-hand side of the page (reading up and down, as Japanese does) was printed the Imperial General Staff's text. On the left-hand side of the page was a detailed explanation of the policy and general orders as well as Imamura's instructions to every unit—from the 17th Army Command down to the divisional and even regimental level—concerning their specific responsibilities under the new orders. He used the word *rei* meaning servant and follower—but also slave—to define the relationship of every serviceman to the emperor and to country.

That usage indicated the seriousness with which General Imamura regarded the obligation to defend the positions to which they were assigned. Something new had been added: for the first time the spirit of Bushido was being invoked as a matter of military policy.

In essence, what General Imamura said was that each unit had the responsibility to fight the delaying action asked by Tokyo—to fight to the end.

As the troops from Kolombangara and the other central Solomon islands were brought back to safer Japanese areas, they were concentrated on Bougainville. Actually, the buildup of Bougainville as a base had begun under Admiral Yamamoto many months earlier. This big island was to be the staging area for renewed attacks on Allied positions to the south and east. In terms of material and installations, Bougainville was in a better position to serve that purpose than had been either New Georgia or the abandoned Kolombangara.

Admiral Yamamoto, too, had supervised the cleanup of enemy intelligence activities on this island. He was helped in this by German missionaries, who had no sympathy for the Americans and Australians, and who secured for the Japanese native support in locating the Allied coast watchers. By the end of June 1943, coast watcher Jack Read had to report that after fifteen months of occupation, Bougainville had become thoroughly pro-Japanese. None of the native Bougainvilleans could be trusted. Several parties of coast watchers and downed fliers had been betrayed to the enemy. He was unable to secure up-to-date intelligence about Japanese movements and unable to move around the island safely.

Read called for evacuation of all the coast watchers from the island. Consequently, all of these coast watchers were withdrawn in July 1943, and for the first time since the opening of the Guadalcanal campaign, the Allies seemed to have lost the intelligence advantage. After the initial impact of return to civilization had worn off, as the planners planned at Noumea and Brisbane, several of the old Bougainville coast watchers schemed and agitated in Sydney, trying to convince higher authority that they could go back into Bougainville before the invasion and make themselves useful.

As for the Americans, the realization that the Japanese army forces on the ground were far more formidable than they had appeared at Guadalcanal brought about a change in Halsey's plans for the move northward, even as the fighting wound down in the Central Solomons.

Originally, the step after New Georgia and Vella Lavella was to be up to the Shortland Islands. Since the beginning of the South Pacific campaign these islands had been a major Japanese base for sea and air operations. But in September, Halsey's subordinate commanders agreed that this approach must be abandoned. At first they suggested an attack on Choiseul, the next big island up the Solomons chain, almost opposite Vella Lavella. But the main object of this whole drive was to isolate and destroy Rabaul as a base, and Choiseul was still too far away from Rabaul to permit ready air attack. This point was made by General MacArthur when the South Pacific plans were brought to him, and since he was the overall commander, those plans were changed. The next move was to be to Bougainville.

Learning of this, the coast watchers renewed their battle to return to Bougainville, and in October it was agreed that the attempt would be made. Captain Eric Robinson, usually known as Wobbie because of a lisp, led a party that would land in the north. Coast watcher Keenan, another veteran of Bougainville, led a party to the south. Keenan's party was landed on the southwest coast on October 26 by the submarine *Guardfish*, and the submarine then continued north to disembark Wobbie's party. The latter landed between two Japanese camps and played hide and seek with the enemy for the next day or so, before getting situated so as to call for numerous air strikes on Japanese positions when the time came.

By the end of October, the Japanese had moved many men onto Bougainville. The island was headquarters for the Northern Solomons Defense Force. Around the Buin airfield, the 17th Army and the Sixth Division had 15,000 men. The navy's Eighth Fleet had several hundred more men there and at the No. 1 Base Headquarters at Shortland Bay, which consisted of about 6,800 men. Also the South Seas No. 4 Garrison consisted of 5,000 men, plus the navy's coast artillery battalions at the Shortlands and Ballale Island. Ballale with its airfield was a completely navy operation.

In the Gazera Bay (Empress Augusta Bay) area the army had stationed about 3,000 men, most of them in the south. The navy had 200 men there. At the Buka air base and the installations around it, the army stationed 5,000 men and the navy 1,000 men.

Most of the force was in the south where Kahili, Kieta, and Kara airfields were located. By far the most important of these was Kahili. The next largest force was established on the north tip of the island, on both sides of the narrow Buka passage that separates Buka Island from Bougainville. Two important airfields were located there, Bonis and Buka.

The area chosen by Admiral Halsey and his staff was at Empress Augusta Bay, a large semicircular indentation on the western side of the island. The specific point of landing would be at Cape Torokina on the north end of the bay. In a sense the choice was inevitable; the only other practical landing place was on the other side of the island, and that would have involved running the gamut of Japanese air bases from Choiseul to Rabaul. The great deficiencies of this landing place were the terrain, a low, swampy coastline, and the anchorage, which was unsuitable for large vessels. But Empress Augusta Bay it was to be.

By mid-October the Japanese were certainly expecting something, but they did not know quite what. Admiral Koga, the chief of the Combined Fleet, had been bringing in aircraft to reinforce the Eleventh Air Fleet for two months, and more than seven hundred planes had come down the pipeline from Japan. Some of these had been lost in the battles over New Georgia and Kolombangara, but the strength of the force was growing. In October, Koga added to it by assigning planes from the carrier fleet to the shore. He was planning another major air operation to slow the Americans down.

The Allied air forces were still making inroads into the Eleventh Air Fleet with heavy air raids. The Fifth U.S. Air Force on New Guinea was devoting its attention to Rabaul, which was still too far from American bases in the Solomons for effective attack. Admiral Halsey's planes were attacking Bougainville. Here again, the war was reversed. The Japanese had staged at Munda to attack Guadalcanal. Now the Americans at Guadalcanal staged at Munda to attack Bougainville. The new Munda base worked day and night to service aircraft that came in, many times after dusk.

The failure of the Japanese airmen to come to grips with new technology and new problems was more apparent than ever. Japanese fighter discipline was limited. Once a fracas in the air began, it seemed to be every man for himself. The Allied airmen, to the contrary, stuck together, and almost always a fighter pilot had a wingman alongside for mutual protection. This difference led to such incidents as the second mission of P-38 Squadron 339 on October 10.

During the first mission of the day, the P-38s had escorted a B-24 bomber force on a raid of Kahili airfield at the southern tip of Bougainville. In this mission the pilots' job was to stick with the "big boys" and protect them from enemy fighter runs. They followed doctrine and still managed to shoot down or damage four Zeros, with no losses of their own.

In the afternoon, after refueling at Munda, the P-38s went on a second mission to escort a PBY Dumbo (rescue plane) that was looking for survivors from a crashed B-24 of the morning mission who had been seen floating in the waters of the Coral Sea. Halfway along, the rescue force was jumped by fifteen Zeros, and a melee began. The Japanese used their old "dogfight" technique, each pilot selecting a target and then going off on his own. The Americans followed discipline, two plane sections sticking together and using scissor tactics for mutual protection. As a result five Zeros were shot down and five more were damaged, while the U.S. loss was limited to one plane that crash-landed at Munda and had to be junked. The pilot walked away.

The American air effort was also causing serious destruction of planes on the ground, as on October 12 when the Fifth Air Force made a major strike of B-25s and B-24s against the Rabaul port and airfields. They caught many planes on the ground and destroyed a number of them.

Admiral Kusaka was eager to begin the new air effort against the American planes that were harrying Rabaul and Bougainville. Even now the myth persisted that Admiral Yamamoto's Operation I of the spring had been effective. Kusaka certainly did speed up his efforts, aided by those planes coming down the Tokyo pipeline.

Admiral Koga's plans were delayed, however, when on October 5 the American Pacific Fleet staged a carrier raid on Wake Island. This was the first carrier raid since the raid on Marcus Island early in September, and it was a part of the training program for the growing carrier force that would pave the way for the invasion of the Gilbert Islands in November. Admiral Koga had no way of knowing this, and he suspected that the Americans were preparing to recapture Wake.

Koga's contribution to Japanese strategy since he took over the Combined Fleet from the late Admiral Yamamoto had been to divest himself of day-to-day responsibility for the Southeastern Theater operations, so he could move the Combined Fleet out at a moment's notice to meet any American naval threat. With this suspicion about Wake, he clustered the Combined Fleet at Truk and waited for further developments. They did not come. The Americans were also clustering, at Pearl Harbor, for the forthcoming assault on Tarawa and Makin atolls.

In mid-October, the Japanese renewed their power play, but Admiral Koga and the Rabaul authorities misread the signals. Instead of concentrating their air attacks on the Guadalcanal area, where Admiral Wilkinson was building up his amphibious landing force, the Japanese sent heavy raids against New Guinea.

On October 15, a large formation of Aichi-type 99 dive-bombers (Vals) set out to attack Allied shipping in New Guinea's Ormoc Bay, escorted by about twenty fighters. They took heavy casualties from the P-38s and did little damage. Two days later the Japanese tried again, this time with army planes, the Kawasaki light bombers called Lilys by the Americans. Again, the plane losses far outweighed the damage done.

In the last days of October the Allied raids on Rabaul were staged every flying day. B-24s and B-25s kept plastering Rabaul shipping and the airfields.

American planning for the Bougainville invasion was complete. The ships and men were assembled and assigned to the intricate bits of the jigsaw puzzle that would be the invasion.

From a naval viewpoint, the big problem was shortage. Admiral Halsey wanted as much support from heavy fleet forces as he could get, except for carriers. With the capture of Vella Lavella, he now had a nice string of air bases—three on Guadalcanal, two in the Russells, a big one at Munda, and one on Vella Lavella. Kolombangara having been evacuated, that island's strips were also available if needed.

What he did want was ships—destroyers, cruisers, and battleships. And ships is what he did not get, because Admiral Nimitz estimated that Admiral Koga would not risk the major elements of his fleet in the Solomons. Halsey would have to make do with what he had, except for one exchange of cruiser forces. Admiral Ainsworth's cruisers were returned to Pearl Harbor for work, and Admiral Laurance DuBose's cruiser division was to replace them. Halsey had one group of two carriers, two antiaircraft cruisers, and ten destroyers under Rear Admiral Frederick Sherman, Admiral Merrill's cruisers, and Captain Arleigh Burke's destroyers, plus perhaps another dozen destroyers to cover the Bougainville landings. Later on he would get another carrier group and those cruisers under Rear Admiral DuBose, but they were not yet in place.

On the plus side, what he would have, however, was a ground force—marines—about which there could be no doubt. At the end of the Guadalcanal campaign, Marine General Alexander Vandegrift had been relieved. After he was rested he had drawn the plans for the next major operation, which was to be commanded by Major General Charles Barrett. But Barrett died suddenly on the eve of the invasion and Vandegrift was asked to take over command of the Marine I Amphibious Corps.

At the end of the Central Solomons campaign, the Allied air forces concentrated on blasting the Japanese air installations between Vella Lavella and Rabaul. It was necessary to keep the Japanese down, if possible, on the occasion of the landings. Empress Augusta Bay is just about 200 miles from Rabaul, and if the enemy air force was in full flower, it could do immeasurable harm to the invasion. So every day that weather permitted operations, the Allied planes were in the air, hitting the enemy. As usual, the Allied claim to planes destroyed in these forays was high, about 125, and the claim to planes lost was low, about 25. But what was evident was that the constant attack was keeping the Japanese from mounting effective raids against the American staging areas.

Finally, in the last week of October, all was ready at Guadalcanal, and the forces began to move. The first points of attack would be the Treasury Islands and Choiseul—for two widely different reasons. The landing at the Treasuries was to secure those islands as advance bases for small craft, including PT boats. The landing at Choiseul was simply a feint, to keep the Japanese guessing and take their minds away from Bougainville.

The Treasuries were defended by only a few hundred troops. Rear Admiral George H. Fort was put in charge of the amphibious operations. The initial landings would be carried out by 3,700 troops of the 8th New Zealand Brigade Group under Brigadier R. A. Row. The date was set: October 27.

In the last few days before the invasion, the Allied forces were understandably nervous. Although Admiral Halsey had ordered his air force to neutralize the Japanese fields in the area that day, Admiral Fort and Brigadier Row knew that the Japanese had about 25,000 troops stationed in the Buin–Shortland area at the southern tip of Bougainville and about eighty-five daihatsus to transport them. If they caught wind of the invasion, and acted, they could make it across the seventeen miles from Shortland Island in an hour or two. So surprise was the key word.

The other heartening element was the knowledge that on the same day a landing would be staged at Choiseul, which ought to keep the Japanese off balance.

In mid-October, the New Zealand soldiers and the American sailors practiced landings on Florida Island until they were used to each other's ways. Then, they were loaded aboard transport destroyers and (LCIs landing craft, infantry) for the trip into battle. They were escorted up the Slot by Admiral Merrill's cruiser-destroyer force. As the ships sailed north on the evening of October 26, the Japanese float planes were out, and they dropped a number of flares. Admiral Fort was certain that his invasion fleet had been spotted and looked for trouble that night and the next morning. But Japanese communications were not what they had once been, and the float planes did not get the word back to Rabaul, at least not in time for any serious action that night.

At 5:40 on the morning of October 27, in pea soup weather with rain falling, the first seven destroyers arrived off Stirling Island, which controls Blanche Channel. They began to unload their troops. With the rising of the sun came a northeast wind that blew the clouds away, and for most of the rest of the day the weather was fine and clear.

At six o'clock a fighter cover of thirty-two planes arrived over the invasion beach and began orbiting, prepared for enemy reaction. Destroyers laid down a barrage of five-inch shells on the beach as the small craft carried the invading troops in. The barrage stopped five minutes before they were to land.

The landings were carried out at several points, and they drew very little reaction from the Japanese. On Stirling Island, some boats came under fire from machine guns, mortars, and one 40 mm gun. One boat

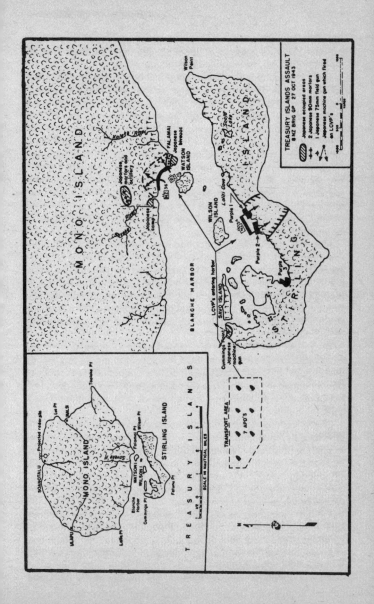

was disabled and thirteen men were wounded. Several LCIs had been converted into gunboats, as an answer to fire from the shore. One of them knocked out the twin-mounted 40 mm guns.

There was no doubt that the Japanese had been surprised. Defensive fire was spotty and slow in coming. In some areas of the landing there was no fire at all. But when the ships began to move into Blanche Harbor, several mountain guns began firing on them. When LST 399 came in to land, she was subjected to mortar fire and received several direct hits. Also, only twenty-five feet back of her landing place was a strong pillbox, which spouted machine gun and rifle fire. When the ramp was lowered and men began moving forward, the first man off was shot dead. So were the second and the third. The captain ordered the ramp closed up. The men aboard could not bring their guns to bear on the pillbox while aboard, and they could not get off. The skipper of the LST asked for permission to back off the beach. It was denied.

Impasse.

Then one of the New Zealanders saw that they had a bulldozer aboard the LST. He climbed aboard and raised the blade of the bulldozer to protect himself against frontal fire. The ramp was lowered, and the bulldozer went rumbling down onto the beach, with a half dozen New Zealanders behind sheltered by the side of the LST, firing their Bren guns to cover him. The bulldozer driver moved around to the blind side of the pillbox, lowered the blade, and plowed. Exit pillbox. Enter New Zealanders.

The Japanese in Rabaul were surprised, as the Allies had hoped, and so no surface forces tried to interdict the early morning landing. But as the landings began, the word flashed to Rabaul, and the first air strike of the day started out for the Treasuries. Zeros arrived in midmorning and began mixing it up with the Allied air patrol, with casualties on both sides.

On the land, the defenders got better organized by noon and began directing effective gunfire from 75 mm mountain guns and mortars against the beach and the ships off Stirling Island. LST 399 took several hits, one of which wrecked her capstan machinery. Then a shell exploded in a dump of ammunition that had just been unloaded, and threatened to destroy LST 399. At last she was given permission to back off the beach and delay her unloading.

The first Japanese bombers arrived over the Treasuries but were met by P-38s at high altitude and P-39s and P-40s down low. A number of the Japanese planes were shot down, and, as important, the attack was frustrated so that no ships were hit, although unloading on the beach had to be suspended for an hour.

The same pattern occurred on the other beaches of the Treasuries where the Allies landed. The most stringent resistance was encountered by the New Zealanders' 29th and 36th battalions that landed near Falamai on Mono Island. They attacked the Japanese headquarters, which was west of the Saveke River. The Japanese here had several heavy machine guns, heavy mortars, and 75 mm mountain guns. The New Zealanders moved in steadily and effectively. Before noon, Second-Lieutenant L. T. G. Booth led a platoon to capture two of the mountain guns, and an hour later he and his men captured a 90 mm mortar. They had only twenty-seven casualties (wounded).

By nightfall, the Japanese had been pushed back into the jungle, and the New Zealander beachhead was secure. That night the Japanese tried to recapture their headquarters area, which held most of their food supply, but they were driven off. The tactics of noise and confusion that had now become familiar to the Americans were new to the New Zealanders, but they weathered the storm well, although they lost two men dead and nine wounded to rifle grenades and sniper fire. Altogether that first day had been successful. The New Zealanders held the islands, and all together Americans and New Zealanders had suffered 115 casualties to take them. The Japanese had removed their dead and wounded, and their casualty figures were unknown.

At Truk and Rabaul, the Japanese high command puzzled over the meaning of the Treasury Islands' invasion. Admiral Koga could not resist the thought that it was a feint. Caught off base at the time of the Vella Lavella landings that had bypassed Kolombangara, the Japanese were now not quite sure what to expect. Their difficulty was increased by the activity on the New Guinea front. For Admiral Koga felt like a cat forced simultaneously to watch two rat holes on opposite ends of the kitchen.

One could draw the conclusion that the air raids on Rabaul, the feint at the Treasuries, and the increased air pressure from New Guinea meant an immediate invasion of New Britain Island.

With that in mind, Admiral Koga watched what the Allies were doing in the Solomons, but he did not take decisive action.

On the other hand, Imperial Headquarters in Tokyo was much aroused by the events of October 27. Tokyo did not much care whether the invasion was to be Bougainville or Choiseul or New Britain. What the Imperial General Staff did care about, desperately, was the maintenance of its long-range plan, called then the Ro Operation. The Ro Operation called upon the Combined Fleet to force the decisive battle on the Americans. Until that time it was absolutely essential that the Southeast Area Command hold out every step of the way, and Tokyo so reminded Admiral Koga on the night of October 27.

On October 28 it rained hard all day. The New Zealanders moved around on the islands, extending their perimeters and investigating. The Japanese moved back doggedly. A few Zeros appeared, and several made low-level strafing attacks on the beaches and exposed positions. Enemy bombers came over and dropped thirty bombs, but these fell harmlessly in the jungle.

The most vigorous fighting in the campaign came at the end, beginning on the last day of October, when the Japanese began a series of strong attacks near Soanatolu on the far side of Mono Island. These troops, the main body of the force on Mono Island, had moved from the Falamai area through the jungle of the Soanatolu River valley. After several skirmishes, they attacked toward the beach on the night of November 1, hoping to seize the American landing craft and get away. The fighting was fierce. Some of the Japanese reached the beach, but there they were stopped and did not get through. The New Zealanders suffered ten casualties. The Japanese left fifty dead on the field. The next night the Japanese tried again to break through, and they were once more driven back. The New Zealanders noticed that the second night's attack did not have the force of the first. That was because the Japanese force was cut in half, and this time it was virtually wiped out. That attack of the night of November 2 was the end of organized Japanese resistance in the Treasury Islands. The first phase of the invasion of Bougainville had been carried off.

18

THE INVASION OF BOUGAINVILLE—2

Choiseul

THE second phase of the Bougainville invasion was much more chancy.

In the planning of the Bougainville invasion, Admiral Halsey had recognized the need for a real diversion in case the Japanese decided to resist in force this new move north. The logical choice was a feint against Choiseul, for if the Americans had not adopted the bypass strategy, Choiseul, as the next island up the chain, was the obvious target for invasion. In fact Choiseul was Halsey's choice until General MacArthur objected to it. So Choiseul had always been in the minds of the South Pacific planners.

To strengthen the Japanese suspicion that this island and the Shortlands would be the next target, Admiral Halsey decided that on the same day that the Allied forces landed in the Treasury Islands, they would stage a commando-type raid on Choiseul. The unit chosen for the action was the 2nd Parachute Battalion of the 1st Marine Parachute Regiment.

For several weeks in September and October 1943, the Choiseul coast watcher, Sub-Lieutenant C. W. Seton of the Royal Australian Navy, had been collecting information about the Japanese and the best landing areas on Choiseul. All this was presented to General Vandegrift and

Admiral Wilkinson at Guadalcanal. Late in October, Lieutenant Colonel Victor H. Krulak, commander of the 2nd Parachute Battalion, was ordered to Wilkinson's headquarters to confer on this raiding operation. At that meeting General Vandegrift laid out the plan. What he wanted was the appearance of a major landing, without the investment of many troops. It was decided that the landing should be made on the beaches of Northwest Choiseul, in the vicinity of Voza Village. Seton had reported that the Choiseul natives were friendly to the Allied cause, unlike their neighbors at Bougainville. The beaches were good for landing. The Japanese installations in the area did not include many troops, although several thousand Japanese were known to be on the island. The 2nd Battalion of the Japanese 23rd Infantry Regiment was located in the northern part of the island, with an outpost at the village of Sangigai.

So the plan called for the landings, an attack or two to establish the fact that a force was ashore, and then the establishment of a patrol base for PT boats.

With that information, Lieutenant Colonel Krulak went back to his 750-man battalion in camp on Vella Lavella, to figure out how to make that number seem like ten times as many.

On the afternoon of October 27, as the Japanese at Rabaul were still reacting to the New Zealand landing in the Treasury Islands, Krulak and his men loaded up four destroyer transports and eight landing craft. Since Japanese air activity around Choiseul had been heavy recently, they stayed alongside the shore until after dark and then headed across the water to Choiseul, escorted by the destroyer *Conway*. The night was just what they wanted, dark and moonless. The sea was calm. There were no Japanese in sight.

But that calm did not last all the way across the Coral Sea. Shortly before midnight, the force was sighted by a Japanese float plane, which dropped a bomb or two. The bombs scored a near miss on one destroyer transport but did no real damage. It was uncomfortable enough, however, for Krulak and his officers to know that they were no longer alone.

At about midnight, the ships reached a point a little more than a mile off the northwest coast of Choiseul and pulled up. The landing began. Coast watcher Seton was waiting for the marines with about eighty natives who would carry supplies.

Another Japanese float plane came over and dropped two bombs near the *Conway*. No harm was done, except to increase the tension of the men on the ships and those going ashore.

By two o'clock in the morning, the landing was complete and the ships were beginning to move away from Choiseul, leaving behind only four small landing craft for the marines' use in scouting.

Coast watcher Seton led the battalion across the beach, then into the jungle and up a trail until, at six o'clock in the morning, they had reached a wooded plateau a mile above Voza. This point was to be the base of operations, with outposts up and down the beach.

The Japanese now knew the Allies had come—but just where they had landed was a different matter. After the marines had moved inshore, a party of natives had gone back to the beach and brushed away every boat mark, every boot track, every sign of a landing of foreigners. In the morning, Japanese planes came over, searched the area, and bombed, but without effect. They had not discovered the hiding place of the marines.

The next step for Lieutenant Colonel Krulak was to let the Japanese know, incontrovertibly, that the marines had landed. He led a patrol to the bank of the Vagara River, where the marines discovered a handful of Japanese unloading a daihatsu. The marines took cover and ambushed the Japanese. They sank the landing barge, killed seven Japanese, and left the bodies on the beach. That would make the point.

That same day, a squad of marines of Company F went out on another patrol in the Vagara River vicinity. They were supposed to set up an ambush for any Japanese patrol that came along, too, but they did not fare so well. They encountered a Japanese patrol and got into a fight. When it was over the sergeant in command could find only two of his men. So who had ambushed whom?

On October 29, Lieutenant Colonel Krulak decided to make an attack on the Japanese positions at Sangigai. It was scheduled for the next day. He ordered up an air strike. Dutifully, at 6:10 on the morning of October 30, a dozen TBF bombers and twenty-six navy fighters came in to drop two tons of bombs in the area.

At that point there were about 150 Japanese at Sangigai, but reinforcements were not far away to the south, and they could be expected to show up soon after the bombing. The marines were already in motion, moving up to Voza Village, where they found the rest of the missing squad, intact.

The battalion then waited for landing craft to come up and take them to the vicinity of the Vagara River. When the boats showed up, however, they were mistakenly identified by some of those attacking planes as Japanese and strafed until one marine pulled out an American flag and began waving it. The aviators then ceased and desisted, and buzzed them, giving the thumbs up sign. Since nobody had been hurt, the marines could return it without too many curses.

The "friendly" air attack had damaged one landing boat, so the battalion had to give up the idea of approaching by sea. Led by local scouts, the men marched until they reached a point near the Vagara River where they ran onto a Japanese outpost.

After firing a few shots, the Japanese fell back to their base at Sangigai. Lieutenant Colonel Krulak then began his attack. He intended to envelope the position; one company would move down the beach line and attack from the north; the rest of the battalion would move inland around Sangigai and attack from the east. They set out.

Company E, coming down the coast had little trouble. Company F, going inland, found the terrain difficult. They were marching through rain forest with its high trees cutting out the light, slippery footing on muddy ground, lianas, creepers, and roots to trip them up. Further, this unit was accompanied by the machine gun section and part of an experimental rocket platoon, and this meant heavy equipment. The going was slow.

H-Hour was supposed to be 2:00 P.M. but at that time E Company was still more than a mile from its objective. When the time came, Krulak listened for the sound of gunfire. There was nothing and he began to conjure visions of ambush. But then the sound of the E Comapny rockets broke the silence. And just then the scouts reported to Krulak that the enemy was dead ahead.

When the small Japanese garrison of Sangigai learned of the impending attack by a much larger force, they withdrew from the village toward prepared positions in the mountains. Thus the coastal column had no difficulty in entering Sangigai, which was deserted. But at almost that moment, Krulak's force moved up to the perimeter of the Japanese mountain position, which the Japanese garrison had just reached.

Krulak's men began to move forward, firing. They found the Japanese in bunkers and rifle pits among the huge banyon trees with their multiple trunks that gave such good shelter. Snipers had climbed into the trees and were firing down on the marines.

Krulak sent one platoon around to the enemy's left to flank. It was accompanied by the regimental machine gun platoon, which put two heavy guns forward. The Japanese in the forward line were thus threatened and fell back. But they did not leave easily or quickly, and in the fighting, Colonel Krulak and Captain Spencer Pratt of F Company were both wounded.

The Japanese fell back but almost immediately executed a "banzai charge," in which the Japanese riflemen crawled and wriggled up to the line, and then rushed forward shouting, screaming, hurling grenades, and bayoneting. They penetrated the marine line. The cost was heavy, and this first wave fell back. But it was followed almost immediately by

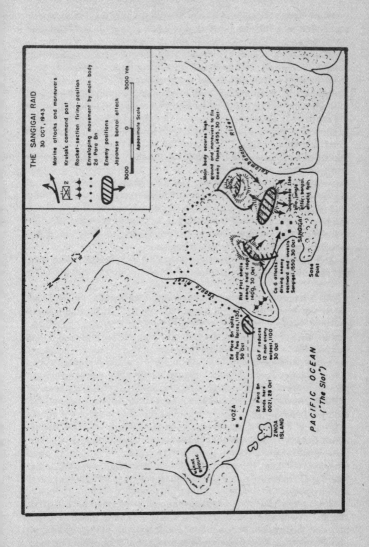

THE SANGIGAI RAID
30 OCT, 1943

Marine attacks and maneuvers
Krulak's command post
Rocket-section firing-position
Enveloping movement by main body 2d Para Bn
Enemy positions
Japanese banzai attack

3000   0   3000 Yds
Approximate Scale

Main body secures high ground and maneuvers to fix enemy flanks, 1455, 30 Oct

Japanese flee into jungle after banzai charge, fails

Rnf Plat meets enemy hold ridge, 1400, 30 Oct

Co G attacks, driving enemy seaward and wrecks Sangigai, 1550, 30 Oct

SANGIGAI

Sosa Point

2d Para Bn splits into two forces, 1130, 30 Oct

Co F reduces 12-man enemy outpost, 1100, 30 Oct

2d Para Bn lands here 0021, 28 Oct

VOZA

ZINOA ISLAND

Inland bivouac

PACIFIC OCEAN
("The Slot")

Colombangara River

another charge. Again the marines' M-1 rifles and the machine guns took a heavy toll. After the Japanese had again retreated, the Americans counted seventy-four Japanese bodies on the field.

But Krulak also had his casualties: six men dead and twelve men wounded, two of them seriously. The marines stopped to bury their dead and then went back to the Vagara River to wait.

Company E had an easy time of it. The men entered Sangigai without opposition and blew up all the Japanese installations with demolition charges. They also destroyed a new daihatsu, and captured a number of Japanese papers, including charts of the Bougainville-Choiseul area that showed a Japanese mine field of the Shortlands area and the daihatsu routes. Company E then turned about and returned to the Vagara River.

The next day, the navy landing boat crews had repaired the damaged boat, and the craft were able to return Krulak's force to the base at Voza. On the afternoon of November 1, a Dumbo plane arrived at Voza and evacuated the wounded to Guadalcanal. The charts of the Japanese mine field were also sent back to Admiral Halsey, and he ordered up a minelaying mission for the Shortlands area.

During the battle for Bougainville at least two Japanese ships were sunk in the middle of channels that appeared on their charts to be perfectly safe.

After destroying the Sangigai garrison, Lieutenant Colonel Krulak had to be ready for a swift Japanese countermove from the south, where the majority of troops were located. He waited. Meanwhile an airdrop replenished the supply of hand grenades (250) and explosives as well as rice for the native carriers and scouts.

The orders had been to make a big noise to frighten the Japanese, and so on October 31 Major Warner Bigger, the battalion executive officer, set out to the north with a large patrol. He learned that the Japanese had already reoccupied Sangigai and were rebuilding the installation there. What the marines did not know was that the immediate area was actually teeming with Japanese who had been brought over from Kolombangara. Bigger encountered several small units but had no way of understanding the significance of these "patrols."

Bigger returned with his report to the base that night, and the next day he set out with ninety men to move up the coast, destroying Japanese outposts, and then shell the small craft base in Choiseul Bay. There was another smaller base on Guppy Island, south of the bay. That was given as an alternative target.

Major Bigger had his difficulties. The maps showed that the Warrior River, which he wanted to use for movement, was navigable by small schooners. But the landing craft continually grounded and the boats had to be abandoned. Bigger's scouts did not really know the terrain and got the unit hopelessly mired down in a swamp. Bigger sent Lieutenant Rea Duncan back with the radio to get in touch with Krulak, and the Japanese moved in between Bigger and Duncan and surrounded Duncan. The lieutenant and his squad managed to break through the line, get to the boats, and make their way to Voza, where he reported that Bigger was cut off.

Lieutenant Colonel Krulak then asked Guadalcanal for an air strike and a PT boat mission against the Japanese in the area, to cover Bigger's retreat.

But Major Bigger did not know that the Japanese were behind him, and on the morning of November 2 he moved on toward Choiseul Bay with the help of a local warrior who did know the terrain. He sent a small patrol back to the Warrior River to tell the boat crews to meet them up

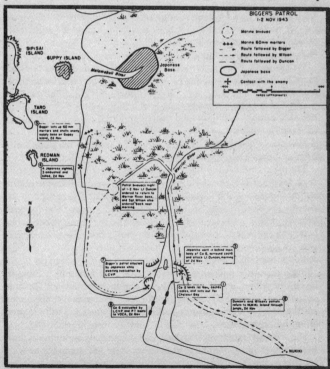

the coast. The patrol ran into the Japanese and had to fight its way through, losing one man, Corporal Winston Gallaher.

Bigger pushed on through the swamp and jungle to Choiseul Bay. He ran into a four-man Japanese patrol. The marines opened fire and killed three of the Japanese, but the fourth man escaped into the jungle, and Bigger had to assume that the American presence would be reported. It seemed too risky to move further toward Choiseul Bay, so he elected to hit the alternative target at Guppy Island, which was a supply dump for the Choiseul Bay area.

The trouble was that the shore facing Guppy Island was overgrown with trees and bushes that hung to the water's edge, so the mortars had to be set in the water, with only their muzzles protruding. It was not the easiest mortar position in the world, but the mortar men managed to put 120 rounds of high explosive shells into the area, and they hit something for a large fire erupted.

Satisfied that he had made enough of a racket to impress the Japanese, Major Bigger then headed back toward his base. He still knew nothing of the Japanese behind him.

When he reached the mouth of the Warrior River, Major Bigger first set up the defense perimeter and then settled down. After a rest, he would send a patrol across the river to make contact with Lieutenant Duncan's patrol, which was supposed to be there. Several of the marines asked for permission to go for a swim, and Bigger gave it.

The marines dove in and began swimming. Upstream, a Japanese patrol was moving along the bank of the river, when one member saw the swimmers. The Japanese immediately opened fire on them—and that is how Major Bigger became aware that he was in the presence of his enemies.

The Japanese moved swiftly down the bank of the river and attacked the marine position, not knowing how strong it was. The paratroopers were not caught napping, and in the firefight their heavier weapons and more rapid rate of fire of the M-1 rifles made the difference. No Americans were hit, but several Japanese were killed or wounded, and the Japanese patrol retired.

Obviously it was not a good idea to bring boats to this side of the river, with the Japanese upstream. Major Bigger sent Lieutenant Samuel Johnston, Platoon Sergeant Frank Muller, and Private Paul Pare to swim across the river to find Duncan and see that the boats did not move across the river. They swam across. What happened next is still a matter for conjecture. One story has it that just as they were about to stand up and walk to the beach, another Japanese patrol fired on them. Private Pare escaped because he was a slow swimmer and had lagged way behind the other two. In any event, it is definite that he turned around and swam back to the western shore of the river and reported to Major Bigger what was happening.

One story has it that Lieutenant Johnston was wounded by the Japanese volley and sank into the water. Sergeant Muller was killed. As Pare swam away, he said he saw a Japanese come to the water's edge and haul Johnston's limp body ashore.

Another story has it that Johnston went on ahead, and managed to make contact with a Choiseulian member of the coast watcher team who led him toward the headquarters. They ran into a patrol, said the coast watcher, and Lieutenant Johnston surrendered.

Whatever had happened, Johnston and Muller were lost.

When Private Pare told his story, at first Major Bigger believed that his patrol had been fired on by Duncan and his men, who had not correctly identified them. Consequently he brought out a large American flag and waved it at the river. The result was a burst of gunfire. That answered the question.

Meanwhile, Lieutenant Duncan was bringing the boats down to the Warrior River. They had just turned in toward the mouth, when the gunfire began. The navy officer in charge of the boats wanted to turn back, but Duncan persuaded him to go on to the west bank. The landing in the rough surf was covered by the marines ashore who turned their full firepower across the river and upstream.

All went well enough, despite the roughening weather and the heavy seas, until one boat took a big wave and the motor flooded. The crew couldn't get it started again. The boat began to drift toward the enemy shore and it seemed inevitable that both the men and the vessel would be lost. Then, like the U.S. Cavalry in the cowboys and Indians movies, a PT boat appeared on the scene.

The marines and the navy crew leaped aboard the PT boat, and the landing craft scuttled itself on a coral reef. Another PT boat came up and the two vessels covered the remaining landing craft while loading and then on the trip up the coast to Voza and safety.

Through captured papers, the Japanese had become aware that the American force on Choiseul was very small. They brought troops up from the south to the village of Vagara, and on November 1, the day that Bigger left to make his alarums and excursions, the Japanese began a concerted move to wipe out the paratroop unit. Their patrols around the perimeter became increasingly aggressive and there were many brief firefights. The Japanese lost several men, and the marines did also.

The coast watchers had reported back to Guadalcanal that the Japanese were moving on the Sangigai area and that at least a thousand of them were there already. General Vandegrift then decided that the best move would be to withdraw the marines while there was time.

There was no way a PT boat base could be built on that shore without bringing in many more troops.

To do that would make Choiseul a major center of action in this phase of the advance, and inviting a major action on Choiseul was not in the Halsey plans.

Vandegrift gave orders that the paratroops were to be prepared to withdraw on the evening of November 3. Since the enemy was closing in on the marines from north and south and had reached a point only five hundred yards from Voza, the preparations had to be elaborate. The marines set up land mine fields and booby traps, using 1,100 pounds of explosive for the mines and 243 booby traps.

After darkness fell and the marines assembled to withdraw, the results began to become apparent. The Japanese were up to their old tricks, but this time, when approaching a marine foxhole, they found not a marine inside but an explosive charge that went off with a satisfying (to the marines) noise. The Japanese infiltration that night slowed down remarkably.

Around midnight, three LCIs showed up on the beach, and the marines began to embark. In twelve minutes they were off the beach and aboard the landing craft. The perimeter remained unbroken, and the movement out was uneventful. The Choiseul feint was ended.

How much good had it done?

It had not, as Halsey's staff had hoped, caused the Japanese to move any large segment of troops into Choiseul. It had cost the Japanese some men, but it had also cost the Americans nine men killed, fourteen wounded, and two missing. What had happened to the missing men was questionable.

As we have seen, there are indications that at least one was captured and that he had enough of the overall Bougainville plan in his possession to show that the Americans had made a feint here and that the major action was to be at Empress Augusta Bay. But as so often happened with the Japanese, the officers at headquarters did not believe the soldiers in the field, and they ignored the warning about place and time. So the captures did not have the significance they might have had.

As far as the American effort was concerned, it had really accomplished very little except the destruction of a few landing barges and several hundred tons of Japanese supplies. To counter that was an unexpected negative. The Japanese jeered that they had driven off a major American landing, and the Choiseul natives tended to believe them. This belief made the coast watchers' job much harder and tended to turn more natives pro-Japanese, as were the Bougainvilleans. The coast watchers, needless to say, were not pleased with the outcome.

But overall, the two feints—at the Treasuries and Choiseul—had kept the Japanese guessing and unprepared at the moment that it was important, those last few hours before the troops were to be put ashore at Empress Augusta Bay. Whatever else they had done, they had bought time and kept Admiral Kusaka and General Imamura a little bit off base.

19

THE INVASION OF BOUGAINVILLE—3

Empress Augusta Bay

IN one sense, the Americans could never have chosen a better spot for a landing on Bougainville than Cape Torokina.

As the Central Solomons campaign had progressed and the 17th Japanese Army had begun to realize that there was a good possibility that they would be defending Bougainville soon, they had looked over the beach areas with an eye to Allied possibilities. They had rejected Cape Torokina as most unlikely because of the low, swampy ground.

Consequently, Lieutenant General Masatane Kanda, the commander of the Japanese Sixth Division, had sent only a single company of the 2nd Battalion of the 23rd Infantry to maintain an outpost there.

But the Americans saw Cape Torokina in a different light. It was the best possible landing spot on the west coast of Bougainville; by landing there the Americans would cut off the Shortlands to the south and bypass a large number of troops. To be sure, these troops could be brought up to fight, but that would take some time. Further, by putting an airstrip in quickly, they would be close enough to Rabaul to attack that base. And Halsey did not forget that the whole reason for this march northward along the Solomon chain was to knock out Rabaul.

To make this landing, Halsey had chosen the 3rd Marine Division. He felt more comfortable with marines than with army soldiers, which was

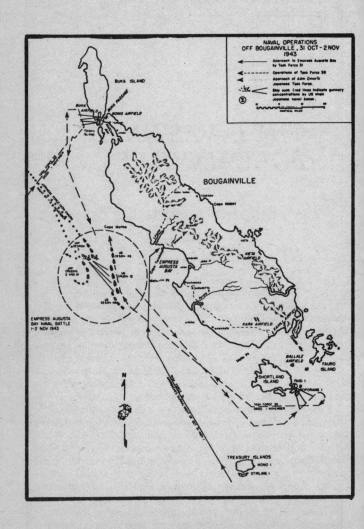

NAVAL OPERATIONS
OFF BOUGAINVILLE , 31 OCT - 2 NOV
1943

Approach to Empress Augusta Bay
by Task Force 31

Operations of Task Force 39

Approach of Adm Omori's
Japanese Task Force.

Ship sunk (red lines indicate gunnery
concentrations by US ships
Japanese naval bases.

BUKA ISLAND

BUKA
AIRFIELD   BONIS AIRFIELD

TSIOH
ISLAND

BOUGAINVILLE

Cape Moari

Cape Moltke

US
DESRON 45

US
CRUDIV
3 AND 40   US
CRUDIV 12

US
DESRON 465

EMPRESS
AUGUSTA
BAY

EMPRESS AUGUSTA
BAY NAVAL BATTLE
1-2 NOV 1943

KIETA
AIRFIELD

KARA AIRFIELD

KAHILI AIRFIELD

BALLALE
AIRFIELD

FAURO
ISLAND

SHORTLAND
ISLAND   FAISI I

POPORANG I

TASK FORCE 39
0400 I NOVEMBER

N

TREASURY ISLANDS
MONO I

STIRLING I

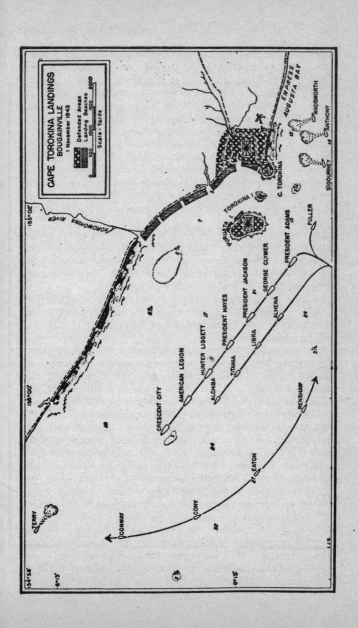

certainly understandable, and particularly so given the performance of the army on New Georgia. Major General A. H. Turnage would command the reinforced marine division, which meant 14,000 troops.

There was plenty of transport for this invasion—troopships and cargo vessels. A dozen of them, guarded by eleven destroyers, eight minesweepers, and a number of other support ships began heading for Bougainville at the end of October. They took several different routes, so that the Japanese search planes would be thrown off. If one unit of four ships was seen, that's how it was reported. The idea was to conceal from the enemy the size and power of the Bougainville landing force.

Before dawn on November 1, the convoys had converged and were moving in along the west side of Bougainville. The ships would stand off, about three miles from the beach, and unload their troops into landing craft.

The day dawned bright and clear. The sun came up at 6:14, and the wind was so slight that the troops lining the rails of the transports could see wisps of smoke curling upward from Mount Bagana, the live volcano that towered over this section of Bougainville. The scene was lush and green, the epitome of the tropical paradise.

As day dawned, the minesweepers moved in ahead of the transports to look for trouble. They found no mines and reported that there was enough water for the transports to follow their plan.

The transports moved in.

The Americans looked toward Cape Torokina and saw no evidence of the enemy. Small wonder, for the total enemy force there was the reinforced company of 270 men, with a single 75 mm gun and a wireless connection to the world. General Kanda had been sure that the Allies would land east of Cape Torokina. There were about 2,500 troops in the area, but they were not readily available for defense.

No one was deceived that this landing would be a cakewalk, however. Rabaul was only a little over two hundred miles away, which meant that within an hour after landing things could start to happen.

Although the army's Fifth Air Force had twice claimed to have knocked out virtually the entire Rabaul air force, it was not true and Halsey knew it was not true. In defense of the army claims, it must be said that the Japanese had become masterful at the arts of camouflage and concealment. All base personnel, even pilots, had to participate in the building of fake aircraft that were cleverly designed to look like Zeros, dive-bombers, torpedo planes, and twin-engined bombers. These were built by the score out of bamboo and paper.

Fifth Air Force planes came over and bombed and strafed, and the mock-up planes burned beautifully. Every pile of bamboo and paper ash became a statistic in the Allied reports. The exaggerated reports of destruction were a real tribute to the Japanese camouflage experts.

Admiral Wilkinson had been director of Naval Intelligence in 1942, and shortly after a stint as a battleship division commander he had gone to work for Halsey as Deputy Commander, South Pacific. So Wilkinson knew all about what had happened in the Guadalcanal campaign before he ever took over from Kelly Turner as commander of the amphibious landings. He had no illusions about Japanese air power. Remembering what had happened at Guadalcanal, he built his whole plan for Bougainville around quick turnaround: get in, get the men and supplies off, and get the transports and cargo ships out of those waters before the Japanese air and sea forces began showing up.

H-Hour, Admiral Wilkinson announced, would be 7:30 A.M.

At 5:45 four destroyers began sporadic fire on the beach.

At 6:45 the transports were anchored in a line with the cargo ships in another line five hundred yards further out. The troops began moving down into the landing craft.

At 7:10 the boats from the *President Adams* began their run in toward the beach. The destroyers increased their rate of fire and began firing patterns aimed to destroy enemy concentrations. Thirty-one TBF bombers from Munda showed up to bomb and strafe along the beach line.

All this softening up had ended by 7:26 when the first wave of marines from the 2nd Battalion landed.

Five minutes later, troops were coming in to the rest of the twelve beach areas assigned. In that first wave, eight thousand troops went ashore.

Eight thousand against 270. But those 270 Japanese were dug in. They had eighteen pillboxes, and connecting tunnels and trenchworks to protect them.

One Japanese platoon with several heavy machine guns was stationed on Puruata Island and a squad was located on Torokina Island. The 75 mm gun was set on the northwest shoulder of Cape Torokina, above the landing area.

The Americans soon became aware of all these facts.

As the landing craft came in line with Puruata Island, they came under fire from machine gun crossfire from the cape, the tip of Puruata Island, and Torokina Island. It was murderous fire, but the boats sped on. They had chosen the only sensible course. The number of casualties was fairly light.

Once the landing craft got inside that deadly crossfire, they were again in trouble, from fire that originated on Cape Torokina itself. The 75 mm gun was so placed as to range along the beaches. During the morning the gunners fired fifty high explosive shells and did a good deal of damage.

Boat No. 21 from the *President Adams* got the full treatment. As the boat neared the beach, it took three shells from the 75 mm gun in rapid succession. The first shell killed the boat's coxswain and the boat went out of control. The second and third shells killed the two officers aboard the landing craft as well as twelve enlisted men. Fourteen others were wounded.

The survivors got over the side and swam to the beach, where they began fighting with rifles and hand grenades.

Meanwhile the dead boat had drifted ashore, still filled with the wounded and the dead. Corporal John McNamara saw that the wounded had to be gotten back to the ship, and he tried to get the landing boat under control. He tried to push the boat off the beach.

It would not move.

He found another man to help him. He and the other man finally got the boat into the water again, got the engine going, and backed the boat into the sea. Having been holed in a number of places, the boat promptly sank. Most of the wounded went down with the boat and the dead. Only four or five men survived.

That 75 mm gun shot up the boat group commander's craft and did so much damage to others that the landing became disorganized. The men began landing catch-as-catch can, and the minute they hit the beach they ran into rifle and machine gun fire from the defenders.

The result was that whole units lost contact with their officers. Surprisingly, however, the individual marines were able to keep moving. Each marine had been told what the mission was, and in spite of the confusion each kept moving ashore and fighting the enemy.

Sergeant Robert A. Owens of the 3d Marines' A Company got ashore and realized that the 75 mm gun was creating havoc on the beach. He set out with his squad to destroy the gun.

He located the gun, which was inside a palm log and sand bunker.

He posted four men to cover the bunkers next to the gun position. Then he started up the hill to hit the gun himself. As he went, he saw that his men were being shot down, one by one, by snipers. But there was no stopping, even though he was soon wounded several times himself. In this instance the small caliber of the enemy rifles worked in one American's favor. He could keep on going, though badly hurt.

He moved up to the gun, crawled through the fire port, firing his weapon, and killed several members of the gun crew. The others fled out the back, where they were shot down by other marines.

Owens emerged through the back of the emplacement and then fell dead from his wounds. When the marines examined the 75 mm gun, they saw that the crew had just placed a new round in the breech as Owens came up, and he had caught them in the act of firing again. They had plenty of ammunition on hand.

This action obviously prevented the enemy from causing many more casualties on the landing beaches, and Owens was awarded the Congressional Medal of Honor, posthumously.

But the 75 mm gun was not the only difficulty. The handful of Japanese were skillful and dedicated. The 2nd Battalion of the 3rd Marines and the 2nd Raider Battalion found themselves all mixed together on the beach. The effective enemy fire had caused the boat crews to hurry in and land at the closest point rather than where they were supposed to.

Lieutenant Colonel Joseph P. McCaffery, commander of the 2nd Raider Battalion rallied his men as they came, confused, out of the boats, and got them going. He kept fighting until he was mortally wounded. By that time the situation was beginning to come under control.

The 3rd Battalion of the 3rd Marines and the 9th Marines landed on beaches that were not so heavily defended as those near the cape, but they had something else to worry about: terrain. The beach dropped off sharply in this area, and the boats could not come in and hold their position. The jungle grew right down to the edge of the water, which did not help any. Soon, boats began to broach, and before the day was out sixty-four LCVPs and twenty-two LCMs were stranded. Many of them did not get unloaded.

The 3rd Battalion of the 2nd Raiders was assigned to take out the Japanese on Puruata Island. The task was harder than it looked. The Japanese had dug in well, their positions were nicely camouflaged, and they were firing from rifle pits and pillboxes. As usual, they had established interlocking fields of fire.

Guadalcanal had taught its lessons; the marines were ready for this development. It was slow going, but inch by inch they combed the island. As night fell, they dug in and kept alert for Japanese activity. When morning came, they went back to the combing, and by noon they had eliminated the Japanese from Puruata Island. They did not take prisoners.

On the first wave, more than half of the 8,000 marines of the assault force got ashore. The rest kept coming. In view of the sheer numbers of Americans, that single company of Japanese defenders did an astounding job of slowing down the marines for most of a day. Those interconnecting trenches seemed to run everywhere. They had snipers in the trees and fallback positions for their machine guns.

By 7:30 in the morning, the Japanese air attack that had worried

Admiral Wilkinson was beginning to come in. The American air force had produced fighter cover over the beaches but the Japanese sent down Zeros and bombers, using the usual technique of stalling the American fighters with the Zeros, while the dive-bombers tried to work their way in. The result was a number of Japanese planes shot down, but some bore in to bomb.

The destroyer *Wadsworth* was hit, and two men were killed. Five others were wounded.

Japanese fighters came roaring over the beaches, strafing, but the marines had been taught that the first thing to do when you stopped moving was to dig—they dug. The strafing casualties were minimal.

All day long the Japanese sent in air attacks, and for the most part they were driven off by the fighter cover. Occasionally a plane got through, but even then the results were not serious, except in one respect. Every air raid caused the stoppage of unloading. Twice during this first day the transports had to haul out and move into deep water to maneuver defensively. That meant the unloading was slowed down. But by the end of the second day all that problem seemed to be solved and the supplies were ashore.

The Japanese fought bravely all the way. By the end of the first day the marines had established three main defensive positions. The Japanese defense force—or what remained of it—had been driven back to a prepared position not far from the west bank of the Piva River, about a mile above the beach.

On the map the marine situation looked good, but in fact the marines were in a dangerous fix. The terrain was virtually a trap. Except for two lines of approach to Cape Torokina, the land was swamp and dense jungle. Attempts to establish lateral communication created enormous difficulties. The jungle was so thick that the troops were lucky to push ahead fifty yards in an hour, whether there were Japanese in front of them or not.

The marines discovered that an old trail to a mission down by the beach led from the Vira River. The 2nd Raiders put up a trail block between the beach and the Japanese position up the mountain.

And the unloading continued.

On November 2, patrols went out all along the beach line to probe up the mountains. On November 3, two platoons from the 3rd Raider Battalion moved to Torokina Island under cover of a bombardment by 75 mm pack howitzers. They found the Japanese had disappeared. At this point, organized resistance in the Torokina area had come to an end. The Seabees began to come in to build roads. Parties set out to find and bury the dead Japanese. They found 192 enemy bodies.

The Japanese, who had retreated from the area, reassembled and counted the men of the 2nd Company, reinforced. Of the 270 men only seventy-eight had survived.

On the Japanese side that day there had been many heroic deeds, but there were no medals for Japanese servicemen. They were expected to die heroically for nation and emperor. In fact, the officers of any unit that gave up its position were subject to a certain criticism for not dying on post. But those Japanese of Torokina (which they called Tarokina) did not deserve the criticism. There had been just too many marines and too much firepower for them to do any better than they had.

On Guadalcanal and the other islands, the American troops had been sorely troubled by the Japanese ability to infiltrate, or to remain silently in position as the battle surged past them, then emerge at night and raise havoc inside the American perimeter. At Bougainville, the Americans had a new weapon—the war dog.

These dogs were Doberman pinschers, long known for their aggressive dispositions. At Bougainville they paid their way immediately by pointing out snipers and concealed Japanese positions. The effectiveness of the old Japanese techniques was reduced, and the worry of the marines at night was lessened.

On the second day, the beachhead was now established to a depth of a little more than a mile. Construction was to be the next step. First, roads and a fighter strip had to be built to make the island defenses work. A bomber field site had to be located and then captured, and various supply dumps had to be located and protected from the air attacks that would be coming.

Right now, the marines had a toehold on Bougainville, and not much more.

20

THE BATTLE OF EMPRESS AUGUSTA BAY

ADMIRAL Halsey knew that Bougainville was too important to the Japanese for the landing there to go unchallenged. He suspected that the Japanese would counter first with an attempt to force a sea battle. Thus, as the amphibious landing ships set out from Guadalcanal and the newer bases in the Central Solomons, so did U.S. Task Force 39—four cruisers and eight destroyers under Admiral Merrill.

The ships sailed at 2:30 on the morning of October 31 to bombard Buka and the Shortlands and to seek battle with any Japanese ships that came down.

Soon they were in the Slot, moving northward. A Japanese search plane spotted them there that morning and radioed the word to Rabaul.

As noted, the Japanese had been surprised by the Allied landings. The landing in the Treasuries had been so inconclusive that Admiral Koga had been unwilling to react. The landing at Choiseul was quickly recognized as a feint, and then it was apparent at Truk and Rabaul that the real landing had to be either on Bougainville or on New Britain if the Allies believed they could take on Rabaul at this particular moment. Still, Admiral Koga had to wait.

But the Japanese counterplan was already in motion. It was the Ro Operation. It was a three-pronged response to the Allied move—on land, on sea, and in the air.

To prepare for Ro Go, the Japanese had been funneling planes down to Rabaul by the score. No American carriers except escort carriers had been reported in the area recently, and Admiral Koga, not expecting to use his carriers, had stripped them of many of their planes and pilots and added these to the strength of the Eleventh Air Fleet.

With the word that the American marines had landed at the Treasuries, the Ro Operations began. Admiral Koga sent a large force of cruisers down to Rabaul. They would escort the counterlanding force to Bougainville and then seek battle with the American cruisers expected to come up from Guadalcanal.

Admiral Sentaro Omori had arrived at Rabaul within the past few hours in the heavy cruiser *Myoko*, with the heavy cruiser *Haguro*. They had escorted a large merchant convoy down from Truk.

Having some second thoughts, Koga had also sent for Admiral Ozawa and the carriers *Shokaku*, *Zuikaku*, and *Zuiho*, but these were at sea and it would be several days before they could reach Rabaul.

Thus, for the first time in months, Admiral Samejima, the commander of the 8th Fleet, had at his disposal a force powerful enough to send out to do battle with the enemy cruisers. He prepared to dispatch Omori southward to find the American cruiser force and destroy it. Omori had the two heavy cruisers, the light cruisers *Sendai* and *Agano*, and seven destroyers.

The one commander in the whole force who was familiar with these waters was Admiral Ijuin, who was assigned to assist Omori. Ijuin went to the flagship on the afternoon of October 31 to confer with Admiral Omori and Admiral Matsubara, who was in command of the *Agano* and three destroyers. Omori had just returned from the homeland and was not up to date on battle tactics. Matsubara was not experienced in night fighting, which Ijuin knew was going to be a problem. At best the Japanese would see the Americans before they were seen, but the American radar had proved to be a growingly effective curse to them. Matsubara's lack of experience could make a difference.

But there was nothing to be done. Imperial Headquarters was adamant that the Americans must be held in this area as long as possible, to give General Tojo's government time to regroup its forces on the new defense line. It would have been helpful if they could have waited for the carriers to come down, but there was no chance of it. The American move had triggered Operation Ro. The pressure was on Admiral Koga from Tokyo, and he exerted it in turn on Omori. They were to get going and engage the enemy.

The Eleventh Air Fleet was to put everything it had on the line, against the landing forces and the American air and naval forces. The

17th Army was to mount a land action. This would consist of a drive up from the south by the 23rd Imperial Army Regiment (less the 2nd Battalion, which was stationed on Choiseul) and a counterlanding near the American landing beaches on Bougainville. The land drives would be simultaneous, and the 2nd Regiment was supposed to link up with the landing force and drive the Americans into the sea.

But once again, the Japanese Army showed its appalling ignorance of American military techniques. The Americans already had 14,000 troops in motion, and nearly three times that number were expected. The 23rd Regiment troops available on Bougainville numbered about 2,500. The detachment of shock troops selected to make the initial landing was the No. 2 Ken Butai. The Japanese called these troops a "decisive battle unit." They were, in fact, commandos, and No. 2 Ken Butai had long years of experience in the China war.

They were to be delivered to a landing point just east of the American position at Point Torokina, to assemble and attack along the beach as the 23rd Regiment came down the Piva Trail.

They would catch the Americans in a vise.

Just after midnight on November 1, the American ships were approaching Buka to begin the scheduled bombardment, when they made contact with an unidentified plane. They assumed that it was Washing Machine Charlie, one of the ubiquitous float planes that served the Japanese so well during the entire Solomons campaign.

Twenty minutes later, Admiral Merrill's flagship, the cruiser *Montpelier*, opened fire on the Buka airstrip. If there had been any question earlier that the Japanese were aroused, it was settled then. Rabaul had the word in minutes. Admiral Samejima called Admiral Omori. He was to prepare to go out and do battle with the Americans—immediately.

The American task force bombarded the Buka bomber strip and several other installations. Just after midnight a Japanese plane attacked the force, but one of the destroyers shot it down. A little later the lookouts aboard the cruiser *Cleveland* reported seeing torpedo wakes and two small craft they believed to be Japanese torpedo boats. They did no damage. Shore guns also fired back at the ships, but these did no damage either.

Several times during the night Japanese planes came over the force, but the destroyers kept after them and drove them away.

After bombarding Buka, the ships moved down to the Shortlands, to bombard the enemy troops and installations on Faisi Island and Poporang Island. By 7:00 A.M. the shooting was all over, and the task force steamed back toward Vella Lavella. Several of the destroyers were short of fuel, so they moved down to Hathorn Sound to refuel from a barge there.

Admittedly the Japanese high command at Rabaul had been caught napping by the American invasion of Bougainville. But once the word reached Rabaul, General Imamura had swung into action.

He had conferred with Admiral Samejima, and they had discussed the "cooperation" orders from Tokyo. So within a matter of hours after the marines landed at Point Torokina, the Japanese were loading four transport destroyers with 880 army troops of the No. 2 Ken Butai.

Admiral Omori's force sailed just before 2:30 on the afternoon of November 1, and the transport division came along a few miles behind. The *Amagiri, Uzuki, Yunagi,* and *Fuzuki* were supposed to reach the southern part of Gazere Wan (Empress Augusta Bay) where they would land their reinforcements. At that point they were supposed to meet the attack squadron that would cover their activity.

In midafternoon, Admiral Merrill learned of the movements of the Japanese and set a course north to meet them.

The first sign of trouble for the Japanese came shortly after dark. A B-24 broke out of the clouds and bombed the cruiser *Sendai* but did not score any hits.

Then came word from Japanese scout planes that a large American force was standing off Empress Augusta Bay. The planes erroneously reported three battleships among the vessels, and when Admiral Samejima had that news, he suddenly ordered the troop transports to turn around and return to Rabaul without unloading their troops.

Admiral Omori was freed of the protective responsibility. His task now was to sink enemy ships.

The Japanese were steaming through squalls, and visibility was just about three miles. That was a disadvantage already to men who would have to use their eyes alone to make contact with the enemy.

At about 10:30, an American reconnaissance bomber reported to Admiral Merrill the sighting of a Japanese formation of eight ships. (Omori actually had ten.) The pilot gave position, course, and speed and then announced he was going to attack. He attacked the *Haguro* but did no damage. The attack over, the *Haguro* then launched one of its float planes, which soon found the enemy about twenty miles south of the Japanese formation.

Admiral Omori then turned around, to confuse the enemy about his position. That tactic worked fine when one was fighting enemies who relied on visual observation, but for Omori this night it did nothing but waste fuel. The American task force was tracking the Japanese already by radar.

Admiral Omori was confused by another report of many ships in

Empress Augusta Bay. These were actually three American minelayers, escorted by a destroyer, which had just laid a mine field north of Cape Torokina. They then retired south, passing the task force, and further confusing Omori as to the number and sort of ships he was facing.

Omori turned toward Empress Augusta Bay, to attack the "transports" he had been told were just unloading there. Admiral Merrill moved his cruisers across the mouth of the bay to prevent the Japanese from entering.

The forces grew closer and closer. Admiral Merrill knew precisely how the Japanese were coming and where they were. The big blips in the middle of the radar screens were the heavy cruisers, with the two lines of destroyers, each led by a light cruiser, on the flanks. The battle was fast approaching, and Admiral Omori still did not know where the enemy was.

Admiral Merrill, for the first time in South Pacific history, was going to make classic use of his destroyers. They were to make a torpedo attack and then retire back beyond the range of the Japanese guns. Admiral Merrill would start the fight at ranges he believed to be beyond those of the Japanese torpedoes.

At 2:31 in the morning, Captain Arleigh Burke's four destroyers slipped away from the American formation to head in for their attack. They were the *Charles F. Ausburne, Dyson, Stanly,* and *Claxton.* As they moved, Merrill turned around to get out of the way, and let the second group of destroyers, the *Spence, Thatcher, Converse,* and *Foote* have a clear field for their attack.

Just about then, a Japanese float plane did Omori the service of dropping a flare over the American cruisers, and aboard the *Sendai,* Admiral Ijuin's men saw the American ships for the first time. Ijuin then ordered his destroyers to begin firing torpedoes on a right turn, and they did so as they turned.

Just then, Admiral Merrill ordered his cruisers to open fire on the nearest enemy ships. The nearest blip of any size happened to be the *Sendai,* and she caught the fire of all four cruisers, which were firing by radar.

In a minute the *Sendai* was in desperate trouble. Her rudder jammed, which made her virtually useless as a fighting ship. She began to burn.

Meanwhile, in trying to avoid the sudden blast of cruiser gunfire, the destroyers *Samidare* and *Shiratsuyu* collided, and both suffered so much damage that they pulled away from the battle.

Ijuin's order to turn saved the Japanese destroyers from Captain Burke's torpedo attack. The American torpedoes slid harmlessly by into the waters where the Japanese would have been had they stayed on the old course.

The Japanese opened fire on the American ships with their guns, but the range was too great for the destroyers. The two heavy cruisers still had not found the enemy, and they were going around in a great circle. The second group of destroyers was thoroughly confused and milled about, following the heavy cruisers.

The American gunfire was now concentrating on the heavy cruisers, and it was coming so close as to throw at least one destroyer captain into a panic. The skipper of the *Hatsukaze* tried to duck oncoming salvoes by cutting between the *Haguro* and the *Myoko*, and the *Myoko* hit her, shearing off part of the bow and wrecking two torpedo tubes.

So, half an hour into the battle, the Americans had set one light cruiser to burning, and the Japanese had damaged three of their own ships.

Admiral Merrill had studied all the night actions of the past, and he could see that his problem was to avoid the Japanese torpedoes, which had always caused trouble for the American warships. To do so he kept in constant motion, changing direction, so that no matter when the Japanese launched torpedoes, he would be somewhere other than the point indicated when they arrived.

Moreover, with radar fire control, all the while he was doing this his guns continued to work. However, they did not work as well at thirty knots, under violent maneuver, as they would at a lesser speed that offered a more stable platform. The cruiser guns were not doing much damage to the enemy.

By this time—about 3:15 A.M.—Admiral Omori had finally located his enemies and was returning fire with his eight-inch guns. The cruiser *Denver* was hit several times and damaged badly enough that she had to slow down to twenty-five knots.

Admiral Omori was trying to close the distance so his destroyers could work, and a few minutes later he seemed to have done so. The range was about eight miles, well within the capability of the "long lance" torpedoes.

Japanese planes did all they could to help Admiral Omori, and just at this point they were of considerable assistance. They dropped flares over the American cruisers and lit them up brightly. Admiral Omori continued to shoot with his eight-inch guns, but the Japanese gunners' aim was off this night, and they scored many near misses but few hits. Admiral Merrill began making smoke to conceal his ships, and Omori made the error so common in these night flights—confusing manufactured smoke with the smoke of heavy fires. He believed he had hit several big ships and put them out of action. Actually, among the U.S. vessels, only the *Denver* was hurt.

Captain Burke's destroyers, which had charged forth so bravely to make the first torpedo attack then lost each other in the night; it took Burke a long time to get them into formation again. The ships then approached the sinking *Sendai*, and they put some more shells into her as they passed by.

Burke's ships next caught the damaged *Samidare* and *Shiratsuyu* on the radar screens, and Burke announced that he was going to start firing. But through a failure in communication he got the idea that the ships ahead were those of the other destroyer division, and he did not fire. So the two Japanese ships moved off, safe.

Commander B. L. Austin's four destroyers had caught the damaged *Hatsukaze* after her collision and had set her afire. Burke's destroyers came up to help sink her.

That second destroyer division never did get off a torpedo attack because Commander Austin misunderstood Admiral Merrill's signals and got completely out of position. One of his destroyers, the *Foote*, ran smack into a torpedo that had been fired at the cruisers, in that mad maneuvering of mid-battle. Her stern was blown off and she skidded to a stop in the water. The cruiser *Cleveland*, coming by at thirty knots, just managed to miss hitting her.

It certainly was the night for collisions. The destroyer *Spence* side-swiped the destroyer *Thatcher*. The *Spence* then took a shell at the waterline that effectively eliminated her from the high-speed battle.

The battle ended raggedly with neither group of cruisers ever really coming to grips with each other. The destroyers sank the damaged *Hatsukaze*, which went down without any survivors. Admiral Ijuin stayed aboard the sinking *Sendai* to the last, but almost miraculously he was saved along with a small number of men.

He owed that rescue to Admiral Omori. When Omori retired, he sent a message to Rabaul, asking for a submarine to come to the battle scene and pick up survivors. The submarine *I-104* did come, and did rescue the admiral, the captain of the *Sendai*, and seventy-two other men. Still more *Sendai* survivors managed to get aboard rafts and reach Bougainville.

When dawn came both Americans and Japanese were eager to be away from the scene, because both expected air attack from the enemy. The Japanese did put forth an enormous air effort, getting a hundred planes into the skies over Empress Augusta Bay, but the effect of their raid was dismal. They managed to hit only the cruiser *Montpelier*, and the two small bombs wounded only one man and did little damage. Many of the Japanese planes were shot down by New Zealand and American fighters before they reached the cruiser force. Many more were shot down by the antiaircraft guns of the cruisers and the destroyers.

From any standpoint, it was not a very satisfactory battle. Admiral Merrill had commanded with great skill; the same cannot be said for

Admiral Omori, who never came to grips with his enemy. Captain Burke had launched a brave destroyer attack, but the second division of destroyers became almost as confused as the Japanese destroyer divisions.

Considering all the ships involved, the damage done by guns and torpedoes was minimal; intraservice collisions seemed almost as damaging in terms of ability to fight. Admiral Ijuin was unlucky to have his flagship in the van against the radar-controlled fire of the Americans.

The victory this time went to the Americans for sinking one Japanese light cruiser and one destroyer. The Japanese lost about 880 men.

All the American ships made it back to base and only the *Foote* was badly damaged. The Americans had lost only six men killed and seven injured.

Admiral Merrill won the praise of his superiors, and Admiral Omori was sacked and sent back to Japan to run the submarine school. Admiral Matsubara, the commander of the ineffectual second destroyer division, was also assigned to shore duty. Only Admiral Ijuin came out of the battle with his reputation intact.

But as for settling anything about the Bougainville invasion, the Battle of Empress Augusta Bay was a draw. The American beachhead was intact, and so was the Japanese naval fighting force at Rabaul. It would all have to be fought over again.

21

BOUGAINVILLE IN THE BALANCE

THE Fifth U.S. Army Air Force had been hitting Rabaul hard for a month, with major attention to the ring of airfields around this important base.

It was no milk run. The bases were ringed by antiaircraft guns, and the fighter fields put up fighters every time. Japanese action and the weather were almost equal enemies, too. Some days the raids had to be called off because of foul weather over the target.

On October 27, when the Bougainville assault began with the landing on the Treasury Islands, General Nathan Twining's Thirteenth Air Force lent a hand. But the Fifth Air Force continued to strike Rabaul. On October 29, the bombers were there again. But on November 1, the day of the invasion of Bougainville, the bombers could not make the run. Weather again. The next day, however, they tried to make up for it.

The fighters and bombers tried to fly low, to avoid detection along the way, but in St. George's Channel they encountered two large Japanese warships that opened fire with everything they had. So, by the time the American planes reached Rabaul, the sky over the harbor was dark with antiaircraft fire.

Warned, the Japanese had put a hundred fighters into the air that day. The fighting was fierce, and both sides lost a number of planes. The

Americans, as usual, overstated the case, claiming sixty-five Japanese fighters shot down to nine of their own fighters and eight bombers. The Japanese said that only eighteen of their planes were shot down, and Captain Tameichi Hara, skipper of the destroyer *Shigure,* claimed five American planes for his ship, plus a number of others badly shot up.

But the most important aspect of the fight was that once again it prevented the Japanese from sending off the reinforcements to Bougainville.

The Imperial General Staff in Tokyo had no illusions about holding Bougainville or even Rabaul for an indefinite period. But they had a timetable, which involved shoring up the defenses of the inner empire, and these southeastern area bastions played a most important role in that schedule.

The Ro Operation was designed to win that time.

On Bougainville, the Americans awoke on November 2 to discover all was quiet. The Japanese had not mounted a counterattack. General Turnage soon saw that the Japanese on the west side of them did not intend to begin an offensive, so he moved the 3rd Marines to that side and transferred the 9th Marines to the west. The 3rd Marines had taken something of a beating in the landings, and the 9th Marines were fresh. The move was accomplished on foot for the most part. There simply were no trails along the beach, and few anywhere on this west side of the island.

The marines were as secure as they could be on the uncomfortable beachhead. On their left, about seven miles west of Cape Torokina, was the Laruma River, which was a fair stream. On the right flank was the Piva River, which twisted through the jungle. And behind the center was the 840-foot Mount Bagana, the smoking volcano.

On November 3, the 2nd Raider Battalion was assigned to take over the roadblock on the Piva Trail. For the next three days action along the beachhead was confined to patrols, in which the marines captured some papers and killed thirteen Japanese. From the papers and the progress of the action, it seemed apparent that any Japanese reaction to the landings was going to come from the south.

But the Japanese at Rabaul were having more than a little difficulty in moving the troops down to Bougainville to start a counteraction.

At Truk, Admiral Koga received the news of the defeat at Empress Augusta Bay with considerable agitation. The setback put a big hole in his Ro Operation before it had scarcely started. The counterlanding was already late.

Koga's next step was to send those heavy cruisers, a light cruiser, and four destroyers to Rabaul to prepare for a new naval strike at the Americans. These were followed by a pair of oilers and three troop transports escorted by the light cruiser *Isuzu*.

However, the oilers *Nichiei Maru* and *Nissho Maru* were bombed by planes from the Solomons and so badly damaged that they had to be towed back to Truk for repairs. This was a real shock. The loss of an oiler always troubled a naval commander, even more than the loss of a capital ship. It was a reminder of the frailty of oil-bound warships.

The heavy cruiser *Chokai* towed one of them, and a destroyer took the other.

Then on November 4, as the troopships and their escort were about fifty miles north of Kavieng, they were attacked by B-24s, and one of the transports was damaged so badly that it had to be towed into Rabaul. These forces were destined for Bougainville, but they were obviously very much delayed.

When Admiral Halsey learned of the concentration of Japanese cruiser power in the Rabaul area, he was more than a little disturbed. What he needed were some heavy ships in a hurry. But there were no heavy ships for the South Pacific Command just then, because everything Admiral Nimitz could get his hands on was being used to mount the offensive against Tarawa and Makin atolls in the Gilberts, an assault scheduled to occur in just a little over three weeks.

Admiral Halsey did have one card in the hole, although he could not be certain whether it would turn out to be an ace or a joker. He had been lent one carrier task force, Rear Admiral Frederick C. Sherman's Task Force 38, built around the carriers *Saratoga* and *Princeton*. These had been lent him for the first days of the Bougainville campaign and were supposed to be going back to Nimitz, but Halsey still had them.

The problem was that American carrier doctrine still held that attacks by carrier forces on stoutly defended air base complexes were to be avoided at all costs. The Japanese were thought to have 150 planes at Rabaul just then. That would classify as stoutly defended. Actually they had nearly twice that number.

But Halsey, who had been the first to try something new (the Marcus Raid, the Doolittle Tokyo Raid) was not a great respecter of formal doctrine. Furthermore, unlike a number of senior commanders, Halsey believed that ships were built to be risked in war, and he had no hesitation in risking them.

So when Halsey learned that the cruisers *Takao, Maya, Atago, Suzuya, Mogami*, and *Chikuma* were all at Rabaul, along with the *Myoko* and the *Haguro* and several light cruisers, he gave orders to Admiral Sherman to make a strike at Rabaul on the morning of November 5. Sherman was to go after the cruisers first of all, and then the destroyers. He would be supported by planes from the Southwest Pacific Command, which were supposed to hit Rabaul around noon.

But that didn't mean much. By the time MacArthur's planes got to the big Japanese base, the carrier planes would have won or lost everything. And, if one looked at the figures coldly, the chances of their winning seemed slight. By speeding to the launching point and putting everything that could fly into the sky, Admiral Sherman was able to throw up ninety-seven planes from the two carriers, fifty-two of them fighters. That meant twenty-two dive-bombers and twenty-three torpedo bombers would go against all those ships and the fighters the Japanese could put up in a hurry.

At nine o'clock on the morning of November 5, Admiral Sherman had reached the launch point, about 230 miles southeast of Rabaul. That was a comfortable enough margin of safety in terms of gas, but that aspect was the only comfortable part of the mission.

The American pilots did not really know where the Japanese ships could be found in the big complex that was Rabaul Harbor. But they were lucky because the sky over Rabaul was clear and blue that day, and when they were fifty miles out they could see the enemy ships: eight heavy cruisers and twenty light cruisers and destroyers. It was the sort of target the Fifth Air Force would have given some eyeteeth to have.

The carrier pilots were even more fortunate than they knew. A number of those ships had just arrived in port at six o'clock that morning from Truk. If there was anything they were not expecting, it was an air attack from carrier planes.

Commander Henry Caldwell, the leader of the American air attack, recognized from the beginning that he had a special problem with Rabaul. The Japanese had many ships, and that meant all the shore antiaircraft guns plus the guns of the fleet would be turned on the carrier planes. In addition, they had to look for a very large number of Japanese fighters right above their own major base.

Therefore Commander Caldwell brought his pilots in a large traveling formation, fighters on top, and this time they held the formation as they came in toward the volcanoes, passed over them, and moved into the harbor area to bomb. Only at the last minute did the planes break off into small groups to dive-bomb or go low and drop their torpedoes.

The Japanese reacted too slowly. Instead of attacking the main formation when it was still outside antiaircraft gun range, they waited for the formation to break up, and when it did not they found themselves in the position of flying into their own flak. So the effectiveness of the fighters in stopping the strike before it began was minimal.

The ships were caught unaware. One was fueling. But by the time the attack was launched the shore and ship guns were putting up a hellish field of fire that the Americans had to fly through. The result was a scattered attack, and no Japanese ships were sunk. But that does not tell the real story: so much damage was done to the cruisers that they were withdrawn from the Bougainville operation.

The heavy cruiser *Mogami* was hit by only one bomb, but it damaged her so badly that she had to be sent back to Japan for repairs. The bomb penetrated below decks and started a number of fires. The major damage was to the hull, engine rooms, and one magazine. Nineteen men were killed and forty-one wounded.

The cruiser *Maya* took one bomb in the port engine room through her main stack, and she had to be towed back to Truk. That remarkable delivery of bombs was made by Lieutenant Commander James Newell, leader of the *Saratoga*'s dive-bombers. The *Maya*'s casualties were heavy: seventy men killed and sixty wounded.

The cruiser *Takao* was hit twice, and a hole below the waterline on her starboard bow and damaged steering meant she, too, would have to go into dry dock. Her casualties were twenty-three men dead and twenty-two wounded.

The cruiser *Atago* was damaged by three near misses, and the destroyer *Wakatsuki* was also damaged by near misses.

The light cruiser *Agano* was damaged by bombs that knocked out her forward turret and wounded eleven men. The light cruiser *Noshiro* was hit by a torpedo, apparently a dud, which wounded fourteen men. The destroyer *Fujinami* was slightly damaged by a dud torpedo, which wounded thirteen men.

Most of the damage was done by the dive-bombers. The Americans were having a great deal of trouble with their torpedoes, aerial and undersea. In fact, for the amount of effort expended, the torpedo squadrons produced very little except when they were using bombs instead of torpedoes. The reasons were two: an inferior exploding device and a poor system of drop control.

The following year the latter would be remedied in part by development of control devices that kept the torpedoes from skipping or submarining when dropped at high speed at low altitude. Altogether, however, torpedo plane performance was a disappointment, and it had nothing to do with the skill or willingness of the pilots.

Another problem on November 5 was that there were too many targets for the planes involved. As it was, the Americans lost five fighters and five bombers. They could thank the aircraft designers and builders for a number of lives saved that day; many of the American planes arrived back on the carriers so badly shot up it seemed remarkable that they got home.

Lieutenant H. M. Crockett of the *Princeton* was wounded but brought his F6F fighter back to the carrier and landed. The "airedales" (aircraft handlers) counted two hundred holes in the aircraft. Commander Caldwell, who directed the operation from above, was attacked by Zeros, one of his crewmen was killed and the other wounded, and his gun turret went out. So did the radio, and one aileron, the flaps, and one wheel. Still he got the TBF torpedo bomber back to the *Saratoga*.

As to the attack, from the Japanese point of view it had completely destroyed a major effort to shore up the defense of Rabaul. As the Imperial General Staff's history noted: "For some reason, the Southeast Area reinforcement's efficiency was lacking."

That same day, since many of the ships had not been in port for twenty-four hours, the force was withdrawn to Truk, and (again in the words of the Imperial General Staff) "no profit resulted."

The Japanese that day attempted to recoup somewhat at least by getting at the carriers. The Eleventh Air Fleet sent out a number of torpedo bombers.

But they did not find the American carriers. Instead, they found a small force consisting of *PT-167*, *LCI-70*, and *LCT-68* on their way south from the Torokina beachhead. The Japanese planes attacked and damaged the ships but did not sink any of them because the vessels were so small the torpedoes passed under their keels. The LCI had the unique experience of having a porpoising torpedo bounce into the engine room and still not explode. One man was killed by the impact, but the torpedo sat there smoking—and still not exploding. The men of the LCI abandoned ship, but when the ship remained afloat eventually they reclaimed her and got her back under tow to Torokina.

The Japanese pilots who returned to Rabaul from this action claimed to have sunk one carrier and set fire to a second, which sank later. They also claimed two heavy cruisers and one light cruiser and a destroyer. These claims are not mentioned in the official Japanese history of the war, because there was not a shred of truth to them.

The American pilots were prone to exaggeration in the heat of the moment, but at no time did they ever claim so much when so little had been accomplished. Those torpedo bombers had not even sunk a rowboat and had lost at least two of their number in the one-sided fight against three small craft.

When the results of the Rabaul strike were in, and Admiral Sherman could announce that he had accomplished all this with the loss of only ten planes, Admiral Halsey was delighted. He had expected heavy losses and had also put those carriers at risk by moving them so close to Rabaul. The gamble had paid off magnificently: Admiral Koga had been planning to use those heavy ships to break up the Torokina landing. He had nothing left that he wanted to risk, and by the time he thought it over more, the Gilberts landing was in progress and he had a third major front to worry about.

22

COUNTERLANDING

JUST because Operation Ro had suffered a serious reverse did not mean that Admiral Koga had given up or that the Southeast Area Command was surrendering Bougainville without a fight.

On November 2, after the counterlanding force had to turn back on the eve of the Battle of Empress Augusta Bay, Sixth Division Headquarters sent a message to the 23rd Infantry at Moshiguta on the southwest side of Bougainville ordering the immediate relief of the small garrison at Torokina.

Based on these orders, Colonel Shunaki Hamanoue, the commander of the Twenty-Third Regiment decided to lead a detachment to arrive on the west side of the island not later than the afternoon of November 6. Altogether he had about 2,400 troops, but this initial detachment consisted of about 300 riflemen with artillery and machine gun squads that included knee mortars, (eighteen of them with ten grenade rounds each), light and heavy machine guns (each heavy machine gun had 7,400 rounds of ammunition), and artillery that ranged from 75 mm pack howitzers to 37 mm guns.

When the rescue operation was set up, it was planned that there would be plenty of supplies for these troops. The army engineers had

four daihatsu barges in the area, and five days' supplies could be
brought up on these.

But on the morning of November 4, Allied planes found the daihatsus
and strafed them, rendering all four *hors de combat*. The troops would
have to go into battle with a prayer and two and a half days of iron
rations. That wasn't going to stop them. The colonel entrusted the
regimental colors to those left behind and set out.

They were harried all the way along by urgent messages from the 18th
Area Army through the 17th Army, through the Twenty-third Regiment, through the Sixth Division, urging them to hurry and get into
battle to save the Torokina detachment. It was as if this little detachment was responsible for the Torokina outpost being left out there on
the vine in the first place.

Eighteenth Army Headquarters staff officers, looking at their small-
scale maps far away at Rabaul, somehow had the idea they ought to get
into position to attack on the morning of November 6 at dawn.
Obviously these Japanese staff officers had never climbed through the
Bougainville jungle. The beautiful spiky vine named for the island was
just one of the hazards of foot travel.

The loss of time in the destruction of the daihatsus and the problems
of assembling such a striking force so quickly had brought delays, and
there was really nothing that could be done about it, in spite of the
radioed urging of the various headquarters.

From Sixth Division Headquarters came a message giving the detachment its battle plan:

The enemy main force had concentrated at four o'clock on November 4 on the right bank of the Jaba River. By going overland northwest
along the Jaba, the Japanese troops would find Noboi nine miles away.
To hit the enemy they could depend on fire power from heavy weapons
aboard its small boats. After reaching this point, the troops were to head
for Point Torokina, which was about four miles to the northeast. They
would advance to the Peku vicinity and wait there. The attack would
begin at dawn on November 6.

It was very important that one platoon of the 1st Battalion move to
Jaba and advance along the Noboi-Peku Road to Peku, there meet the
Torokina defense detachment, and scout the enemy camp.

Specifically, the infantry of the 1st Battalion on November 5 was to
advance down the Jaba to the Piva River where the small boat force
would be on the right bank. The infantrymen were then to land behind
the enemy and make a surprise attack from the rear.

The Hamanoue detachment moved as quickly as possible, but that
road mentioned in the orders simply did not exist. They found them-

selves slogging through the deep rain forest, with its jungle growth toward the seacoast.

They stumbled along through hip-deep water, crossing small streams and swamps. When they got to the mouth of the Jaba River, they discovered it was very deep, and crocodiles appeared and disappeared on the banks and in the water.

The colonel ordered the men into the water to swim across. But one of the first men to put his foot in ran into trouble. A log moved, there was a small splash, and then a large one, a scream, the water turned pink for a moment, and then the swirls disappeared as the crocodile dragged its prey to the bottom.

Fighting the enemy was one thing, but being eaten by crocodiles was something else, and the troops balked at trying to ford the river. The engineers came to the rescue with rubber boats and ferried the men of the unit across.

Next came the crossing of the Korogi River, which once more they found to be too deep to ford. Again the boats were employed.

By this time darkness had fallen, and they moved through the blackness, stumbling and sliding, until at ten o'clock they reached Noboi Village on the right bank of the Korogi River and sank down, exhausted.

At dawn the seashore was clearly indicated by the captive balloons that the Americans were flying above their bridgehead to discourage Japanese strafing. The air was full of American planes, orbiting around the beachhead, and every time the unit moved, they got strafed. Finally they gave up attempts to move forward for the moment.

At this stage, Colonel Hamanoue was not at all confident of the success of the coming assault.

Events certainly bore out his feelings of concern.

Colonel Hamanoue was to await the coming of reinforcements before launching his attack. They were to arrive early on the morning of November 6 by sea.

These were the first one thousand troops of the counterlanding force. Another two thousand men would come along later. This detachment was the No. 2 Ken Butai, that unit of shock troops with long experience on the China front. They were the troops scheduled to land on November 1, who had been turned back by order of Admiral Samejima when the Omori force discovered the presence of what the admiral thought was a very powerful American fleet.

The No. 2 Ken Butai had returned to Rabaul at that time. In fact, they were lucky because no one had told the officers where they were going or what they were going to do, and they were brand new in the South Pacific. The commander, Major Mitsuhiro Miwa, and his officers took the next few days for intensive training in the tactics of jungle warfare, which gave the men a new confidence.

On November 5, the orders had come again: board the destroyer transports and prepare to land on Bougainville. The plan was precisely the same as the last one.

But on November 5, Admiral Samejima made a change in the destroyer command (a result of the poor performance of the destroyers at Empress Augusta Bay). So the move was again delayed. The attack was to be at night on November 6. But then the word came from Bougainville that Colonel Hamanoue's force was being eaten by crocodiles and otherwise delayed, and so the attack was again postponed.

The No. 2 Ken Butai finally boarded the destroyers on the morning of November 6 and sailed from Rabaul at one o'clock in the afternoon. Lieutenant Colonel Hisano of the staff of the 8th Area Army went along as liaison officer with the navy.

They would land that night and attack at dawn.

As it turned out the destroyers did not reach Bougainville until the early hours of the morning, and then the destroyer commander decided he would lie offshore about two miles. He had been involved in the Kolombangara reinforcement operations and that was the way they did it there.

But a reinforcement of friendly troops and a landing on an enemy beach were two different matters, and the army men protested that they were being thrown to the wolves. This meant more discussions before the destroyers finally moved in a little closer.

So much for interservice cooperation.

Lieutenant Colonel Hisano watched anxiously through his field glasses as the landing boats moved off toward the beach. Only when the signal flare that showed a safe landing went up did he relax. He sent a message then to Eighth Area Army Headquarters at Rabaul announcing the safe landing of the troops.

At Rabaul, when the message was received General Imamura heaved a sigh of relief, gave thanks to the emperor, and sent a message to Imperial General Headquarters.

But from that moment on radio contact with the detachment was spotty.

At 7:00 A.M. on November 7, the navy reported that the landing seemed to be successful. But the landing force still had not been heard from.

By five o'clock in the evening the detachment still had not been heard from.

The first word came through a radio intercept. At 8:35 an American message was picked up, reporting that the enemy was on the left and

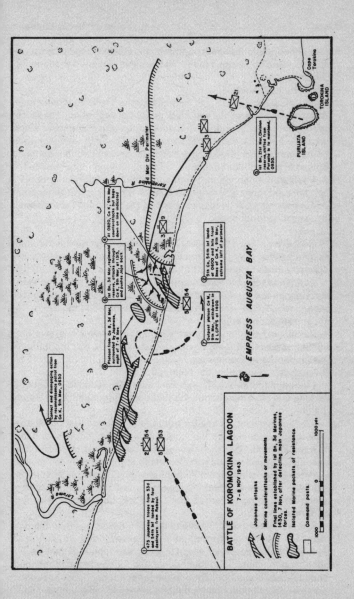

BATTLE OF KOROMOKINA LAGOON
7-8 NOV 1943

Japanese attacks

Marine counterattacks or movements

Final lines established by 1st Bn, 3d Marines,
1400, 8 Nov, after detecting main Japanese
forces.

Isolated Marine pockets of resistance.

Command posts

1000   0   1000 yd.

EMPRESS AUGUSTA BAY

1st Mar Div Perimeter

Contact and disengaging action
by secondary patrol from
Co K, 9th Mar, 0830

475 Japanese troops from 53d
and 54th Inf landed by four
destroyers from Rabaul.

Platoon from Co B, 3d Mar,
surrounded by Japanese,
rescued in 2 hrs.

1st Bn, 3d Mar, regimental
reserve, attacks through
Co K, 9th Mar, at 1345,
and pushes Japs back.

At 0820, Co K, 9th Mar,
counterattacks but bogs
down on line indicated

Outpost platoon Co K,
9th Mar, withdrawn in
2 LCVP'S at 1400

5th Co, 54th Inf lands
at 0400 and hits front
lines of Co K, 9th Mar,
extreme left of perimeter

1st Bn, 21st Mar, Division
reserve, ordered to
Puruata to be maintained,
0630.

PURUATA
ISLAND

TOROKINA
ISLAND

Cape
Torokina

that about fifteen daihatsus had been seen on the northern beach near
the mouth of the Rovuma River. The message requested an immediate
air strike.

After that, nothing.

The No. 2 Ken Butai landed in three sections. The main force of about
650 men landed near the east bank of the Karumu River. The second
group, the Fifth Company of the 54th Infantry, about a hundred men in
all, landed near the Keiki River's west bank. The Sixth Company of the
54th Infantry, a hundred men with a field gun and two machine guns,
landed near the Kuko Stream.

Major Miwa directed the landing energetically and then went off to
join the main force. The three forces never did get back together again.

Almost immediately, following orders, the No. 2 Ken Butai rushed in
to stage a "surprise attack."

On the American side, the four Japanese destroyers were seen coming
in, and landing craft were seen to debark and begin to load men, and
then come into shore just east of the Laruma River.

They were seen, but since warships in the dark look the same even to
navy men—and American landing craft and Japanese landing craft
looked much alike—no one paid attention until it was too late to stop
them from getting ashore.

But in the hurry to get ashore the Japanese scattered over a wide
section of the beach. They also ran into the problem that had bothered
the marines in the first landing: swamp and jungle. Thus they could not
immediately concentrate their forces for attack.

Company K of the 9th Marines was holding this flank, dug in between
swamp and sea. One platoon was patrolling upland along the Laruma
River.

The marines saw about fifty troops landing from two boats, some
four hundred yards away, but what was happening did not sink in for a
few minutes—and then the Japanese attacked. The marines drove them
off. The Japanese moved into the swamp and disappeared.

When Lieutenant Colonel Walter Asmuth, Jr., commander of the 9th
Marines 3rd Battalion, got the message about the attack, he ordered
Company K to counterattack and called also for mortar and artillery
support.

The marines attacked at 8:20 and moved west about 150 yards before
they ran into the Japanese, who had already dug in. The Japanese had light and heavy machine guns, and soon they had the left
platoon of Company K pinned down. The center and right platoons
tried to come around and encircle the Japanese, but they were slowed
down by the same thick jungle that had given Colonel Hamanoue's men

such a hard time. The marine advance wasn't helped by the fact that in some rearrangement of the perimeter, other marines had left entrenched positions that the Japanese now occupied.

The Japanese ashore gave fire cover to more troops who came ashore in landing craft, and soon they had all three platoons of Company K pinned down. The fighting then slowed to a sharpshooting match. Five marines were killed and thirteen wounded by 1:15, when the 1st Battalion of the 3rd Marines was ordered to attack, and the mauled Company K was withdrawn.

The fighting now became a slugging match. The marines advanced, foot by foot, behind grenades, machine gun fire, and mortars. The Japanese threw the grenades back sometimes and added their own knee mortar shells. The Japanese machine gunners gave ground slowly and reluctantly, one gun covering another.

Sergeant Herbert J. Thomas of Company B saw that his squad was held up by a Japanese machine gun. He gathered the men and told them what he was going to do. He would get up and throw a grenade into the machine gun nest. The men were to wait for the explosion and then pour small arms fire into the position.

But when Thomas threw his grenade it arched too high, got caught in a vine hanging from the trees above, and fell down among the marines. Thomas leaped forward and smothered the grenade with his body as it exploded, thus saving the lives of at least most of his squad. For that his family received his posthumous Congressional Medal of Honor.

The Japanese soon had two hundred men ashore in this sector, and those machine guns. The machine guns caused plenty of trouble for the marines and had much of Company B pinned down.

Seeing this, Captain Gordon Warner, the commander of Company B, got a helmet full of grenades and found a tank to help knock out the machine guns.

Warner had studied Japanese and had an idiomatic command of the language. With the tank behind, he led his riflemen to the Japanese position, then began issuing orders in Japanese.

"*Juken de sasite!* (Fix bayonets)."

"*Teki o gekimetsite!* (Annihilate the enemy)."

The Japanese soldiers, unaware of the source of the orders, dutifully followed them. They fixed bayonets and charged forth into the steady rifle fire of the marine riflemen.

Warner moved forward time after time, got the Japanese attention by shouts that confused them, and hurled his grenades. The tank came along and cleaned up. Before the afternoon was over, Captain Warner and the tank had knocked out six machine gun posts. He was wounded in the leg and later traded it for a Navy Cross, awarded because the

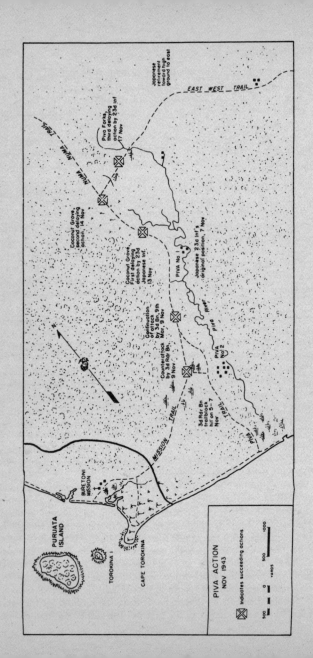

PIVA ACTION
NOV 1943

⊠ Indicates succeeding actions

YARDS
500   0   500   1000

marines knew that his action had let them build up a firing line and prevent the infiltration of the marine positions that day.

The patrol up the Laruma River got into trouble before the afternoon was over. It was attacked and withdrew to the east. Its members came back within the marine lines that evening.

Then the outpost platoon of Company M, on the beach, was hit by Japanese coming from the Laruma River. What seemed to be a company of Japanese attacked and soon had the marines pinned on three sides. Help came up from the beach in the form of Lieutenant Frank Nolander of the navy, who brought a pair of amphibious landing craft up to the position and evacuated the besieged patrol. He got sixty marines out without losing a man.

By evening the Japanese had taken over the extreme west side of the beach, from the Laruma River to a point about a mile to the east. They had also driven a wedge between marine positions and thus surrounded the first platoon of Company B of the 3rd Marines.

The marines set up a perimeter and held their position through the long night. At dawn they moved back and made it to the marine lines.

As Colonel Hamanoue had feared, the seaborne counterlanding had failed to drive through the American lines. The No. 2 Ken Butai was fighting now for its existence. Its only hope was to fight through to Colonel Hamanoue's unit.

Given the results, General Imamura called off the next wave of landings in the bay, and the 2,500 additional troops were not committed.

The only decent trail in the whole Empress Augusta Bay region of Bougainville was the Piva Trail that more or less followed the Piva River from the southeast toward the Mission Area, where the marines had taken up temporary residence.

The marines had set up a roadblock across the Piva Trail about a mile from the beach and had held it against sporadic Japanese attack by the remnants of the Torokina detachment.

On the night of November 6, Colonel Hamanoue had bivouacked on the east side of the Piva. The next day he moved down to a point opposite the roadblock, and early in the morning he crossed the river. He was to coordinate his attack from the inland side with that of the troops coming into the beach. But, alas, from the Japanese point of view, the troops coming into the beach never got very far, and although Colonel Hamanoue attacked at 2:30 in the afternoon to drive through and meet them, the attack was repelled. He backed off until the next day and retreated to dig in west of Piva Village.

The situation had developed in a most unpleasant way, and the brave plan for a breakthrough on the first day had failed. But that did not mean the colonel had quit. The night was punctuated by a continual mortar barrage levied against the marines in the trail block positions. At 7:30 in the morning, the colonel led his men out to attack. The fighting was fierce for seven hours, until the marines brought up reinforcements and pushed the Japanese back again.

The colonel was bothered most by the marines' big guns, which seemed to follow his men wherever they went and kept him constantly off base.

On November 7, in the afternoon, the Japanese had broken through the marine lines at the roadblock, but when the colonel sent a new wave against the position, the marine artillery had broken up his attack, and he had been forced to give it up.

On the 8th, before launching his morning attack, Colonel Hamanoue had tried to respond in kind with a four-hour mortar preparation for his attack. But it was not the same. His infantrymen had been forced to fight for every foot of the advances they made that day, and then to hold against a determined marine counterattack. But they had held. It was the artillery that made the difference.

That night the colonel considered a plan to drive on through the marine lines to reach the anchorage and destroy the artillery there.

But Major Tanaka, his intelligence officer, looked over the plan and sent out a small patrol, and then announced that it would be extremely difficult—*muzukashii desu nee* . . .—which, in the polite way that a subordinate talked to the colonel, meant that he was out of his head to try. The trouble was that the support from the seaward side had completely evaporated, and at Rabaul General Imamura was not prepared to commit any more men to what he saw as an improbable situation. And it was down along the beach that the artillery operated.

On the night of November 8, the marines planned a new and heavier artillery barrage, and it began at 7:30 on the morning of November 9. The 2nd Raider Battalion was chosen to make the new attack half an hour later. It was slow going, since Colonel Hamanoue's troops fought every inch of the way. At the end of an hour and a half the marines had progressed only fifty yards. The marines brought up reinforcements and continued to press on, but the Japanese resisted, until suddenly at 12:30, they pulled out. Neither Rabaul nor Colonel Hamanoue's detachment picked up any messages from the No. 2 Ken Butai that night. But during the night and in the morning Colonel Hamanoue's men heard constant gunfire. At eight o'clock on the morning of November 8, Hamanoue sent a message to Sixth Division headquarters reporting that the fighting seemed to be concentrated around the southwest entrance to the bay.

There was no communication from the No. 2 Ken Butai during the remainder of that day.

On the morning of November 8, the marines to the east of the Japanese thrust attacked to drive the enemy back to the beach and consolidate the line. The attack was preceded by an artillery barrage that killed an estimated three hundred Japanese, and it was supported by light tanks. When the assaulting troops moved forward to the Japanese positions, they found there were no living Japanese to oppose them then.

On the night of November 9, the Japanese received word that the No. 2 Ken Butai was in the middle of a battle. No more.

On November 10, the remnants of the No. 2 Ken Butai straggled into the Biba River landing.

The Hamanoue detachment had also pulled back out of sight.

The marines could not understand it, but they were not about to refuse a gift, so they moved on rapidly up the Piva Trail. They saw that the Japanese had inexplicably left everything behind: machine guns, mortars, and even rifles. They saw a large number of casualties. By 3:00 P.M. they had reached the junction of the Piva and Numa Numa Trails and had not caught sight of a live Japanese for more than an hour.

They stopped, dug in, and consolidated their positions. Security patrols sent out in front discovered a large bivouac area—empty. They encountered some Japanese stragglers, moving back along the Numa Numa Trail. But that was all.

The marines had lost a dozen men and thirty were wounded. They counted a hundred Japanese bodies in the area.

The reason for the Japanese pullback continued to puzzle them.

The reason was simple enough. On the night of November 8, a discouraged Colonel Hamanoue had assessed his situation. During the past forty-eight hours the Americans had enlarged their perimeter, and the beachhead seemed to be established beyond the possibility of destruction. The failure of the seaborne attack had certainly shown that much. The Americans held the only usable trail. Their concentration of artillery seemed to be growing and the guns were firing faster. Much as he might admire this as a professional soldier admired a good job well done, he decided to move back to escape the shelling. He did move that very evening from the old bivouac and did escape the night shelling.

In the morning, the colonel prepared to launch a new attack. Then, from the Piva Trail, came a message from the commander of his 1st Battalion. The enemy's morning artillery barrage and air strike had caught the entire heavy weapons section in their bivouac on the trail and had virtually wiped the section off the face of the earth. The casualties were very heavy and virtually every weapon and much of the ammunition had been destroyed.

The Japanese situation was serious to the point of desperation. It would take seven days for a round trip back to base to secure a new supply of ammunition for the machine guns and mortars. And not only had most of the ammunition for these heavy weapons been destroyed, but the ammunition carriers were then handling much of the supply for the riflemen.

The artillery barrage had not caught the Japanese who were immediately opposite the marines. So when the morning attack had begun those Japanese soldiers in the front line had fought with their usual tenacity.

So had the marines. Private First Class Henry Gurke and Private First Class Donald Probst were sharing a foxhole on the front of the line. The Japanese discovered them first thing in the morning and began to pour machine gun fire into the position. They followed that with grenades.

Two marines in the next hole were killed, but Gurke and Probst hung on. The firing grew more intense. Gurke observed that Probst's Browning Automatic Rifle was a damned sight more effective under these circumstances than his M-1, and that if anything happened—such as a grenade falling into their hole—he would take care of it while Probst continued to fire.

Suddenly a grenade landed squarely between them. Without hesitation, PFC Gurke threw himself onto the grenade and smothered it so that Probst could continue to fire and hold the position. Probst did and won the Silver Star. Gurke's relatives received his Congressional Medal of Honor, as had Sergeant Thomas's.

The Japanese fought like tigers until those grenade hurlers began to run out of ammunition and sent the word back. The runner returned with the answer that there was no ammunition for the machine guns and there were no grenades.

The Japanese suddenly fell back.

So the pullback had been a result of the enormously effective artillery barrage.

The marines were not giving enough credit to their own guns.

The marines planned to attack again the next day, November 10. Before moving out they waited for a fifteen-minute artillery barrage and an air strike, and these were both delivered by 9:45 on the morning of November 10.

When the riflemen began to move ahead, there was no resistance. As the marines moved on toward Piva Village, they saw that the Japanese had left equipment, ammunition, and even some rifles behind as they moved out. (These were the weapons destroyed or damaged in the previous day's shelling.)

Before noon the marines had moved into Piva Village where they stopped and established a new position. The battle of the Piva Trail seemed to be over.

Once again, on the night of November 9, the Japanese commander considered his problem. What nagged him was that the artillery made all the difference. On a ratio basis, the American firepower outdid him by 150 to one.

He was convinced that without this discrepancy in firepower, he could defeat the Americans. He could have worked his theory all out on paper.

And that was all very nice, but the discrepancy in firepower was going to continue.

23

THE FOOTHOLD
ESTABLISHED

BY the end of the first week of the invasion of Bougainville, the Americans were bringing in fresh troops.

The Army 37th Infantry Division was slated to take over at Bougainville as soon as possible. Parts of the Army 148th Infantry arrived on November 8. The 21st Marines began to come in on November 11. The Army 129th Infantry began arriving on November 13.

The troops down below on the beach began building roads up into the hills. Until the roads were completed, only tracked vehicles could start for the front lines with much hope of getting there through the mud and swamp.

If they could get as far as Piva Village they could go on, for the ground hardened there.

But up the Piva River, Colonel Hamanoue and his men still held their defensive positions, while the colonel worried about the artillery and the inequality of this war that had made his attack into a virtual slaughter.

The point, as far as the Americans were concerned, was that the Japanese had to be pushed back far enough into the hills to prevent them from launching an attack on the vital airstrip once it was completed.

To do that General Roy Geiger, the new marine commander (General Vandegrift had just been promoted back to Washington), decided to establish a powerful outpost at the junction of the Numa Numa and East-West trails.

This time the marines neglected to start with an artillery barrage. It was a costly mistake.

The marine attack began at 7:30 on the morning of November 13. Company E of the 21st Marines moved up the Numa Numa Trail and ran smack into an ambush. The Japanese, as was their habit, were dug in. Once again they had shown that remarkable ability to make the best of the terrain. Log blockhouses protected their heavy and light machine guns. The riflemen given the knee mortars were scattered around the perimeter.

The dugouts were deep and had overhead cover of logs. Most of the machine gun positions were augmented toward their own rear by interconnecting trenches. And all this had been done without bulldozers or cement or virtually any equipment at all other than the infantryman's entrenching tools.

The defending troops had been able to obtain ammunition and automatic weapons from the 3rd Battalion of the Japanese 23rd Infantry, and they had many snipers in the trees.

The marines of Company E advanced without any knowledge of these defenses. They began to take casualties.

Company E called for help, and the 2nd Battalion commander, Lieutenant Colonel Eustace R. Smoak, came up with the battalion. Company G was sent in to relieve the pressure on Company E. Company H was ordered to set up a mortaring operation with the 81 mm mortars.

Major Glenn E. Fissell, the battalion executive officer, was sent up front to assess the situation. He saw that Company E was slowly being decimated by enemy fire. The answer, he figured, was artillery, and he called for it—to focus on the east side of the trail where the heaviest Japanese firepower seemed to be concentrated.

But Battalion Commander Smoak was getting conflicting reports. Instead of believing his exec and setting up the firing pattern for the artillery, he came up to look for himself.

By this time Fissell was wounded. Company E was still being cut down and no artillery was firing.

Smoak then ordered Company F to come up and relieve Company E. Company F started off bravely, then slanted away and got lost. Nobody could find hide or hair of them.

Company G was ordered to hold, and Company E, sensing a lull in the firing, began to withdraw, leaving a big hole in the center of the marine line. Still there was no artillery action.

Lieutenant Colonel Smoak now became worried about the various companies and sent more officers out to find them.

Still, no one but Major Fissell had thought about using the artillery.

All the battalion officers who searched did not find Company F. They did find a big hole in the center of the line between Company G and Company E. The battalion situation, says the marine history, was "precarious."

Even now, no one called for that artillery fire that Colonel Hamanoue hated so much.

Lieutenant Colonel Smoak then ordered Company E back into the line to close up the gap. It was growing late, and the time had come to dig in, even though the position was terrible. So the marines dug in at 4:30 in the afternoon.

The search for the missing Company F continued.

Down on the beach the patient artillerymen waited for information so they could begin firing. None came. Then Japanese infiltrators cut the telephone line, and Colonel Smoak was out of communication with the artillery and regimental headquarters.

The evening went by without any artillery fire.

At 5:00 P.M. a bedraggled sergeant showed up at battalion headquarters to report that Company F had managed to march around behind the Japanese lines without being discovered and was now worried about the situation. The platoons were all mixed up and no one seemed to be giving any coherent orders.

Lieutenant Colonel Smoak told the sergeant to go back and get the company, and he did. Perhaps miraculously, Company F marched back to the battalion command without getting decimated. The Japanese must have been stunned by it all.

During the night, Colonel Evans O. Ames, commander of the 21st Marines, came up to make a little sense out of the battlefront. He brought along the 2nd Raiders to protect supply and communications lines back to headquarters. He reestablished communication with the artillery and set up a firing pattern for the next morning (barrage on three sides of Smoak's battalion). He brought up tanks and called for an air strike in the morning.

In other words, the colonel did all the things that Colonel Hamanoue hated, which maybe should have been done in the beginning.

At eight o'clock on the morning of November 14, the air strike was overhead, waiting. But Colonel Smoak had patrols out, so the planes hung around and waited while he got them back in. The artillery obligingly fired smoke rounds right on target around the battalion to mark the areas where the planes should bomb and strafe, and the planes came down to do their work.

Eighteen TBFs plastered the area with high explosive and machine gun bullets.

Then Company E on the left and Company G on the right were supposed to step out in attack, with companies F and H in reserve. A platoon of five medium tanks would lead the way.

H-Hour was set for 11:00 A.M..

At 10:45 the telephone wires to the regiment broke down again. For reasons that will become apparent, it seems likely the Japanese had a hand in it.

The attack had to be delayed.

At 11:15 the wires were reestablished. H-Hour was moved back to 11:55.

The 12th Marines' splendid artillery promised a twenty-minute preparation and then a rolling barrage.

At 11:50 the attackers moved out.

The Japanese poured in a rain of heavy machine gun fire, light machine gun fire, and mortar rounds. The tankers became confused and turned. They ran over a number of marines. They began firing at positions. The trouble was they were marine positions.

Colonel Smoak decided the whole problem was the artillery barrage, which was confusing the troops, so he stopped it. He moved forward and halted the advance while he straightened out his officers and reorganized the assault.

The Japanese were thoroughly confused by these irregular tactics and stopped shooting while they tried to figure out what the enemy was up to.

Colonel Smoak issued orders to all company commanders to stand fast and send out patrols to see what the Japanese were up to. The tanks were sent back into reserve before they could kill any more marines. Two of them could not go. They had been knocked out by Japanese antitank guns.

And where were these guns?

They were behind the marine lines. It seems that the marines and the tanks in all the confusion had overrun the Japanese lines without knowing it and now they faced pockets of resistance behind their front. That seems to have accounted for the several breaches in communication lines.

Several squads of riflemen had to be detailed to find and wipe out the Japanese positions with grenades. They did so very effectively, using dogs, who sniffed out the positions and then waited while the riflemen blew them up.

Meanwhile, the Japanese facing the marines moved out, and when the American advance was resumed at 2:15, it moved ahead without much trouble. By 3:30 Lieutenant Colonel Smoak's men had achieved their objective, and they dug in for the night. For two days the reinforced battalion, supported by planes and artillery, had been fighting a single Japanese company.

The marines lost twenty men killed and wounded. They did not know how many Japanese they killed but it was probably many fewer than the forty they estimated. The fact is that this attack was an indication that Colonel Hamanoue was not talking through his hat when he said that if it wasn't for the fire power . . .

24

HANDWRITING
ON THE WALL

THE Japanese Eleventh Air Fleet at Rabaul was largely responsible for the defense of that center during the stepped up Allied air offensive. The Eleventh Air Fleet had been strengthened by November 1 for the Ro Operation. The Combined Fleet's Third Air Group was called The Tiger Cubs, a name given for its ferocity in the air. That air group's 1st Squadron was informed on November 1 that it would go to Rabaul that very day. On November 2, it arrived and flew two missions. On November 3, it flew one mission. On November 5, it went into the air to help with the defense of Rabaul, and when the fighting ended this squadron had done very well for itself. Only four planes were lost, and the fighter pilots had accounted for several of the American attackers.

The big raid on November 5 did not really slow down the Eleventh Air Fleet, but it did play hob with Admiral Koga's attempt to secure supremacy on the sea.

Rabaul harbor was cleared of warships. The heavy cruiser *Maya* remained in the harbor—but only because she could not move until internal repairs were made. The light cruiser *Agano* was still in harbor, too, and for the same reason. But the only other fighting ships to remain were the light cruiser *Yubari* and several destroyers, which had to be kept to protect, and sometimes to make, the reinforcement and resupply missions.

On November 6, the *Yubari* and the destroyer *Shigure* were sent to Buka. General Imamura was following his orders. The Americans would not get any of these bases easily. This time the destroyer and light cruiser landed seven hundred men and twenty-five tons of supplies for the Buka base.

The Americans were moving as quickly as they could to build those airstrips at Bougainville for land-based aircraft to use in attacking Rabaul. But in the interim, Admiral Halsey had the use of another of Admiral Nimitz's carrier task forces. This one consisted of the new *Essex*, the *Bunker Hill*, and the light carrier *Independence*. That meant five carriers in all for the next air operation, which would occur on November 11.

In the meantime, Admiral Kusaka's Eleventh Air Fleet was continuing the air battle with all its resources.

From the Shortland Islands lookout station on the morning of November 8 came a report to Japanese headquarters at Rabaul that a large force of Allied transports was heading north, obviously bound for the Torokina beachhead.

The alert was sounded, and at 10:15 (U.S. time) that morning a force of seventy-one Zero fighters and twenty-five Aichi 99 dive-bombers set out for Bougainville.

They arrived off Cape Torokina at noon and moved immediately to attack.

The convoy coming up consisted of the three big presidential liners that had brought the original contingent of troops. They were bringing the first load of reinforcements and more supplies. They were escorted by a number of minesweepers and destroyers.

The Japanese fighters and bombers managed to put two bombs into the *President Jackson*, causing some serious damage in the holds and twenty-five casualties, five of them dead.

Then the bombers were augmented by a force of Betty bombers and they found Admiral DuBose's covering cruiser force, which consisted of three light cruisers and four destroyers. The cruiser *Birmingham* took one bomb that blew the hatch off her airplane hangar, another on a gun turret, and a torpedo in the bow. She kept on going.

The Japanese who returned to Rabaul announced that they had sunk two transports and three destroyers, badly damaged a cruiser, left another transport burning, and shot down twelve American planes with another two probables.

The Japanese losses, they said, were ten bombers and five fighters, and two planes were damaged.

With this sort of reporting it was impossible for Admiral Koga or anyone else to have a real feel for the way the air battle was proceeding.

On November 11, about a hundred of Admiral Sherman's planes from the *Saratoga* and the *Princeton* were launched near the Green Islands, about 250 miles southeast of Rabaul. When they arrived over the target it was overcast, and they did not get much of a look at the whole harbor. But there down below were the *Yubari* and four destroyers, and the American planes attacked. The Japanese managed to duck in and out of rain clouds and the attack was not a success.

Admiral Montgomery's three carriers launched about 185 planes against Rabaul. They had moved in to a point about 160 miles southeast of the base for their attack. They ran into a surprise. For some reason the Americans had developed a habit of underestimating Japanese air strength at Rabaul. They did not then understand the pipeline system, which kept a steady stream of aircraft funneling into the headquarters of the Southeast Area Command. The almost constant bombing of Rabaul was reported through the various commands, and as the Allied pilots returned day after day to report the destruction of twenty, thirty, forty planes, the air intelligence officers had to believe that the Japanese strength at Rabaul was way down. In reality, on the 11th of November, the Japanese had 270 planes at Rabaul, and when the American air strike reached the area, it was met by sixty-eight Zeros.

The fight that ensued was a fierce one, but this time the Americans did to the Zeros what the Zeros had done so many times to the U.S. fighters. They lured the Japanese fighters into combat, and the dive-bombers and torpedo bombers sneaked through to attack the harbor.

The torpedo bombers performed better than they usually did: they put a torpedo into the crippled *Agano* and knocked off her stern. They also damaged the destroyer *Naganami*. And the dive-bombers sank the destroyer *Suzunami*.

The Japanese put up even more Zeros and chased the American attackers off. The Zeros then landed. Some of them would rearm and go off on the counterstrike against the American carrier force.

At noon the Eleventh Air Fleet launched its counterstrike, about a hundred and fifty planes. They were guided to the American task force by an orbiting Zero that had hung around all morning in spite of the efforts of the combat air patrol to get rid of it.

They attacked, but the combat air patrol and every fighter that could be moved off the decks of the three carriers got into the air. The fighters and the antiaircraft gunners disposed of the majority of the Japanese planes that afternoon. At the end of the day, Rabaul's air force was again in disrepair, with only about a hundred and fifty planes available.

The Japanese pilots came home to Rabaul bragging that they had sunk a cruiser, damaged two carriers, and also damaged three other warships. There was not a word of truth in the claim; they had not hit a single ship with a bomb or torpedo. Their one accomplishment, about which they were ignorant, is that they had forced the cancellation of the second American strike of the day against Rabaul.

The worst casualty of that day's fighting for the Japanese was the loss of many of the carrier planes lent to Admiral Kusaka's Eleventh Air Fleet by the carriers at Truk, including the Tiger Cubs.

The planes could be replaced relatively easily, but trained and experienced carrier pilots could not. The loss of these pilots in November 1943 was still to be felt by the big carriers *Shokaku* and *Zuikaku* during the following summer when they set out to engage the Americans in the "decisive battle" of the Philippine Sea.

The Japanese called the encounter on November 11 "the third Bougainville air battle," and at the moment their appraisal was that it, like the other two (on November 5 and 8), had been an enormous success.

The American buildup on Bougainville was constant. The waters off Torokina were busy with ships coming and going, bringing troops and all sorts of supplies. Every day that the weather permitted the Japanese attacked from the air. Every night Washing Machine Charlie brightened the sky with his flares and the fireworks of his bombs.

By November 11, the amphibious forces had brought in their fourth round of supply and troop reinforcements. The men who manned the ships were growing tired. A voyage up from Guadalcanal meant a constant harassment by the Japanese air forces, which were out every day. At night the "snoopers" were always around, keeping the lookouts and the gunners on their toes. By day a raid could be expected at any time. And there was the constant worry about submarines, which caused the dumping of hundreds of depth charges against bubbles and currents and the wreckage of the Slot.

On the night of November 12, for example, the destroyer *Fullam* was operating as part of a force escorting a convoy up from Guadalcanal to Bougainville. The force was under the command of Commodore L. F. Reifsnider.

The sky was clear, with a full moon and scattered clouds. There was virtually no wind; in other words, it was a wonderful night for snoopers.

The Japanese were still fighting the great air battle with the feeling that they were winning it. There were difficulties. Among the planes that returned to Rabaul, so many were damaged that the mechanics were making two planes out of three.

As soon as the Japanese learned that American ships were operating in this area, they launched an air strike, in what they were to call "the fourth air battle of Bougainville."

The Japanese planes began to appear at 9:15 but in their usual annoying way they stayed out of gun range, perfectly visible on the radar but refusing to close, and obviously reporting on the progress of the convoy up the Slot.

At midnight one plane closed in on the destroyer *Wadsworth*. All this while, of course the gunners had to be alert. As this plane came in to a point four thousand yards off the starboard bow of the convoy, those gunners fired nine rounds of antiaircraft fire. The plane withdrew.

More planes approached and withdrew. At 1:50 A.M. planes began dropping flares, red ones, white ones, and green ones. (The green ones indicated the presence of destroyers in the convoy.)

The snoopers grew bolder. One plane approached the *Wadsworth* again, and her gunners fired twelve rounds. The plane withdrew. Another plane approached the *Bennett*, and her gunners fired twenty-four rounds. The plane withdrew.

A number of "bogies" showed on the screens of the destroyers, and it seemed that an air attack was forming up. But the planes then went away. They came back, one by one.

It was indeed an air attack, mounted from Rabaul, but the attackers were not nearly so much interested in Reifsnider's destroyers as they were in Admiral Merrill's cruisers, which were not far away. The flares were to alert the torpedo bombers, and indicate the nature of the ships in each grouping.

The torpedo bombers found the cruisers and torpedoed the *Denver*, killing twenty men and injuring eleven.

She was towed back to the relative safety of Guadalcanal, where the air attacks had slowed down remarkably.

The attack on the *Denver* was again lumped in as a part of the strong effort the Japanese had been making for nearly two weeks to counteract the invasion of Bougainville.

The Americans were really unaware of Operation Ro as a major initiative until after the war. The reason was simply that the whole operation was so disconnected. It was supposed to have begun with the major strike by those cruisers from Truk in combination with the air strikes and the land push from the coast and by Colonel Hamanoue's 23rd Infantry from the inland side of Bougainville.

Since none of these attacks was ever coordinated and none of them really got off the ground, an American commander would have been flabbergasted to learn that the Japanese really believed that they were successful.

This night's activity was another example.

At 4:21 A.M. a stick of bombs exploded alongside the destroyer *Anthony*, without doing any damage. Somebody up there obviously identified her as one of the cruisers.

At 5:18 the destroyers *Wadsworth* and *Anthony* were attacked by torpedo planes. The men on deck saw at least two torpedoes dropped, but none hit the ships nor were any tracks seen. The gunners were firing constantly and claimed to have shot down one plane.

Those torpedo bombers, Betty bombers from Rabaul, were among the last of the attackers. As the survivors winged off, the light of false dawn was breaking, and it was not long before they were heading home.

When the pilots got there, they were again full of the most exaggerated tales.

The Japanese propaganda machine claimed that the Imperial forces had sunk five battleships, ten carriers, and nineteen cruisers, plus dozens of other ships. The claims made fine propaganda for Tokyo, and fine anti-Japanese propaganda for Washington.

By this time at Rabaul the reality of the Ro Operation had begun to sink in.

If so many American carriers and battleships had been sunk, then why were there still so many afloat?

That was the sort of question that sensible Japanese officers were beginning to ask themselves.

The fact was that the Japanese at every level were uncomfortably aware of the change in their fortunes in the past six months. They were losing the South Pacific campaign on the land, in the air, and on the sea.

As Colonel Hamanoue put it from his rough bivouac on the hillside above the Puma Puma Trail, "our advance was not on strong legs."

How true.

As of November 10, the colonel assessed his casualties. He had lost five officers dead and ten wounded. He had lost a hundred and four men killed and a hundred and eighty-four wounded. Forty men were missing. So the casualties against his force of about two thousand were about fifteen percent. But the problem was that there had been no noticeable assistance from the rear. He was going to have to fight on with these men, many of them near exhaustion. For example his assistant regimental commander and adjutant, Lieutenant Colonel Tanaka, was so tired that each night he collapsed in his foxhole and slept like one dead.

By November 13, the Americans had 34,000 troops ashore on Bougainville. The Japanese had strong defenses up north around the Buka airfield, but these showed no indication of coming south to fight against the Torokina beachhead. The Japanese also had strong defenses in the south, about 11,000 troops, but these had not moved from their prepared positions. The Americans were facing only Colonel Hamanoue's 23rd Infantry combat team, what was left of the thousand men who had attacked the beachhead's flank on November 7, and the remains of the Torokina defense force.

General Geiger saw as his major task the building of the airstrips. But before this could be done, the area around their proposed sites had to be cleared of Japanese, and roads had to be built for supply of the front lines.

As it was, two weeks after the invasion the only way to the front was via the narrow Piva Trail, which met several other trails upland. A man wounded at the front might require the assistance of a whole squad of men to get back to the beach area hospital.

The Japanese south of the Piva River had no such luxury. They were a long way from their base. And with every engagement, every skirmish, there were fewer of them.

Between the 14th and 16th of November the survivors of No. 5 Company of the 54th Infantry straggled in to Colonel Hamanoue's camp. They were pitifully few; all the officers were dead, and only sixteen enlisted men still lived.

On November 17, what was left of the 54th Infantry's No. 6 Company arrived with the remainder of the 53rd Infantry's No. 6 Company: twenty-three soldiers with two machine guns.

On the night of November 16, the fifth convoy for Cape Torokina was moving toward Bougainville. Another force of destroyers moved up to Buka to bombard the Japanese army airfield there.

Both of these reports were radioed to Rabaul and brought instant action.

The reinforcement flotilla consisted of eight LSTs and eight transport destroyers carrying marines to Bougainville, accompanied by six protective destroyers.

At sunset, a Japanese seaplane scout had sighted the force, which it misidentified as containing cruisers and aircraft carriers.

The reinforcement flotilla was approaching Torokina and had nearly reached Mupina Point at about one o'clock in the morning, when nine Japanese bombers and five torpedo bombers found them and prepared to attack. But the visibility from the air that night was bad, and the Japanese pilots attacked one by one over about a four-hour period.

One torpedo plane got through to the transport destroyer *McKean* and put a torpedo into her. The torpedo set off an explosion in the magazine and depth charge storage area. It was very quickly apparent that the ship was finished, and many of the marines aboard began jumping over the side. This turned out to be a fatal error, because nearly all of them were caught in pools of oil burning on the surface and burned to death.

Lieutenant Commander Ralph L. Ramey, the captain of the destroyer, moved her out of the area of the burning oil, and then ordered the passengers and crew to abandon ship.

The men then went off, the captain last. Three other destroyers stood by and picked up survivors, although the Japanese attack was still in progress.

During the rescue operation the *McKean* sank. Altogether fifty-two marines were lost, plus three of the officers of the *McKean* and sixty-one men.

The Japanese pilots went back to Rabaul to claim that they had sunk one large carrier, two middle-sized carriers, three cruisers, and one warship of an unidentified type. They reported the loss of four land bombers (Bettys) and one torpedo bomber.

These claims were made with great vigor. For example, referring to the big carrier, the Japanese could have said simply that it was sunk. But no, the report came in that it *gochin shite ita*, it sank immediately (and there could be no doubt about it).

On the basis of further scout reports, another force of fifty-five torpedo planes and ten dive-bombers left Rabaul early on the morning of November 17.

When they came back (minus six torpedo bombers and four dive-bombers), they reported having attacked a large group of transports and sinking three transports, forcing one to run aground after a near miss, leaving one destroyer dead in the water and burning, and shooting down two Allied planes.

Both reports were transmitted to Imperial General Headquarters that day, and as usual, Imperial General Headquarters accepted them without question and issued a communique, which was then broadcast by Radio Tokyo.

Since there were no carriers on that side of Bougainville that day, and since the only warship or transport sunk that day was the *McKean*, the Allies found it hard to understand what the Japanese were talking about. As with so many of the Japanese claims, reality seemed elusive. For whatever damage it did in Japanese planning, only the Imperial General Staff was to blame.

Admiral Yamamoto had seen this coming from the day after the disastrous Battle of Midway, when Imperial General Headquarters had trumpeted a victory in spite of his truthful report of the affair. He told his chief of staff that it would be disastrous in the end. But as the war worsened for Japan, the Imperial General Staff grew ever more impervious to advice and criticism. Such ridiculous reports were now the norm.

On Bougainville, little by little the marines expanded the perimeter, moving upland and to the east of the Torokina beachhead. On November 17, they occupied a Japanese roadblock on the Numa Numa Trail that had apparently been abandoned. They moved in. The Japanese decided to come back, found the marines, and a fight ensued. A number of Japanese were killed, and the marines held the position.

Colonel Hamanoue's 23rd Infantry was now being forced back south along the East–West Trail, and the main body was dug in approximately a mile from the Torokina River. But the Japanese advance parties were far to the west.

On November 19, the marines cut the Japanese line of communication by capturing a promontory known in marine history as Cibik Ridge, after Lieutenant John Cibik of the 3rd Marines. He led a platoon on patrol, found the ridge, which had been used as an observation post by the Japanese, and took control.

The Japanese attacked on November 21, but the marines held. On the 22nd and 23rd, the Japanese attacked, but still the marines held, and by the end of the 23rd the position was consolidated and the line brought up with it.

The Japanese were in deep trouble. They had lost their point of observation of Empress Augusta Bay. A number of troops were cut off on the west and had to either make their way up around the lines or try to fight through. The marines were building pressure along the Numa Numa Trail toward the main Japanese position astride that trail.

Colonel Hamanoue's force was by now down to about 1,500 men.

On November 23, the 3rd Marines planned a major attack on the Japanese who were located on both sides of the East–West Trail. To prepare, they did what Colonel Hamanoue hated most: they brought up seven battalions of artillery that were programmed to fire a twenty-minute barrage the next morning into an area 800 yards square. They would put several thousand rounds of 75 mm and 105 mm high explosives into that small area. Behind were the 155 mm guns and howitzers that were prepared for firing on call.

The marines had forty-four machine guns and a dozen 81 mm mortars and nine 60 mm mortars trained on the area.

H-Hour was set for nine o'clock on the morning of November 24. It was (for the Americans) Thanksgiving Day.

For twenty-three minutes before H-Hour, the artillery fired 5,700 rounds into the Japanese positions. It was the greatest artillery barrage yet delivered by the marines in this war.

However, Colonel Hamanoue had finally gotten some help. His messages about the devastating power of the American artillery had brought from the Sixth Division some artillery support. And as the Americans fired at the Japanese positions, a single Japanese 75 mm battery fired up and down the American line.

"This successful use of artillery by the Japanese," said the official marine history of the Bougainville campaign, "seemed to the Marines the worst feature of the entire fight."

They were getting a taste of what the Japanese had been taking for three weeks.

But just a taste. For in the middle of barrage and counterbarrage, a marine artillery observer up front spotted the Japanese battery and directed the guns of the 4th Battalion of the 12th Marines onto the position. A handful of shells knocked out two of the guns and silenced the Japanese battery.

At H-Hour the marines advanced. But instead of facing the usual hail of fire from Japanese machine guns and rifles, they found themselves in a zone of silence. The only Japanese soldiers they saw were dead. The Japanese positions had been completely knocked out by the artillery.

The marines advanced five hundred yards before the enemy was able to offer any resistance. Colonel Hamanoue had committed some reserves by that time, and they fought fiercely, launching a flanking counterattack against the marine left. The 3rd Marines 3rd Battalion bore the brunt of it.

The fighting started with more Japanese artillery fire. It was worrisome to the marines, and effective.

Fighting then dropped into a hand-to-hand pattern, with marines and Japanese killing each other for possession of individual trees and declivities. In the end, the marines destroyed the effect of the flanking force, and the surviving Japanese moved back.

The frontal force also moved ahead against strong Japanese opposition. The mortar platoons worked hard to plaster the Japanese positions, and they succeeded. The mortar was the key weapon, because the Japanese were really dug into a virtual maze of slit trenches, pillboxes, and foxholes that were mutually supporting. But the artillery and the mortars did the job for the riflemen. The marines reached their destination. The 23rd Japanese Infantry melted away before them.

Again on November 25 the marines moved forward in attack. Again the artillery softened up the ground for them. The marine line extended

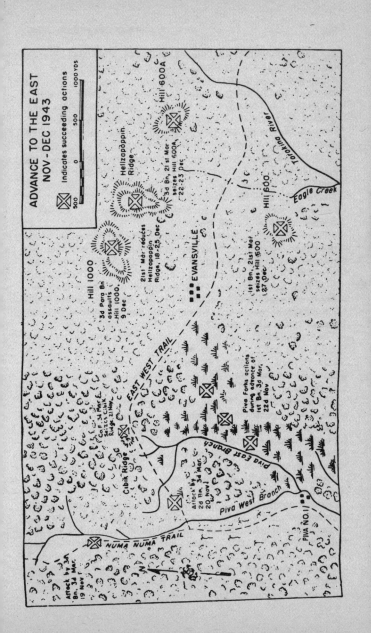

ADVANCE TO THE EAST
NOV - DEC 1943

⊠ Indicates succeeding actions

500   0   500   1000 YDS

Hill 600A

Hellzapoppin Ridge

3d Bn, 21st Mar
seizes Hill 600A,
22-23 Dec

Hill 1000

21st Mar reduces
Hellzapoppin
Ridge, 18-25 Dec

Hill 600

3d Para Bn
assaults
Hill 1000,
9 Dec

EVANSVILLE

Torokina River

Eagle Creek

1st Bn, 21st Mar
seizes Hill 600,
27 Dec

EAST WEST TRAIL

C of F, 3d Mar
seizes Cibik
Ridge, 21 Nov

Cibik Ridge

Piva Forks actions
during advance of
1st Bn, 3d Mar,
22d Nov

Piva East Branch

Attack by
2d Bn, 3d Mar,
20 Nov

Piva West Branch

PIVA NO. 1

⊠ NUMA NUMA TRAIL

Attack by 3d
Bn, 3d Mar,
19 Nov

around Cibik Ridge. The Japanese defense position was atop a promontory the marines were to call Grenade Hill.

There the Japanese had accomplished overnight another of their brilliant defenses. Some seventy Japanese soldiers were dug in on the ridge, with four heavy machine guns, a number of light machine guns, and lots and lots of grenades. Thus the marine name for the hill.

The marines surrounded the position completely and tried to work their way to the top. But no matter from which direction they came, as they reached the summit the Japanese began throwing grenades with considerable accuracy, and the marines had to fall back.

All day long the battle continued, and at the end of the day the Japanese still held Grenade Hill.

But that night the Japanese moved out, and the next morning the marines moved in without opposition.

The next day, the marines moved forward along the line and straightened it out. They had accomplished their objective and now controlled the trail to the Torokina River. For the next four months the Japanese would try no more than to put patrols across the river. The Americans controlled the heights above their beachhead and the site that was to become the Piva bomber field. Since this was what General Geiger wanted, the marines dug in and a few days later turned over the area to the U.S. Army's XIV Corps.

By this time, the 23rd Japanese Infantry had taken a tremendous beating. The marine figure for the total number of Japanese dead since D-Day was 2,000. That had to include the casualties from the 300 original defenders and the one thousand men brought from Rabaul to attack the beach. But the vast majority of the dead were men of the 23rd Infantry. The 1st and 3rd battalions of the regiment were in tatters. The two-pronged attempt to strike the bridgehead had failed miserably, the Americans were ensconced on the beachhead in great strength, and there was no way the situation could be reversed by moving along the mountain trails from the south.

Colonel Hamanoue's campaign was over.

As if to emphasize the change, on November 24, the first U.S. plane landed on the fighter strip down by the beach. Although it was premature—Marine Captain J. C. Richards's dive-bomber had been damaged by antiaircraft fire in a raid on northern Bougainville, and he had to put down somewhere—the strip held up and the plane was safe.

For all practical purposes the Americans had their first airfield on Bougainville. It was just a question of time before planes would begin operating from there against Rabaul.

The Americans did not realize, however, that the 23rd Regiment was about to pull out of the area. They worried about a force coming up along the south side of Empress Augusta Bay to somehow reinforce or link up with the colonel. And without sufficient intelligence to justify it, they planned a raid inside the Japanese lines on the southern side of the bay to destroy communications and supplies.

The trouble probably lay in the failure of the Allies to convince the Bougainvilleans, as they had the natives of Guadalcanal and the Central Solomons, that the Allies and not the Japanese were going to win the war. On Bougainville, as noted, the Allies did not have the advantage of a friendly native population that could have warned them against precipitate action to the south.

On November 23, the 1st Marine Parachute Battalion arrived at Bougainville, and General Geiger decided to send them in to make the raid to the south, along with Company M of the 3rd Raider Battalion and several specialists and native guides.

Major Richard Fagan was in command. He was to land on a beach about 3,000 yards northwest of Koiari. No one knew much about the beach except that it was there. The native guides were useless. No one knew how many Japanese were in the area, or where they were. Fagan's mission was to establish a base and then send out raiding parties as far inland as the East-West Trail. If he encountered any large force of Japanese, he was to retreat to the Torokina beachhead.

At three o'clock on the morning of November 29, the parachute force loaded aboard landing craft and an hour later was landed on the coast at Koiari Beach.

They were greeted by a Japanese officer, who marched out from the jungle and began a conversation with the incoming marines. He was wearing his sword, but it was scabbarded, and he obviously was expecting Japanese reinforcements—not Americans.

The moment an American spoke, the Japanese officer ducked back into the jungle and was gone.

The marines moved fast. Soon they had a beachhead, 350 yards wide and 180 yards deep. But this did not include the 3rd Raider company, which had been landed about a thousand yards east of the other troops.

Within a few minutes firing began. It soon became obvious that the Japanese force ahead was large. In fact, Major Fagan had stepped into a hornet's nest; he had arrived in the middle of a Japanese supply area.

The 3rd Raider company was cut off. They began to fight their way up the beach toward the rest of the force, but it was costly, and by the time they arrived at 9:30 in the morning, they had suffered thirteen casualties.

The parachute troops were also under fire. Major Fagan was in touch with Torokina, until his radio receiver went out, and from that time on it worked sporadically.

At dawn the Japanese attacked. They used 90 mm mortars and heavy machine guns. The marines were pinned down on their beachhead. They fought off the attacks but as the morning wore on these continued and became more fierce.

By eight o'clock in the morning, Fagan had decided that he was in real trouble and that if someone did not get him out, all of them were liable to be killed. He sent a message back to General Geiger asking that the landing craft come and pull them out of their predicament. Obviously the landing craft would have to have some support.

General Geiger agreed, and he proceeded to instruct Fagan in his next steps. But the message did not get through.

So the marines dug in and waited. The Japanese attacked, and attacked again. The marines fought them off. But after several attacks their ammunition supplies were diminishing rapidly, and Fagan wondered whether they would last through the night if the attacks continued.

Meanwhile the landing craft came back and tried to get in to take the men off. But every time they approached the shore, the Japanese laid down a heavy mortar barrage and drove them off.

However, Major Fagan had another weapon: that artillery again. He could not receive messages but he could transmit, and his artillery spotters began to set up coordinates for fire from the 155 mm guns back on Torokina.

The guns responded, great splashes of dirt and greenery rose up from the jungle, and the marines' situation took a turn for the better.

It improved more when strafing planes came zooming down over the area and fired into the jungle.

At six o'clock that night, the destroyers *Fullam, Lansdowne,* and *Lardner* appeared off the beach and began shelling the Japanese, covering the right and left flanks of the beachhead.

With this firing, at 7:20 that night the landing craft were able to get to shore. The night was pitch black, and under this cover the marines moved into the water and the boats. But in the darkness much of the equipment of the detachment was missed or had to be abandoned. There was no help for it; the marines had to get going.

By 8:40 they were in the boats and moving out to sea under the covering fire of the destroyers.

Seventeen marines had been killed or received mortal wounds, and ninety-five were wounded. When they came back to Torokina, they claimed to have killed 145 Japanese, but there is no way this could be substantiated, and the figure is undoubtedly exaggerated.

The mission was a complete failure. The members of the detachment were lucky to get out with their skins. It was a good lesson that the Japanese were still very much alive in Central Bougainville.

25

THIRTY-ONE
KNOT BURKE

ADMIRAL Halsey was moving faster now. In the middle of November the pace of the air war stepped up.

Guadalcanal was now a rear area. The American planes came from Munda on New Georgia Island and from Barakoma on Vella Lavella, and they ranged up and down Bougainville, strafing and bombing. The bombers from the various Central Solomons airfields could now reach Rabaul, but the range was still too great for the fighter planes. So Halsey pushed the work on the fighter strip down by the Torokina Beach even harder.

The Japanese effort also continued, and that beach at Torokina was hit night after night. More antiaircraft guns were brought up to Bougainville, and they paid their way in knocking down the Japanese night birds.

But they did not stop Japanese air activity.

By November 24, Rabaul's air force was building again, despite constant raids by B-24s and B-25s. Scout planes counted more than two hundred Japanese planes on the Rabaul airfields.

The Americans continued to resupply the Bougainville beach with big convoys, and the Japanese continued to attack them. The combination of American fighters and antiaircraft gunners aboard the ships kept damage to a minimum, and many Japanese planes were shot down.

Three weeks after the invasion of Bougainville, the Japanese command at Rabaul was still not convinced that this move into Torokina represented the major American effort on the island. The move was completely unorthodox; major Japanese bases existed on the north end (Buka) and the south end (Buin and the Shortlands), and it seemed unreasonable that the Americans would not seek to capture at least one of these. West Central Bougainville, where they had landed, did not even have a decent harbor.

So, even though the Japanese Army on the island outnumbered the original landing force of 34,000 by almost two to one, the Japanese chose to build up the northern and southern bases for the expected attack, instead of pitting their major effort against the Torokina landings.

On November 24, the Pearl Harbor radio intelligence team intercepted messages between Rabaul and Truk concerning a new supply and reinforcement mission for Buka, the site of major air bases. The navy was to send three destroyer transports with two protective destroyers down to the Buka passage with nine hundred and twenty-five troops and thirty-five tons of food and ammunition. They were to take off seven hundred incapacitated sailors and soldiers for return to Rabaul. The date was to be November 24. The destroyers were to sail at 3:30 in the afternoon, Tokyo time. Commander of the mission would be Captain Kiyoto Kagawa in the *Onami,* a two thousand-ton ship about a year old. With him for protection would be the *Minami,* another ship of the same class.

To be protected were the three older destroyers *Yugiri, Amagiri,* and *Uzuki,* which would be carrying the troops and supplies.

All three destroyers and their crews were veterans of the Slot. The *Amagiri* had been making such runs to Kolombangara for months. The *Uzuki* had been in these waters since the Guadalcanal days; she had been through Admiral Tanaka's Guadalcanal resupply battles. The *Yugiri* had been involved in one of the earliest successful American air attacks on Japanese warships: August 28, 1942, when U.S. bombers completely stopped a Guadalcanal resupply mission, sank the destroyer *Asagiri,* and caused such damage to the *Yugiri* that her whole superstructure had to be rebuilt at Truk.

When Admiral Halsey received that "Ultra" message about the coming Japanese supply run, his staff moved to act quickly. On November 24, Captain Arleigh Burke's Destroyer Squadron 23 was refueling at Hathorn Sound, when a message came addressed to "31-knot Burke" from Halsey. The U.S. Navy loves meaningful nicknames, and Burke had gotten his from his habit of traveling in enemy waters at top speed, just as his destroyer squadron had earned the name "The Little Beavers" because of an unusual willingness to take on all sorts of jobs not sought by destroyer outfits (such as transporting troops) and doing them swiftly and well without complaint.

On this day Burke's message from Halsey had the ring of a message that Admiral Lord Nelson might have sent one of his captains:

> Put your squadron athwart the Buka–Rabaul evacuation line about 35 miles west of Buka. . . . If enemy contacted you know what to do.
>
> Halsey

The operating ships of Burke's squadron that day were the flagship *Charles F. Ausburne*, the *Claxton*, and the *Dyson*, all of Division 45, and the *Converse* and *Spence* of Division 46. Commanding the second division was Commander B. L. Austin. Burke himself led Division 45.

At Rabaul all went according to plan. The troops and supplies were loaded, and the Japanese ships set out for the relatively short trip to Buka. This same voyage had been made a few weeks earlier without opposition.

But times had changed drastically in those few weeks. The Japanese had then still controlled the air and sea around Buka passage. The Americans raided, but the raids were brief and dangerous for the attackers. Now, in November, the Americans were wresting away that control.

On the night of November 24, nine of Halsey's PT boats had been sent up to lurk off Buka Passage and make a pass at the destroyer reinforcement team if they came along that way. And as Halsey sent his orders to Captain Burke to find the enemy, he also instructed the Solomons air force to give Burke night fighter cover, which meant that Burke had an extra advantage not enjoyed by the destroyer commanders in the days of Guadalcanal.

The Japanese convoy steamed on that evening toward Buka, not really expecting trouble. The transport destroyers peeled off and entered Buka Passage, then closed on the shore, where they stopped, desposited their troops and supplies, and took on the sick and wounded from the Buka base. Then they began to move out to join the protective destroyers.

Just outside, three of the U.S. PT boats observed these actions on their radar screens but failed to understand the significance. At about midnight, Commander Henry Farrow saw the ships moving but believed them to be the ships of Captain Burke's force, and so he politely moved inshore to get out of the way.

But suddenly, two of the ships altered course and headed directly toward the PT boats, something that Burke's destroyers would not be likely to do. And one, the *Onami*, speeded up and gave the PT boat skippers something of a scare. It ought to have, *Onami* Captain Kiyoto Kagawa was heading toward the pestiferous PT boats with the intention of cutting as many of them in two as possible, in the same fashion that the *Amagiri* had destroyed PT 109 in the Slot.

Still, most of the PT skippers believed the problem was one of mistaken identity and did not move to attack, even when five-inch shells began whistling through the air around them. They evaded the oncoming destroyers by ducking into a rain squall. Only one, PT 64, fired a single torpedo. It missed.

Nevertheless the PT boats served a useful purpose that night, because Commander Farrow radioed the story of his encounter, and Captain Burke's destroyers picked up the message.

Burke was moving toward the western approaches to St. George's Channel, which separates New Britain Island, where Rabaul is located, from New Ireland. This was all considered to be Japanese water. From the mouth of the passage, off Cape St. George, the distance to Buka passage was only about a hundred and fifty miles.

When Burke learned that the PT boats had encountered ships he was sure would be those of his enemy, he began preparations for the attack. Down from thirty-one knots to twenty-three went the U.S. destroyers, so that the south sea phosphorescence of their wakes would decrease, and they would be less likely to be spotted by aircraft from afar.

The destroyers changed course, moving across their assigned patrol area. It was a fine night for American radar and a bad one for Japanese night vision, for the clouds hung low and those rain squalls were all about, breaking the regular horizon of the sea. The clouds just hung there, low in the air, for there was almost no wind.

Having already had one encounter with the enemy, and now being on the last leg home to Rabaul, Captain Kagawa was not expecting a destroyer attack. He was, in fact, much more anxious about the slowness of the transport destroyers to join up with the *Onami* and the *Makinami*.

At 1:40 in the morning, the American destroyers changed course to the north, and this put them on a line that would converge with Captain Kagawa's ships. Just moments later, the radar operators of all three of Burke's Division 45 ships picked up a pair of blips on their screens. The blips were eleven miles away, to the east.

Captain Burke then ordered his ships to point toward the enemy. The *Charles F. Ausburne, Claxton,* and *Dyson* were leading, with Commander Austin's *Converse* and *Spence* a little more than three miles behind. According to Burke's battle plan, his three ships would attack with torpedoes, then turn to evade enemy torpedoes and reload, whereupon Commander Austin's destroyers would have a clear sea on which to attack.

The American ships now sped on toward the enemy, the matter of wakes no longer worrying anybody. The Japanese destroyers moved on serenely, close now to Cape St. George and the protected waters of Rabaul. Captain Kagawa had absolutely no hint that there was an enemy near.

At 1:56 Captain Burke's three destroyers were in position and the calculations were complete. The torpedomen fired fifteen torpedoes and then turned sharply to the right to avoid any incoming torpedoes the enemy might have fired. This was a maneuver that too many American destroyer skippers had forgotten in the past.

The torpedoes headed for the Japanese ships, about three miles away. Captain Kagawa's lookouts saw them—the first indication they had that enemy ships were anywhere about—just thirty seconds before the torpedoes began to hit. It was too late to turn away, and the *Onami* crewmen watched with horrified fascination as the torpedoes came right at them, and two struck the side of their ship. For most of the crewmen of the *Onami* the violent explosion that came next was their last experience on earth: one of those torpedoes obviously found a magazine, and the destroyer exploded in a ball of flame that shot three hundred feet in the air and scattered like a giant Roman candle charge.

A third torpedo struck the *Makinami,* and it, too, must have found some explosives inside the ship, for the *Makinami* also erupted in explosions and broke in two. But the halves continued to float.

Waiting for the torpedoes to hit, the men of the *Charles F. Ausburne* radar crew stayed tense and then saw three more blips on the screen. When they called Captain Burke on the bridge, he had stopped waiting; the first explosions were in the air. He issued terse orders to Commander Austin to take his second division and finish off the enemy destroyers, and then Burke set out in hot pursuit of the next three enemy ships.

The *Amagiri, Yugiri,* and *Uzuki* were trying to catch up with the lead destroyers, but they were still eight miles behind when the *Onami* and *Makinami* erupted in balls of fire.

Captain Katsumori Yamashiro was in command of the transport

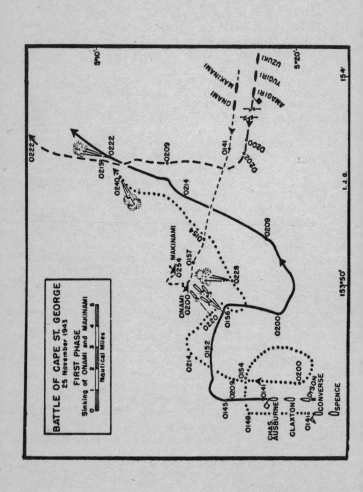

BATTLE OF CAPE ST. GEORGE
25 November 1943

FIRST PHASE
Sinking of ONAMI and MAKINAMI

Nautical Miles
0 1 2 3 4 5

destroyers. He decided to make a run for it, north to Rabaul. The problem was that his three destroyers were all badly in need of refit and could not make thirty knots. But he was close enough, perhaps eighty miles off Cape St. George and the safety of St. George's channel.

He had a chance.

The Japanese destroyers fled at their best speed, but Captain Burke managed to bring his three pursuers up to thirty-three knots and close the gap to eight thousand yards.

Suddenly, Burke had the feeling that he ought to get out of the way of something, and he ordered a high speed turn of forty-five degrees to the right, held that course for a minute and then turned back to his base course.

Somebody up there was looking after the Americans this night, for just at the moment that the three U.S. destroyers turned back to the original course, three sharp explosions were heard behind them. Torpedoes were detonating in the turbulence of the wakes of the ships. The captain of the *Yugiri* had slowed long enough for his torpedo men to fire a spread of torpedoes at the pursuing American ships.

It was a gallant effort, but it cost the Japanese dearly. For in slowing to fire the torpedoes, the *Yugiri* fell behind the other Japanese destroyers and into range of the Americans.

Captain Burke pursued and in pursuing ordered his ships to open fire with their forward guns. They did so and began scoring hits on the *Yugiri*. They also fired on the other two destroyers but did not do so well. The *Uzuki* was hit by one dud five-inch shell and the *Amagiri* by none at all.

But the *Yugiri* began to take punishment.

At 2:30 in the morning, Burke's guns were scoring consistent hits on the tail end Japanese ship. Not long afterward a shell destroyed the steering of the *Yugiri*, and she began to move in circles. Explosions poured up over her new superstructure.

Shortly after 3:00 in the morning, the *Yugiri* sank.

Captain Burke chased the *Amagiri* and the *Uzuki* as far as he dared, to within thirty-five miles of Cape St. George. By that time, the darkness of night was racing toward the dawn, and it might be suicidal to be caught in daylight so close to the airfields of Rabaul. Burke broke off the chase and turned south.

The *Amagiri* and the *Uzuki* sped onward into the safe waters of St. George's Channel. There Captain Yamashiro sent an urgent message to Rabaul to dispatch assistance for the men in the water from the sinkings of the three destroyers lost that night.

The navy hurried to help and dispatched submarines to pick up survivors. But when the waters where the *Onami* and *Makinami* were

reached, the rescuers found nothing. A few men from the *Makinami* had
been able to get into rafts and eventually they made the shore and
rescue. The *Onami* had gone down immediately. Only at the site of the
sinking of the *Yuguri* were the rescuers rewarded. The submarine *I-177*
picked up nearly three hundred men from this ship and brought them
back to Rabaul.

Meanwhile, Captain Burke went back to safer waters, south of Bougainville. When dawn broke, the men of the destroyers began to scan
the skies anxiously for aircraft. But they were lucky; when the planes
came over, they were American planes, not Japanese. The Burke force
had got off scot-free in what was to that point the cleanest and most
effective American multi-ship action of the war. Not a man was hurt,
not a scratch was administered to an American ship, and three Japanese
destroyers had gone down.

When praised for the action, Captain Burke attributed his squadron's
success to "a force beyond its control." Whether he meant a supreme
being or luck, it was certainly true. Something had put Burke's ships in
the right place at the right time.

A fifteen-minute delay in getting to the position where he sighted the
Japanese destroyers would have meant missing them, Burke pointed
out.

Even more subject to speculation is the reason for Burke's sudden
decision to change course when in hot pursuit of the *Yugiri*. He had not
seen the ship slow down, nor had he any physical indication that he was
coming under attack. Still he turned and by turning saved his ships from
almost certain damage and possible destruction.

But attributing the success of Burke's action to luck or the Almighty is
an oversimplistic solution. The fact is that in the past few months the
American fighting captains had come of age. The U.S. Navy began the
Pacific War with a large number of superannuated destroyers, and
skippers and officers virtually unskilled in battle because they had never
fought before. Furthermore, what was important in peace was no
longer important in war. In the prewar navy, one of the quickest ways to
oblivion for a naval officer was to risk his ship. It had taken some
adjustment and some experience for these professional officers to learn
that there were worse things in life than running aground.

Despite his modesty, Captain Burke was a superior officer. He was
well loved by his men for his earthy ways and his level-handed discipline and for that indefinable characteristic that arouses superior
loyalty.

Further than that, Burke was a good student. Undoubtedly at least
part of the reason that he turned to avoid the *Yugiri*'s attack was his

realization that it was precisely what the enemy should have done. A hunch he said it was, but a reasoned hunch it must have been. Like Commander Moosbrugger and Admiral Merrill, Captain Burke was one of a new breed.

Admiral Halsey was responsible for much of this change in attitude in the South Pacific, as those earlier anecdotes about Burke and Halsey indicated.

Now it had all begun to pay off. The Japanese, once so contemptuous of American naval prowess, were staggering under a multiplicity of blows. They blamed everything on American technological prowess, but it was not as simple as that, as Burke's action shows.

And as far as Buka was concerned, General Imamura now gave up. He issued orders that no further attempts would be made to resupply or reinforce the Buka garrison from Rabaul. From now on the responsibility was to be that of General Hyukatake's Seventeenth Army, based on Bougainville.

For all practical purposes, Captain Burke's successful foray had caused the Japanese to draw the new line of defense at St. George's Channel. Bougainville was still crawling with Japanese soldiers (about 70,000 of them). But except for air support, they were going to have to take care of themselves.

That's what Captain Burke and his Little Beavers had done on the night of Thanksgiving 1943.

26

GENERAL IMAMURA'S MISCALCULATION

GENERAL Hitoshi Imamura was an intelligent man and a highly experienced officer in His Imperial Japanese Majesty's Army.

He had studied in England and later served in the military attache's office in London. As early as 1917 he had been a member of the all-important Military Affairs Bureau of the War Ministry, which really ran the Japanese Army and later the government. He was, then, one of the important clique (some called them arch-conspirators) who ran Japan.

As for experience, he above nearly all others could scarcely claim that he did not understand his enemies. Not only had he served in England, but he had traveled widely in Europe, observing other armies there, and had also served in India as resident Japanese military officer—the equivalent of military attache.

Imamura had hitched his star to the group of men who captured control of the Kwantung Army in Manchuria as a power base, and thereafter his rise was rapid. By 1930 he was a section chief in the Military Affairs Bureau, and the next year he held the same position in the Army General Staff.

Then came the requisite period of commanding troops in the field: his command was the 57th Infantry Regiment. From there he went on to run the Narashino Army School and after two years to become a brigade commander (47th) in 1935. By this time he had achieved the rank of major general.

A hitch as deputy chief of staff of the Kwantung Army showed where he stood in the military hierarchy. The year was 1936, the year the Japanese made their plans to carry the war into China.

Then came the prestigious job of commanding the Army Infantry School, a division, and finally in 1942 the Twenty-Third Army. When the enormous expansion of Japanese military power across the Pacific brought staggering problems of military administration, General Imamura was advanced to the post of commander of the Eighth Area Army, which included everything the Japanese might ever capture, down to Samoa, Australia, and New Zealand.

It was fitting that what happened in the South Pacific, whether Japan triumphed or fell, should be in his hands.

After the failure of the Hamanoue detachment and the counterlanding force to wrest control of the Torokina beachhead from the Allies, the Japanese did virtually nothing for several weeks to carry the war on Bougainville.

Meanwhile the Americans kept landing reinforcements, supplies, and heavy artillery.

The major Allied effort (by American and New Zealand engineers) was to build the airstrips—one down on the beach and two on the uplands. The remainder of the troops on Bougainville were there to protect the airstrip builders.

Had the Japanese concentrated their forces on Bougainville, either at the beginning of the invasion or at any time within the three or four weeks, the outcome of that battle might have been quite different. Actually Bu Shima, as the Japanese abbreviated the name, offered the sort of battle conditions where the major American advantages were largely vitiated. Thick jungle made air strikes of only limited value. The same held true of naval bombardments. If there was a place in the Pacific where manpower and infantry skills (plus artillery) meant the difference, it was this island.

Yet General Imamura of the 8th Area Army and General Hayakutake, commander of the Japanese 17th Army, ignored their own advantage of numbers of troops and did not make the major effort that might have driven the Americans from the small area of Bougainville that they held.

The reason was disbelief.

What General MacArthur was planning was the encirclement of Rabaul. The only reason for invading Bougainville at all was to establish airfields. That could be done without taking on the thousands of troops to the north around Buka, or to the south around Buin and the Shortlands. Japanese troops on Bougainville still numbered more than 70,000, but only two or three thousand of these were anywhere near the Torokina perimeter. The Japanese generals persisted in a belief that the Americans would now move a major effort against either Buin or Buka. Almost all their effort was devoted to improving and extending the defenses of these areas.

But there was never any possibility of Halsey undertaking such a complex operation in these times. The South Pacific was always known as the Shoestring Theater, and so it would remain. While Halsey was moving on Bougainville, Nimitz at Pearl Harbor was directing the investment of the Gilbert Islands and immediately thereafter planning for the capture of the Marshalls. The navy war plan had always envisioned a drive across the Central Pacific and the only reason for the Guadalcanal invasion had been to stop a dangerous Japanese effort to cut Australia and New Zealand out of the Allied camp.

But in its way, adversity had become a blessing. By landing in the relatively deserted middle of Bougainville, Halsey had obtained the foothold he wanted, and at a price for the airfields now building that was much cheaper than anyone could have expected in terms of lives and effort.

At Truk, Admiral Koga suggested that the Americans might be serious in what they were doing, but the generals were not used to taking instruction from an admiral, and they ignored him. Koga's own efforts persisted: he stripped the rest of his command of first-class aircraft to keep them flowing into Rabaul, and despite constant attrition through warfare with Halsey's Solomons air force and MacArthur's Fifth Air Force, admirals Koga and Kusaka did keep the Japanese Eleventh Air Fleet constantly in motion. If the number of planes fell below two hundred in any one day, immediate effort was made to reinforce the fleet.

So ineffectual was the Japanese "air war" against Bougainville that Admiral Halsey was some time in discovering the importance the enemy attached to it. And the record does not indicate that anyone in the South or Southwest Pacific was cognizant of the most compelling reason for the continuation and blowing up of the Japanese air effort.

It was, in a word, political.

At home Japan was beginning for the first time to feel that the war was not going well. The overblown reports of the Ro Operation were distributed to the membership of the Greater East Asia Co-Prosperity Sphere, whose representatives were then meeting in Tokyo. The report of the great victories (the claim was four battleships sunk and two left burning, two cruisers sunk and four sinking in the second "battle") was distributed to the conferees, and care was taken that the reports were circulated in Manchuria, Taiwan, the Philippines, Burma, and all the other corners of the Japanese empire.

The Japanese were worried about the coming Cairo Conference of the Allies, and it was for that reason that the "great air battle" was continued, even when Admiral Koga had to at least suspect that the results were being faked.

For the Imperial General Staff felt something must be done to shore up a sinking Japanese morale. In Tokyo, General Soichiro Sanada, one member of the Imperial General Staff, had some private thoughts, which he confined to his diary only:

> As for what is happening in the South Pacific, pardon me for saying, it is windy. This talk about return to Guadalcanal is idiocy. Malaria and other evils make it totally impossible.
> The Bougainville battle is having enormous repercussions here. Business is declining. Wheat hoarding has begun. Confusion has begun to hang over market conditions. . . .

As the war situation began to worsen a number of the Japanese leaders recognized the truth of what Admiral Yamamoto had been saying for a long time before his death: that the best that could happen to Japan after Midway was to secure "an honorable peace."

Thus Japan's diplomatic and military establishment in the neutral world was on the lookout for favorable signs that might lead to a softening of the tough Allied position that demanded unconditional surrender of the Axis powers. The Bougainville "air victories," Tokyo believed, provided just the sort of ammunition that was valuable.

From the Japanese embassy in Madrid came the word that the Spanish press had aroused considerable excitement in that city with the reports of the great Japanese victory in the South Pacific. (The Spanish government and press were all but members of the Rome-Berlin-Tokyo axis.) Further, reported the Japanese embassy, sources in Madrid indicated that Great Britain was showing more and more war weariness and that the leadership in London was not pleased with attempts by the Americans to draw them into further participation in the Pacific War.

Another report in mid-November, from the Japanese diplomatic group in Stockholm, indicated that while at first the reports of the great Japanese victory were greeted there skeptically, the constant repetition, with no American denials, had brought many people to believe in the Japanese claims. This was useful, Stockholm reported, because it indicated that the antipathy toward Japanese statements on the war was beginning to break down.

Even from Bern came favorable comment. The Japanese in Switzerland operated under considerable difficulty, because various American agencies (including the OSS under Alan Dulles) waged an incessant and generally successful campaign to keep Japanese "news reports" out of the Swiss press. But in spite of all this, the minister to Switzerland reported, the "great victories" had aroused a reluctant admiration for the Japanese effort, and this could be valuable.

So, in December, the Japanese naval air force continued what it called the great air battle of Bougainville and sent air strikes over the island almost every day. The pilots returned with extravagant claims of damage done, as was becoming usual.

The major land defense effort of the Japanese in December came midway through the month. The U.S. Marines wanted to consolidate their line north of the East-West Trail, and they found a Japanese strongpoint on a ridge north of the position of the 21st Marines. It turned out to be a natural fortress, about three hundred yards long, with two almost vertical sides and a narrow and highly defensible crest about forty yards wide. It was all heavy jungle.

Needless to say, the Japanese had done the best they could with the terrain at hand. The ridge was occupied by a reinforced company of Colonel Hamanoue's 23rd Infantry Regiment. They had done something that the marines would find new: they treated their position as an island and defended it on all sides. Thus there was no "tender" spot at the rear, which could be outflanked. Of course, this sort of defense presupposed willingness to fight to the last man; that was becoming a cornerstone of Japanese defense in this war. Not many of the Allies involved in the South Pacific had any direct information about what had occurred at Tarawa late in November, so they were not quite sure what to expect.

On December 12, the marines began their assault on this position, which they quickly named Hellzapoppin Ridge (after an Olsen and Johnson vaudeville show then popular back home). The ridge lived up to its gaudy name, producing more fireworks than any other Japanese position on this island. During the lull of late November, the Japanese, probably advised by Colonel Hamanoue, had brought up a considerable amount of artillery to this point.

The battle lasted for six days, and the marines fought for every foot of the terrain. The Japanese defenses were so well concealed that the marines did not find them until they stepped into them, and by that time it meant bursts of fire and casualties.

The marines used every weapon at their disposal. They tried 60 mm mortars, but these turned out to be too small. They switched to 81 mm mortars, but these were only of limited effectiveness against the dug-in positions. They turned on the artillery, but it was not very effective against reverse hill positions. They called for air support, but it, too, had serious limitations against defenses in dugouts.

Finally, after five days of heartbreaking fighting, the marines utilized everything at once. They called for three air strikes, an artillery barrage, and then a fourth air strike. They got them all.

Then troops of the 1st and 3rd battalions of the 21st Marines moved forward on two sides of the hill, and up, squeezing the Japanese like one squeezes an orange. Under this pressure, the Japanese troops moved upward and out of their dugouts and foxholes, and they were pushed off their hill. When the battle was over and the marines held the position, they had twelve men killed and twenty-three wounded. They counted about fifty Japanese bodies.

The next Japanese position that had to be eliminated was Hill 600A, another high point, not far from Hellzapoppin Ridge, from which the Japanese were shelling supply dumps in the area with 75 mm guns and 90 mm mortars. The battle began on December 21.

For two days this attack languished, in the face of determined Japanese resistance and the usual carefully built defensive positions. On December 23, the marines called up a heavy artillery barrage, but even this did not do the job. The infantry that attacked after the barrage was again repulsed by heavy machine gun fire from concealed positions along the hill.

But what the artillery did do, once again, was convince the Japanese that their hours on the hill were numbered. And on the night of December 23, they pulled out. On Christmas Eve, when the marines moved up, they found a Christmas present: Hill 600A, abandoned by the enemy. They found twenty-five prepared positions on the hill and one dead Japanese soldier.

After the Allied capture of Hill 600A and Hellzapoppin Ridge, once again the fighting died down. The marines held their perimeter, and the work on the upper airfields continued.

On December 10, Marine Squadron VMF 216 had begun operations from the lower airfield. Ten days later the Army 339th Fighter Squadron and the 347th Fighter Group began operations from the new airstrip built on Stirling Island in the Treasury group. Part of the Army 69th Bombardment Squadron moved up to the Treasuries as well. Soon three army heavy bomber squadrons were operating from Munda. It would not be long before the two upper strips were ready at Bougainville.

During December, Major General Oscar Griswold of the Army XIV Corps took over the defense of the perimeter from General Geiger. The marines began to move out to the beach and into transports. On

December 28, Major General John R. Hodge, commander of the Americal Division, took over the active eastern front of the island from the Third Marine Division.

The assault phase of the invasion of Bougainville was officially over. General Griswold's job was to hold the perimeter and protect the airfields.

One reason the Japanese generals were so loath to undertake activity on Bougainville was the nature of the island. There were virtually no roads (save those the Japanese had built around their major bases). A movement north from Buin meant that the troops either had to take Colonel Hamanoue's crocodile route or come up along the seacoast. Since the Japanese Navy would not commit destroyers for this activity, the army had only its own resources, and that meant the daihatsu barges. There were hundreds of them in the area, but they were lightly armed and no match for anything larger than PT boats. By this time a number of U.S. destroyer squadrons were ranging all over these waters, looking for trouble, and not finding it often enough to suit them.

There was also another problem: the army's sailors were not such good navigators. Thus, although many daihatsus were dispatched around the island, they had a tendency to get lost—when they were not attacked. It was not a very satisfactory system of troop movement.

Yet at the end of December 1943, General Imamura of the 8th Area Army finally realized that the Americans were dug in around Torokina and that they apparently were not going to move elsewhere in Bougainville. This meant that they were now capable of assaulting Rabaul as they liked.

The occasion for this change of heart was the assault by General MacArthur's Southwest Pacific forces on New Britain Island's Cape Gloucester. Since Cape Gloucester was on the same island that housed Rabaul (although at the other end of the heavily jungled island), the Japanese had to begin to rethink their entire South Pacific strategy. Next came Southwest Pacific moves that cut off Dampier Strait as a usable waterway, and it was soon apparent to General Imamura that the Allies were bent on surrounding Rabaul. They were coming too close.

Therefore, he ordered General Hayakutake to prepare a battle plan and be ready to carry it out within the next two months. Its objective would be to drive the Americans from Bougainville and put an end to the American air superiority that was developing in the South Pacific.

At that point, General Hayakutake moved to act.

The Japanese 17th Army and its supporting forces numbered about 44,000 troops. Many of these were in and around Buin, but some were as far away as Choiseul. Another ten thousand troops were stationed in the north, around Buka.

The Japanese Navy, with its Shortlands and Buin bases, had some

20,000 personnel in Southern Bougainville, ranging from pilots to Special Landing Corps Units (marines). The Southern Bougainville base also controlled units on Choiseul.

So when the Japanese decided it was time to do something about the Americans in the middle of their Bougainville Island base, they had the troops. Hayakutake spent the next few weeks planning the assault that should have come in November.

He detailed General Kanda's Sixth Division to lead the attack. Altogether twelve thousand troops would be employed, with another three thousand in reserve. They would make the arduous overland trek along the trails, and they would take plenty of artillery.

This was the plan.

So important had it become suddenly that on January 21 General Imamura bestirred himself to make the arduous (and dangerous) journey to Bougainville to confer with General Hayakutake and see the Seventeenth Army's battle plan for himself. He came, he saw, he put his stamp of approval on the plan. Furthermore, Imperial General Headquarters did the same.

The reason it was going to take three months to get into action was that Imamura and Hayakutake had so far underestimated the power of motion of the Allies that they had relaxed combat training. Now they felt the need for at least a month of training and preparation before the men would be ready to go into battle.

The urgency of the Japanese situation was made even more grim on January 31, when suddenly out of the blue, it seemed, some three hundred troops of the New Zealand 30th Division landed on Green Island and remained there for twenty-four hours. During this period they scouted some good landing beaches and a site for an airfield.

Green Island lies northwest of Buka Island, and it is 117 miles directly east of Rabaul. The Japanese had no particular use for the island except as a barge staging area and port of refuge, but in Allied hands it would be another link in the steel chain that was tightening around Rabaul.

Sure enough, less than three weeks later Halsey ordered troops landed on Green Island. About 5,800 New Zealanders landed and quickly wiped out a seventy-man Japanese garrison. Then the Seabees came in and began building an airstrip. By March 7, the day the Japanese attack against the Torokina bridgehead was to begin, the airstrip was completed and ready for traffic.

The noose was tightening around Rabaul, and Admiral Halsey and General Griswold knew that the Japanese would have to try something to relieve the pressure.

As for the Americans, they now had around 27,000 combat troops on Bougainville. They included the Army 37th Division, General Hodge's

Americal Division, and the 3rd Marine Defense Battalion. But General Griswold would also have the services of the Solomons air force, now operating out of Bougainville strips too, and a destroyer fleet on which to call for fire support.

The Japanese had no naval support at all and no air support that would do them any good, even if Rabaul were able to move planes down to fight. The problem was that by March 1944, Rabaul was getting pasted so often that the number of planes was decreasing sharply, and many key personnel were already being evacuated from New Britain Island.

So General Hayakutake was about to fight, in March, that much delayed battle for Bougainville, but it was under far less salutary conditions for his troops than had existed four months earlier.

As the two sides prepared, Halsey did his best to interdict supply movement to Bougainville and movement around the islands, but this campaign was not particularly successful since the Japanese were using the elusive daihatsu landing craft. The presence of four different squadrons of destroyers, ranging around Bougainville, did keep the Japanese from managing any resupply missions. Not that they were really needed. The Japanese had plenty of troops and plenty of guns and ammunition on Bougainville. What they did not have was air and sea control. The air bases at Buka and Buin were kept under surveillance by the Allies and were bombed, bombarded, and strafed regularly.

The troops were in movement early in March. Three main assault points, around the upper perimeter, were chosen by the Sixth Division as keys to the battle. The Japanese also brought in as much artillery as they could, to place on the heights overlooking the battle area.

One column of Japanese, the Iwasa Detachment, would approach along the Numa Numa Trail and attack from the northwest against the height the Japanese called Hill 800 and the Americans called Hill 700.

Another, the Muta Detachment, would attack from the north, against Hill 600.

The third, the Shinkata Shibu, would attack from the east. Their objectives were the upper airstrips. Once those were taken, they would move down to the coast and wipe out the coastal airstrip and drive the Americans into the sea.

The attack began on March 8 with a simultaneous Japanese bombardment of the lower airstrip and the movement of the 13th Japanese Regiment's 1st Battalion. (The Americans did not consider the attack of the 8th the main thrust.) By day's end, the Japanese had moved up to a position close to the American lines and were pleased to note that the attack seemed to have got off to a good start.

On March 9 the Japanese attacked with enormous enthusiasm and secured a stronghold on the bottom of the height they called Hill 800. But they could not attain the top, no matter how hard they tried. As night fell, they gave up and prepared for the next day.

It was the same. The Japanese reinforced the position and attacked other high points nearby, but they could not dislodge the Americans. The big difference was provided by the American planes that dropped high explosive and fragmentation bombs that did great damage to the Japanese.

The 23rd Infantry was supposed to move in and make its assault that day, too, but for some reason it did not. The combination of fierce American air activity and the Japanese failure took the edge off the primary attack.

That night the 23rd Regiment did make an attack, and although it was pressed hard, it still did not succeed, largely because the Americans were able to call on destroyers off the Torokina coast for spot fire. Once again this was useful—not only in what it destroyed but in its effect on the Japanese troops, who had no such support.

As noted, General Imamura had believed that all the columns would swing into action on the same day and that within forty-eight hours the decision would be made. But as it turned out the Muta Detachment failed to get into position to make its attack on Hill 600 until March 12.

This battle for the Bougainville perimeter was by far the most sophisticated encounter of the land war to date. The Americans used tanks and flamethrowers. They brought up loudspeakers to the area around Hill 800 and called on the Japanese to surrender. The Japanese answered with a hail of bullets. There was not going to be a lot of surrender here.

The battle raged for nearly three weeks. The story of this battle is complex enough to deserve a book of its own. Several times the issue seemed to be in doubt, but in each case the preponderance of American military power turned the scales. The stories of the Japanese are tales of deadly valor, for they literally attacked at times by coming up over the dead bodies of the comrades slaughtered in the attack before.

Finally, on March 23 the Japanese launched a last desperate attempt and managed to come within a few yards of one airstrip before they were hurled back again. This was the last time. The Army's Americal Division and its 37th Infantry Division proved themselves to be as effective fighters as the marines had been on Bougainville. Before the end of the month, the Japanese withdrew, exhausted. They would not again try in force to break the American line.

And for good reason. Their officers had from the beginning of the China war instilled in the Japanese soldier the belief that his patriotism and loyalty to the Imperial system made him virtually impervious to defeat. And why would it be so hard to believe?

Historically, the system of the warrior class who were willing to sacrifice life for a master was very much a part of the Japanese ambience. The idea of "honorable suicide" had persisted for a thousand years. Given the belief that a death in battle guaranteed a soul's future, the Japanese did not find it hard to accept the spirit of self-sacrifice.

Further, in all their history the Japanese had never lost a foreign war; they had defeated the Chinese, the Russians, and the Germans in wars past. Since 1941 they had defeated the English, the Dutch, and the Americans.

The 9,500 shock troops of three crack regiments had given the attack their every effort, and one had only to look at the casualty figures to prove it. The Americans claimed to have lost only 263 men killed or dead of their wounds and listed their casualties in the hundreds.

The Japanese had lost three thousand men dead and four thousand wounded, or about eighty percent of their fighting force. It was no wonder then that they had to give up the field to the victorious Americans.

So Bougainville was as secure for the Americans as it would ever be. There was just one more effort to be made in tightening the belt around Rabaul. On March 20, as the Bougainville perimeter battle continued, Admiral Halsey's forces landed on Emirau Island, in the St. Matthias group, some seventy-five miles northwest of Kavieng and two hundred and fifty miles north of Cape Gloucester on New Britain. The small Japanese garrison was eliminated in a matter of hours. Then the ring around Rabaul was complete.

The campaign for the Northern Solomons was not very well understood by either the Japanese or the Americans at home. After the initial landings at Cape Torokina on Bougainville, the land fighting seemed to lose direction. The war correspondents, who wanted excitement, found the Bougainville campaign too dull for them. So they left, after issuing some parting shots about Halsey's waste of time by getting bogged down in the jungle of Bougainville when he could be attacking big bases. They went off either to explore General MacArthur's well-oiled press machinery or to wait back in Pearl Harbor where the action of the next few months would originate.

The criticism of the Bougainville campaign was anything but warranted. The fact was that the struggle on New Georgia had shown how disastrous it could be to get bogged down in jungle warfare. On Bougainville, the Allies avoided that trap, and their casualties were minimal, while they tied up some 70,000 Japanese troops who were certainly not going to be fighting elsewhere.

After the establishment of the ring of bases around Rabaul, General Imamura and Admiral Kusaka found themselves completely cut off from the mainstream of the war. In February, the American carrier fleet had attacked Truk, "the Gibraltar of the Pacific," with the result that Admiral Koga decided to remove his headquarters from that atoll and in essence declared that it was abandoned as a major base.

After that happened, the fate of Rabaul was indeed sealed. No longer were aircraft brought in from the pipeline to defend the southern base. What were left were withdrawn that spring, and Rabaul became an air base without aircraft. Once in a while a resourceful mechanic managed to piece together enough parts to put a Zero into the air, but against the seven hundred planes or so of the Solomons air force plus the hundreds more of MacArthur's Fifth Air Force, these little forays were meaningless.

While Admiral Halsey was moving up the Solomon chain, General MacArthur was moving around the Papua peninsula of New Guinea, sewing up the top of the circle around Rabaul. With the capture of the Admiralty Islands in March the Allies not only had sealed off Rabaul but had acquired an enormously important new base at Seeadler Harbor off Manus Island.

So, by the first of April 1944, there sat General Imamura and Admiral Kusaka and perhaps a hundred thousand soldiers and sailors, cut off completely from their home bases.

They had no immediate problems of survival, because Imamura had laid in thousands of tons of supplies and guns and ammunition for the Port Moresby operation and other forays that never came off.

However, from that point on the only contact between the South Pacific islands and the Japanese command was kept up through infrequent submarine missions, bringing in medical supplies and other elements of survival. The survival rate was not as high as it might have been. Deprived of proper medical treatment and condemned to sinkholes of fever, the Japanese soldiers and sailors languished, and while there were perhaps two hundred thousand bypassed troops throughout the South Pacific, when the time of surrender came, only about a hundred and twenty-five thousand of them were left alive.

Rabaul, Bougainville, Choiseul, and a dozen smaller island bases languished, immobile for the rest of the war. Except to defend themselves from Allied air attack, which came almost daily for the next few months, the soldiers and sailors had nothing to do but plant gardens and raise crops.

For a time, General Imamura expected an Allied attack on Rabaul, and he welcomed it because his defenses were strong. Indeed, the antiaircraft defense of Rabaul continued to be troublesome all through the rest of the war.

The attack never materialized. The Allies had shown that the process of bypass could save thousands of lives and months of time. And the events in the Solomons were enormously important in the shortening of the Pacific War. In fact, after the war was over General Tojo, the defeated enemy, told General MacArthur that the one great unexpected move the Allies had made was to bypass the strongest Japanese base system in the Pacific.

The Imperial General Staff had miscalculated badly, and the errors of General Imamura had not helped. The glory of the Solomons, which had belonged to Japan for a brief two years, turned out to be a major factor in their defeat in the Pacific War.

NOTES

1. The South Pacific Tide

THE story of the Jápanese destroyer rescue mission at Guadalcanal comes largely from the *Boei Kenshujo Senshi Shitsu* series, the official Japanese history of the Pacific War, published by the Self Defense Agency of Japan. The volumes that deal with this are Volume 28, which deals with Japanese army operations through the Guadalcanal period, and Volume 83, which covers navy operations until the withdrawal of the troops from Guadalcanal. I also used Morison, Volume 5, which deals with the Guadalcanal campaign, and *Admiral Halsey's Story*. The *War Diary of the South Pacific Command* also gave certain details.

The account of the Imperial Communique of February 9, 1943 is from Volume 3 of the account of the Japanese army operations in the Solomons (*Rikugen Sakusen Vol. 3, Munda, Salamaua*).

The account of the quarrel within the Japanese government is from *The Last Banzai* (Tojo biography), and *Kogun*. Some indications are to be found in *Rikugen Sakusen, Vol. 3*.

The account of the American reaction to the Guadalcanal victory is from the pages of *The New York Times*, for January 1943, and from Halsey. Morison goes into some detail here. The background material is from my own previous researches into Pacific War history, which have been published in *Blue Skies and Blood, How They Won the War in the Pacific*, and the Yamamoto biography. The Imperial Rescript of December 31, 1942 is from the *Boei* series.

The accounts of the supply missions to Kolombangara in February come from the army history also.

2. Confusion in Command

THE development of the army-navy quarrel over command of operations in the Pacific is nicely detailed in Grace Hayes's history of the Joint Chiefs of Staff. The observations about Major General John Marston's command problems come from the History of the Second Marine Division, in the files of the Operational Archives of the Navy. That command problem was never solved during World War II.

The discussions of the tactics and strategy of the Japanese come from the *Boei* series. For this period the most useful volumes were among those of the *Boei Kenshujo Senshi Shitsu* (Japanese Self Defense Agency War History). They are: *Nan Taiheiyo Rikugun Sakusen (3) Munda, Salamaua (South Pacific Army Operations Vol. 3)* and *Nanto Homen Kaigun Sakusen (3) Ga Shima Tekyo Nochi (Southeast Area Naval Operations After Withdrawal from Guadalcanal)*.

Also, I used Admiral Matome Ugaki's *Dai Toa Senso Hiki (Secret War Diary)*, published after his death.

Various accounts of the MacArthur-Nimitz staff meetings in March, 1943 generally agree on the facts. I depended on the research done for my *How They Won the War in the Pacific*. The CincPac files have a considerable amount of material on this subject, including comments from various officers. Other sources used here for the feeling of cooperation in the two commands were Admiral Halsey's memoirs and General MacArthur's *Reminiscences*.

3. Step One: The Russells

THE story of preparations for the next step in the U.S. climb up the South Pacific ladder of the Solomons is largely from the files of the South Pacific Command. Many of these files have now been filmed, and I used a number of them on microfilm, obtained from the Navy's Operational Archives. There is an account of the development of Camp Crocodile (Admiral Turner's Amphibious Command base) written by Rear Admiral Paulus P. Powell. Admiral George Dyer's *The*

Amphibians Came to Conquer, Vol. 1, was useful since at the beginning of the Central Solomons campaign Turner was in command of amphibious operations. (He went on to the Central Pacific operations during the period.)

I followed the invasion of the Russells through the *War Diary of the South Pacific Command* and the action reports of the vessels involved. The account of the arrival of various ships in port and the reactions of the sailors comes from the South Pacific Command records, and particularly those of Admiral Merrill's new cruiser task force.

The account of the pre-Russells convoy that fought off the Japanese air attacks is largely taken from the reports of Captain Ingolf Kiland of the *President Hayes.*

The story of the Japanese resupply mission of February 19 is from the Japanese Navy's *After Guadalcanal* and the Army's *Munda.* (See above, chapter 2.)

The account of the March 5 Munda bombardment is from the action reports of several vessels in Admiral Merrill's Cruiser Division 12. The account of the sinking of the Japanese destroyers *Murasame* and *Minegumo* is from the Japanese sources cited above and from the Merrill task force action reports. This action, by the way, had the most devastating effect on the Japanese naval officers at Truk and Rabaul. They were not used to seeing the Americans score total victories and get away scot-free. The technological superiority with which the Japanese began the war—best torpedoes, best fighter planes—was rapidly being wiped out by developments in radar and American aircraft production.

4. Naked Power in the Air

FOR the Japanese side's story in this chapter, I relied on *Rabauru,* the story of the Japanese Eleventh Air Fleet, and the *Boei* Volume 3 (Army), which goes into considerable detail about an event the Japanese found extremely disturbing. The loss of an entire convoy of reinforcements and several destroyers represented the first such defeat in Japanese history, and it forced an entire rethinking of the problems of reinforcement of troops in combat areas. To the army the shock was greater because the navy admitted that there was nothing to be done to rescue the several hundred survivors of the Battle of the Bismarck Sea who were struggling in the water for two days. Heretofore the Japanese Navy had appeared (from the outside) to be invincible. The Japanese were also flabbergasted by the skip-bombing techniques that had been worked on so hard by the men of the Fifth Air Force and that proved so successful. The appearance of the B-25, the

A-20 attack bomber, and the P-38 fighter plane were evidence of the
rapidly changing balance in the war in the South Pacific. I also used
Sensuikanshi (Submarine History) of the *Boei* series for the accounts of
the attempts to rescue survivors of the battle by submarines *I-17* and
I-26.

For the American side, I relied on William N. Hess's *Pacific Sweep*
and on Morison.

5. Yamamoto's Offensive

THIS chapter is the story of Operation I carried out by
the Japanese naval and air force in the spring of 1943. Admiral Yamamoto observed the Allied buildup in the Solomons and the efforts and
growing power of the Fifth Air Force in the New Guinea area. He saw
that unless something was done to stop this activity, there would be the
devil to pay. And so he launched Operation I against both fronts. It was
difficult, and extremely costly in terms of men and aircraft, to do this,
but he had no choice, he was bound by Imperial General Headquarters
injunction to devote maximum strength in support of the army's Papua
campaign, which was seen in Tokyo as the key to Southeastern Area
operations. Had he been able to concentrate on one area or the other, he
might have succeeded. But the big raid of April 7 on Guadalcanal could
not be repeated in the following two or three days as it should have been
because Yamamoto was constrained to devote the same effort that
week to an attack on New Guinea. There was, in fact, very little reason
to do so just then but the army was obdurate. As it turned out, Operation
I could be used as a shorthand justification for the continued separation
of American South Pacific and Southwest Pacific commands, had
Admiral King known all the facts. The effect on the Japanese was to
divide and conquer; Yamamoto had too many rat holes to watch.

For the American side, I used the South Pacific Command records
and Morison. The story of the raid on Guadalcanal indicates that it was
more successful than the Americans really admitted at the time.

For the story of the Japanese resupply missions, I relied on the
Japanese official sources, and Captain Tameichi Hara's *Japanese De-
stroyer Captain*, which gives a good feeling for the emotions of the
Japanese naval officers involved during the period.

The stories about Lieutenant Miyano come from *Rabauru* and *Nihon
Kaigun Sento Kubu (Japanese Navy Battle Squadrons)*. The stories
about Admiral Ainsworth's cruiser task force come from the official
South Pacific Command reports, the action reports.

6. The Assassination of an Admiral

THE material for this chapter comes from a number of important sources. Primary is the biography of Admiral Yamamoto. Also the war diary of Admiral Ugaki, Yamamoto's chief of staff, which Ugaki kept all through the war. Burke Davis' *Get Yamamoto* is a minute-by-minute account of the American operation, with some references to the Japanese. A full account of the Japanese fighter escorts appears in *Rabauru*. I used the Halsey memoirs and the SoPac official records. *Fighter Sweep* has some reference to the mission. Jasper Holmes's *Double-Edged Secrets* tells a good deal of the story. I also used materials collected for my *How They Won the War in the Pacific*, regarding Nimitz's reactions before, during, and after the ambush. The *Boei* naval volume on Guadalcanal contains a complete account of the Japanese side of the story, including the mention of the suspicions of staff officers at Rabaul and Truk that the Japanese naval code had been broken, and the short shrift they received at Tokyo for daring to make such an appalling suggestion.

7. Attrition

THE *Boei* naval and army volumes on Guadalcanal operations were vital to this chapter. I also consulted Hara's *Japanese Destroyer Captain*. *Rabauru* is the source of the note "Blood Bath over the Solomons." The Miyano story is from *Rabauru* and the naval *Boei* volume. The Japanese history contains a complete study of the characteristics of the P-38 fighter, as it does of every American plane. The accounts of Japanese air missions to Guadalcanal are from *Rabauru* and the *Boei* series. SoPac records and Morison were used for the American accounts. The account of Miyano's last mission is from *Rabauru*.

8. Rendova

THE discussions of the American planning to move north in the Solomons are described cogently in Morison. Halsey's book adds little to them, and the record gives little but the bare facts. Admiral Dyer's biography of Admiral Turner adds some insight.

The material about General Sasaki comes from *Kogun* and from *Boei*.

The raw material of the Halsey-Nimitz interchanges is in the CincPac files in Washington. The account of Turner's plans comes from Dyer's biography.

The Japanese histories show that the Japanese were expecting a straightforward island-hopping campaign and were prepared for a major battle for New Georgia, and then an even tougher fight to hold Kolombangara, which was their major base in the Central Solomons. What they did not realize was that the whole Allied Solomons campaign after Guadalcanal developed into a move to isolate Rabaul. There is no reason they should have realized it, because the development was gradual and, at the time of the invasion of New Georgia, even Halsey did not know where he was going to go next. MacArthur was the genius who insisted on the bypass campaign.

The story of the investment of Segi Point is from *The Coast Watchers* and from *The Marines in the Central Solomons*, the official USMC study of that campaign.

The story of the Rendova assault is from the South Pacific Command files and the Marine Corps study. The tale of the fate of the USS *McCawley*, Admiral Turner's command ship, is from his action report on the invasion.

The stories about Japanese air activity are from *Rabauru* and *Boei*. The account of the Imamura-Kusaka exchange is from the army volume of the *Boei*.

9. The Battle of Kula Gulf

THE account of the invasion of New Georgia is from the South Pacific Command files. The Operational Archives archivists at the Washington Navy Yard have packaged much of this material in recent years and it is available on film, thus saving a good deal of slogging effort on the part of the researcher.

The account of the Battle of July 4 is from Morison on the U.S. side and the *Boei* naval volume on the Japanese side. For the naval activity of the period I also consulted Hara's *Destroyer Captain* and the action reports of the U.S. destroyer *O'Bannon*, which was mixed up in most of the fighting.

The account of the Battle of Kula Gulf depended on the naval volume of the *Boei* series for the Japanese side, and for the American side, the action report of Admiral Ainsworth's flagship the *Honolulu*.

10. Jungle War

THE discussion of the battle for New Georgia indicates the basic Japanese misunderstanding of the progress of American power by this stage of the war. Given their own production difficulties, it is understandable that the Japanese high command would be unable to comprehend the fact that the Americans were moving toward a production schedule that would bring literally scores of carriers off the ways. At the Kaiser shipyards on the west coast of the United States the shipbuilders were producing escort carriers in less than ninety days from keel-laying to launch. Save Admiral Yamamoto, there had been virtually no one in the Japanese military hierarchy who understood America or its potential—and he was gone. Even at this stage, the Japanese Army tended to belittle the fighting qualities of the Americans.

The story of Colonel Liversedge's Northern Landing Group is from the group's action reports over the period of the New Georgia invasion.

The army volume of the *Boei* series includes a long section on the New Georgia fighting, giving some detail about Japanese jungle methods. The editors observe that the New Georgia campaign is notable as a lesson in what not to do in defense. The basic problem was the lack of communication between the headquarters at Rabaul and General Sasaki's field force. Neither did it help that a careless communications watch officer at Rabaul made a serious error of omission that prevented the landing of sufficient reinforcements at a critical time. Also, the reluctance of the Japanese Navy to carry on such activity as the shelling of the American positions, which would have been easy enough, showed the difference between a Koga and a Yamamoto.

The story of the dismal record of the army troops under General Hester is from the South Pacific files. After Hester's relief by General Griswold, the Americans began to get on track. The 172nd and 169th regiments were composed of perfectly able and willing American soldiers who were simply not properly trained for the job at hand. They had been given only minimal instruction in amphibious warfare at Guadalcanal and virtually no effective training in jungle fighting. They learned everything the hard way.

The marines up north, on the other hand, were effective from the first, facing some of the toughest Japanese troops, the Special Landing forces of the navy, which are Japanese marines.

The story of Major Kikuda's battalion is from his own postwar memoirs. The story of the young lieutenant of the Japanese 229th Infantry Regiment who wandered into the plantation area seeking help is from the army *Boei* volume.

11. The Battle of Kolombangara

THE material for the Allied side of this action depended on the action reports of Admiral Ainsworth's ships, available at the Navy Operational Archives. The Japanese side is told in the *Boei* navy volume.

In *Breaking the Bismarcks Barrier*, Samuel Eliot Morison raises the question of continued American failure to understand the Japanese superiority in torpedoes; this nearly a year after the invasion of Guadalcanal. The failure is even more remarkable when one realizes, as Morison notes, that a spent torpedo washed up on the beach at Guadalcanal, was found by the Americans, taken apart, and shipped back to Pearl Harbor. What happened after that might be the subject for a study by a professional naval student, because the information was never disseminated through the fleet, and when Admiral Ainsworth sallied forth to do battle with the enemy, he hadn't the slightest idea that the Japanese torpedoes were anything special.

12. Munda

FOR this account, I used Admiral Dyer's book, the Northern Landing Force action reports, the *Marines in the Central Pacific*, and Morison. For the Japanese side, I used the applicable army and navy volumes of the *Boei* series.

All the way through it was apparent that the problem of the American army forces on Southern New Georgia was leadership. Leadership had failed in training, and leadership failed in the field. General Hester's men simply could not get going and could not cope with the Japanese harassment. The 169th Regiment was bogged down on the main trail, and the 172nd wasn't a lot better off back on the seacoast.

13. In the Balance

THE account of Japanese air activity from Rabaul is from *Rabauru* and the *Boei* army volume. The stories of the Japanese resupply missions come from the *Boei* army volume. The stories of Colonel Liversedge's force are from *Marines in the Central Pacific* and the action reports of the Northern Landing Group.

The account of the Halsey-Burke interview comes from several interviews with Admiral Burke in 1972 and an article I wrote for the *Reader's Digest*.

The account of the last days of the Munda campaign come from the *Boei* series and from the South Pacific Command records and the marine story.

14. Awkward Victory

FOR this chapter, I depended on the South Pacific Command records, the *Boei* volumes, and *PT 109*.

The relief of General Hester was one of those awkward changes that embarrass the military hierarchy. But in the appointment of Major General John R. Hodge to command the division, the army made no mistake. General Hodge later led the Americal Division to glory at New Guinea and fought a totally distinguished war throughout, ending as commander of the XXIV Army Corps.

The study of Halsey's planning comes from his own story and from the records of the South Pacific Command. I also used materials gathered from the CincPac files for my earlier study of Nimitz and his admirals.

The tale of Commander Moosbrugger's foray is from the action reports of Destroyer Division 12 for the period. This action was more than a little significant: it was the first time the American destroyer men began to show any proficiency with torpedoes. For the Japanese side, I relied on the *Boei* naval volume and Hara's *Japanese Destroyer Captain*.

The story of the fighting on Arundel Island is from the South Pacific Command records and *The Marines in the Central Pacific*. The Japanese side is from the *Boei* army volume.

15. Vella Lavella

THE material about the Japanese high command's changing defense plans comes from three volumes of the *Boei* series, the two already mentioned and Volume 3 of the accounts of the *Dai Hon Ei*, the Imperial General Staff. The Japanese war history is organized into volumes covering area operations, but the major command decisions of the Imperial General Staff are treated separately in fifteen volumes (eight army and seven navy). This literary organization quite properly represents the Japanese military attitude. In a way the *Dai Hon Ei* volumes are like the *History of the U.S. Joint Chiefs of Staff*. Interesting insights into the Japanese army operations are to be found in *Kogun*, the work of Saburo Hayashi, a Japanese army officer and staff officer of the Imperial General Staff. Insights into naval attitudes are also to be found in *Rekishi no Naka no Nihon Kaigun* (*The Inside History of the Japanese Navy,* by Minoru Nomura, a much more recent graduate of the Japanese naval academy—1942).

For the accounts of the Japanese air raids of August 12, I relied on *Rabaru, The Marines in the Central Pacific,* and Morison.

The South Pacific Command records were the most important source of the materials on SoPac's Vella Lavella invasion plans. The leapfrog concept had been around for some time. Nimitz had discussed it. But it was MacArthur who insisted that this method of isolating Rabaul, which was the essence of his plan, would result in fewer casualties and less time lost.

For the Japanese reactions to the landing, I depended on the *Boei* army volume. The surprise was enormous because it had not occurred to the Japanese high command that the Allies would bypass such a major base as Kolombangara.

The account of the discussions between General Imamura and Admiral Kusaka at Rabaul are from the *Boei* series. The story of Admiral Ijuin's August 17 operations comes from the *Boei* naval volume and from the Hara book.

The story of the night Japanese air attack on the beach is from *Rabauru* and from the Morison book.

16. The Battle for Vella Lavella

THE study of Japanese operations on the island comes from the *Boei* army volume. The Allied story is from the South Pacific Command records.

The diary excerpts regarding Japanese operations are from the war diary of General Sasaki's Southeast Defense Detachment. The stories of the Japanese efforts to evacuate Kolombangara are from both the army and the navy *Boei* volumes. The counterstory of American efforts to stop the evacuation comes from the reports of the PT squadrons and destroyer squadrons to the South Pacific Command.

When, at the end of September, the Japanese Rabaul commands agreed that operations to rescue the Kolombangara troops were too expensive and ought to be stopped, the action aroused a tremendous reaction among the field officers, as opposed to the staff officers who dreamed up the plan. The problem was General Imamura's faulty reading of the wishes of Imperial General Headquarters in Tokyo. At that point Imperial Headquarters was calling for defense in depth but not for a fight to the death at every position. General Imamura backtracked, announced that the troops would all be rescued, and then proceeded to develop his plans for defense to the death at future positions. The reason was simple enough: Imamura was finding it more and more difficult to resupply and reinforce outlying positions as the steel ring of Allied power closed around Rabaul.

The story of the events of October 6 is told from the Hara book, which was invaluable for setting the tone of the Japanese activity that day, and the *Boei* volumes. The account of American activity comes from the ComSoPac records and from Morison.

17. The Invasion of Bougainville—1

ADMIRAL Turner had been the first to see that the troop differential with which the Allies were working at New Georgia was not enough. Even three to one against the sort of defenses the Japanese put up was not an adequate margin to assure minimal Allied casualties. He had asked for thousands more troops for New Georgia, but they were not then available. But when it came time to invade Bougainville, the situation had changed. Admiral Halsey gave Admiral Wilkinson the troops. In the very beginning, the ratio was enormous; the New Zealanders landed at the Treasury Islands against about two hundred Japanese defenders. The Japanese did not react swiftly to the Treasury invasion because they really did not know what to expect next. Was it to be Choiseul or Bougainville, or New Britain itself, site of the Rabaul base? In that sense, Allied planning was a roaring success. The island bypass technique used at Vella Lavella had thoroughly confused General Imamura, and until he could see light, he waited.

The account of the Japanese defense plans is from the *Boei Dai Hon Ei* volumes. The story of General Imamura's interpretation of the Imperial Headquarters orders is from the *Boei* army volume dealing with the Rabaul defenses.

The notes about the difficulties of the Allied coast watchers on Bougainville come from *The Coast Watchers.*

The Japanese troop statistics are from the *Boei* army volume.

The notes about Japanese air operations during the Bougainville battle come from *Rabauru,* and the story of marine air operations is from *The Marines in the Northern Solomons,* another official marine history.

During the entire battle, most Americans were completely unaware of any special Japanese effort, which is, in a way, a sad commentary on the brave Ro Operation launched by Admiral Koga. The trouble was that by November 1943 the Japanese naval air force at Rabaul had lost most of its experienced fliers. The army had withdrawn its planes from joint operations because of army limitations. The army's bombers were built and the army pilots were trained to carry out operations on land against troops and installations not to fight warships. Thus the heavy bombers came in too high and missed their targets for the most part. The light bombers tried skip-bombing techniques, but the pilots did not have the experience and the results were dismal and expensive. General Imamura decided his army air forces were needed to combat the Allies in the larger land areas of New Guinea. Thus the navy was alone.

The Japanese never stopped trying. But these new pilots were so eager to make a showing that they exaggerated wildly. Further, they simply did not know the differences between types of ships. To a pilot who is for the most part at a distance and comes in to attack at high speed, usually in partial cloud cover, with antiaircraft guns barking below and perhaps a handful of fighters zooming up to counterattack, one ship looks like another, and all of them look enormous. Thus tankers and transports and even little minesweepers were called "carriers," near misses were too often taken for hits, and if a ship made smoke to divert the enemy, the pilots believed it was in extremis and would sink within the next ten minutes. These are the sorts of reports that the Japanese pilots brought back to Rabaul during the Ro Operation, and as indicated, the self-perpetuating myths got abroad and multiplied. The story of the reactions in Europe is from the *Boei* army volume.

18. The Invasion of Bougainville—2 (Choiseul)

THE story of the Choiseul raid by the marines is not one of the chapters of greater glory for the planners at Guadalcanal and Noumea. Why it was done is still something of a mystery since the objectives were so loose and limited. The events are described completely in Major Rentz's *Bougainville and the Northern Solomons,* and the course of those events indicates once more the immense resilience and strength of the marines.

As for the Japanese, they were not fooled in the slightest for even a moment. They knew from the beginning that this force was too small to have any but raiding objectives, and so the thousands of troops of the 17th Army in Southern Choiseul did not move. Instead a small detachment was sent out to clear up the trouble if necessary.

That assessment takes nothing away from the troops of the 2nd Parachute Battalion, who performed very well in the heart of enemy territory.

19. Bougainville—3 (Empress Augusta Bay)

THE story of the invasion of Bougainville on November 1, 1943 comes from the reports of the marines, the reports of the South Pacific Command, and the action reports of the various ships involved in the operation, which have been collected in a package by the Navy Operational Archives in Washington.

The various air claims are made in the operational records of Japanese and American air forces. Altogether they are not very accurate, adding up on each side to more planes than the enemy ever had.

One thing is obvious: by this time the Americans had begun to underestimate the ability of the Japanese to deliver new planes to the area. The Fifth Air Force "knocked out" the Japanese Eleventh Air Fleet not once but several times, according to the claims, yet as of November 1943 the Eleventh Air Fleet continued to be resupplied and its average air strength for the month was probably still around 275 planes. The really desperate times were yet to come.

As for troops, the Americans at Torokina Point attacked about three hundred Japanese troops with a landing force that numbered four thousand marines at the end of the first wave and double that number a few hours later. Considering that disparity, the Japanese did very well for themselves, and their single 75 mm pack howitzer knocked out about twenty landing craft before it was silenced by Sergeant Owens's gallant sacrifice. All this is told in Major Rentz's official history.

The story of the Japanese troops originally in defense at Torokina is from the *Boei* army volume. It is brief because there were not many left to tell the tale at the end of the campaign. Only a handful escaped the first two days' fighting to link up with Colonel Hamanoue's 23rd Regimental Combat Team.

20. The Battle of Empress Augusta Bay

THE attack on Bougainville's unprotected belly was a great surprise to General Imamura and the staff of his 18th Area Army. They had expected nearly anything else. Most bets were cast for an attack on the Shortlands and Buin area at the southern end of the island, but Admiral Halsey simply bypassed another important point, leaving more Japanese troops hanging on the vine. What the Americans did do was blast these installations so hard and so often that Buin airfield was useless to the Japanese, and the Shortland base, which had housed Washing Machine Charlies by the dozens and had been the kicking off point for destroyer resupply missions to Guadalcanal in times past, became no more than a communications outpost. Its value was reduced to that of a forward observation post, from which the Japanese could tell when the Americans were coming up the Slot to resupply the Torokina beachhead.

The first attempt to land Japanese troops on Bougainville failed when the American cruiser force appeared just as Admiral Omori was about to send the troop carrying destroyers into the bay above Torokina Point. As it turned out they could have gone in easily enough, but Omori was a nervous man and not well versed in South Pacific fighting. So he sent the troop carriers packing back to Rabaul while he prepared to engage the Americans. The story is all in the navy volume of the *Boei* series. Captain Hara adds an assessment of Admiral Omori that is not very flattering.

Then came the battle, which is described by the Japanese in the *Boei* naval volume and by the Americans in Admiral Morison's history. I used both plus the records of Admiral Merrill's task force. It was not an inspired battle, and the results at the time seemed cloudy. Captain Burke was probably the most effective destroyer commander in all the Pacific but he had no luck this night. His first torpedo attack missed because the canny Admiral Ijuin had a hunch that something was coming and turned away. Then Burke never really got back into the main action. Even the arm of the Pacific called the Solomon Sea is a big body of water.

Admiral Merrill went home low in spirit, depressed by what he considered failure, but he had won, and he was properly congratulated back at Guadalcanal for an excellent effort. Admiral Omori's sun set that day, and afterwards he was quietly retired to less dangerous waters to become superintendent of the torpedo school back in Japan. This seems a bit odd since one of the failures Omori showed that night was an inability to manage torpedo operations, but the ways of naval general staffs have always been mysterious. It is not the first time a naval high command operated on the principle: "Let those that can't do, teach."

21. Bougainville in the Balance

AS the records of the U.S. South Pacific air forces (Airsols) and the Southwest Pacific Fifth Air Force show, claims and fact are often far apart. So it was with the attacks on Rabaul. By November 1, if one believed Fifth Air Force reports, there should have been not much left at Rabaul but smoking ruins. The fact was that damage was still relatively light. But all this changed on November 5, when Admiral Frederick Sherman's carrier task force planes hit Rabaul. They did not do the job they hoped to do, but they did enough, and they were followed by Fifth Air Force bombers that helped matters along. At the end of the day, Admiral Koga's proud cruiser force, with which he had hoped to sweep Admiral Merrill out of the South Pacific, lay in shambles in Rabaul Harbor. Most of the ships managed to limp back to Truk for major repairs. They were not sunk, but—what might be worse in terms of operations—they were laid up for months, eating up more valuable resources and not fighting.

The reason for this disaster still remains something of a mystery. Generally speaking, the Japanese air patrols around Rabaul were extremely effective, yet Admiral Sherman got within 250 miles of the base without detection. His planes came in and completely surprised the Japanese naval forces, which had just arrived. In fact, one or two of the ships had just put down anchor after the voyage from Truk. Surprise under those conditions means that a lot of people were asleep at the switch. That day the Eleventh Air Fleet fighters racked up a good account of themselves, but the carrier bombers did better, getting inside the fighter screen and getting out so fast that the really formidable ring of antiaircraft guns around Rabaul Harbor, and the ships themselves, were unable to cope with the attack properly. It was one of the most successful surprise air attacks of the war.

It took a Halsey to launch it. Rabaul still had a fearsome reputation and a lesser commander would have feared to risk a single carrier air group under such circumstances. Not Halsey. He told Sherman to go full speed ahead, and Sherman did. The result established Halsey's reputation for all time. This action came just as the American fast carrier forces were getting into stride. Back at Pearl Harbor, the "battleship" men, such as Admiral Raymond Spruance, and the new carrier breed, typified by Sherman and led by Vice Admiral John Towers, had been quarreling for months over the proper use of carriers. A few weeks later Admiral Spruance was to take the Gilbert Islands Invasion Force to sea and worry every minute about protection from the carriers, not about what the carriers could do for him.

The results of Sherman's November 5 raid were held up by the carrier men as proof positive of their argument. None of that, of course, appeared in the action reports.

The story of the abortive efforts that day of the Eleventh Air Fleet to find the carriers is a sad little tale of a declining Japanese naval air force, indicated in *Rabauru*. The details of the attack on *LCI-70* come from that vessel's action report for the day.

22. Counterlanding

THE story of Colonel Hamanoue's 23rd Japanese Infantry Regimental Combat Team on Bougainville comes from the *Boei* South Pacific army operations volumes 3 and 4. The story of the adventures and eventual landing of the No. 2 Ken Butai come from the army volumes and from navy volume 3.

The No. 2 Ken Butai was an ill-fated special unit. Most of the troops had fought in China and they were well trained, although not in tropical warfare. That difficulty was remedied at the last minute, as the chapter indicates. Their landing was muffed by the navy, because Admiral Ijuin had been invalided home after the last naval battle, and Admiral Samejima, who was in command of the 8th Fleet at Rabaul, had some ideas of his own about destroyers. So a new skipper, who knew nothing about the previous destroyer landing operations, was in charge of the landing destroyers. First of all, he arrived eight hours late. The troops were supposed to be landed in darkness and then have a chance to form up and prepare positions for an attack.

Then the naval vessels stopped three miles out at sea and dropped over the daihatsus (landing barges). As the 18th Army staff officer accompanying the force indicated, the troops were dismayed, but in fact the error did not make too much difference, because the Americans ashore mistook the Japanese destroyers for American APDS landing American troops. So the Japanese were ashore before the Americans realized what had happened, and it was not hard for them to slip into the jungle just above the beach and form up for the attack.

But there were not enough of them. How could fewer than a thousand troops, even charged to the gills with the spirit of Bushido, expect to take on some 15,000 troops?—because this was what the Americans had ashore by this time. The trouble here, as at Guadalcanal and at New Georgia, was that the staff officers at Rabaul who set up the plans seemed to have no sense of what was happening in the field and what it took to launch a counter offensive. The original three hundred defenders of Torokina Point gave an excellent account of themselves because they were in place, with machine guns and mortars zeroed in. The No. 2 Ken Butai had no such advantage. Those troops had to come in off the sea to the beach, land, and then get ready to fight. In fact, what happened to them had happened to the marines and would happen again. Some of the boat coxswains missed their landings for one reason or another, the troops of those boats failed to land in their assigned areas. In the case of No. 2, Ken Butai, the commander got separated from his command post headquarters unit and never did get back to it again.

The story of the marine reaction to the Japanese landing is from Major Rentz's book, as is the remarkable story of Captain Warner and his misleading of the enemy. Such deception was possible because at this stage of the war the Japanese still reveled in what was becoming a fairyland view of the enemy. They did not believe it possible that Americans could understand Japanese. Based on the American prewar record, of course, they had a good deal of justification for that view. But with the coming of war the Americans had swung into high gear with a language program that was now beginning to bear fruit. In this particular case that change was not responsible—Captain Warner had a command of Japanese that came from prewar service in Tokyo. But the Americans were now making efficient use of Japanese Americans (nisei) and a few trained officers and men. At about this point the *Boei* notes the change: the use of public address systems at the front by nisei, calling on the Japanese in their own language to give up. This was all new to the Imperial forces. But the Americans had long since ceased to be surprised when Japanese troops spoke to them in faultless (except sometimes for Rs) English. Japanese army arrogance was deep-seated indeed.

The failure of the No. 2 Ken Butai to land properly and then to give a good account of itself discouraged General Imamura at just the wrong time. Had he sent in the other two thousand shock troops he had planned to send, he might have given the marines a very bad time indeed. But at this point, Imamura decided that all further reinforcement of the Torokina area would have to come from the 17th Army troops on Bougainville, and communications were so imperfect that General Kanda of the 6th Division did nothing. He, like Imamura, was waiting for that other shoe to drop, for the "real" invasion that was supposed (Japanese thinking) to come at Buin or up north at Buka.

The army *Boei* volumes devote a good deal of space to Colonel Hamanoue's operations and even to personalities, which is somewhat unusual for the *Boei* series. The colonel's musings about the American artillery and his troubles are from that volume. Ultimately, after staging an heroic defense, the colonel was killed in the latter stages of the fighting against the marines.

23. The Foothold Established

THIS chapter depends largely on the Rentz account of the latter days of the marines on Bougainville and on the South Pacific

Command reports as the army moved in to take over. The story of the near disastrous battle of the 21st Marines on the upper trails is from the Rentz book. The material about the Japanese is from the *Boei* army volume.

24. Handwriting on the Wall

THE story of the Japanese Eleventh Air Fleet operations in November during the Ro Operations is from *Rabauru* and the naval volumes of the *Boei*. The Japanese numbered the air battles: Bougainville Air Battle No. 1, etc. up to Air Battle No. 6.

The reality of the air battle is better indicated by the adventures of the American destroyers *Anthony* and *Woodsworth*, which I drew from their action reports for November 11 and 12. The sinking of the *McKean*, also from action reports, tells another bit of the story.

In 1943 and 1944 most Americans knew virtually nothing about the fighting on Bougainville. In late November the war correspondents, an itchy bunch, found the going dull and so hied themselves off elsewhere seeking excitement with a few parting shots at Admiral Halsey for allowing himself to be "bogged down" on Bougainville instead of fighting heroic battles there.

The fact is that the press, as so often happens, was dead wrong in its assessments. Halsey had bypassed about 50,000 troops in southern Bougainville, who could have killed a lot of Americans. He was doing just what he set out to do—establish airfields that would bring Rabaul within 250 miles, easy fighter and bomber range. The action might not have been exciting, but it was drawing the noose around the enemy's major South Pacific base.

The story of the near disaster of the 1st Marine Parachute Battalion comes from the SoPac reports and the Rentz book on Bougainville. The problem was that the Americans had no inside intelligence on Bougainville because the natives were not with them, and so they had no way of knowing that the place they chose to land on was a major supply base for the Japanese. They could thank the Rome–Berlin–Tokyo Axis for that. The poisoning of Bougainvillean minds against the Allies by the German missionaries (a tradition left over from the days when the Solomons were part of the German South Pacific colonies) was one of the few services the Germans did the Japanese during the Pacific War. It provided an interesting side note and warning about future treatment of enemy alien missionaries in occupied territory.

25. Thirty-One Knot Burke

THE note about the situation in which the Japanese found themselves at the end of 1943 comes from the *Boei* books. The material about Captain Burke's big fight and the other operations comes from the action reports of the *Charles F. Ausburne* and other vessels and the reports of Destroyer Squadron 23.

26. General Imamura's Miscalculation

GENERAL Imamura's career was a distinguished one. He was obviously one of the major figures in the military regime of Japan, and he had all the right credentials: service in the General Staff and with the Kwantung Army in Manchuria. The Kwantung Army was a sort of mother matrix for the militarists. Nearly all the principal figures who engineered the takeover of civil government were nurtured there. So it was fitting that General Imamura, one of the crowd, should have to eat some of the bitter fruits of the army's harvest of aggression. Notes on his career come from the *Boei* and from *Kogun*.

At home in Japan, the highly exaggerated results of the Ro Operation air battles were further exaggerated to the point that they caused comment around the world. One reason for this manufactured claim was to impress a meeting of the Greater East Asia Co-Prosperity Sphere special committee, just then meeting in Tokyo. Domei, the Japanese news agency, tried to get articles planted in the major newspapers of the neutral countries. In Sweden they were successful, in Madrid they were more so (Madrid not being very neutral). But in Switzerland the "victory" was greeted by silence and *Neue Zuricher Zeitung* and *Le Journal de Genève* would not print a line of the propaganda. The Japanese minister blamed the Americans, who, he said, conducted a constant campaign to keep Japanese news out of the papers. It was true all right. Allen Dulles, the OSS and later CIA honcho, was very active in Switzerland against the Axis powers.

Since the war correspondents had left, the battles of December 1943 on Bougainville were almost unknown to the public. The marines had been relieved by the Army's 37th Division and the Americal Division under General Hodge. General Imamura made another of his miscalculations: his intelligence indicated that the Americans had only a single division of fighting troops on Bougainville, so he employed parts of two divisions to counterattack and throw them into the sea. But General

Hodge was not marching toward the sea. The men of the Americal Division (and the 37th too) distinguished themselves in some of the hardest fighting of the Pacific War. This almost unknown Bougainville campaign is worth a book unto itself.

The struggle ebbed and flowed, but it continued into March 1943, as the finishing touches were being put on the three airfields that would send planes to work over Rabaul and all the seas around it. Actually the lower airfield, down by Torokina Beach, had been in operation since late November. But the other fighter strip and the bomber field were just getting into action when the Japanese launched their March offensive. They brought up artillery and they fought like tigers. But so did the Americans, and once again in the end the American superiority of firepower carried the day. The Japanese have devoted a good deal of attention to this campaign in the *Boei* volumes.

BIBLIOGRAPHY

Records
(From the Operational Archives, U.S. Navy)

Occupation of Bougainville and Supporting Operations. Action Reports
  assembled and filmed by the U.S. Navy Operational Archives.
War Diary ComSoPac 1943-4
CincPac Fleet Reports, Solomons
Camp Crocodile Paper, R. Adm. Paulus P. Powell
Guadalcanal Advanced Base II-225
Occupation of New Georgia and Vella Lavella; filmed materials
  assembled by the U.S. Navy Operational Archives.
CincPac Fleet Report, Solomon Islands, February 18, 1943
Hayes, Grace P. Lt.; Joint Chiefs of Staff History, World War II
Radio Intelligence History (filmed)
History of the Second Marine Division (2) (filmed)

Books

Agawa, Hiroyuke, *The Reluctant Admiral*, Tokyo and New York:
  Kodansha, 1981.
Boei Senshishitsu.
(*History of the Pacific War* compiled by the Japanese Self Defense
  Agency.)

Army:

Nan Taiheiyo Rikugun Sakusen (3) Munda, Salamaua.
(South Pacific Ground Forces Operations (3) Munda, Salamaua.)
Nan Taiheiyo Rikugun Sakusen (4) Finschhafen, Tsurubu, Torakina.
(South Pacific Ground Forces Operations (4) Finschhafen, Tsurubu, Torakina.)

Navy:

Nanto Homen Kaigun Sakusen, Ga Shima Tesshu Made.
(Southeast Area Naval Operations, Guadalcanal Until Withdrawal.)
Nanto Homen Kaigun Sakusen, Ga Shima Tesshu Ato.
(Southeast Area Naval Operations, After Guadalcanal Withdrawal.)
Sensuikanshi.
(Submarine History.)

Imperial General Staff:

Dai Honei Kaigun Bu, Rengo Kantai, Showa Juha Nen, ni getsu, made.
(Imperial General Staff, Combined Fleet, until February, 1943.)
Dai Honei Kaigun Bu, Rengo Kantai, Dai San Dan Sakusen Maezenki.
(Imperial General Staff, Combined Fleet, Third Stage, Early Operations.)

Browne, Courtney. *Tojo: The Last Banzai.* New York: Holt, Rinehart and Winston, 1967.

Bryan, J. and Halsey, William F. *Admiral Halsey's Story.* New York: Da Capo Press, 1976.

Cant, Gilbert. *Great Pacific Victory.* New York: John Day Co., 1946.

D'Albas, Andreiu. *Death of a Navy.* New York: Devin-Adair, 1957.

Davis, Burke. *Get Yamamoto.* New York: Random House, 1970.

Dyer, George C. *The Amphibians Came to Conquer* (biography of Admiral Richmond Kelly Turner) Vol. 1. Washington, D.C.: U.S. Government Printing Office, undated.

Feldt, Eric A. *The Coast Watchers.* New York: Oxford University Press, 1978.

Francillon, Rene J. *Imperial Japanese Navy Bombers of World War II.* Windsor, England: Hylton Lacy Pub, Ltd.

Hara, Tameichi, with Fred Saito and Roger Pineau. *Japanese Destroyer Captain.* New York: Ballantine Books, 1961.

Hayashi, Saburo, with Alvin D. Coox. *Kogun: The Japanese Army in the Pacific War.* Quantico: The Marine Corps Association, 1959.

Hess, William N. *Pacific Sweep.* New York: Zebra Books, 1974.

Holmes, W. J. *Double Edged Secrets.* Annapolis: Naval Institute Press, 1979.

Horton, D.C. *New Georgia: Pattern for Victory.* New York: Ballantine Books, 1971.

Hoyt, Edwin P. *How They Won the War in the Pacific: Nimitz and His Admirals.* New York: Weybright and Talley, 1970.

Morison, Samuel Eliot, *Breaking the Bismarcks Barrier* (U.S. Naval Operations in WW II, Vol. 6). Boston: Atlantic, Little, Brown, 1950.

Nomura, Minoru. *Rekishi no naka no nihon kaigun (Inside History of the Japanese Navy),* Genshobo, Tokyo.

Ochi, Harukai. *Gadarakanaru. (Guadalcanal).*

Okumiya, Masatake. *Rabauru Kaigun Kokutai (Rabaul Navy Air Force).*

Rabauru. (The story of the Japanese 11th Air Fleet) Tokyo.

Rentz, John N. *Bougainville and the Northern Solomons.* Historical Section, U.S. Marine Corps, 1948.

Rentz, John N. *Marines in the Central Solomons.* Historical Branch, U.S. Marine Corps, 1952.

Rikusenshi Kenkyu Fukyukai *(Gadarakanaru to Sakusen) (Japanese Army War History, Guadalcanal Operations [and After]).* Tokyo.

Takenawa Tomoshibi Sha. *Nihon Kaigun Sentoki Bu. (Japanese Navy Fighter Squadrons).* Tokyo.

Ugaki, Matome. *Dai Toa Senso Hiki, (Secret War Diary).* Gensho Moshi, Tokyo.

INDEX